SECRETS & SOVEREIGNS

E. Phillips Oppenheim was the Prince of Story Tellers. In his lifetime he published over 150 books—novels, story collections, plays, travel books and autobiographical works. But a handful of his stories were never published in a book. They appeared in magazines like *The Strand, Windsor* and *Cosmopolitan* in the early 1900's, and have never been reprinted since. Editor Daniel Paul Morrison scoured major research libraries to put together the first new collection of Oppenheim stories in over sixty years: nineteen tales of mystery and political intrigue, duplicity and romance. Oppenheim could always be counted on to tell a good story, and this collection is guaranteed to keep you entertained.

Secrets and Sovereigns also features the most comprehensive bibliography ever published of the works of E. Phillips Oppenheim. Beginning with his vast collection of Oppenheim books and paraphernalia, Morrison has crosschecked all publication data with information from the Library of Congress and the British National Library. This bibliography resolves difficult questions regarding phantom, pirated and posthumous titles that have long plagued Oppenheim collectors. In his introduction, Morrison spotlights Oppenheim's life – as riveting and romantic as any story ever told by the Prince of Story Tellers.

Whether you are a reader or a collector, there is something here for you. So pull up an easy chair and enjoy these newly-unearthed tales from E. Phillips Oppenheim.

Daniel Paul Morrison lives in Princeton, New Jersey, with his wife and two children.

SECRETS & SOVEREIGNS

The Uncollected Stories of

E. PHILLIPS OPPENHEIM

Edited with Introduction and Bibliography
by Daniel Paul Morrison

STARK
HOUSE

Stark House Press • Eureka California

SECRETS & SOVEREIGNS:
THE UNCOLLECTED STORIES OF
E. PHILLIPS OPPENHEIM

Published by Stark House Press
1315 H Street
Eureka, CA 95501, USA
griffinskye3@sbcglobal.net
www.starkhousepress.com

Originally published 1900-1911, 1927
Windsor Magazine, Harmsworthy London Magazine,
Strand Magazine, Cosmopolitan, Little Brown
This edition published and © 2004 by Stark House Press

The Prince of Story Tellers (Introduction)
A Collector's Bibliography of Oppenheim Books (Annotated Bibliography)
© 2004 Daniel Paul Morrison

ISBN: 0-9749438-0-0
ISBN 13: 978-0-9749438-0-0

Cover design and book layout by Mark Shepard, SHEPGRAPHICS.COM
Cover illustration by F. H. Townsend

First Stark House Press Edition: May 2004

REPRINT EDITION

TABLE OF CONTENTS

THE PRINCE OF
STORY TELLERS

Life on the French Riviera

They called him "The Prince of Story Tellers." And it was a fitting title for E. Phillips Oppenheim, a man who earned a king's ransom from the torrent of books and magazine stories he wrote.

By 1923, when he moved into Villa Deveron, a rambling house on the French Riviera nestled between a golf course and the Mediterranean shoreline, Oppenheim had more than 30 books simultaneously in print, both in Great Britain and in the United States. On top of royalties from book sales, he earned even larger sums from serializations of his books in such leading magazines as *Collier's* and *The Saturday Evening Post*.

The money poured in and Oppenheim used this wealth to create a world in which he reigned like an oriental potentate. At home, he was indulged by servants and secretaries who anticipated his every need. At the finest restaurants in London and Paris, he was a well-known and pampered customer. And at the Casino of Monte Carlo, which he could reach in a few minutes by his chauffeured Rolls Royce, Oppenheim was a regular at the most glamorous gaming tables in the world.

The nearby principality of Monaco, awash in celebrity, money and royalty, was an irresistible lure for Oppenheim. He found characters for his novels just by watching the beautifully dressed passers-by as he dined in the restaurant of the Hotel de Paris or enjoyed a martini at the bar of the Métropole Palace. Between luncheons with the King and Queen of Siam, tennis with the Prince of Greece, and dinners with the King of Sweden, Oppenheim found time to talk shop with the likes of Somerset Maugham, Sax Rohmer and Baroness Orczy – successful writers who also found Monaco conducive to their work.

Life in Leicester

But it wasn't always that way.

Born in October 22, 1866 in London, Oppenheim was raised in Leicester, an industrial city of more than 200,000 people located in England's midlands. His father, Edward John Oppenheim, was a moderately successful leather merchant selling wholesale to shoe manufacturers. From the business, his father was able to support his family comfortably and to send

Phillips to the nearby Wyggeston Grammar School, a private boarding school with a middling reputation.

But when a financial crisis struck the family firm in 1883, Phillips, at the age of sixteen, was forced to leave school and join his father in the business. It was a bitter blow to the shy, secretive boy who envisioned himself graduating from Wyggeston and making his way to Oxford or Cambridge.

Among the treasures the young Oppenheim hid in his trunk when he left Wyggeston was a 400-page handwritten draft of his first novel.

Though he worked hard and had a good head for business, Oppenheim always resented working in his father's leather firm. Six days a week, eight hours a day, Phillips helped his father in the family concern. At home, he spent every spare moment, late into the night, clandestinely laboring over his novel. Finally, in 1887, when he was 21 years old, Oppenheim's first novel, *Expiation*, was published. While the book earned no money for Oppenheim – in fact, his father had to underwrite a part of the production costs – it did open the door to selling stories to local and regional publications such as the *Leicester Mercury* and the *Whitehall Review*.

It would be another seven years before his next novel, *A Monk of Cruta*, was published in 1894. But during those years, Oppenheim worked like a man possessed with the demon of ambition – putting in long days in the leather business, and long nights writing story after story.

In 1892, Oppenheim traveled to the United States to transact business in Boston for his father's firm. A few months later he returned to England with an American bride, Elsie Clara Hopkins. The couple bought a small house about eight miles outside of Leicester and settled into the life of newlyweds. The family was completed when the couple's only child, Geraldine, was born. During these years, Phillips continued to commute into Leicester six days a week to work with his father. Evenings at home were devoted to writing.

A Turning Point

In 1898, when he was thirty-two years old, Oppenheim published *The Mysterious Mr. Sabin*. An espionage thriller, it was Oppenheim's first commercial success and allowed him to believe that writing could become his full-time occupation. Today, Oppenheim is best remembered for his many spy novels and the suave and unscrupulous Mr. Sabin was the hero of the novelist's first excursion into international intrigue. Mr. Sabin reappeared in *The Yellow Crayon*, a spy thriller published in 1905.

Unfortunately, shortly after the publication of *The Mysterious Mr. Sabin*, Oppenheim's father died unexpectedly of pneumonia. The full burden of running the family's leather business then fell onto his shoulders. Not only did he have to support himself and his wife, he was now also responsible for supporting his mother and his sister.

The success of *The Mysterious Mr. Sabin* allowed Oppenheim to dream of leaving the leather business, but the new obligations he faced in the wake of his father's death postponed his dream. Though he longed to be rid of it, Oppenheim continued to oversee the operations of the firm, searching all the while for a buyer so that he might pursue his literary career.

In the end, it was *The Mysterious Mr. Sabin* that made possible Oppenheim's dream of forever leaving behind the leather business. While conducting business in New York City, Oppenheim met Julian Stevens Ullman, an American leather mogul who had read and enjoyed *The Mysterious Mr. Sabin*. Ullman was looking for a toehold in the English market and offered to buy Oppenheim's leather business. The author jumped at the opportunity and felt enormously relieved to be free of the pressure of keeping the business afloat.

Oppenheim stayed on as a director in the business for a while, drawing a salary from Ullman. But when he was forty years old, Oppenheim finally left the firm and was completely free of the workaday obligations of commercial life. It had been nineteen years since he saw his first novel in print – and already he had published no fewer than thirty-three books.

Every one of them written in his spare time.

Popular Magazines: A Road to Success

The road between the grimy factories of Leicester and the glittering palaces of the French Riviera was paved by the nearly 13 million words Oppenheim wrote in his lifetime. Between 1887 and 1943, E. Phillips Oppenheim published one hundred and fifteen full-length novels, thirty-nine collections of short stories, as well as a travel book and an autobiography.

Due to his enormous popularity, by 1910 most of Oppenheim's books, whether they were novels or short story series, were first serialized in magazines. Thus we see *Peter Ruff and the Double Four*, a collection of detective stories, first appearing in the August 1909 through June 1910 issues of *Pearson's Magazine*. It was not published as a book until 1912. The novel, *Million Pound Deposit*, was first serialized in the April 20, 1929 through May 25, 1929 issues of the *Saturday Evening Post*, and later published as a book in 1930. Due to the enormous reach of popular magazines and the high fees they paid, Oppenheim actually earned more money from the serializations than he did from book sales.

In his early days as a writer, Oppenheim published an uncounted number of individual stories in popular magazines, both in Great Britain and the United States. These stories never appeared in any book and, as a result, quickly disappeared from the view of all but the most zealous archivists and collectors.

Now, nearly sixty years after Oppenheim's death, I am delighted to be writing this introduction to *Secrets and Sovereigns: Uncollected Stories of E. Phillips Oppenheim*. This is the first-ever collection of long-forgotten stories from Oppenheim's formative years.

The stories in this collection – published between 1900 and 1911 – appeared during the glory days of British popular magazines. Periodicals such as the *Strand Magazine* and the *Windsor Magazine* reached hundreds of thousands of British households with a regular diet of short fiction, cultural notes, news about royalty and celebrities, and reports about the latest colonial exploits and scientific developments – all profusely illustrated.

The most popular of the illustrated monthlies was the *Strand Magazine*. Launched in 1891 by George Newes, the first issue sold out immediately and had to be reprinted three times, eventually selling 300,000 copies. By the turn of the century, the circulation of the *Strand Magazine* exceeded a half million – a figure towering over the paltry 40,000 circulation of *The (London) Times* during the same period.

Oppenheim published dozens of stories in the *Strand Magazine*. And in those pages, he rubbed elbows with the literary lights of his generation: H. G. Wells, the early science fiction author who wrote *The War of the Worlds*; Arthur Morrison, the realist chronicler of life in London's East End; P. G. Wodehouse, wry humorist and creator of Jeeves; and Arthur Conan Doyle, whose ever-popular Sherlock Homes stories first appeared in the *Strand Magazine*.

While fiction has a small place in magazines in the twenty-first century, short stories and serialized novels filled more than half the pages of monthlies such as the *Strand Magazine* and the *Windsor Magazine*. This fact is hardly surprising when we realize there was neither radio nor television during the heyday of these magazines. They were the equivalent of our primetime television. When radio came along in the 1930s, the entertaining stories provided by illustrated monthlies came in over the airwaves. Radio was such a threat to the kind of entertainment Oppenheim produced that his British publisher blazed the slogan, "Switch off the wireless – it's an Oppenheim" across the dust jackets of his books.

The Uncollected Stories

The stories in this collection first appeared in three British magazines – *Strand*, *Windsor*, and *London* – and one American magazine – *Cosmopolitan*. In them we can see the wide range of Oppenheim's literary styles as well as early appearances of themes that would later become his hallmarks.

"The Ambassador's Dilemma" takes up Oppenheim's favorite topic:

international diplomacy and espionage. Here were meet the deadly-serious work of spies and foreign service agents and are reminded that not all is as it seems in the double-dealing world of international intrigue. Mixed in with the twists and turns of the unfolding plots are healthy dollops of romantic interest and nerve-racking brinksmanship.

The themes of Oppenheim's 1931 novel, *Simple Peter Cradd*, are clearly anticipated in "The Perfidy of Henry Midgley" and "The Deserter" – two stories that explore the consequences of inherited money on a hard-working, but henpecked man and his crass and socially-ambitions wife. Money does change everything and the heroes of each of these stories must figure out how to turn a windfall into a boon and prevent it from becoming a new oppression.

No matter what topic Oppenheim tackles, romance is never far away. "Mr. Hardrow's Secretary," and "John Garland the Deliverer" tell the tales of women saved from loneliness and destitution by rich and caring men, while "The Outcast" and "Quits" show the power of a woman's cheerful love and clear common sense to rescue dissolute aristocrats from total destruction.

While Oppenheim may have tailored his love stories for women, he knew men would enjoy his stories of revenge. "The Sovereign in the Gutter," "The Ill-Laid Scheme of Mr. Ambrose Weare," and "The Turning Wheel" let loose characters who have been done some grievous injury and have for years schemed and planned the perfect revenge. The unleashed wrath of these wronged men makes for frightening situations. But best-laid plans can go awry.

This collection even offers two old-fashioned detective stories. In "Mr. Ashley's Failure" we meet an amateur detective who fails to resolve the mystery of a stolen necklace. Or does he? And "The Man Whom Nobody Liked" is the twisting and unpredictable tale of a man trying to extricate himself from a false accusation of murder.

And then there is money. Like romance, money is never far from any Oppenheim story. "The Money-Spider" and "The Three Thieves" explore the effects, both good and evil, of oppressive poverty and extravagant wealth. As a man who went from a leather shop in Leicester to the palaces of the French Riviera, making money is a topic Oppenheim understood well.

Kicking off this collection of Oppenheim short stories is a rare example of his nonfiction. "E. Phillips Oppenheim: The Prince of Story Tellers Tells His Own Story" appeared as a small pamphlet in 1927 to celebrate the publication of his one-hundredth book. In this autobiographical essay, Oppenheim offers a bit of his personal history and a glimpse into his writing methods.

The Enduring Charm of E. Phillips Oppenheim

I have read more novels and stories by Oppenheim than I can count – the walls of my study are lined with his books – and still I find that he charms and satisfies.

As a storyteller, he is hard to beat. Oppenheim sets out to entertain, not to impress. And you cannot help but imagine that he had a ball writing these tales.

The characters Oppenheim creates are people we would love to be. Lively and capable women. Refined and companionable men. Vicariously, we enjoy their struggles and their successes. We respect them for their determination and applaud when they shape their own destinies and realize their fondest dreams. While there can be plenty of suspense and heartache as a story progresses, by the end, the author resolves the difficulties and the reader enjoys a happy resolution. You do not walk away from an Oppenheim story feeling gloomy or defeated.

Oppenheim understood the aspirations and daydreams of his readers – ordinary people from a wide swath of British and American society. He convincingly brought to life dreams of adventure and the thrill of besting an oppressor, dreams of the comforts and refinements that come with wealth, dreams of true love with the perfect mate. Oppenheim consistently served up a cozy dish of what people most hankered for.

It is a long way from Leicester to the French Rivera. Especially for a boy forced to leave school and labor long years in his father's struggling business. But like a character from one of his stories, Oppenheim never lost sight of his dreams and laid hold of them through dint of ceaseless labor. He took control of his destiny, overcame extraordinary obstacles and created a life of glamour and pleasure. In the end, the life of "The Prince of Story Tellers" was proof that his stories were not mere fictions.

Daniel Paul Morrison
Princeton, New Jersey
February 2004

E. PHILLIP/ OPPE/HEIM: THE PRI/CE OF /TORY TELLER/ TELL/ HI/ OW/ /TORY

Story writing is an instinct. I write stories because, if I left them in my brain, where they are endlessly effervescing, I would be subject to a sort of mental indigestion.

Story writing was my ambition from the first. My father was a clever story teller — he never printed anything, though. When we were small children he made each of us write a story on Christmas evening — he wrote one himself — and they were read out and we voted as to which we liked best. My father always won. We were not allowed to vote each for himself! I shall never forget my father's astonished face when one Christmas I won the prize. I was only thirteen, and was quite considerably pleased with myself.

I was eighteen years old when my first short story was published, and only twenty when my first novel appeared. I have therefore had more than forty years of story writing, and the first thing which it occurs to me to say about it is that I do not think there can be another profession in the world which maintains its hold upon its disciples to such an extraordinary extent. I do not know how else to account for the fact that to-day I sit down to commence a new story with exactly the same thrill as I did at twenty. The love of games, of sport, of sea and mountains, the call of strange cities, wonderful pictures and unusual people, however dear they may still remain to one, lose something of their first and vital freshness with the passing of the years. Not so the sight of that blank sheet of paper, waiting for the thoughts and picture which crowd their way into the brain. For every story has about it something new; every slowly unwinding skein of fancy leads along some untrodden paths into virgin fields. The lure of creation never loses its hold. Personally I cannot account for the fact. Perhaps it springs from the inextinguishable hope that one day there will be born the most wonderful idea that has ever found its way into the brain of a writer of fiction, an idea, dim glimmerings of which have passed through the mind when one is half awake and half dreaming. Every imaginative writer knows those will-o'-the-wisps. With the morning their light has gone, but they do their good work — they keep hope alive.

I do not know how a novel will develop when I begin it. I get a vision of about two good characters — the man (he's the main thing) and the woman (very secondary). These two elements, together with my first chapter, constitute my preparation. Then I live with my characters for a while — eat with them, walk with them, play golf with them. Finally they begin to act according to their own wills; then I let them go, and they work out their own destiny. I simply pull the strings. Soon, the first thing I know, I have another book ready for my publishers. It's great fun, really.

If I were to attempt to work from a synopsis I should be done. My story would be stilted and untrue. My characters would resent it and at once kick over the traces. They would line out in sulky and lethargic indifference. My readers would at once say "Pshaw! He has written too much." And my publisher would hint at the high price of paper and an old-age pension. So I leave the synopsis alone. And as to plots — there are only about a score in the world, and when you have used them all, from A to Z, you can turn them around and use them from Z to A.

The measure of success which my stories have attained enables me to write them in a manner I like best. When I'm not in the country or in London I'm down on the Riviera, where I've a small villa. I generally go there at the beginning of the year and come back in the Spring — sometimes later. I have built a summer house in the garden there, looking over the sea, where I do my writing. There are excellent golf links near at hand.

Generally speaking, half my time is devoted to actual writing and the other half is divided between exercise and sport, visits to London, and travel. My work itself is accomplished with the aid of a secretary, to whom I dictate my stories as they unfold themselves in my mind, in Summer out-of-doors into a shorthand notebook, and in Winter in my study onto a typewriter. Many a time, earlier in life, when I used to write my stories with my own hand, I have found that my ideas would come so much faster than my fingers could work that I have prayed for some more speedy method of transmission. My present method is not only an immense relief to me, but it enables me to turn out far more work than would be possible by any other means.

I find my best time for writing is in the morning — namely, from about nine or nine-thirty till about one o'clock. Unfortunately, however, my scheme for the day is complicated by the fact that this is also the time during which I prefer to play golf. I have, therefore, schooled myself into an artificial preference for working between the hours of four and seven in the evening.

Large numbers of people have noted that in certain of my earlier novels I prophesied wars and world events that actually did come to pass. In "The Mysterious Mr. Sabin" I pictured the South African Boer War seven years before it occurred. In "The Great Secret" and several others I based plots upon the German menace and the great war that actually did occur. In "The Great Prince Shan" I tried to picture the consequences that would result if Great Britain abolished her international secret service, her army and navy, and relied on some form of a League of Nations solely for protection and peace. First of all, it must be understood that what I write is done absolutely from the standpoint of fiction. But I try to put more into the books than romance. Plausibility is one of the things I aim at. Indeed, I think that no novel can stand sturdily upon its own legs unless it possesses sufficient plausibility to make the theme possible in actual life.

I'm afraid that I cannot lay any claim to being an actual prophet of world events. I don't go into trances and neither do I gaze into a crystal and read the future. But I do try to keep abreast of contemporary events and put two and two together. If there is "writing on the wall" I try to see it. I was not the only one who prophesied war with Germany. The signs were there for all to read who took the trouble.

The war was, of course, a great hindrance as well as a great stimulus to the writer of imaginative fiction. After having written some fourteen novels foretelling exactly what happened and preaching national service, the actually falling of the thunderbolt was none the less stupefying. I was in Florence in the early Summer 1914, and what I heard in political circles there brought me home just in time to fetch my daughter from boarding school in Brussels and reach London before the fateful fourth of August. I remember in those first few months I was inclined to take almost seriously the badinage of my friends, who opined that now war with German had actually come to pass, there would be nothing left for me to write about. That, however, was only in the first few clouded weeks. Now that the cataclysm is over, the stage is set for even more tragic happenings. So long as the world lasts, its secret international history will continue to engage the full activities of the diplomatist, and suggest the most fascinating of all material to the writer of fiction.

It will be noticed that in the majority of my novels I display considerable familiarity with foreign capitals, but I am sorry to say that, outside of Europe, I have never been a great traveler. I have visited more or less frequently most European countries and those in Northern Africa, and I have been to the United States a dozen times. I have made it a hobby for many years to frequent the cafés in all the cities which I visit on my travels. I make the acquaintance of the maître d'hôtel whenever possible and in my conversation with him, and by studying the types represented among the patrons, a good idea for a story inevitably suggest itself. Once, in a little café in Paris, a café frequented by all classes, I started one of my novels. As I was seated at one of the small tables, a young French dancing girl told me the story that formed the plot. Then and there I actually wrote the first chapter.

It is no gift of mine to impart reality to scenes and events taking place in a country in which I have not actually lived. Half a dozen thoroughfares and squares in London, a handful of restaurants, the people whom one meets in a single morning, are quite sufficient for the production of more and greater stories than I shall ever write. The real centres of interest in the world seem to me to be the places where human beings are gathered more closely, because in such places the struggle for existence, in whatever shape it may take, must inevitably develop the whole capacity of man and strip him bare to the looker-on, even to nakedness. So the cities are for me!

It is in these great cities, too, that men meet and mingle who shape the destinies of nations. There is no more thrilling subject than the activities of these men. The romance of secret diplomacy has enthralled me for years; I have tried to reason out the desires and ambitions of various nations through these secretive individuals. I have reasoned to myself, "This nation is aiming toward this", and, "That nation is aiming toward that"; then I have invented my puppets representing these conflicting ambitions and set them in action. If I have frequently reached conclusions that later developments in the real world have established as true, it is because I have reasoned in a logical manner and not through any supernatural insight. After all, the roadways that great nations desire to travel are plain enough.

To end these personal matters where I should have begun, I may say that I was born in London in 1866, married in the United States, and have one daughter. My chief interests, outside my work, are the theatre, travel, sports and games of all sorts. I enjoy my country life and my club life in London, and the thing I enjoy better than anything else in the world (need it be stated again?) is writing stories.

No, after all, I am not a prophet. I try to be, first of all, a teller of tales, and the sort that will hold the interest of every adventurously minded man and woman, and whether or not I have succeeded or failed rests entirely with that public which has greeted me so sympathetically for many years. To them I send my greetings.

E. Phillips Oppenheim

THE AMBASSADOR'S DILEMMA

The Ambassador looked at me and I looked at the Ambassador. It was not by any means the first pause in an exceedingly awkward conversation.

"You see," he remarked, suavely, "you also are concerned in this affair. I am glad to observe that you contrive to retain your cheerfulness, but I am bound to point out the fact that – diplomatically, at any rate – you are in a parlous state."

I assumed as lugubrious an expression as possible and ventured to contest his point of view.

"I don't exactly see —" I began, but he stopped me.

"Perhaps not. I will explain. If I am – what shall we say? – removed, my First Secretary will certainly go with me. He is supposed to be equally to blame when anything goes wrong; he shares the reward when a small triumph is gained. Now, you are my First Secretary, Hamblin, and we are in no end of a mess; in your own interests I should recommend you to bestir yourself."

I drew a little breath. If I had not been in a way attached to my chief, I should certainly have used it for a different purpose. As Sir George had remarked, we were certainly in no end of a mess, but it was he himself and alone who had landed us there.

"If you could suggest any way, sir, in which I could be of the slightest use," I remarked deprecatingly, "nothing would give me more pleasure. Unfortunately, we seem to be sitting down before a great wall; it's too high to climb, and there's no way round."

"A very charming simile," Sir George said dryly. "Nevertheless, if you don't get over, yourself, or help me to, you won't marry my daughter."

I came to the conclusion promptly that Sir George was an unreasonable and disagreeable old man; but I kept my conviction to myself.

"I hope you will reconsider that, sir," I said most respectfully. "I am very fond of Clara, and I think she cares a little for me."

"Work for her, then," was the prompt answer. "Here's your chance. Get us out of this wretched muddle, and you shall have her – as soon as she likes!"

I pondered. I was very fond of Clara. I began to wish that the situation were not so hopeless. Sir George took up his penholder and marked time with it.

"The affair," he said, "lies in a nutshell; it is as simple as A B C."

"Oh, it's simple enough," I assented – "painfully simple!"

"England," the Ambassador continued, ignoring my interruption, "is at war with the Transvaal Republic. Last week there appeared in an issue of a foreign newspaper what purports to be an interview between the monarch of this country and the European representative of the Transvaal Republic. The interview – or, let us say, purported interview – you have read yourself. It is sufficient to remark that, if it was authentic, it was tantamount to a declaration of war against England. Now, you know what an artful old beggar Highbury is! He sends me across by Queen's messenger two sealed dispatches for the Emperor, addressed to him privately. One is marked 'A,' the other 'B.' Now, if the interview had been genuine, I was to have dealt the first blow by presenting 'B,' which is tantamount to an ultimatum couched in most formal and war-like language. If, on the other hand, its authenticity is denied, I present 'A,' which is a friendly little note assuring his Majesty that no notice was taken in England of what was obviously a ridiculous canard. You know, of course, what has happened."

"The Emperor has denied the whole story contemptuously from beginning to end," I remarked. "The Transvaal representative was never accorded an interview."

Sir George flourished the penholder with new vigour.

"Precisely. I accordingly left at the Palace the letter marked 'A,' and, returning here, proceeded to open and destroy letter 'B.' I read it first, and to my horror found that its contents were as per specification of letter 'A,' and that consequently the lettering must have been wrong, and the ultimatum left at the Palace."

"I don't quite see where we are to blame, you know," I interposed.

"Perhaps not," my chief remarked dryly. "You see, you are very young. But there is an axiom in diplomacy which you will do well to lay to heart. If anything goes wrong at your charge, no matter who is to blame, you are responsible. Those letters have been changed by spies, most likely, and I think I know who is at the bottom of it. It was probably done while they were in the possession of the Queen's messenger – he admits that he took no extra precautions. That is of no consequence. It is upon us that the blame will fall. There awaits for the Emperor a letter which will either plunge us into a ruinous, unnecessary, and unpopular war, or else will mean Highbury's resignation, our retirement to a Colony, and a most awful climb-down."

"The Emperor," I remarked, "is still at Meritzburg – manoeuvering?"

"Yes. He returns to-morrow. To-morrow night that letter will be handed to him."

"You're sure it hasn't been sent on to him?"

"Certain. I happen to know that his commands were most absolute.

Nothing was to be forwarded. Von Butz has the letter, and knows its contents."

"Sure of that?" I ventured.

Sir George tossed an evening paper over to me.

"You see what the beast is doing," he said. "Strange rumour at the barracks, all-night work at the arsenals, mysterious notices to railway companies. It all means one thing – mobilisation."

"Von Butz has read the letter by fair means or foul. The Emperor will receive it in person to-morrow night. The letter awaits him at Von Butz's house," I remarked thoughtfully.

"Marvellous!" Sir George remarked with sarcasm. "You have the insight of a Mazarin."

One must put up with sarcasm from one's prospective father-in-law, especially when he is in as tight a place as Sir George undoubtedly was. I had sufficient magnanimity to ignore it.

"Have you made any effort to regain possession of the letter?" I asked.

Sir George shook his head.

"I might as well try to fly," he said, "as attempt to regain possession of it by fair means. Von Butz is our enemy and the enemy of our country. All the ill-feeling and friction of the last few years has been his making and his alone. This letter is the summit of his desire. In the light of the Emperor's frank and downright statement, it is nothing more nor less than a brutal insult. I cannot imagine any apologies which could possibly be offered sufficient to atone for it. It will mean war for England and the Colonies for us."

"If the Emperor reads it," I remarked softly.

"If the Emperor reads it," Sir George repeated, looking over at me.

I buried my face in my hands and tried to think. There came a knock at the door and a telegraphic dispatch. Sir George fetched out the code-book with shaking fingers. He groaned as he read it out.

"Understand mobilisation secretly commenced. Panic on Stock Exchange owing to rumours from Badenberg. Presume you only delivered letter 'A.' What does it mean? Have you blundered? Reply.

"HIGHBURY"

"We haven't much time, have we?" I remarked. "Let us make the most of it."

"How?"

I took up my pen and the code-book, and wrote a telegram.

"To HIGHBURY, Downing St., London.

"Discredit all rumours. Mobilisation ridiculous. All quite here. Duly delivered letter 'A.' Probably Stock Exchange rig. Will request audience to-morrow."

"We'll start boldly, at any rate," I said, rising. "Send this, and I will be back in an hour."

"Where are you going?" Sir George asked.

"To call on Fräulein von Butz," I answered.

✳

Youth is dauntless and excitement is sweet. So I walked through the broad, sunlit streets of Badenberg with a smiling face, a cigarette of delicate flavour between my lips, and tried to persuade myself that it was not a forlorn hope upon which I had embarked. In my pocket was letter 'A,' which should have been marked 'B,' in my right hand a fragrant bunch of Neapolitan violets, whose faint, sweet perfume had stolen out to me from a florist's shop in the Avenue. As I passed up the broad steps of the mansion where Von Butz lived, the Fates did me a good turn. The door before me opened and Fräulein von Butz came out, dressed for driving.

I bowed low and held out the flowers.

"A farewell gift, Fräulein," I said sadly. "You will deign to accept them, I hope!"

She held out her hands, and her bright smile of welcome changed to a look of interrogation.

"I will accept them," she said, "with very much pleasure, and I thank you indeed for thinking of me. But why a farewell gift, Mr. Hamblin? Are you going away on leave again?"

I shook my head sorrowfully.

"It is no matter of leave, dear Fräulein," I said. "I am quitting the Service. I should have left to-day, but I wanted to say good-bye to you."

She turned back into the hall.

"Come inside," she said. "I do not understand."

I heard her instruct the hall-porter to send back the carriage. She led me into her own tiny sitting-room, as neat and dainty as herself, and motioned me to an easy-chair. She sat down close to me and loosened the furs from her neck.

"You are giving up the Service," she said, "you are leaving Badenberg! Is it not very sudden, Mr. Hamblin?"

"It has come upon me," I said gloomily, "like a thunderclap."

"You shall tell me," she insisted, raising her bright eyes to mine, "all about it. Have you come into the title, is your heath bad, or are you promoted?"

I was silent for a moment. It was silence which told. Then I shook my head.

"Fräulein," I said, "when I have gone you will hear from others what I would rather tell you myself. I have longed for this opportunity, yet now it has come – it is not easy!"

Her piquant little face was full of sympathy. By accident my hand fell upon the arm of her chair and touched her fingers. She drew them away – slowly.

"Fräulein," I said, "there is one profession in the world in which a single mistake is fatal. That profession unfortunately is, or was, mine – and that mistake – I have made."

"Oh!" she cried.

It was enough. My humiliation now required no pretence. It came naturally to me. I felt that I was a cad.

"Won't you tell me a little more?" she begged. "I am so very sorry for you – and sorry that you are going away."

Her hand once more fell upon the arm of her chair. Never were fingers more soft and velvety to the touch.

"Fräulein," I said, "if I may tell you, I will. I should like you to know the truth. It is this. Two letters were entrusted to me, one of which was to be delivered to the Emperor, the other destroyed. I delivered – to your father, as it happens – the wrong one."

She was perplexed.

"Is that all?" she asked.

I nodded.

"The action," I said, "is a small one – but the result is terrible."

"Terrible?"

"It is too weak a word," I assented. "Do you know what war means, Fräulein?"

She shuddered.

"Do not speak of it!" she begged.

"You will hear it spoken of before long, Fräulein," I said; "and, alas! I shall be the unhappy cause. War between your country and mine! It is fearful!"

I am afraid my fingers tightened upon hers. I am sure that the pressure was returned.

"The letter you spoke of," she asked – "has the Emperor received it yet?"

"Not yet," I answered; "your father has it. The Emperor returns to-morrow night."

She leaned forward, suddenly pale.

"He returns to-night!" she exclaimed. "Only an hour ago my father had a telegram from him."

"To-night or to-morrow night," I muttered – "what matters? The letter has gone from my hands beyond recovery; he opens it, reads, and war is as certain as to-morrow's sun. Oh, it is enough to make a man mad to think of it! War between the two nations who have brought the science of killing to perfection! It will be the greatest massacre the world has ever known, and the everlasting shame of it will be upon my head."

"Don't," she cried – "please don't!"

I drew myself up.

"At least, Fräulein," I said gently and with real tenderness, "I have no right to come here and make you miserable. Only I could not go away without seeing you and asking you to sometimes remember – a most unfortunate man!"

I stretched out my hand for my hat. She stopped me.

"No, no," she cried; "sit still! Let me think."

I watched the colour come and go from her cheeks. She pushed back the pretty fringe from her forehead. Ah, Gertrud von Butz, you wrote the memory of your dainty little self into my heart for ever in those few minutes!

She turned toward me.

"What if the letter were destroyed?" she asked slowly.

"It is impossible," I answered, with thumping heart.

"But if it were?"

"There would be no war," I said. "There would be no disgrace for me; I should remain in Badenberg. But it is impossible!"

"Should you know it if you saw it?" she asked.

"Of course."

She rose up.

"Come with me," she said. "Do not speak. If we meet my father it will be a convent for me. You must do what seems best to you."

She was as pale as a sheet, but she walked firmly and without hesitation. As we crossed the hall where several servants were standing she turned to me.

"Your own conservatories," she said, "are so much more beautiful. But there, you shall judge."

We turned off down a long passage. At the end was a conservatory, but she paused and listened at the last door on the right. It was empty. She turned the handle. We passed inside. She took a bunch of keys from her pocket and unlocked a cabinet which stood in the centre of the room. A pile of letters were there. My head swam with joy.

"Quick," she whispered. "Ah! We are lost. It is my father."

I dashed at the letters, seized a handful, but dropped them again as the lid of the cabinet fell upon my wrist. She whirled me across the room, behind a curtain into a long annexe to the conservatory. I could have cried with the disappointment. But for her sake I would have rushed out and torn the letter to pieces before Von Butz's eyes. Gertrud came close to me. I passed my arm round her waist; she was trembling violently.

Voices approached, and footsteps. The door of the room opened. Through the crack in the curtain I saw Von Butz enter, and my heart stood still. For behind him came a tall, familiar figure in a brilliant uniform partially covered by a long military cloak.

"And now, Von Butz, the letter at once," he exclaimed brusquely.

"Your Majesty shall have it," was the quiet answer, as Von Butz produced his keys. "When you have read it, you will say that I have done well in starting the great engine which your Majesty has constructed with such marvellous and wonderful forethought."

There was a moment's pause. Then I saw the letter pass into the Emperor's hands.

"You yourself, Von Butz," I heard him say, "are well acquainted with the contents?"

"My secret agents," Von Butz answered, "ever keen in the service of the Fatherland, borrowed it from the Queen's messenger and brought me a copy. We have saved hours which are worth millions."

The Emperor broke the seal. He stood up and a fierce light burned in his eyes.

"Von Butz," he said, "you will be my witness that these things which are to come are of God's ordination, not mine. With the finest army in the world, trained and brought to perfection under my own care and governance, I, the certain master of this great continent from the firing of the first guns of battle, have ever refrained from violence or provocation. With the warlike spirit of my forefathers in my veins, I have yet held out to all nations the olive branch instead of the iron grip. History must acknowledge this. Though I am all-conquering and almighty, I have yet been slow to strike. You will remember this, Von Butz."

"Always, your Majesty."

The Emperor tore open the letter and bent over it with serene forehead and expectant eyes. He read, frowned, re-read, and flung it passionately upon the table. He turned upon Von Butz with a fury which was paralysing.

"Dolt! Fool!" he cried. "You have been tricked! You have made me a laughing-stock! You have betrayed the nation!"

"Your Majesty," Von Butz faltered, "the copy I sent you was a faithful one. My agent copied it himself in the express."

"Listen, then," cried the Emperor.

He read out letter 'A.'

*

I walked home, my nerves tingling with excitement, relieved, but very puzzled. Sir George called me into the study immediately I arrived.

"Hamblin," he said, in an airy manner, "I'm afraid you have been disturbing yourself about a mare's nest!"

"Oh, indeed!" I found breath to say.

Sir George, nodded and tapped an open letter with his finger.

"It seems," he continued, "that Bucknell, the messenger, is rather a smart fellow. He found out that his dispatches had been tampered with, so wired Highbury for instructions. Immediately he received them he destroyed letter 'B' and duplicated 'A.' The duplication was to catch the thief, if possible, and I should imagine that it did."

"I should think so, too," I answered, smiling.

"One word more," Sir George said, coughing and assuming his most dignified deportment. "With regard to Clara, I have talked to her seriously, and found her, as I expected, amenable to reason. You are both too young to think of marriage, and an engagement does not seem to us desirable. In short, we have other views for Clara."

I drew a long breath – not of despair, but of resignation. That night, at the Russian Embassy, I sat out four dances with Gertrud von Butz.

MR. A/HLEY'/ FAILURE

A somewhat short, precise-looking young man stood on the steps of a mansion in Hyde Park Gardens, deliberately scraping his boots; for the weather was showery, and he had walked from the Foreign Office. Having concluded that operation, he turned to the opened door, and instantly perceived, from the disturbed expression of the usually most impassive of doorkeepers, that something was wrong.

"Is anything the matter, Burditt?" he asked condescendingly, as he stepped into the hall. "Mrs. Tregarron and Miss Alice are quite well, I hope?"

The man first carefully secured the door, then turned round and bowed.

"The ladies are quite well, my lord," he said gravely; "but we are all a good deal upset this afternoon. Mrs. Tregarron will see you at once in the morning-room, if your Lordship will be so good as to come this way," and he ushered the visitor down the hall into a small room on the left-hand side.

Curiosity was not one of Lord Maclenie's failings, neither was impatience; so he did not question the man further, merely desiring him to at once inform Mrs. Tregarron of his arrival.

In less than a minute his prospective mother-in-law – a tall, aristocratic-looking woman, wearing a widow's cap and looking about fifty years old – swept into the room.

"My dear Robert," she exclaimed, holding out her hand, "how good of you to come so soon! Of course you have had my note?"

His Lordship shook his head. "I have had no note from you today," he answered. "Alice is —"

"But I wrote you to Cadogan Place nearly two hours ago," interrupted Mrs. Tregarron.

"Which note I have not yet had the pleasure of receiving," he returned. "We are busy at the Foreign Office, and I have not been home to lunch. Alice is —"

"Then you don't know anything about it?" broke in Mrs. Tregarron. "Dear me! I —"

"If you were to tell me —" he ventured to suggest.

Mrs. Tregarron became all impressiveness.

"You remember that diamond necklace you gave Alice yesterday morning?"

Of course he remembered it. Had he not spent nearly the whole of the previous afternoon at Filmoy and Morton's, undecided whether a less magnificent present would not be deemed a more suitable offering to a portionless fiancee? and had he not, after finally deciding upon its acquisition, then and there written out a cheque for fifteen hundred guineas, and left the shop with the little morocco case in his breast-pocket? Certainly he remembered that diamond necklace.

"Well, what about it?" he inquired almost impatiently. He was proud of his self-control, this rising young diplomatist, but Mrs. Tregarron's manner was irritating.

"It has been stolen," she said impressively, and then leaned back in her chair, waiting anxiously to see what effect her communication would have upon him.

It was instantaneous. Lord Maclenie was self-controlled, but parsimonious; and fifteen hundred guineas is a good deal of money.

"Stolen!" he exclaimed, starting from his seat. "Stolen!"

"Yes, stolen," repeated Mrs. Tregarron, gently pressing a little lace handkerchief to her eyes, and watching all the time with deep anxiety his disturbed expression. "Sit still, and I will tell you all about it. You have no idea how upset we have all been."

"Upset! I should think so!" exclaimed his Lordship vigorously. "Have you any idea what that necklace was worth, I wonder?"

Mrs. Tregarron knew quite well her future son-in-law had taken care that she should not remain in ignorance, but she shook her head.

"Don't tell me, please," she pleaded. "I really cannot bear it just now. Let me tell you how it happened."

"Just what I want to get at," he exclaimed impatiently. "Do you suspect anyone?"

"At present, no one; but I think, when you hear the circumstances, you will agree with me that the theft must have been carried out by someone resident in the house; and, if so, they can have had no opportunity of disposing of it, for I have allowed no one to go out on any pretext whatever. I look upon it as somewhat a suspicious circumstance that Ann (Alice's maid) has twice asked for leave to absent herself this afternoon. Of course I refused it."

"Of course. But please tell me exactly how it happened," entreated Lord Maclenie.

Mrs. Tregarron cleared her throat and proceeded in her recital of the affair. Told in her own way and in her own words it took some time; but, briefly, the facts – very simple facts they were – appeared to be as follows: —

Directly after breakfast that morning, Alice (Mrs. Tregarron's only daughter and Lord Maclenie's betrothed) had left the room, and, a few minutes later, had summoned her mother into the apartment in which they now were to look at the diamonds by daylight. After admiring them for some time, Mrs. Tregarron was called away for her morning's interview with the cook, and about half an hour later Alice had come to her and announced her intention of visiting old Lady Somerville, her godmother. She did not return for luncheon – she very seldom did when she went to visit Lady Somerville – but got back early in the afternoon. She met her mother in the hall, and explained that she had hurried away immediately after lunch as it had suddenly occurred to her during that meal that she had left her necklace on the mantelpiece of the morning-room. Mrs. Tregarron and her daughter then entered the morning-room together and found that the necklace had disappeared. They searched everywhere, high and low, and then questioned the servants, who one and all denied having even entered that particular room during the whole morning.

"You can imagine what a state Alice and I were in then," concluded Mrs. Tregarron. "Poor girl! It made her quite ill, and she has gone to lie down for a while. Of course, I forbade any of the servants to leave the house, and sent round to you, and also a note to Scotland Yard. Did I do right?"

"I don't see that anything else could have been done," replied Lord Maclenie thoughtfully. "It seems a strange affair altogether. Could the room be entered from outside, I wonder?" and he crossed the room and looked out.

"Easily; but the window does not appear to have been tampered with, and you must remember it was in the middle of the day. Anyone getting through the window would certainly have been seen."

Once more the interior of the room was carefully examined. Nothing was to be discovered. All was in order. Neither could the sagacious officer from Scotland Yard, who arrived a quarter of an hour later, find anything at all suspicious in the entrance to or general appearance of the room. The servants one by one were had in and examined, and the trunks of all of them, from the newly installed scullery-maid to the gray-haired butler, thoroughly ransacked, but nothing affording the faintest shadow of a clue was discovered.

"Would you like to see my daughter herself?" inquired Mrs. Tregarron of the astute-looking detective, who stood sucking his pencil and looking thoroughly bewildered.

"Quite unnecessary," he declared. "I should be sorry to have her disturbed. There is really nothing to ask her beyond what you have told me. It's not a pleasant thing to say, ma'am," he continued, "but the thief must be one of your servants. I should like the name and address of each of them, and also, if you can oblige me with it, particulars of their last place;

and I must ask you to let me know at once if one of them leaves your service or give notice."

"I suppose a reward had better be offered?" remarked Lord Maclenie. The officer assented.

"Decidedly it would be better that there should be a reward."

"Then you can make it £250."

"Very good, your Lordship." And, after making a few more notes, the detective departed, with the usual promise that, should he discover a clue, etc.

A fortnight elapsed and nothing was heard from him. At the end of that time Lord Maclenie had a conversation at the club with an acquaintance concerning the mysterious robbery.

"In the hands of Scotland Yard, is it?" remarked the latter. "Well, I don't want to revile any of our institutions, but I really do think that, so far as our established detective force is concerned, we are a long way behind the other countries of Europe. Scotland Yard very seldom discovers anything more than clues nowadays. Now, look here, Maclenie," he continued in a lower tone, "I could introduce you to a man – he's not regularly in the profession, but he'd do anything for me – who would find out all about this little affair for you, if anyone could. He's a regular sharp fellow, is Ashley; and only say the word, and I'll tell him to call and see you."

Lord Maclenie shook his head doubtfully.

"I don't believe in amateur detectives much," he remarked disparagingly. "I'm afraid if Scotland Yard can't make anything of it, that it would be waste of time and money trying anyone else. Of course, if he likes to take it up on the chance of the reward – I've offered £250 reward, you know – well, then I don't mind helping him with any information. If he likes to come down to Hyde Park Gardens tonight, I shall be there."

"Well, I'll tell him," replied his friend. "Detective business of any sort is his hobby, and I dare say he'll come."

The surmise was a correct one. About nine o'clock of the same evening a respectable-looking, middle-aged man, who gave his name as Mr. Ashley, called at Mrs. Tregarron's house in Hyde Park Gardens and asked for Lord Maclenie, who was spending the evening with his betrothed. His Lordship immediately explained the circumstances to Mrs. Tregarron, and begged leave to have the man shown in.

"You really must excuse me, then," pleaded Miss Tregarron, rising from her chair with a languid gesture and a slight frown of annoyance. "I'm perfectly sick of the whole matter, and shall go to my room until the man's gone."

"As you please," and Lord Maclenie rose and opened the door.

"Ask Mr. Ashley to step this way," he said to the servant, who had remained in the room. And, accordingly, Mr. Ashley was shown in.

The simple story of the theft was repeated to him in a few words. He listened attentively and grew thoughtful.

"I should rather like to see Miss Tregarron," he remarked, after a long pause, "if not inconvenient."

Mrs. Tregarron looked rather doubtful.

"Is it necessary?" she inquired, with her hand on the bell.

Mr. Ashley bowed in a deprecating manner.

"If she is engage, pray don't disturb her," he said suavely. "Any time will do; but I should like to see her."

Mrs. Tregarron rang the ball, and, through the servant, conveyed Mr. Ashley's request to her daughter. In a minute or two he returned. Miss Tregarron was suffering from headache and had retired. She was sorry that she could not see Mr. Ashley.

The detective did not seem in the least disappointed; in fact, his eyes brightened as he received this message.

"It is of no consequence," he declared. "No doubt I have all the information available. I should like just a word with the coachman, though. May I step down stairs and speak to him?"

Mrs. Tregarron would have had him summoned, but the detective seemed bent on descending to the lower quarters, and, accordingly, he was ushered into the servants' hall, and the coachman brought to him; but when he arrived, Mr. Ashley seemed to have lost interest in him, and merely asked him carelessly a desultory question or two.

"Miss Tregarron kept you a good time waiting at Lady Somerville's?" he remarked.

"We didn't wait for her, sir; we had orders to come back and fetch her again in an hour and a half's time, which we did."

The detective seemed mildly surprised.

"I should have thought," he said reflectively, "that it would have been scarcely worth while for you to have come back again. It must have taken you all your time."

"It did that, sir, and no mistake," assented the coachman; "but young ladies never think of the 'osses. Anyways, them were her orders, and, of course, I was bound to obey them."

"Just so; and then she kept you a good time waiting, I expect, when you got back?"

"Not so very long, sir – not more than a quarter of an hour."

"Ah! well, good evening," said Mr. Ashley, turning away. "I am much obliged to you. Sorry to have disturbed you, though. I ought to have remembered that you were away during the time that the jewels were stolen."

"Seems a very mysterious affair, madam," he admitted, on his return to the upper regions. "If anything occurs to me, however, I will, of course, let you know. Good-night, ma'am; good-night, my lord," and Mr. Ashley bowed himself out of the room.

"Clear as daylight," he murmured to himself, as he walked slowly homewards; "but a nasty job to tackle."

Nevertheless, the quiet smile on his lips did not denote any great distaste in his task.

Early on the following morning he took the 'bus up to Highgate, and alighted at the road at which Lady Somerville resided. There was a cabstand near, and he entered the shelter and made a few inquiries, the result of which appeared to be perfectly satisfactory. Then he took down a name and address, after which a certain coin of the realm found its way into the dirty but eager palm of one of the Jehus.

He seemed to be getting on. He set off, after leaving the shelter, for a very different part of town, and entered a low, dirty-looking little shop, from behind the counter of which a somewhat dirty-looking Jew bowed to him obsequiously.

"A few words with you, Jacob," said the detective shortly; and, in obedience to a gesture, he followed the man into a little back room.

The few words lasted fully an hour, at the end of which time Mr. Ashley emerged from the shop with a confident smile upon his lips.

His morning's work was not yet finished, though. He made some more calls, but chiefly now upon his most distinguished patrons, including Lord Maclenie's friend, who had recommended him. As a rule, Society doings possessed no manner of interest for him, but today he was incessantly asking questions about different people, and at the end of the morning his satisfied smile had not decreased.

The next day he called again at Hyde Park Gardens. Mrs. Tregarron was out; but the announcement of her absence did not appear to be an overwhelming shock to him. In fact, he had just watched her drive away. He would see Miss Tregarron.

The servant to whom he conveyed his request was not at all sanguine as to the young lady's willingness to see him, but he was shown into the morning-room and his message taken. In a very few minutes a tall, handsome girl swept into the room and confronted him. The detective rose and bowed.

"You wish to speak with me, Mr. — Mr. Ashley, I believe?" she said, slightly acknowledging his salutation. "Be as quick as you can, please, as I'm particularly engage."

"I will not detain you a moment longer than is necessary, Miss Tregarron," he said quietly. "Permit me to offer you a chair."

She sat down and fixed her dark eyes upon him, full of impatient inquiry. Mr. Ashley hesitated. He had a delicate task before him, and he knew nothing of this young lady's disposition.

"Will you permit me," he said slowly, "to tell you a short story which has come under my notice lately? It will not detain you long, and you will, perhaps, find it interesting."

She arched her magnificent eyebrows, as if somewhat surprised at his presumption, but motioned him to proceed.

"We detectives come across some strange incidents sometimes," he began, "and unravel some curious tangles. Listen to this story, for instance, none the less interesting, perhaps, since it is strictly true. There was a young lady and young gentleman who fell in love with one another. Both were poor, both were in Society, and the young lady was everywhere expected to make a brilliant match, for she was beautiful and her mother ambitious. This young gentleman with whom she had unfortunately fallen in love, although of excellent family, was not only poor, but was also hopelessly in debt; and so, seeing the utter impossibility of ever being married to the man she loved, the young lady yields to her mother's solicitations and becomes engaged to a rich young nobleman.

"She has resolved to see no more of her unhappy lover, nor does she; but she hears of him often, for it happens that her maid and his manservant are brother and sister. She hears of his despair at the news of her engagement, of the terrible worry of his debts, and of his unsuccessful attempts to raise a certain sum of money to enable him to leave the country and start life afresh. Her pity for him is great, and she resolves anonymously to help him. At first, however, she is powerless, for she, too, is of a poor family, and the sum is an impossibility to her. Whilst she is striving hard to think of some means whereby to raise the money, her betrothed, a very rich but somewhat stingy young nobleman, makes her his first present – a diamond necklace of great value. An idea occurs to her. She cares nothing for the stones, and they are her own. Can she not secretly realize them, and thus obtain the money for her desperate lover? She resolves to do so, and lays her plans with considerable shrewdness. The necklace is believed by everyone to have been stolen; her lover receives the money in such a fashion that he imagines it to come from someone else from whom he has no hesitation in accepting it, and joyfully carries out his plans. Only two persons know the true facts of the cases – the young lady and myself."

"A very romantic story, Mr. Ashley," said the young lady quietly, with her eyes fixed upon the carpet. "I should like to know the end."

The detective smiled and cleared his throat.

"Well, the fact of – er – the second party becoming acquainted with this little story was most annoying to the young lady, as, of course, his disclosure of it would mean the breaking off of her marriage and social ruin. Fortunately, however, this second party was quite amenable to reason, and had not the slightest wish to ruin the young lady's prospects. He suggested to her, therefore, that she should promise him (on paper) to pay him twice the amount of the reward after her marriage and give him a small sum down to cover expenses." She, being a sensible girl, at once agreed to this.

Miss Tregarron rose and moved toward the door.

"You will excuse me for a moment?"

"Certainly," and during her brief absence Mr. Ashley occupied himself in drawing up a little document.

She was not gone long, and re-entered the room with a roll of notes in her hand.

"To continue your story, Mr. Ashley," she said, with a levity in her tones which scarcely harmonized with her pallor-stricken face, "the young lady handed over fifty pounds in notes — all she could spare before her marriage, for she was, as you observed, very poor — and signed the document which the second party had prepared for her," and, sitting down at the table, she signed with a firm hand the slip of paper which lay before her. "That ends the story, I think, Mr. Ashley," she added, rising.

"That ends the story, Miss Tregarron," the detective replied. "I wish you a very good-morning," and he bowed himself out of the room.

"Your detective didn't turn up trumps, after all," remarked Lord Maclenie to his friend in the smoking-room of the club, about a fortnight after his return from his honeymoon. "A regular duffer, I thought him."

"I can't make it out," replied his friend thoughtfully. "Ashley doesn't often fail."

Perhaps Mr. Ashley, after all, does not reckon this little affair as amongst his failures.

THE MAN WHO SAVED
THE PRESIDENT'S LIFE

It was the second day out, and people were beginning to settle down into their steamer clothes and manners. The girl had already established a little court, as was usual with her wherever she went. The man had not yet appeared.

He came just as the deck-steward appeared with the afternoon tea. He was tall and pale, with dark, deep-set eyes and a sensitive mouth, notwithstanding its straight, firm lines. His features were hard and cleanly cut, his clothes hung loosely about him, as though his gauntness were merely the temporary result of some recent illness. He stepped out from the gangway with some hesitation; but once there, he swept the deck with a keen, masterful glance. A lurch of the steamer threw him against the side of a chair. He calmly seated himself in it and commenced to look bored.

The chair was next to the girl's, but he did not appear to notice the fact. Several of the young men who were in attendance upon her had coveted the chair, but in vain. The girl, however, made no remark at this act of calm appropriation. It was left for his servant, who appeared a few minutes later with rugs and a small library of books, to point out to him that he was a trespasser.

"I beg your pardon, sir," he said, "but I don't think that this is your chair."

The man looked annoyed.

"It will do," he said shortly, "unless," he added, turning to the girl, "it belongs to one of your friends."

The girl smiled upon him pleasantly.

"It is my aunt's chair," she said; "but I think that you may safely occupy it for the present, at any rate. She will not be on deck this afternoon."

The young man raised his cap, but he seemed curiously bereft of words. His thanks were barely articulate, and if it were possible for him to have become paler, he certainly did so. His long, white hands clutched nervously at the rug which covered his knees. Every now and then he cautiously studied the girl's profile. Under his breath he groaned to himself.

"This is the beginning! What a fool I am! What a fool I have been!"

There was a change also in the girl. Her high spirits seemed to have deserted her. Her laughter was forced, the sallies of her cavaliers failed to amuse her. She, too, was apparently conscious of the sudden approach of tragedy. One by one her attendants deserted her. Soon she was alone with the man.

They did not begin to talk at once. They both seemed interested in the tumbled gray waste of waters through which the steamer was plowing her way. But presently her rug slipped, and she felt it replaced with firm, skillful hands. She thanked him — almost shyly for her — and they began to talk.

Their conversation took its tedious but necessary course through the desert of the commonplace, but long before the dinner bell rang the probationary period was past. He had learned that she was the Miss Ursula Bateman whom New York society papers loved to allude to as the prototype of the modern American young woman of fashion. She was tired of Newport and Lennox, and, although she did not tell him so, she was also tired of being ceaselessly importuned to marry one or another of a goodly number of eager young men. She was an orphan and her own mistress. In a moment of inspiration she had planned this flight, a Continental tour amongst the unvisited places of Europe with an elderly aunt of purely negative tendencies. She was very enthusiastic over her escape.

"You can't imagine how it feels," she told him, as they leaned over the rail together to watch a shoal of porpoises, "to be really free from it all for a month or two, at any rate. We're too much in earnest over our pleasure. We make a business of it, as we do of everything else."

He looked at her with a faint smile.

"I'm glad to see," he said gravely, "that you have emerged from the holocaust without any ineffaceable signs of the struggle."

She laughed good-humoredly.

"Oh! I know what you're thinking," she exclaimed; "but it isn't in the face alone one carries the marks of deterioration."

"I suppose not," he answered thoughtfully. "Yet the face is a wonderful index."

She turned and surveyed him coolly.

"You would trust your own impressions of a face, then? It would be sufficient for you?"

"I think so," he answered. "Corroborating evidence would, of course, be reassuring."

"But suppose the evidences — all appearances were against your impressions, which should you rely upon?" she persisted.

"I dare say I should find it hard to make up my mind," he admitted.

She nodded and brushed back the hair from her forehead.

"That is exactly how I feel," she said, turning and walking back to her chair.

✳

At dinner-time she was in unusual spirits. She increased at every
moment the circle of her admirers. She sat at the captain's table, and everyone seemed to catch a little of the reflected glory of her bright sayings and
infectious laughter. But someone asked her a question, about half way
through the meal, which for a moment checked her flow of spirits.

"Who was the man who turned us all out this afternoon, Miss Bateman? We can't put up with that sort of thing all the way over, you know.
No one man has a right to two whole interrupted hours alone with you
— not even the President of the United States!"

"His name is Geoffrey Paish," she answered. "I really don't know much
more about him than that."

The name awakened plenty of interest.

"Why, he's the fellow," someone eagerly exclaimed, "who's come in for
the whole of the Paish estate. The old man was a banker in New York, you
know — his uncle, I think it was. Mighty queer family, too."

"The old man died worth seven millions," the boy who sat on her left
hand remarked enviously. "Nice little pile for him to step into."

"Did anyone ever hear of this Geoffrey Paish at college or anywhere?"
asked Andrew Bliss, the man who sat opposite her.

No one had. A man from little higher up the table leaned forward.

"There were some very queer stories going about New York concerning
this young man only last week," he remarked.

The girl caught him up sharply.

"There are queer stories about everyone," she said, "if people care to listen to them. Let us talk about something else."

✳

She was a little later than the others when she came up on deck after
dinner. As usual, she wore no hat or wrap of any sort. The wind blew her
fair hair about her face, and she was obliged to gather up and hold the
skirts of her black dinner-gown. Several young men came hurrying toward
her, but she waved them away. She crossed the deck to where the man was
sitting. He had just finished a frugal dinner which had been brought out
to him by his servant.

"Will you come for a little walk?" she said. "I should like to go out to
the bows."

He rose at once and led the way. The journey to the fore-part of the ship
was a little devious, and once, after a moment's hesitation, he offered her

his hand. She took it frankly, and a sudden rush of colour came into his cheeks. The willing touch of her fingers possessed a certain significance for him.

They leaned over the white railings, and the fresh breeze blew strong and salt in their faces. She stood quite close to him.

"I wanted to come here," she said, "because we are safe against interruption. There is something which I have to say to you."

He moistened his dry lips. His interjection was scarcely audible.

"I was telling you only this afternoon," she said, "how monotonous my life had been. I seem to have been moving along the plane all the time. But once, for a few minutes, things were different. I had what I suppose people would call an adventure. It was while I was staying in Virginia with an aunt — not this one. I do not think that I will tell you the name of the place."

"Don't!" he muttered.

"It was a large, old-fashioned house, very low, and my room was on the first floor, only a few feet from the ground. One night we had a dance there. I fell asleep in my chair afterwards, leaving my jewels scattered about the dressing-room. When I woke up, there was a man in the room calmly filling his pockets with them."

"Pardon me," he interrupted, "but I hope you are noticing the phosphorus."

"We will talk about the phosphorus afterwards," she continued equably. "I suppose the slight noise I made disturbed him, and he wheeled suddenly round. He was a tall man and he wore a mask.

"A mask! Yes!"

"Which afterwards slipped," she continued. "Just at that moment all I could think of was that I was looking into the muzzle of a revolver.

"Of course you were not frightened?" he remarked, with a queer little smile.

"Not in the least," she answered him.

"I looked upon the revolver as a sort of harmless but necessary toy. At that moment I had no fear. But afterward —"

She shivered.

"Let me fetch you a cloak," he begged. "The breeze is too strong here."

"I am not cold," she answered calmly. "It was a memory. But to go on with my story. Naturally I asked the man what he was doing in my room, and as naturally he pointed to what were left of my jewels. For a burglar he was a terrible bungler. The hand which held his revolver shook so that I could have knocked it out of his hand."

"Look here," he said, "I've got to have some of these. It's life or death to me. I'm very sorry."

"I told him that he was welcome to all of them, that I was quite tired of them, and dying to get some new ones. I warned him of the bloodhounds, and told him of the nearest way to the State Road. And all the time he stood looking at me in a queer sort of way. I was absolutely certain that the man would never harm me. Perhaps I took advantage of my conviction. I began to laugh at him for his clumsiness. The man got mad. The first part of the whole thing ended very much as I had imagined it would. He threw down the jewels and made for the window. He was clumsy with the fastening, and I got up and helped him. It was then that his mask slipped. It was then also, for the first time, that the burglar misbehaved himself."

Again that queer little smile. The man looked up from the tumbling mass of cloven waters into the face of his companion.

"What did he do?" he asked.

"I shall not tell you," she answered severely. "Only, I think that I would rather have lost my jewels."

"You are not sure about it?" he demanded eagerly.

"It is not a matter which concerns you, is it?" she asked innocently.

He did not reply, and when she spoke again, her tone was graver.

"The comedy ended there, the tragedy began a few seconds later. The man was met upon the lawn by a confederate. There was a quarrel between them, presumably because the burglar declared that he had no jewels to share. I heard the second man declare that he would give his companion up to the police and earn the reward offered for his apprehension. I shouted to them softly to go away. They did not hear. Then I think that the second man decided to break into my room himself. I am surprised that he did not think of it before. It was absurdly easy. They quarreled. I could see that the first man was determined to stop him. Then there was the shooting. I saw it all. I could not move. I was terrified to death. They carried the second man into the house. I saw him clutch at the air and fall. It was horrible. The other man —"

"Yes?"

"He escaped. It was wonderful, but he escaped."

The man by her side touched his forehead lightly. There were great drops of moisture there, though the wind was still blowing about them.

"Well?" he said.

"The mask slipped," she murmured. "I have never forgotten his face for a single second."

They stood side by side, and the young men on the promenade-deck grumbled. The strains of shuffling feet came to them from the steerage. Then the man began to laugh softly, but very bitterly, as he tore open his coat.

"You think that he did not rob you — at all," he said. "You were wrong! See!"

It was a cracked and bent little ring of very thin gold, holding a single moonstone. He drew it from an inner pocket and held it out to her.

"You took that?" she exclaimed.

He nodded.

"That — and a memory," he said, looking into her face, "were the sole proceeds of my little attempt."

Her cheeks flushed a fiery red.

"How dare you remind me of that!" she exclaimed. "And I have always wanted to tell you — you took me by surprise, or I should have called out. Of course I should have called out."

He bowed.

"Well," he said, "I believe it. I took you by storm. All my life, I think — bah! What folly is this! I am quite ready, Miss Bateman."

"Ready?"

"You will tell the captain, of course, I shall not make any resistance. I always fancied that this would come some day, although I never thought that you would be concerned in it. I shall not deny anything. I had broken out of prison with the man Willard, and I shot him."

"Did you think that I was going to give you up?" she asked, looking at him with wide-open eyes.

"Of course. Why not? It is your duty," he answered.

"My duty?" she repeated.

"Certainly," he answered. "It will be quite simple. I shall deny nothing."

She was silent for a moment, leaning over the rails with her head resting upon her hands.

"Please to go away," she said to him. "I want to be quite alone — to think!"

He left her without a word.

II.

"Sure?"

"Dead sure. We've got him, Jake. It's a thousand dollars sure."

The girl turned her head cautiously. She saw the red tips of two cigars. She herself was out of sight behind a ventilator.

"Pity we had to take the trip," the first voice remarked. "We could have nabbed him in New York."

"I guess we're all right, anyway," was the answer. "An ocean trip won't do either of us any harm, and I wasn't taking any risks."

There was a moment's pause. The girl felt herself shaking from head to foot.

"What bothers me is how he has managed to escape detection all this time," one of the men remarked.

"Guess everybody thought he was a pauper," the other answered. "Nobody thought of looking for him amongst the millionaires."

"Sure! Old man Paish left him all his pile. I forgot that."

"Guess he'll try and square this thing. He's been clever enough at keeping out of the way. He won't fancy being dropped on just as he's off."

"Won't do," was the terse answer. "Besides, it won't pay us. This is a big thing!"

The men moved on, the girl lingered there. Her eyes were fixed upon vacancy. This was to be the end of it, then. A prison cell, perhaps worse. A sudden shriek of the foghorn broke in upon her thoughts. They had steamed right into the midst of a dense bank of white sea mist. Under cover of the gray floating shadows she stole away to her state-room and locked the door.

✳

Almost before the decks were dry the next morning she was out, and, curiously enough, she found him the only other early riser. A fresh, strong wind was blowing salt and vigorous, and the white spray was leaping high into the dazzling sunshine. She held on to the rail, and he came at once to her side.

"You see, I am not yet in irons," he said, with an attempt at gaiety which went ill with his beringed eyes and white cheeks. "What have I to thank for this respite?"

She looked at him in the face, and the breath seemed to die away in his body.

"I think," she said quietly, "that you know very well — that — that —"

The wonder of it kept him speechless, motionless. There was something in her face which he had never seen in any other woman's. He felt like a man mocked by a mirage of impossible joys. It was surely a miracle, this. He could not find any words, but for a moment their hands were clasped together.

"I wanted to speak to you," she said hurriedly. "There are one or two things which I must ask you."

"You shall ask me whatever you will, and I will answer you truly," he assured her.

"Are you really Geoffrey Paish?"

"Yes."

"You are very rich, then?"

"Very."

"Why did you break into my room?"

"I had just escaped from prison. I needed money to get away."

"And you were in prison for —?"

"For nothing I ever did. Please believe that. It is my only excuse for many things."

"I want to believe it," she answered simply. "I certainly shall, if you tell me so. Tell me what your plans are now?"

He shrugged his shoulders.

"My fortune," he said, "was a tardy recompense for the act of injustice which sent me to prison. I know that I risked a great deal in coming forward to claim it, but I had had enough of poverty. I was never known in my younger days by the name of Paish, and I have had a fever lately, which has altered me. I decided to risk it. I thought that if I could once reach Europe safely, I could find a dozen hiding-places."

Her eyes filled with tears.

"I am afraid," she said, "that you will not reach Europe safely."

"You mean that you will give me up?" he asked quietly. "It is your duty."

"You know very well that I shall not," she answered. "But there are others here on board, following you."

She told him of the conversation which she had overheard. He listened intently.

"I know the two men," he remarked. "I have seen them watching me."

"You must try and make terms with them," she suggested, eagerly. "Those sort of men are to be bribed, are they not?"

"Generally," he answered; "and yet, after all, I am not sure that it is worth while. I shall be hunted from corner to corner of the earth all my life. I shall bring disrepute and scandal upon my friends. Nothing worth having in life will be possible for me. I think that I will not struggle any more against fate."

"You must not talk like that," she answered. "You are a young man, and you should have a long life before you."

He laughed bitterly.

"The life behind has been too long!" he exclaimed.

She dropped her voice.

"For my sake," she whispered.

Again he looked at her in amazement. He was still weak from his fever, for his hands were trembling.

"You cannot mean — that you really care?" he said, in a low tone.

She smiled encouragement upon him. The breakfast-gong had sounded, and they were no longer alone.

"Should I be here if I did not?" she whispered.

✱

She played shuffleboard badly that morning, for only a few yards away Geoffrey Paish and two men were sitting together and talking earnestly. Their chairs were pulled almost to the rail; their heads were close together. It was not possible for her to hear a word of their conversation, yet she found her attention continually diverted toward them. At last the two men departed. Geoffrey Paish was left alone. He sat with unseeing eyes fixed upon the sky line. She came softly to him.

"Well?"

"The men are honest," he answered. "They are not to be bribed. I have offered them half my fortune."

She reeled for a moment and then sat down in one of the empty chairs.

"What are we to do?" she murmured. "Oh! what can we do?"

"For you," he answered, "there is only one thing. You must forget. Our acquaintance must end here. We may renew it, perhaps — in the police-court."

She looked at him reproachfully. He was instantly ashamed of himself.

"Forgive me," he whispered; "but indeed I scarcely know what I am saying. Either I am a little mad, or those two men were. They talked like lunatics."

"In what way?" she asked.

He laughed shortly.

"Well, they seemed to think that the notoriety I should gain would be a sort of recompense for any minor inconveniences such as imprisonment, for instance, which I might have to undergo. They talked of the whole affair as a capital joke, and they seemed amazed that I should have attempted to keep my secret at all."

She shuddered a little.

"That is the American of it," she exclaimed bitterly.

He looked cautiously around. Her chair was behind a boat. He took her fingers into his.

"I'm going to adopt your philosophy," he whispered. "Let us make the most of these few days."

✳

Of course, all sorts of stories went around. The one most favoured by their fellow-passengers, and which she herself had certainly encouraged, was that they were old friends who had parted years ago under some misunderstanding. No one else ventured to claim even a share of her time. The colour came back to his cheeks; his step upon the deck became positively buoyant. No one would have guessed anything of the shadow which lurked behind their apparent gaiety. Now and then they came across the two detectives, whose greeting was always perfectly respectful. He laughed once with a momentary bitterness as he returned their bow.

"What a devil's comedy!" he murmured.

Her fingers touched his, and the bitterness fled away.

"You are a witch," he declared.

At Queenstown she found Hoyle, the senior of the two men, in the saloon writing cablegrams, with a messenger at his side. He had covered them with his hand at her approach.

"You are determined to send those, Mr. Hoyle?" she said.

"I have no alternative, Miss Bateman," he answered.

"I, too, am rich," she said hesitatingly, "and I am engaged to Mr. Paish."

"Delighted to hear it," Hoyle answered heartily. "You mustn't let him get downhearted. Most of the men in the world would enjoy a little affair like this" (he tapped the cablegrams). "I guess it won't do him any harm in the long run. You'll excuse me now, Miss Bateman."

He was busy with another cable. She made her way on deck again. Only once during the rest of the way to Liverpool did she address the detective again.

"I want you to tell me," she said, stopping suddenly in front of his chair, "is — will — have you sent word to Liverpool?"

"Well," he answered slowly, "I guess so. I hated to do it, Miss Bateman, with you both so set against it; but there wasn't any use in bottling it up. I shouldn't be surprised if something didn't happen to Mr. Paish in Liverpool."

"At the docks?" she asked.

"At the docks," he answered.

✳

Early the next morning came their farewell. She drew him behind one of the boats and pressed her lips passionately to his. She dared not trust herself to words. Then he went overboard into the gray mists and was lost to sight in a moment.

✳

Twelve hours later he was shown into a sitting-room at the small private hotel which they had selected as their rendezvous. He was properly dressed, but he had the appearance of a man grown suddenly younger. His smile, as she rushed into his arms, was a trifle apologetic.

"You have seen the papers?" she cried.

He nodded.

"I must have been the densest of idiots!" he exclaimed. "I couldn't see what Hoyle was driving at all the time; and I suppose my head was full of the other thing."

"And all the time," she cried, half laughing, half sobbing, "you were a hero, and I didn't know it. You were the man who saved the President's life at Metrofuzo, and for whose discovery he offered a thousand dollars reward."

"It came my way," he said. "You can imagine that I was a bit reckless just then, and odds didn't scare me much."

She wiped the tears from her eyes.

"You have made yourself the laughingstock of the country, sir," she declared. "Fancy jumping overboard, even though it was in the river, to escape being lionised and interviewed! Why, it will be worse than ever now, when they do find you out."

He sighed.

"They mustn't find me," he said. "You forget, Ursula, the other affair remains."

She shrugged her shoulders scornfully.

"Pooh!" she exclaimed. "I guess the President will have to settle that for you. It isn't as though the man had died, you know."

He turned toward her suddenly.

"What? Say that again."

His voice sounded strange and harsh. He was suddenly pale again.

"I thought you knew," she murmured. "We took care of the man, and he got well. They took him back to prison."

He sat down heavily.

"And I," he said, "I carried with me all the way to Cuba, all through the fighting, and through many sleepless nights, that dead man's face! Great Heavens! Not dead! I never saw a newspaper. I never doubted but that he was dead. Not dead!"

He was trembling. She came and sank down by his side.

"If you hadn't met me," she murmured, "you would have never known."

He took her into his arms.

"Ursula," he said, "I am a free man. I can prove myself innocent of the thing they sent me to prison for. It was Paish's son who stole the bonds. He found it out, and that is why he left me his money. His son died in Cuba. I have his confession."

She laughed softly.

"Aren't you glad," she murmured, "that the mask slipped?"

He slipped a battered little ring on to her finger.

"After all," he remarked, "I wasn't such a clumsy burglar."

THE MAN WHOM
NOBODY LIKED

He came into their midst unexpectedly, apparently unconscious of the sudden silence which seemed designed to act as a barrier between him and them. He only smiled — a little malevolently, it is true, but still with some sense of humour. He dragged a chair across the lawn and seated himself in a cool place within a yard or so of his hostess.

"How very enterprising of you, Mr. Lyndham!" she murmured, lifting her parasol a little on one side, and inwardly rebelling against her husband's express instructions to be always civil to this man. "Have you walked all the way from Broom Hill in this sun?"

He assented, but without speech. His gesture was of the slightest. Really his manners were worse than brusque. Mrs. Poynton languidly ordered some fresh tea and turned her shoulder upon the newcomer. He had come without invitation upon an afternoon of some importance — he should entertain himself. There were limits to her tolerance, obedient wife though she was.

So the conversation ebbed and flowed around him. Everyone followed their hostess's lead and made no attempt to draw him into it. Yet never was a casual visitor so little upset by the subtle but unmistakable rudeness of being ignored. He drank his tea absently, and notwithstanding his isolation, he made no movement to depart.

"My dear Eleanor," Lady Martyn whispered to her hostess, "what an extraordinary man! Is he a specimen of your country neighbours? I thought the people were quite decent round here."

Mrs. Poynton gently elevated her shoulders.

"Heaven only knows who or what he is!" she murmured. "We none of us like him except my husband, and you know how anything unusual attracts him."

"But where does he come from? Is he a neighbour?"

"His name is Lyndham, and he has taken a cottage a few miles away. No one seems to have an idea who or what he is, and he is most uncommunicative. He seems to spend most of his time walking in the grounds here and staring up at the house."

"A gentleman — but how uncouth!" Lady Martyn declared under her breath.

Mrs. Poynton looked sideways at him through the lace which drooped from her parasol. There was disparagement, but a certain amount of curiosity in her stealthy gaze. Mr. Lyndham wore old clothes, his beard was ill-trimmed, his necktie a subterfuge. But, after all, perhaps Lady Martyn was right. There was a certain air of breeding about the man, and his voice had the unmistakable quality which attracts. She lowered her parasol again.

"Why he comes here," she said softly — "especially whilst my husband is away — I cannot imagine. No one is civil to him, and he very seldom speaks to anybody. He asked Arthur for permission to walk in the grounds, and since then he seems to haunt the place. I met him one evening striding along the avenue and muttering to himself. I must have passed within a yard of him, and he took not the slightest notice. I was almost frightened to death."

"Your husband was always so good-natured," Lady Martyn yawned. "By the by, how about the lease?"

"Arthur has gone up to see the solicitors," Mrs. Poynton answered. "They do not seem to be able to get any reply from Sir Gervase. I don't think they even know where he is, and they have no power of attorney."

Lady Martyn looked across the terraced lawn to the long, ivy-covered front of the house.

"I hope you do not lose it," she said.

"There isn't another place like it in the county. Isn't it almost time she came?"

Mrs. Poynton leaned forward in her chair.

"I believe," she said, "that I can hear the carriage."

From where they sat, the lower of three terraced lawns, cool with the quivering shade of dark cedar trees, one could see the long approach to the Abbey, a mile of straight white road leading through a parklike expanse of meadowland, yellow always at this time of the year with buttercups and clumps of marigolds. Mrs. Poynton rose to her feet, and there was as much excitement in her manner as a well-bred woman would permit herself to entertain.

"The Princess is coming," she announced.

Only her unwelcome visitor sat still. Everyone else stood up to catch a glimpse of the victoria, now plainly visible. Mrs. Poynton glanced at this man, whom nobody liked, almost with aversion. He represented the one alien note in the little party of immaculately flannelled men, and women in all the glory of muslin gowns and flower-garlanded hats. He ought to have the good sense to go before the arrival of the Princess. He must understand that his appearance and strange humours were in ill accord with a gathering such as this. But Mr. Lyndham did not move. His arms were folded, his eyes were fixed on vacancy. He seemed to have passed into a world of his own creation — obviously a very rude thing to do. Apparently he was not even contemplating an early departure.

He had manners enough to rise, however, when the Princess, seeing them all gathered under the cedar tree, stopped the carriage and came smiling across the lawn to them. A trifle grave-eyed, perhaps, and a little wary, she still justified easily the extravagant praises of a too personal Press. In her white lace dress and parasol, without a vestige of color, her pallor seemed to speak of a fatigue not wholly physical. Yet it was impossible to deny her beauty.

In the midst of a little buzz of introductions, she found herself suddenly face to face with Lyndham, whom Mrs. Poynton had no idea at all of mentioning. In those few seconds of breathless silence which intervened before she held out her hand, there flashed backwards and forwards between the two, nameless things. She, if possible, was a little paler, and her admirable self-possession faltered. He, too, seemed to be struggling for self-control.

"I may be permitted to recall myself to your memory, Princess," he said, looking at her steadily. "My name is Lyndham — Richard Lyndham. May I hope that I am not quite forgotten?"

She held out her hand.

"One does not forget one's oldest friends," she said softly. "I am very glad to see you again, Mr. Lyndham."

Her hostess led her away. The Princess of Berlitz was a personage, even if her husband's estates had lain far away in a corner of Austria; and the suite of rooms into which Mrs. Poynton herself conducted her had once been occupied by royalty. Tea and fruit were ready on a tiny table in the sitting-room. Beyond in the bedroom a couple of maids were already busy unpacking. Mrs. Poynton looked around, and the stream of idle words which had been passing between the two stopped.

"I wonder," she said, "if there is anything else I can do for you?"

The Princess hesitated.

"Yes," she said, "there is something else. I should be glad if I could speak for a few minutes with Mr. Lyndham up here."

Mrs. Poynton was taken aback. She stared blankly at her guest.

"With Mr. Lyndham?" she repeated vaguely.

The Princess bowed.

"Yes."

Mrs. Poynton recovered herself, though she was still steeped in amazement.

"By all means," she said slowly. "I will send him up to you."

Mrs. Poynton returned to the garden. Mr. Lyndham was still there, sitting a little apart from the others. She went up to him.

"Mr. Lyndham," she said, and unconsciously her voice took a new tone in addressing him, "the Princess desires to speak to you in her room. If you will come this way, I will show you where she is."

Mr. Lyndham rose slowly to his feet. He did not appear surprised, but he showed no signs of eagerness.

"I will follow you," he said.

✳

The door was safely closed. They were face to face. The Princess was in unfamiliar guise. Her eyes were full of tears, her voice, as she stood there with outstretched hand, shook.

"Gervase!" she exclaimed, "at last I have found you, then! You cannot escape me now. Come!"

He took her hand and raised it to his lips. He was almost unrecognizable. All the hardness seemed to have passed from his strong, weather-tanned face. His eyes and voice were as soft as a child's.

"Dear Gabrielle!" he murmured. "You believe still? You have not lost your faith?"

"Never! Never for one moment!"

"Thank God! Even though it be you against the world."

They were silent for several moments. There was so much between them which seemed better expressed unspoken.

"You keep still — your borrowed name?"

"I have no other," he answered.

"Yet you are back in England — here, of all places in the world."

"And in this room," he added, with a dash of his old cynicism. "Nothing is stranger than that!"

She stared away and looked around. Her dark eyes were full of shadows of some reawakened fear.

"It is true!" she declared. "The whole place is altered and modernised out of recognition. I did not realize where I was."

He moved to the window.

"It was from here," he said, "that the shot was fired; and there were a dozen people ready to testify that no one save myself passed out from this room."

She held out her hand.

"Gervase!" she exclaimed suddenly, "you are here with an object!"

"And you?"

"Also with an object. Tell me, you received a letter?"

"I did! It brought me from Alaska."

"And me," she declared, "from Austria. Look!"

He glanced at it.

"The same as mine," he declared. "Heaven knows, it seems improbable enough! But dying men sometimes tell the truth."

He was busy already at the wall. With his knife he gashed recklessly at the new and expensive lincrusta walton. For several minutes he pushed and strained and knocked. At last with a little cry he succeeded. A hidden door swung back a few inches. With a poker for a lever he forced it open. The Princess looked over his shoulder eagerly. It was a mere closet of an apartment, dark and empty, save for a single shelf.

"After all," he said despondently, "there is nothing here to help us."

"But do you not see," she exclaimed, "one part of the mystery vanishes from this moment? This is where the man hid who fired the shot!"

He nodded.

"I was an idiot not to have thought of the place before," he said, "but I was told that it had been blocked up whilst I was at school. You are right. One part of the mystery vanishes. But the other remains."

She pointed to something upon the floor.

"What is that?" she asked. "A book?"

He stooped to pick it up — a dingy, faded volume, with the word "Diary" stamped upon it on the outer cover, the sort of thing which was the weakness of the last generation of schoolgirls. It was thick with dust and yellow with age. He opened it carelessly at the last page and bent forward to catch the light. Then he gave a little cry.

"What is it, Gervase?"

"Heaven only knows!" he muttered, and the hand which clutched the book shook as though an ague had seized him. "Read, Gabrielle! I cannot!"

She snatched it from him. Followed by him, she carried it out into the light.

✳

The man whom nobody liked, the man who was Mrs. Poynton's bête noire, remained alone with the Princess in her sitting-room for nearly an hour. Meanwhile Mrs. Poynton and her guests talked. The more tolerant assumed an old friendship; others smiled. The Princess was of ancient family, but in the days before her fortunate marriage she had been poor. It was rumored that she had been a governess. Who could tell what entanglements she might not have formed at that time? The Prince, who had been dead for little more than a year, had left her a wealthy woman. Her place in Society seemed assured. It was supposed that she was ambitious. She was indeed a splendid victim for the intelligent blackmailer. Mrs. Poynton grew weary of explaining how little she knew of Mr. Lyndham. He had come from nobody knew where. Arthur had taken a fancy to him, it was true, but she herself had mistrusted him from the first. Then there was a sudden hush. The Princess and Mr. Lyndham were coming down the steps and across the lawn.

"Dear Mrs. Poynton," the Princess murmured, as she joined them, "my rooms are perfect. But one of them, I think, has a history. Is it true that Sir Knowles Philton was shot from the window of my sitting-room?"

Mrs. Poynton was a little perturbed.

"I am afraid that it is true," she admitted. "It is many years ago, however, and I thought that everyone would have forgotten. I hope you are not afraid of ghosts."

The Princess smiled brilliantly.

"Already," she confessed, "I have seen one."

There was a little murmur of amusement. Then everyone suddenly realized that she was in earnest. She had something to say to them.

"I want you to tell me something about that murder, Mrs. Poynton," the Princess said. "Sir Knowles was shot as he walked upon the terrace, was he not, by some unseen person? Was the mystery ever cleared up?"

Mrs. Poynton shook her head.

"Never positively," she answered. "Never in the courts, that is to say. Of course, all the evidence pointed to Gervase Philton, Knowles brother; and although they never arrested him, he had to leave the country."

"Was there any quarrel between them, then?" the Princess asked.

"No open quarrel," Mrs. Poynton answered, "but it came out afterwards that there had been a great deal of ill-feeling for some time. Very fortunately for Gervase, no word of this transpired at the inquest."

"Dear me," the Princess murmured. "And the cause of the ill-feeling — was that ever known?"

Mrs. Poynton shrugged her shoulders.

"The one eternal cause. She was a governess to Lady Morrey's children — Lady Morrey was their sister, you know, and she was living here while her husband completed his term in India. They say that both brothers were in love with her, and Gervase was supposed to be horribly jealous."

There flashed between the Princess and Mr. Lyndham an illuminative glance which was a source of wonder to Mrs. Poynton.

"Anyhow," Mrs. Poynton continued, "one night Sir Knowles was shot as he walked upon the terrace, and the shot was fired from his brother's window. Some workmen were taking down a picture on the landing just outside, and they saw no one but Gervase himself come out of or enter his room. So, you see, as far as the negative evidence went, it was fairly conclusive. Gervase remained in England for several months; then he went abroad, and no one has ever heard of him since. We took the place a few months afterwards, and for my own part I can't help saying that I hope Sir Gervase never comes back. We could not possibly find another place to suit us so well."

The Princess smiled. Mr. Lyndham, wonderful to relate, followed suit.

"I am afraid that there is a disappointment in store for you, Mrs. Poynton," the Princess said. "Sir Gervase is back in England now. He is sitting by my side."

"Mr. Lyndham!" Mrs. Poynton screamed.

Mr. Lyndham bowed.

"I must apologize for being here under false pretenses," he said, "but I had a very particular reason for desiring to pay a visit to this neighbourhood, and you can understand that I did not care to venture here under my own name. Eight years in the Colonies and a beard will do wonders for a man."

"Yet the Princess recognized you," Mrs. Poynton said.

"It is true," he admitted.

"I, too," the Princess remarked, "have an explanation to make. You have heard that I was a governess for two years before I marred the Prince of Berlitz; but you perhaps did not know that I was a governess at this house, that it was on my account even that poor Sir Gervase here was accused of shooting his brother, who never spoke more than a civil word to me in his life."

A sudden silence fell upon the little group. After all, the evidence had been very strong. Yet they neither of them looked in the least like guilty people.

"Sir Gervase would rather, perhaps, that I told you what has happened — what we have discovered," the Princess said. "It is very simple, and the mystery which has baffled everyone so long does not exist any longer. Adjoining my sitting-room, from which the shot was fired, is a small secret closet, which apparently has not been opened for years. Some months ago we both of us received anonymous letters, dated from a hospital in Paris, advising us to explore this place. Hence Sir Gervase, hence my broken vow — for I had sworn never to set foot in England again. The closet appealed to us, as a likely hiding-place for the person who had fired the shot, but we have been fortunate to discover far more important things."

"You found something there?" one of the guests exclaimed.

"This," the Princess declared, holding up a little volume. "It is a sort of diary, and it is very eloquent. Is it your pleasure that I read aloud the last two extracts only?"

"This is very extraordinary," Mrs. Poynton murmured. "Yes, please do read anything which will elucidate the matter."

The Princess opened the book.

"This," she said, "appears to be the diary of one Jules Letrange, valet of the late Sir Knowles Philton. The first few pages are merely a highly sentimental and romantic account of his affection for Mademoiselle de Caliste, which under the circumstances you will not expect me to read. He admits that he has not dared to betray himself in any way, he pleads guilty all the time to a most becoming doubt as to whether his suit would be in any way acceptable. He works his way through all the stages of frenzy, however, to madness, and he is evidently very near that state when this entry was written. You will observe that it was on the day of the murder.

"September 11th — I cannot bear it any longer! If she is not for me, she is for no one. She favors Monsieur Gervase — a union impossible for her. Me she passes always by. I do not count with her. I am as the dust on which she treads. If she only knew that I have sworn it, perhaps she would not go out then to meet her lover, so blithe, so gay. If she is not for me, she is not for any other man... If I see her with Monsieur Gervase again, it is the end...

"Heaven help me! I tremble all the time! I am afraid! I have shot the wrong man. I have shot Sir Knowles, my master. I heard him cry out! If only I could get away from here! I hid till it was dark — no one suspects. It is all finished. Tomorrow I may go. I leave this book. They speak of Monsieur Gervase. I will hide myself, and send word of this book if they arrest him. I..."

The Princess closed the little volume.

"The anonymous letters we both received were in the same handwriting. On my way through Paris I inquired at the hospital. The man is dead. He left no other confession. He left only this to tell his story."

Mrs. Poynton shut down her parasol with a snap.

"Really, it has been a most exciting afternoon. Only I am very much afraid now that I shall not get my lease renewed."

Sir Gervase and the Princess exchanged smiles. "That depends," he said, "upon the Princess."

THE GREAT FORTUNA MINE

"**M**r. Anderson, I am sure. I recognised you directly. What a strange chance that we should come across one another in this out-of-the-way part of the world!"

I had risen to my feet, of course, immediately she had taken me by surprise by halting in front of my small table. It was not possible to avoid taking the delicate long hand with its white fingers so frankly held out to me. We shook hands solemnly while I ransacked my brain for some coherent speech of apologetic denial. And then something in the expression of her wonderful brown eyes, a faint meaningful contraction of the eyebrows as she looked straight at me, altered the whole situation. She knew quite well that my name was not Anderson; she was perfectly well aware of the indubitable fact that these were the first words which we had ever exchanged.

I mumbled something idiotic, and she turned to glance down the room. The old man with whom she had entered, a decrepit, weak-faced, but aristocratic-looking, Englishman was shaking hands with an Italian, whom I had been told was a native of the place, and who had evidently come in to dine. They were out of earshot, and for the moment were not observing us.

She leaned over towards me.

"I have seen you here for the last few evenings," she said, hurriedly. "Tell me your real name."

"John P. Shrive," I answered. "I am an American."

The corners of her lips twitched slightly, and those wonderful eyes, which for several evenings I had done little else save sit and admire from a respectful distance, were filled with laughter.

"So I thought," she answered. "I wonder – I wonder whether you would care to do me a service?"

My words tripped one another up. I was incoherent, but earnest. For two days I had been vainly trying to find some excuse to speak to her. I had attempted a conversation with her father, and suffered the ignominy of a chilling repulse. A service. There was a very little in the world which I would not have attempted for her.

"After dinner, then," she said, "do not sit out in the front. You will find some seats at the back of the house. Order your coffee there, and I will come when I can. And remember this. If my father or Count Perlitto should speak to you don't be drawn into any conversation at all. Be rude to them if you can. Don't tell them anything about yourself or your business."

"Count Perlitto," I observed, "is the little dark gentleman with the brushed-up moustache?"

"Yes! But it is my father who is most likely to ask you questions. Please don't think that this is a conspiracy, or anything very terrible. I will explain it all to you presently."

With a little smile and a nod she turned away and joined the two men at the other end of the room. I ordered double my usual quantity of wine and began my dinner.

Now, for two evenings I had dined alone at this same little table, which I had carefully chosen because it afforded me the most satisfactory view of the most beautiful girl I had ever seen in my life. She was tall and very slight, her hair was lightish brown, and here and there a glint of gold, and she had that French trick of laughing with her eyes which I never could resist. She wore delightfully cool muslin gowns, and about her whole person, her jewellery, her shoes, and the care of her hands, there was a certain inexplicable daintiness which was as much a part of her as that delightful little laugh which seemed to me the most musical thing I had ever heard in my life. But to-night things were different. I myself had become an object of the most surprising interest to her two companions. I saw the girl lean forward and talk to them as she trifled with some new and highly-seasoned hors d'oeuvre, and the effect of her words was instantaneous. Her father fumbled for a moment with an enormous horn-rimmed monocle, having successfully fixed which in his left eye, he turned and transfixed me with a most tremendous stare. The little Italian displayed a similar interest in slightly different fashion. He kept darting side-long glances towards me, showing his white teeth and curling his black moustache, and all the while talking in most animated fashion to his two companions. This sort of thing went on more or less during the entire progress of the meal, to my great discomfort. No sooner did I raise my eyes to steal one of my customary glances towards the young lady than either the horn monocle with its blank, unwavering stare, or the little Italian's keen black eyes were fixed upon me. Between curiosity and annoyance, my dinner was completely spoilt. I missed a course, and was in the act of rising when I saw the whole party hurriedly leave their places and bear down upon me.

Her father, who only yesterday had responded to some attempted advances on my part with truly British hauteur, stopped at my table and smiled genially upon me.

"If you are taking your coffee outside this evening," he said, "will you join us? This is my friend, Count Perlitto, who is a large landowner in the neighbourhood; my daughter I believe you have already met."

I glanced towards her and found a decided negative engraven upon her frowning forehead. On the whole, though I was burning with curiosity to know what the whole thing meant, I was glad to have an opportunity of asserting my independence.

"I'm very much obliged to you, sir, for the suggestion," I said, "but I'm afraid it's quite impossible. I have a great deal of writing to do to-night, and the mails out here are a trifle scanty."

I distinctly saw the two men exchange rapid glances as I mentioned the writing.

The Count interposed. "The writing. Oh, yes," he said, "but afterwards? The evening is positively too fine to be spent within the doors – beneath the roof – ah, you understand? Besides, you are a tourist, is it not so, from a great country? We would wish, we who live here, to show hospitality to those who come so far from the large cities where all the sightseers find their way. Here it is very different. Here you see the true Italy. You will do us the honour, signor? There is some liqueur, not of the house, which is to be recommended."

Guidance was before me in the frown, now even more forbidding.

"Very sorry, Count," I said firmly. "It is quite impossible for me to join you this evening."

He departed with a polite expression of regret. The girl smiled at me over her shoulder, which I took to mean that so far I had done the correct thing. I sat down in my chair, poured out a glass of wine and tried to puzzle out where I stood. The Count, who was, as I well knew, the great landowner of the place, and whose aversion to tourists was a byword, and who had several times passed me on the road with an insolent stare, was suddenly more than commonly anxious to make my acquaintance. The father of the young lady who had been the object of my respectful, but vehement, admiration, after repulsing my advances in the most freezing manner, was displaying at least a similar anxiety. The change in both of them dated from the moment when the young lady herself had directed their attention towards me. The undoubted inference then was that she had told them something or other concerning me which had aroused their interest. I determined to go and find out what it was.

The place to which I had been directed was deserted when I arrived there, and deservedly so. There were a few iron chairs, a patch of scanty grass, a long line of outbuildings, and beyond the sloping vineyards. I lit a cigarette, but decided not to advertise my presence there by ordering coffee. In a very few moments I heard the soft rustle of advancing skirts, and she came round the corner of the grey stone building.

Whatever this matter was in which I was becoming involved, it apparently savoured more of comedy than tragedy, to judge by the suppressed laughter in the girl's face. I wiped the dust from a chair with my handkerchief, and she sat down beside me with the utmost composure.

"I suppose, Mr. — Shrive," she began, "you have made up your mind that I am a most forward young person."

"If you want me to tell you exactly what I think of you," I answered, moving a little nearer, "all I can say is that I'm ready to go straight ahead."

She nodded composedly.

"Yes," she said, "you look like that sort of person."

"What sort of person?" I asked.

"The sort of person who goes straight ahead. It's a characteristic of your country-people, isn't it?"

"When one's mind is made up," I said, firmly, touching, as though by accident, the back of her chair.

"There are some necessary explanations," she murmured. "Afterwards —"

She looked at me. I withdrew my hand.

"Please go on," I said.

"My father's name is Derwent," she said. "He has come out here to look at a silver mine belonging to Count Perlitto. He wants to buy it."

I nodded.

"Yes," I said, encouragingly. "The Count looks like the sort who have silver mines to sell. We get plenty of them out in Boston."

"My father thinks he is a good business man," she continued. "As a matter of fact, he has lost nearly all his money speculating in things which he doesn't understand a bit. He has about twenty-thousand pounds left. That is all we have to live upon. The Count is asking twenty-thousand pounds for this mine. If my father buys it we shall be penniless."

"Sure the mine's no good?" I asked.

"Absolutely," she answered, with the first note of impatience in her tone. "Ask yourself what the probabilities are. My father knows nothing about mining himself, and he has not even an expert's opinion upon it. He goes entirely upon the Count's word, and what the Count chooses to show him. Why, the mine isn't being worked – hasn't been worked for thirty years."

"Perhaps," I suggested, "the Count hasn't the capital to work it. Labour out here's mighty cheap, but up-to-date mining takes a lot of money."

She looked at him with a faint frown. The smile had gone from her lips.

"The mine is worthless," she said, simply. "I am sure of it. I have read up its past history, and if ever there were silver there at all it has been exhausted long ago. But even granted that there is a chance in favour of the mine – which there isn't – I want you to remember that this twenty-thousand pounds is all that stands between us and beggary."

"In that case," I said, decidedly, "your father is mad even to think about the deal."

"I knew," she said, "that you would agree with me. You can understand, can you not, the trouble I am in? My father's mind is practically made up. He means to buy the mine. I saw a telegram to his lawyers, ordering them to realise our last securities. The moment the money comes, my father will sign the deed of purchase."

"Has he no friends," I asked, "whose opinion he would take?"

"Not one," she answered. "He has always been so foolish that I think everyone is tired of advising him. He always goes his own way in the long run. He is so painfully obstinate. I do not think that there is anybody who can help me – except you."

Her hand fell upon my coat-sleeve, and mine promptly closed over it. She made no movement to draw it away. I felt that I would have pitched the Count down one of his own shafts with pleasure if she had asked me.

"What can I do?" I asked.

"I will tell you," she said. "A plan came into my head when I saw you sitting there alone this evening. Somehow – you looked helpful, and – I had an idea that – you know you behaved rather badly, haven't you?"

"You mean that I have looked at you a good deal," I answered. "I couldn't help it, Miss Derwent, indeed. It wasn't impertinence. I just felt that I wanted to know you badly, and the next best thing was to sit in my corner and watch you. You are rather nice to watch."

"Am I?" she asked, softly.

"You couldn't give me greater happiness," I said, "than to help you – if, indeed, that is possible. You see, helping implies a reward, doesn't it?"

"You want bribing, then?" she asked, with affected coldness.

"Call it an incentive," I answered. "At least – if it is all I can get – a word of gratitude from you will be worth all the trouble you can give me."

"Is that all – you will expect?" she asked softly.

I felt my heart thumping against my ribs. I wanted to raise her fingers to my lips, and draw her close to me, and I dared do nothing of the sort. I knew well that she was half playing with me, that she permitted herself this badinage because she had decided rightly or wrongly that I was a person to be trusted.

"If I dared to ask all that I would wish to claim," I said, earnestly, "I am afraid that you would say that my service was not worth the price."

An incomprehensible smile played about her lips. I have often wondered since exactly what she was thinking of at that moment.

"Supposing," she suggested, softly, "that we waive the question of incentive – or reward."

"I will willingly leave it," I said, "to your generosity."

She sighed. Her tone when she spoke again was more practical. I felt that a delightful little interlude was over.

"To go back to my plan," she said. "What I want you to do is very simple. I want you to transform yourself into one of those creatures who go about and report on mines – experts you know."

I looked at her steadily.

"Ah!" I said.

"In fact," she continued, "so far as my father and the Count are concerned, you are one already. I told them that your real name was Anderson, that I met you at Mrs. Murgatroyd's, and that you were something to do with mining. You must have noticed their sudden change of manner towards you."

"Yes," I admitted, "I noticed that."

"Of course," she continued, "you won't want to give yourself away all at once. Keep up the tourist as long as you can. But in the end I want you to let father think that you have been sent here by another syndicate to report upon the property, and that your decision is most unfavourable. That ought to stop him buying it, and, in short, that is my plan."

I remained silent. I felt her eyes upon me.

"Do you mind?" she asked timidly. "Is it too difficult? Or perhaps you don't like saying what isn't true?"

"I don't mind a bit," I assured her. "I think that your plan is wonderful, and I will do my best to carry it out."

"I shall never be able to thank you enough," she murmured. "Poverty is hard enough as it is, but destitution!"

I took her hand again. It was soft and cool, and faintly responsive. I felt that I would have lied till I was black in the face for her. But I wondered —

II.

The Count was the first upon the field. He caught me smoking an early cigarette in the cobbled square of the little town, and at once waved his hand in friendly salute.

"Ah!" he cried, as though the sight of me were some unexpected boon conferred upon him by Providence. "It is Mr. Anderson, is it not? Good morning! Good morning!"

"My name," I answered, "is Shrive. John P. Shrive!"

The Count shrugged his shoulders. Suddenly he came close up to my side and looked round to be sure that we were alone.

"Come," he said, "you are an American; you are a people of great affairs; you like, I think, that one talks business with you. Whatever your name may be, you are here to make a report upon my mine – the Great Fortuna

Mine. Is it not so?"

"My dear Count," I said, "I guess you are a long way off this time. I know no more about mines than a babe unborn. I'm junior partner and buyer in a firm of dry goods men in Boston, and I'm on my way to Genoa to buy silk. I just stopped over a day or so to get a bit of your country at first hand, and to see your pictures."

The Count listened to me with marked impatience, tapping his leg all the while with his long riding whip. When I had finished he smiled at me serenely.

"Very good, very good, my dear sir. I understand perfectly that it is necessary for you to act secretly. But I will be frank with you. The mine is as good as sold."

I was careful to let an instantly smothered little exclamation of dismay escape me. The Count heard it with a smile of triumph.

"To whom?" I asked.

"To the Englishman, Mr. Derwent," the Count answered promptly. "I am quite open with you – as you see. I cannot treat with your principals, whoever they may be."

"My principals," I answered, "don't buy mines. We deal in dry goods."

"Yes! Yes!" he ejaculated impatiently. "I know all about that. But let us talk like sensible men, eh? The mine being sold, your report is useless, is it not so? Come, you shall not have your labour for nothing. I will buy it from you."

"If the mine is already sold," I remarked, "of what value can my report be – supposing I have made one?"

"As good as sold," he interrupted. "It is the formalities only which await completion."

"Then I still do not see," I said, "of what value my supposed report could be."

The Count fixed me with his little black eyes.

"For the purposes of business," he said slowly, "no! It is not worth the paper on which it is written. But I will show you how frank I am. Mr. Derwent, he, too, knows that you are Mr. Anderson, the mining expert. He will come to you for your verdict. He will, perhaps, try to buy your report. Now, you have had no opportunity to inspect the property properly. It may be – I cannot tell – that you have even prepared an unfavourable report. If so I will buy it from you. I do not wish to cause the good Mr. Derwent any uneasiness."

"The uneasiness," I remarked, "will come later on."

"What you mean?" he asked, quickly.

"I know nothing about mines," I said. "I am a dry goods man. But somehow I don't take much stock in the Fortuna Mine."

"For how much you not say that again?" he asked. "Not any more at all. For how much you say it is a good mine?"

The little Count had got there at last. I pursed up my lips and stood as though thinking. The Count watched my face anxiously.

Fortunately for me intervention came in the shape of Mr. Derwent and his daughter, who called to us from the front of the hotel. I could not but admire the ease and grace with which the Count cloaked his annoyance. He took me by the arm and let me across the square, all smiles and bows.

"For how much, dear friend?" he whispered in my ear.

I shook my head.

"You're rushing this a bit, Count," I answered. "I'll think it over."

The Count muttered something which sounded very much like "damn," but was probably something worse. A moment afterwards we were shaking hands with the Derwents.

Miss Derwent, in a broad-brimmed picture hat trimmed with roses, and a white flannel gown, looked more charming than ever. Her greeting, too, with its delicate insinuation of our secret understanding, was exactly what I had looked for. She had talked to me in undertones of the beauty of the place, the clearness of the sky, the wonderful early sunlight in which the distant vine-covered hills were bathed. But of the other things which lay between us she made no mention, nor did she attempt in any way to draw me apart from the others.

Our déjeuner – I seemed to be included in the meal as a matter of course – was quite a success. The Count chatted gaily and well of the beauties of the country where, he told us, with a little burst of pardonable pride, his family had ruled for ten centuries. He spoke of art and the things appertaining to it with the ease and fluency of one who was master of his subject. Of his mine, too, he spoke vaguely as the repository of hidden treasures which would long ago have been dragged to light but for his love of the quiet countryside.

"You English," he said, "and you," he added, addressing me, "you do not understand that feeling. It is well for you that you do not. You are a utilitarian people. It is you who work hand-in-hand to-day with the great forces of the world. But with us here it is different. We are guilty of the terrible weakness of leaning upon our past. The people round here are my people. I want to see them husbandmen and wine-growers, not miners with pale faces, sowing the seeds of weakness in the next generation. I love to see my hillsides covered with vineyards as they have ever been. I do not love the tall shafts, the roar of machinery, the country made black and scarred with the entrails torn out of the earth. And yet these things must come," he murmured, leaning back and lighting a cigarette. "For many years I have struggled against it, but no longer. Ah, it is not possible."

I looked across at the Count with unfeigned admiration. His beautiful eyes were filled with sadness. He leaned back in his chair, looking out upon the distant hillside as though already those shafts had come into existence. Miss Derwent permitted herself the faintest of smiles as she glanced across at me. Mr. Derwent seemed intent upon the great dish of strawberries which the Count had sent down from his own villa.

After breakfast we were served with coffee and some delicate green liqueur, and then Mr. Derwent took his hand in the game. He began by moving his chair close to mine, and making clumsy efforts to get rid of the Count and his daughter. At this sort of game the Count was his master, and with very faint help from Veronica (I knew her name now), his attempts for some time were unsuccessful. At last, however, in obedience, as I suspect, to a vigorous under-the-table injunction from her father, Veronica rose languidly to her feet.

"I am afraid," she said, "that I am in an extravagant frame of mind this morning. After all, I think that I must have that ivory cross. Count, will you come and interpret for me?"

The Count rose to his feet with much less than his usual gallantry.

"Will you not charge me with the commission, signorina," he said. "My shop-people, when they see an English lady or an American, are, I fear, inclined to be exorbitant. Leave it to me, and I will promise you the cross at much less cost."

Veronica hesitated. Mr. Derwent interposed.

"Nonsense, my dear!" he exclaimed. "I have seen the cross, and I think the price very reasonable. Go with the Count at once and secure it. I insist! It is only fair that we should spend a little money in a town where we have been so well entertained."

Veronica lifted her white skirts just far enough to show me a delightful little foot, and turned toward the Count. It was not possible for him to hesitate any longer. He made a vigorous effort, however, to include me in the party.

"You, too, Mr. Anderson," he said passing his arm through mine. "Oh, I insist. There are, indeed, some valuable curios to be seen. It is an opportunity which you must not miss."

I am convinced that Mr. Derwent would have detained me by main force had I not saved him the trouble. I rose from my chair as Veronica passed, but excused myself with some emphasis.

"Sorry, Count," I said, "but I'm afraid I'm very unlike most of my countrypeople in that respect. I've no use for curios. I like my ornaments and my furniture clean and modern. I'll keep Mr. Derwent company."

The Count threw me a look over his shoulder, evidently intended to remind me of our uncompleted bargain. Veronica nodded to me from underneath her parasol, and crossed the square at a pace which the Count must have found maddeningly slow. Mr. Derwent leaned over towards me and opened the ball straight off.

III.

"I—er—was hoping to have a few minutes' conversation with you this morning, Mr. Anderson," he said, slowly adjusting his eye-glass. "From something which my daughter let drop in—er—the course of conversation, I gathered that you were to some extent interested in – in short, in mining properties."

"You wanted to ask me," I suggested, "about this mine of the Count's?"

"Exactly!" he admitted. "Now I am free to confess that I am not a mining expert. I came out to have a look at the property, meaning—er—to have an independent opinion in case I thought it likely to interest me. I find, however, that there is no room for any delay in the matter. Our good friend the Count – very decent, hospitable sort of fellow he seems – is, between ourselves, hard pressed. He means to sell, and to sell at once. He says that his brother is even now in London with a power of attorney. However that may be, it is certain that I have no time to get an expert out. I must rely upon my own judgment and the Count's honesty."

"Of the two—" I murmured.

"Eh?" Mr. Derwent interrupted.

I stirred my coffee vigorously and disclaimed speech. Mr. Derwent glared at me from behind his monocle.

"It occurred to me," he went on, "that you might in this dilemma be inclined to help me with a word of advice. I am aware," he went on with a little wave of the hand, "that such a course is a little unusual. I refrain from asking you any personal questions. What your position here may be I do not know. I do not enquire. It is not my business. You may be—er—representing other interests. I will take my risk of that. I have ventured to make out this cheque for one hundred guineas;" he pushed it towards me. "Consider me for the moment as a client. Is the Great Fortuna Mine worth twenty-thousand pounds?"

I tore the cheque into small pieces. "It is not worth twenty-thousand pence," I answered.

He suddenly dropped his eye-glass and leaned forward. I scarcely knew him. A certain vagueness of expression was gone. He spoke and looked like a wide-awake astute man.

"Come," he said, "I don't like your tearing that cheque up. You could have given me value for the money, and no man should be ashamed to take what he has earned."

"No man," I answered, "can serve two masters. That's a mighty true saying, Mr. Derwent."

"There's only one thing I'm afraid of about you," he said, eyeing me keenly. "I can't be altogether sure that Veronica hasn't been getting at you."

"Do you allude," I asked guardedly, "to your daughter?"

He ignored my question, but I could see that his suspicions were growing.

"For some reason or other," he remarked thoughtfully, "Veronica is dead set against this deal. I never knew her to interfere in a business matter before. I can't understand it at all."

"Your daughter," I said gravely, "may surely be pardoned if she takes some interest in a matter concerning her so closely."

"But for the life of me," he protested, "I cannot see how it does concern her."

"Speculations such as this," I said severely, "may be the pastime of the rich; but to gamble with the shreds of one's fortune is unpardonable."

He looked at me in amazement.

"You—I—but you must be acquainted with my daughter, I suppose. You must have some idea of what you are talking about?"

"Naturally," I answered tersely.

"Then upon my word, for an intelligent young man," he said, "you're about the best hand at talking nonsense I've come across."

"You ought to be a judge," I answered. "However, for your daughter's sake, here's the best and safest tip you've ever had. Let the mine alone."

"I'm inclined to think you're right," he admitted with a sigh. "It is a risk, especially if your people, whoever they might be, are 'bears.' I hate to come all this way and do no business, though."

"Why don't you stay at home, then," I said, severely, "and for your daughter's sake put the little you have in a good railroad stock?"

He set down the liqueur glass which he had been in the act of raising to his lips, and looked at me for a moment in utter astonishment. Then he leaned back in his chair and laughed till the tears came into his eyes.

"I don't know who you are," he said weakly, "but you're the funniest young man I ever came across. Never mind. I believe you're right about the mine. We'll start back to London this morning."

I was perhaps as astonished as he was, but I said nothing, for the Count and Veronica were close at hand. The former looked at us both anxiously.

"Come," he called out, "we have triumphed. The ivory cross is ours. And now, if you are ready, Mr. Derwent, my carriage is here. The notary will be at my villa in an hour's time."

Mr. Derwent rose to his feet.

"One moment, Count," he said.

They stepped aside. Veronica turned to me. There was the most becoming little pink flush upon her cheek.

"Well?" she exclaimed.

"I think that your father is persuaded," I said. "He will not buy. He is telling the Count so now."

She laughed softly.

"My friend," she said, "I shall be for ever in your debt."

"I would rather," I answered, "that you paid."

She looked at me and down at her feet.

"He would have signed last night," she said, "if I had not invented you."

The Count and Mr. Derwent came towards us. The former was pale with rage. I am convinced that nothing but the arrival of a telegraph message at that instant prevented his assaulting me. He tore open his message, and as he read he became a changed man.

"Alas!" he exclaimed, turning towards Mr. Derwent with ill-concealed triumph, "I can no longer argue this matter with you. Your time was up last night. You have exceeded it, and, behold, the mine is no longer mine to deal with. It is sold."

Mr. Derwent looked sharply at me.

"Sold to whom?" he asked.

The Count shrugged his shoulders.

"It is my brother in London who has arranged the matter," he said. "He has power of attorney, and he has received the money. The purchaser is a Mr. Charles Ellicot.

Mr. Derwent looked at his daughter.

"What do you know about this, Veronica?" he asked.

"Tell you presently, father," she answered. "Just at present I want to talk to Mr. Anderson. Please come here."

I followed her obediently round the hotel to the gardens in the rear. She made me sit down, and took the seat next to mine. As though afraid that I might seek to escape, she laid her hand upon mine. It was not necessary.

"First of all," she began, boldly, "I'm engaged to Charlie."

I held her hand tightly. I was not capable of articulate speech just then.

"Father wouldn't hear of it," she went on. "He said that Charlie was too poor, and had never done anything. He didn't believe in Charlie. I did."

She paused. I think she found my silence a little disconcerting.

"Charlie heard of this mine," she went on. "He sent over two experts and got two magnificent reports. Then he sent about trying to raise the money to buy it. Unfortunately, father heard about the mine too, and he decided to come over and look at it. I came with him to try to stop his buying it, if I could. All the time Charlie was trying to raise the money in London. Yesterday he wired me, 'All promised. Shall conclude to-morrow.' I was almost at my wit's end, for father had arranged to conclude the purchase last night."

"This is where I come in, I suppose," I remarked feebly.

She nodded.

"They really put the idea into my head," she said. "My father wondered whether you were not here in connection with the mine, and the Count looked mysterious and smiled to himself. So I spoke to you last night, and afterwards I told them that you were a mining-engineer. That put father off at once, for he saw a chance of getting an expert opinion."

"He had it," I murmured.

"It was awfully sweet of you," she declared. "You see how beautifully it has all come off!"

"Then it wasn't your father's last twenty-thousand pounds!" I remarked, suddenly.

"Of course not," she murmured. "My father is really Lord Derwent. He prefers to travel incognito because people bother him so."

For a moment the humour of this thing possessed me. I recalled my sound advice to a multi-millionaire, and I laughed till the tears stood in my eyes. Suddenly I remembered that I, too, had a confession to make.

"By-the-by," I said slowly, "did you say that your—your friend—"

"Charlie," she murmured.

"Had had two favourable reports on the mine?"

"Yes."

"And has bought it?"

She nodded. I looked at her sympathetically. After all, it was impossible for her marry a pauper.

"I am very sorry to hear it," I said hypocritically. "Perhaps the most extraordinary part of this affair is that I am really a mining engineer, and have been preparing a secret report upon this property."

She looked at me in amazement.

"Are you in earnest?" she asked.

"I am sorry to say I am," I answered. "I came over on behalf of a New York syndicate, and I posted my report to them last night. I told your father the literal truth. The Great Fortuna Mine is not worth twenty thousand pence."

"What a fraud the Count is," she sighed, "and what a lot of money people will lose."

"Yes, but Charlie!"

She laughed softly.

"Oh, it makes no difference to Charlie," she said. "I believe he had to pay an awful lot of money for those favourable reports, but he's sold out to a syndicate for a hundred-thousand pounds. He got the signatories and raised the money of them to buy the mine. The syndicate will sell to a company, and, of course, the public who buys shares will be the people who will lose their money. I think Charlie's quite clever, don't you?"

"I should imagine there's no doubt about it," I assured her.

We sat for a few minutes in silence. Our hands were still very close together. I was feeling exceedingly depressed.

"We spoke," I remarked, "of something in the nature of a reward."

"It is quite true," she admitted. "You have earned it. Please sit still."

She rose to her feet and bent over me.

"Close your eyes," she whispered.

I obeyed her. To this moment I can remember the touch of the sun upon my shut eyelids, the rustling of the soft, lazy air through the orange trees, the drowsy humming of bees in the garden. I felt her face close to mine – and suddenly the touch of her lips, one whispered word in my ear! I had had my reward.

For a second I remained there, motionless. I lacked the power or the will to tear myself away. Then with a little cry I sprang to my feet and hurried round the corner of the hotel. I was too late. The hotel omnibus, laden with luggage, was rumbling across the square, the Count stood upon the pavement waving a florid farewell. A little white hand flashed out of the window. It was the last I ever saw of Veronica.

But one morning, some two months later, I received a packet in an unfamiliar handwriting. When I opened it I found one hundred shares in the Great Fortuna Silver Mine, and a little scrawl of paper:

"Charlie says these are very good to sell – quickly!"

JOHN GARLAND
THE DELIVERER

A dozen lanterns showed him the sea-stained, rotting steps. A chorus of hoarse, cheerful voices bade him welcome. A score of willing hands dragged him through a cloud of spray on to the wave-swept, creaking jetty. Then, as he stood for a moment to regain his breath, from somewhere behind in that thick, black gulf through which he had journeyed came the sound of a dull grinding, the crashing of timbers, the hideous, far-off shrieking of human voices. A rocket went hissing up into the darkness, piercing with a momentary splendour the black veil.

"By Heaven, she's broken in two!" a voice cried. "She's gone!"

The rescued man turned sharply round. The light of the rocket was waning, yet he was just in time to see the slow heeling over of the huge, indistinguishable mass which a few hours ago had been a splendid liner.

"You're the last one saved," someone muttered at his elbow. "The boat's going back, but it will be too late. God help the others!"

The rescued man nodded solemnly.

"There are less than half-a-dozen left," he said, "and they had their chance. It was a big jump into the boats," he added. "Queer little cockle-shells they looked, too, from the deck. I've stood there for the last two hours, worrying the people in. I've thrown over a dozen, who dared not jump."

A clergyman pushed his way through the group. He was drenched to the skin, bare-headed, and breathless. He carried an old-fashioned lantern in his left hand. His right he extended to the dripping man, who stood there looking like a giant amongst them.

"I've heard of you, sir!" he exclaimed. "You're John Waters, I'm sure. You did a man's work there. There's a mother up at the vicarage now, with her two children saved, sobbing over them and blessing you. You rigged up a windlass, they tell me, and let them down. I only wish that I had room at my house for you, sir, but the whole village is packed."

"You're very good," the man answered. "I'm used to roughing it, and any place'll do for me. Somewhere near a fire, for choice; your salt water's chilly."

The clergyman raised his lantern and looked anxiously round the little circle of faces.

"We're seventy souls in the village," he said; "it's nothing but a hamlet, and we've found beds for over two hundred. We'll fix you up directly. I've one or two names left yet upon my list."

A slim woman's figure came battling her way along the jetty. She heard the clergyman's last words, and laid her fingers upon his arm. He turned sharply round. There were not many women about that night, and this one seemed frail and small to battle her way alone in the storm.

"My dear Miss Cressley!" he exclaimed. "How ever did you get here?"

"I couldn't rest at home," was the quiet answer. "It was too terrible. And I had no one to send. I want to be of use. Can't I take someone in – a woman, or some children? I have a spare room and a fire lit ready."

The clergyman gave a little exclamation of relief.

"My dear lady," he declared, "you are just in time. Here's our last man, and I was at my wits' end to know what to do with him. A hero!" he whispered in her ear. "He has saved no end of lives there. Bless you for coming, my dear, brave Miss Cressley," he added. "It's just like you – just the sort of thing you would do."

She gave a little start, and looked doubtfully at the tall, dripping figure. In his soaked clothes, his long brown beard, and his hair tossed wildly all over his face, he presented a somewhat singular appearance.

"My dear madam," he said, in his deep bass voice, "don't please refuse me because I am not a woman or a child. I'll give you less trouble than either, I promise you. I won't smoke or swear. I'll do whatever I am told, if I can only see something to eat, a bed, and a fire."

She held on to the railing of the jetty with both hands. Her voice sounded thin and quavery against the background of the storm.

"I shall be very glad to take you, and to do what I can," she said, a little doubtfully. "I mentioned a woman or child because I know more about them and their needs, and because I live alone. Will you come this way, sir?"

He turned and followed her, waving his hand in answer to a chorus of "Good nights." They passed down the sea-soaked jetty between a little line of curious, sympathetic faces, and reached the village. She led the way up the steep street, and looked into his face a little timidly.

"My cottage is close here, sir," she said. "It will only take us a few minutes."

A gust of wind almost swept her off her feet. He put out a great protecting hand and steadied her.

"One moment," he said. "Let me help you. So!"

He turned for a last gaze seaward. There was no sign of light or life upon the black chaos of waters – nothing save the clouds of white foam, flung up almost into their faces, and the sullen roar of the breaking waves.

"God help the rest of them!" he said, with a sudden note of reverence in his tone. Then he turned to his companion.

"Madam," he said, "I am ready."

Together they climbed to the summit of the hill. She gently disengaged her arm from his.

"I am so much stronger than I look," she declared, apologetically. "Really, I can manage quite well alone. My cottage is last upon the left. You can see the light. We shall be there in a moment."

He walked by her side in silence. She wondered, with a sudden perturbation, whether he were offended. His face was invisible; she could not tell that he was laughing softly to himself. Perhaps he was mistaken in her years. He had taken her for sixty, at least.

They reached a little wooden gate, over which he calmly stepped while she fumbled with the latch, passed up a trim garden path, and into the tiny hall of the tiniest cottage he had ever seen. Despite her warning, he bumped his head upon the ceiling. She turned up the lamp, and he looked around him a little ruefully. His size made the place appear like a doll's house.

"If you will step upstairs, she said, bravely disregarding his dripping state, "I will show you your room."

He looked at the stairs, with their neat carpet and shining brass rods, and he looked down at himself.

"Look here," he said, "haven't you a back kitchen where I can strip and have a rub down? You'll have to lend me a blanket while my clothes dry. Good Lord!"

He was looking at her in blank surprise.

"Is anything – the matter?" she asked, frightened.

He burst out laughing.

"Nothing!" he answered. "Only I thought that you were a little old lady."

She blushed desperately, and thrust back the curly waves of fair hair which had escaped in the wind. She was certainly not more than thirty or thirty-five, slim, with nice features and grey eyes, colourless, perhaps a little unnoticeable.

The laugh died away. He stood and looked at her as she turned to ascend the stairs, as one might look at a ghost.

"There are some clothes here which belonged to my father," she said. "Will you go to the room on the left? It is the kitchen."

"It is the little Cressley girl, of course," he said to himself, as he stood on the red tiles and reached out towards the fire. "Little Mary Cressley! Shy little baby she used to be."

Suddenly the smile spread once more over his face.

"Great Scot! I kissed her once!" he muttered. "Good thing she doesn't recognize me!"

She came back in a few moments with a bottle and an armful of clothes. He decided that she had been practicing a severe expression in the glass, but she avoided meeting his eyes.

"My father was a minister," she said, "and he was not quite so large as you; but you must please do the best you can with these clothes. There is a bottle of brandy here, and some hot water in the kettle there. When you have changed your clothes, if you will call out, I will come and get supper ready."

He looked at the clothes, clerical and severe in cut, with a grin. She turned her back upon him and went out. He helped himself to the brandy and hot water, and then commenced to strip off his things. All the time he laughed to himself softly. He remembered the Rev. Hiram Cressley well, and the idea of wearing his garments appealed to his sense of humour.

He called out to her as soon as he was ready. She kept her face averted when she entered, but he could have sworn that he saw the corners of her mouth twitch.

"If you would step into the sitting-room," she said, "I will prepare supper."

He shuddered at the thought of the sitting-room.

"I'm such a clumsy fellow," he said. "I shall break half your pretty things. Couldn't we have supper in here?"

"Just as you like," she said, struggling to hide her relief.

He dragged the table into the middle of the room.

"Come on," he said; "I'm going to help."

In the night the wind died away, and the storm passed down the Channel, leaving behind a piteous trail of disasters, small and large. John Garland opened his window, and looked out with a little exclamation of amazement. The sky was a soft deep blue; the sunshine lay everywhere upon the picturesque village, with its red roofs and grey cottages, its background of hills and rolling moors. From the little garden below, all ablaze with colour, came sweet rushes of perfume – of lavender, of rose and pinks, all dashed and drooping with their burden of raindrops, glittering like diamonds in the sunshine. Garland drank it all in with delight.

"England at last!" he murmured, as he began to prepare for his ablutions. "Lord, what a doll's house this is! I feel as though I were going through the floor."

He dressed rapidly and hurried into the garden. Miss Cressley was there, busy tying up some of her dashed flowers. She started a little at his hearty greeting, and avoided his eyes. All night long her conscience had been troubling her. The memory of that supper was like a delightful scourge. She had been much too friendly. She had quite forgotten the impropriety of the whole thing, and had laughed and talked almost like a girl again. With the morning reflection had come – reflection like a cold douche. And with it other things! The perfume of the flowers, the soft west wind, the aftermath, perhaps, of the joyous evening, were creeping into her blood. Had she done anything so desperately wrong after all? It was the vicar himself who had sent this man to her. As she well knew, every cottage in the village was full. Still, her cheeks went furiously red at the sound of his voice.

"Why!" he exclaimed, "forgive me! Good morning!"

"You look different, somehow," he explained. "Forgive my noticing it. I've been so long in a world where manners don't count, that I've forgotten mine."

Her cheeks burned. She could not remain unconscious of what he meant. She had arranged her hair differently – she was tired of the old way – and her white dress was certainly her most becoming one. The cluster of lilac, too, which she had drawn through her waistband – it was so seldom that it pleased her to wear flowers!

"Won't you come in to breakfast?" she said, shyly.

"Breakfast! Hurrah!" he answered. "I'm afraid I'm eating you out of house and home, Miss Cressley."

She led the way into the sitting room, which seemed to him more than ever like a chamber in a doll's house. He sat very gingerly upon his chair, and was afraid even to move his legs. The moment the meal was over he escaped into the garden and produced a pipe.

"I'm off to the village," he announced, "to see some of the people. Won't you come?"

"Thank you," she answered, "I have things to do in the house."

"I'll do the marketing," he announced. "I'll send some things up for dinner."

"It is not in the least necessary," she declared, with her chin in the air. He laughed in her face.

"Necessary or not," he declared, "either I do the marketing or I dine at the inn."

He was an impossible person to argue with – so big and strong and forceful. The things he said seemed somehow right because he said them. She gave in, and the magnitude of his purchases amazed her. He brought them up himself, wearing a ready-made suit of fisherman's clothes, and carrying the clerical garments in which he had started the day in a parcel under his arm. He took not the slightest notice of her protests, and he spent the next hour between the kitchen and the garden, strolling with his hands in his pockets and an air of being absolutely at home.

Three days passed – four. As yet he had not even alluded to his possible departure. At first she had wondered, had been gently troubled as to what the villagers might be saying about her entertainment of this good-humoured, easy-going giant. Gradually the place was being emptied of its unusual crowds. Surely, she thought, he must speak soon of his departure! And, with a sudden start of mingled shame and alarm, she realized that she dreaded the very thought of his absence.

She fled into her room and locked the door. With blurred eyes and beating heart she looked out seawards and fought against this folly – this folly which seemed to her so egregious, so unmaidenly. For ten years – ever since her father's death – she had lived there alone a life of prim and delicate orderliness, quietly useful to many people – a life, it seemed to her now, colourless, flat, impossible. She looked in the glass. Yes, she was a young woman still! Her cheeks were still pink, her eyes bright, her hair soft and full. With trembling fingers she took it down, rearranged it more after the fashion of her youthful days, and pinned a ribbon around her throat – ribbon of the colour which matched her eyes. After all, she was a woman. She had not sought this thing – it had come unbidden, undesired, she told herself, breathlessly. She had a right to do what she was doing. Nevertheless, her cheeks were hot with shame when she saw him again.

He was standing in the garden, reading a telegram, with a frown upon his face. She went out to him shyly, and he looked at her for a moment in amazement – as one might look at a ghost.

"Why – why, what have you done to yourself?" he exclaimed. "You grow younger every day! If only I could do the same," he continued, with a twinkle in his eyes, "you might remember the farmer's son as well as I remember the minister's daughter!"

She stared. Then a wave of recollection came to her. There had always seemed something familiar about his tone and manner.

"Why," she gasped, "you are John Garland – John who ran away from home!"

He smiled.

"I kissed you once, Mary," he said, "up the lane there."

She blushed furiously.

"I do not remember it," she said, mendaciously – a statement which was scarcely likely to be true, considering that it was the only embrace to which she had ever submitted.

"I'd like —" he began, and stopped. She was stooping over her roses.

"You have been away a long time," she said, softly.

"A long time," he repeated. "Everyone seems to be dead and gone. I am afraid I shall find the old country a lonely place."

"Luncheon is ready," she said. "Shall we go in?"

Afterwards he produced the telegram.

"This afternoon," he said, calmly, "I must go."

She caught at her breath. She could not keep the frightened look from her eyes, but she was able to control her tone.

"Isn't it a little sudden," she asked.

He nodded gloomily.

"I'm a man of affairs now," he said, "and I'm wanted."

She saw him off. She scarcely heard his farewell words. Every faculty she possessed was devoted to the desperate effort of preserving her secret. She saw him go, felt the touch of his fingers, heard the sound of his kindly voice, and turned away a little abruptly, just in time to hide the blinding tears. Then she walked back to her cottage, seeing no one, walking like one stumbling through a dream. It was very quiet, very peaceful, there. The smell of tobacco still lingered about her tiny hall. There was nothing else. Her knees shook as she fled up the stairs to her room.

Tragedy that year came not only from the sea, but from the land, to the little village of Pargeth. Dinneford's bank failed in the neighboring town, and half the village lost their savings. Mary Cressley lost more. She lost everything. When the winter came, and the worst was known, she found herself face to face with ruin.

She went to her landlord, a red-faced sporting solicitor of bibulous habits. She had known him all her life, and hated him. He had been expecting her visit, and received her a little grimly in his bare, untidy office.

He interrupted her timid explanations.

"I know all about it, Mary Cressley," he said. "Your money is lost – Dinneford's will never pay a farthing – and you can't pay your rent, eh?"

"Not just yet," she admitted.

"Not just yet or ever," he interrupted. "How should you pay it? You've got nothing."

"I was going to ask you to wait for a little time, and I would try and get some lodgers," she said.

He laughed scornfully.

"You'd get no one before the summer," he said; "and how do you suppose you're going to live and pay your rent out of boarders?"

"I can't think of anything else," she said, desperately.

"I can," he answered. "You must do what you'd have done years ago if you'd been a sensible woman – marry me!"

She rose at once to her feet.

"That," she declared, "is impossible."

"Is it?" he answered. "Well, then, it's also impossible for me to wait for my rent. I'll give you a week."

She went away without a word. For three days she hesitated. Then she sat down and wrote to John Garland. He had spoken truthfully when he said that he had become a man of affairs. His name was everywhere in the papers lately – the new Colonial millionaire, the owner of gold-mines and townships. Pargeth, it seemed, had entertained a Prince in disguise.

She wrote the letter, and as soon as she had finished it she tore it up. Her head was buried in her arms.

"I can't!" she moaned. "I can't!"

Then legal documents came to terrify her. A man made an inventory of all she possessed – a man who handled her precious pieces of china as though they had been jam-pots, and even counted her household linen. The terror came again! She thought of the workhouse – the cold, grey building on the hillside – its bare rooms, the long-drawn-out days of agony. Again she wrote to John Garland. This time she would have posted the letter, but Fate sent in her way a newspaper. She learned that he had purchased a great county estate, and announced his intention of marrying. The name of the lady was mentioned – the daughter of a poverty-stricken peer, a reigning beauty for several seasons.

Mary tore up her letter and went down to look at the sea. If only she had the courage!

Her landlord, Peter Sewell, came once more – the night before the sale. He was flushed, and he smelt of drink. He talked in a loud voice, and he had a good deal to say about her folly. In the end she turned him out of the house. It was her last luxury, and she enjoyed it.

There were barely a score of people at the sale. Amongst them was the vicar, flushed and anxious, with a little list in his hand which he kept consulting. When the auctioneer mounted his chair the vicar for a moment intervened.

"May I," he said, turning to face the few people, "say just one word? You all know the painful circumstances under which this sale has become necessary. You all know very well our dear friend, Miss Mary Cressley. A few of us have subscribed to buy her furniture, and thus keep a home for her amongst us until the spring. Pargeth, unfortunately, is not a rich place, and the sum which we have been able to collect is, after all, very small. But I should like you all to know that when I bid, I bid for those who wish to return to this dear lady her few household goods."

There was a sympathetic murmur from the bystanders, a nod of approval from the auctioneer, and a growl from Sewell. A red-faced lady, who kept the inn, turned indignantly towards him.

"What I say is, let the poor lady keep her bits and bobs of furniture!" she exclaimed. "Who'd be the better off for them, I should like to know? And what's a matter of a bit of rent behind, eh? Hasn't she lived here respectable, and paid her way, all her life? Shame on them as is pressing her like this, I say."

Sewell turned upon them all a little fiercely.

"Look here," he said, "there's been enough of this sentimental rot. This is a business meeting. Get on with the sale, Cobb. If any of you think you're going to indulge in a little cheap charity, you're wrong. I'm here to buy myself. Now then, Cobb."

The sale proceeded. The vicar bid timidly for the first few lots. Sewell scornfully outbid him and secured them. Then there was a commotion outside. A great motor-car had swung up to the door. A man, head and shoulders taller than most of them, pushed his way in.

"What the devil's the meaning of this?" he exclaimed, looking around.

The vicar recognized the new-comer and scented a friend. He ignored the expletive. In a few words he made the situation clear.

"Right!" John Garland said, leaning his back against the wall. "You can leave the bidding to me, vicar. I'll take a hand in this."

Sewell glared across the room.

"Cobb," he said, turning to the auctioneer, "remember this is a cash affair. You can't take bids from strangers without the money."

John Garland laughed dryly, though there was little sign of humour in his face.

"My name is John Garland," he said. "I've a thousand pounds in my pocket, a few hundred thousands in the bank, and a few million behind that. Like to examine these notes, Mr. Auctioneer?" he added, holding a packet out to him.

The auctioneer waved them away.

"Quite satisfactory, Mr. Garland," he said.

"Go on with the sale," Sewell shouted. "Confound you! I'll make you pay for your interference!"

No one else thought of bidding. Without turning a hair John Garland paid twenty pounds for a tea-pot and seventeen for a china ornament. Then came the piano. Sewell started it with an evil smile.

"Ten pounds!" he said.

"Absurd!" Garland murmured. "Twenty!"

"Thirty!" Sewell replied.

"Fifty!" Garland bid.

The room became breathlessly still. These were sums which belonged to fairyland. The last bid was Sewell's – one hundred and forty pounds. Garland paused for a moment.

"Is that Mr. Sewell's bid?" he asked.

"Yes, sir," the auctioneer answered, waiting.

Garland leaned over and struck a few notes upon the piano – a miserable, worn-out affair, barely worth the amount of the first bid. He shook his head.

"I don't believe Miss Cressley cares about this piano much," he said. "Half the notes seem to be gone, too. I think I'll let Mr. Sewell have it."

There was an instant's breathless silence – then an angry exclamation from Sewell, drowned in a roar of laughter from the company. The auctioneer's hammer descended.

"It's a rascally swindle!" Sewell roared. "I sha'n't pay for it. Put it up again."

John Garland smiled.

"I certainly didn't pledge my word to buy everything," he said. "I dare say there'll be pickings for you, Mr. Sewell."

Sewell flung himself out of the room, and the sale was over in half an hour. The vicar wrung John Garland's hand.

"God bless you, sir!" he said. "You couldn't find a better use for your money than this, I promise you. She's the sweetest, most unselfish little lady that ever breathed."

"Glad to hear you say so, sir," Garland answered. "I'm going to marry her to-morrow."

The vicar looked amazed.

"My dear Mr. Garland!" he exclaimed.

"Quite correct," Garland continued. "I've a special licence here. I suppose you can arrange it some time to-morrow?"

The vicar took the document into his fingers.

"To-morrow is Christmas Eve," he said, "and they'll be busy decorating all day. But I dare say we can manage it," he added, with a smile. "By the by, is it a secret?"

"You can tell anyone you like," John Garland answered, "except Miss Cressley, in case you should see her first."

"Doesn't she know?" the vicar gasped.

"Not yet!" John Garland answered.

Late in the evening Mary Cressley came stealing back from the farm on the moors where she had spent most of the day. A fine snow was falling, and a cold wind blew through her thin clothes. She remembered that there would be no furniture nor any fire in her stripped home, and a sob came into her throat. Perhaps they would have left a rug or something –

her clothes she was not sure about. Tears dimmed her eyes as she made her way down the little lane. It was her last home-coming.

Below were the lights of the village – cheerful enough – the ringers were practising a Christmas peal, the sound of the bells came with extraordinary distinctness through the clear air. Then she turned the corner and gave a little start of surprise. There were lights in her own cottage. Some neighbors must be there!

She walked more slowly. When she reached the gate she peered in, and her heart almost stopped beating. The furniture was all there! Nothing had been taken away!

She began to tremble. She scarcely knew how she pushed open the door. From the kitchen came a pleasant smell of cooking – the parlour door was open. She peered in. A great figure rose from his knees.

"It's this infernal grate again," said a familiar voice. "I can't make the thing go. Never mind. Supper's ready in the kitchen."

She swayed upon her feet.

"Mr. Garland!" she exclaimed.

"May as well call me John," he answered, "as we're going to be married to-morrow."

She fell into his arms. Her hat was crushed, and the little fair curls came tumbling out over her ears. He took the pale face in her strong hands, and kissed her upon the lips.

"Mary, you little fool," he said, "why didn't you send for me?"

"I didn't know," she murmured, weakly. "I thought you were going to be married."

"So I am, to you, to-morrow," he answered. "I've fixed it up with the vicar. Come in to supper and I'll tell you all about it."

He led her out of the room, his arm around her waist. She forgot that she had ever been wet and cold and lonely. For a moment she believed that she had died upon the moor and been taken up into heaven. And then he kissed her once more upon the lips, and she knew that she was on earth!

THE MONEY-SPIDER

The man who was lurking in the shadows, close to the heavy curtains which shielded the windows, glanced impatiently at the clock for the third time. It seemed impossible that time could move so slowly. It was barely five minutes since he had clambered in through the window and hidden himself in the silent room. Five minutes! Surely an eternity!

He had none of the coolness of the practised criminal. He was forty-seven years old, and for the first time in his life he was prepared to lift his hand against his country's laws. No wonder that his lips were dry and his breath came in a little short. It was no small thing, this, which he had in his mind. A man's life lay at the end of it.

The room was large, and handsomely furnished. Save for the somewhat conspicuous absence of books, it was the typical library of an English suburban residence. There were handsome prints upon the wall, little statuettes – not ill-chose – upon the mantelpiece, a soft, rich carpet, and several pieces of heavy, solid furniture. In a corner of the room stood a writing-table of dark walnut wood. There were papers there – laid out as though in readiness, a green-shaded lamp, the photograph of a woman, a bowl of roses.

The man who waited felt himself grow harder and colder as the moments went by. So this was where he sat, then, this enemy of his! In this room, probably, that his own ruin had been worked. John Wilkinson felt in his pocket, and his finger closed upon the butt of his revolver. There was no pity in his heart for the man whom he had come to kill. There was nothing but an intense desire to get the thing over – to meet him face to face, to say those few words, and to shoot! Others might call it murder. He knew very well that it was but an act of common justice.

The clock ticked, and a corner of the burning log fell on to the open fireplace. Then at last came a sound from beyond. A door somewhere in the house was opened and closed. Footsteps were coming along the passage. The man's whole frame stiffened. He stole out from his hiding-place and stood waiting.

It was a woman who entered, a woman tall and fair, dressed for the evening, with jewels upon her throat and bosom, only partially concealed by the open cloak of white lace which she wore. The man would have stolen back to his hiding-place, but it was too late. The woman saw him, and stopped short. She looked at him in amazement.

"Who are you?" she asked. "What do you want?"

"A few words with your husband," the man answered.

"With my husband?" the woman repeated. "But he told me that he was expecting no one except his secretary to-night. Does he know that you are here?"

"No!" the man answered.

She turned up the lamp and looked at him more closely. He was tall and thin, and, although his face was not the face of a criminal, there was something in his expression and the nervous tenseness of his answers which alarmed her. She moved swiftly towards the bell, only to find her arm grasped by his fingers.

"Madam," he said, "you must not ring that bell. I have a few words to say to your husband. If he knew that I were here he would not see me. I cannot allow you to interfere."

The woman stood for a moment looking at him, and the fear in her heart grew.

"How did you get in?" she asked.

"Through the window," he answered, grimly.

She opened her lips, but his hand swiftly closed them.

"Madam," he said, "I am not going to allow you to ring the bell. If you call out, you know very well what will happen. Your husband is in the adjoining room, and he will be the first to rush in. The moment he crosses the threshold I shall shoot him through the heart. Understand that. If you call out, you bring him to his death."

He released her. She stood looking at him with white, scared face, but his words had had their effect. She made no further attempt to raise an alarm.

"Sit down in that chair," he said, "and be quiet. I am sorry you came, but since you are here I cannot afford to let you go."

She recovered a little of her courage. After all, the man's face was not an evil one.

"What do you want with my husband?" she asked. "What are you going to do?"

The man laughed – a little nervous, dry laugh.

"An act of justice," he answered. "It's rough luck on you that you should be here, especially as he is your husband. You'd better go over to the window when you hear him coming."

Once more the horror seized her. She read the purpose in his face.

"You have come here to commit murder?" she cried.

The man smiled bitterly.

"I have come to kill your husband, madam," he said, "if that can be counted as murder."

She shrank away from him.

"You are mad," she faltered. "You know what happens to murderers. You will be hung!"

"I think not," he answered, indifferently. "I have friends below waiting to help me, and I shall try to escape. If I fail, I shall shoot myself. As well that as a beggar! Listen!"

He leaned forward towards the door. The woman, too, strained her ears. At the moment she would have screamed, but her voice seemed paralyzed. The man's eyes were upon her. She opened her lips, but no sound came.

"A false alarm!" he remarked, coolly. "Never mind. He cannot be much longer."

"Tell me why you want to kill him?" she faltered.

"Because he is Philip Angus, millionaire, and I am John Wilkinson, beggar," the man answered, bitterly.

The woman's courage seemed to be returning. Her eyes flashed; she drew herself a little more erect.

"You coward!" she exclaimed. "Because my husband has been fortunate, where you have been unfortunate, you would steal in here like a thief, and kill him without a moment's warning! You shall not do it. I will throw myself in the way. You shall kill me, if you want a victim."

The man listened as one might listen to a child.

"If you have a life to throw away, madam," he said, "pray risk it if you will, but you will not save your husband. My revolver has six chambers, and it is very carefully loaded."

Once more the courage left her. She listened frantically for the footfall outside that she knew so well. He could not be more than a few minutes now! There seemed to be no sound whatever in the house, no sound to break the stillness but the ticking of the little clock which stood upon the table. A wild thought came to her.

"You want money!" she exclaimed. "Of course it is money that you want! You shall have it. Take my jewels. They are very valuable – very valuable indeed. They will make you rich."

Her hands were at her throat, but he stopped her with a gesture of contempt.

"You do me an injustice," he declared, coldly. "It is not money that I want, or your jewels. I want your husband's life. Let me tell you this – it is a terrible thing to say, it is a shameful thing for you to hear, but it is the truth. There are hundreds of men and women who, when they read tomorrow morning that Philip Angus is dead, will breathe the more freely."

"It is not true!" she muttered.

His face darkened.

"Madam, it is the God's truth!" he said, with a sudden note of fierceness

in his tone. "Your husband is one of those who have made the name of a
millionaire infamous. He has made a great fortune. Do you know how? I
will tell you. He has built it up by lies, by deceit, by treachery. He hasn't
even been faithful to his friends. He has filled his pockets with the savings
of the working people whom he has ruined."

A shadow of indignation passed across the white, terrified face of the
woman to whom he spoke.

"It is not true!" she declared. "It is not true!"

The long, lean figure of the man seemed suddenly to expand. His eyes
blazed. He reminded her for the moment of some Biblical character – some
prophet, whose words were charged with woe.

"Madam," he cried, softly, "it is God's truth! Do you need to be told what
your husband's reputation is? Are there no newspapers? Isn't it in the air
wherever you go? Can you look me in the eyes and pretend to be ignorant
of it? There isn't a jewel on your body that's honestly earned. Oh, I daren't
think of it, or I know that I should kill you, too, where you stand, for the
things you represent!"

Once more the woman looked toward the door. His coming was long
delayed. Was it a good or evil omen, this?

"Shoot me, then!" she muttered. "I am not afraid."

The man shook his head.

"No!" he said. "I have no quarrel with you. It is your husband whom I
am going to save from one last sin. I am going to kill him before he can
sign those papers."

"What papers?" she demanded, eagerly.

"Nothing that you would understand," he answered. "They simply represent just one more of those wonderful deals which go to the loading of
your body with jewels, and bring honest men to this."

He dropped his hand for a moment. Her eyes were fixed upon his face
almost hungrily. All the time she sought for some sign of weakness.

"You mean the Bridgport Mills amalgamation?" she asked.

"Yes!" he answered. "You know something of his affairs, after all, then?"

"Yes – yes, I know something!" she admitted. "What have you to do
with the Bridgport Mills?"

The man's whole frame stiffened. His eyes flashed. He spoke rapidly –
almost fiercely.

"What have I to do with them? God in heaven! Why, they're my mills.
I am John Wilkinson, who went to Bridgport with two hundred pounds,
saved from my wages, and started business twenty-five years ago in a shed.
I made money honestly. I found employment for hundreds of poor people,
who earned wages which they had never dreamed of earning before.
Bridgport was a poor place when I went to it. I have made it a prosperous

city. My works are the finest in the country. My workpeople are the best paid. I was prosperous, honest, and respected. Then your husband comes upon the scene! He knows nothing of manufacturing, nothing of those honest and legitimate means by which a man can earn wealth for himself, and at the same time add to his country's prosperity. Your husband came like a great spider, hungry for blood, for money with him is the blood of all things. One by one he bought up my competitors. Before I had time to realize what was happening, there was a great trust formed against me. I had money and I had credit, the money and credit of an honest man. But what are these against the weapons with which your husband fights? They are gone, both of them. My mills will close down this week until he chooses to open them. Even my name will be his, to wheedle money out of poor investors, to make a great gambling scheme of an honest business. You were right, madam. It is your husband who has been fortunate, and I unfortunate. But there is a price that he must pay."

The man paused, breathless. She leaned towards him.

"Supposing he doesn't sign those papers?" she asked, eagerly.

"He never will," the man answered.

She listened once more, and wrung her hands.

"Oh, you can't mean this!" she exclaimed. "It is too horrible! Besides, what do you gain? If you kill him, this deal will go through all the same. It will make no difference to you; someone else will take his place. The papers will surely be signed – if not by him, by another. Give me a few minutes. Let me talk to him. I have influence. Often he does as I wish. I will plead with him."

The man shook his head.

"Many have tried to plead with Philip Angus," he said. "What have they gained by it?"

"But I am his wife!" she cried. "I can do more than anyone else in the world with him. Give me ten, five, even three minutes!"

The man laughed – a hoarse, unpleasant sound.

"Three minutes," he exclaimed, "to melt Philip Angus!"

The woman clutched at his arm.

"Remember that I am his wife," she cried. "Let me try. Oh, let me try! A few minutes can make no difference to you. If you stand over there by the curtains, he will never see you. He is almost blind."

She stopped suddenly and turned her head towards the door. A little moan broke from her lips.

"He is coming," she whispered, hoarsely. "You will give me those five minutes! You must – you must!"

The man hesitated – hesitated gravely and deliberately. One gathered from his appearance that it was not a matter of weakness – only of calculation. In the end he pointed toward the clock.

"You see the time? When the clock strikes, your husband dies. Until then, I will hear what you and he have to say together. Hush!"

He stole softly away towards the curtains. The advancing footsteps were now clearly audible. The woman turned towards the door with a little sob.

"So few minutes," she said to herself, "and Philip sometimes is so difficult. God help me! God give me words – show me how to move him. Ah, Philip!"

The door was opened at last. A tall, thin man, in dinner-clothes and smoking-jacket, entered and paused for a moment on the threshold. He wore heavy spectacles and carried a stick, with which he seemed to feel his way.

"Margaret!" he exclaimed. "Where on earth are you? They told me that you were here."

She moved towards him impulsively.

"I have been waiting for you, Philip," she said. "I came in to say good-bye. How long you have been! Let me take you to your chair."

He suffered her arm to rest upon his shoulder, but he frowned a little at the inference of her speech.

"Thank you," he said. "But I am not quite blind yet. You are alone, then? I thought I heard voices."

He seated himself before the table and took up the topmost of the papers that lay there in readiness. She lingered by his side.

"Quite alone, dear," she said. "I was reading. I have been reading those documents."

"Dry work for you, my dear," he answered, calmly.

"I have been reading," she continued, a little tremulously, "of the Bridgport Mills amalgamation. You are not angry, are you?"

He shrugged his shoulders.

"Angry? Of course not! But why do you bother your pretty head about business? Where are you going to-night?"

"I was going," she began, "to Lady Purcell's box at the Opera, but — but —"

"Ah, to the Opera!" he interrupted. "I see you have your jewels on. Good girl! They look well on you, Margaret."

"Do they, Philip?" she murmured.

"No one in the world, mind," he continued, impressively, "can have finer stones than you have in that necklace. In a few days' time, perhaps," he added, glancing fixedly at the paper upon which his hand was still resting, "I may be able to make you a little Christmas present which you will find worth accepting."

She shuddered a little.

"Philip," she said, "I want no more presents. I told you that I was going to the Opera. I have changed my mind. I have a headache. I don't want to go. I want to talk to you instead."

He accepted her decision with the equanimity of a man of placid temperament married to a woman of many caprices.

"Capital!" he said. "Well, I'll just sign these things, and then we'll have a cosy chat."

He took up his pen, but her hand suddenly covered the place where he would have set his signature.

"Philip," she said, "it's about those papers I want to talk to you. Don't sign them."

He turned round in his chair, looking at her in amazement.

"Don't sign them!" he exclaimed. "Why, my dear girl, what do you mean?"

She kept her hand firmly pressed upon the blank space.

"Philip," she said, "you know that I read these over to you when they came up from the office. I have been thinking it all over. You are to buy the mills and machinery and everything, aren't you, for a trifle – seven thousand pounds, or something like that – just as much as the people owe?"

He nodded.

"Well?"

"And they are worth?" she asked.

"To us," he answered, "to the corporation, that is, anything up to a hundred and fifty thousand pounds."

She drew a little breath, and glanced behind her uneasily. That somber-looking figure had drawn a little closer, or was it only her fancy?

"I suppose, then, Philip," she went on, feverishly, "that you have these people – these Bridgport Mills people, I mean – cornered? They can't keep on in business against you? They must either sell or fail?"

Her husband nodded.

"Precisely!" he remarked. "The thing has been engineered in a thoroughly satisfactory manner. They never really had the ghost of a chance."

She drew a little closer to him. Her right arm had stolen around his neck.

"But, Philip," she protested, "I do not understand. These are honest men, are they not, who built up this concern? They had a right to refuse to join you if your terms did not suit them."

The man shrugged his shoulders.

"A right? They had a right, of course. The only trouble was that they ran up against a stronger corporation."

She looked earnestly into his face.

"Tell me, Philip, is this quite honest?" she asked, fearfully.

The slight frown upon his forehead deepened. His voice became almost harsh.

"Honest? What on earth do you mean, Margaret? Honest? I don't recognize your use of the word."

She took up the papers for a moment and replaced them.

"I am thinking of the man whose name appears here – John Wilkinson," she said. "You are ruining him to make another fortune for yourself. I am thinking of his wife and family, Philip. Is it worth while? We don't need the money."

He looked at her as one might look at a child.

"My dear Margaret," he said, "everyone needs money. Very often the more you have the more you need. We'll talk about this presently. Harrison wants these papers down to-night."

He turned a little round in his chair, took up his pen, and dipped it in the ink. Her hand closed upon his feverishly. She glanced around into the shadows of the room. Slowly creeping nearer, she saw the figure she dreaded.

"Philip, you shall not – you shall not!" she exclaimed. "I don't want you to sign those papers."

For the first time he showed signs of distinct annoyance.

"You are hysterical!" he exclaimed, shortly. "The papers must be signed – and in a very few minutes."

"Philip, don't do it," she begged. "Call it a whim of mine. We have enough money. Send for this man Wilkinson, and let him run his mills for himself; or give him a fair price for them."

A fair price! He stroked his wife's hair indulgently. How could one reason with a person so ignorant of every law of finance?

"My dear heart," he said, soothingly, "this comes of a woman trying to understand business. You don't even understand the first axioms of barter. A fair price is the very least you can get the other man to take. It has no relation whatever to value. That is another matter."

She glanced at the clock, and back into the room. The ineffectiveness of her words made her almost hysterical.

"Philip, you are wrong, dear!" she exclaimed. "I do not often ask you for anything," she continued, a little wildly. "I beg you to listen to me now. See, I am on my knees. I have been thinking of the wives and children of these men. The jewels you gave me would seem always like their tears. I could not wear them. I should hate them. Think, Philip, if you were this man John Wilkinson, and I your wife. Think what it would mean if we had to go out into the world again, penniless."

He laughed dryly.

"My dear girl," he said, "you do not flatter me. I can assure you that I should never have placed myself in such a position."

"Dear, you cannot tell!" she exclaimed. "Don't you think that sometimes we – you and I – take life a little too easily? It is all so engrossing. It runs away with us. If we were to die to-night," she continued, nervously, and with a quick glance behind; "if we were to die to-night, Philip, you or I, would you feel that your hands were quite clean if you had signed those papers?"

"Why not?" he answered, sharply. "We are all here to do the best we can for ourselves."

"And for others, Philip!" she cried.

He drew a little sigh, as of one anxious to be tolerant, and yet tried beyond his powers of endurance.

"The man who was in business with those Utopian ideas, my dear Margaret," he said, "would very soon go under. You are talking about matters which you do not understand. Business is a great duel, in which the weapons are brains and opportunity. The man who fails to make use of both goes down. The rules of the game are thoroughly understood. Both sides go in with their eyes open. There is no quarter to be given or expected. The man who allowed sentiment to even creep into his calculations, to weaken for one moment his arm when the time came to strike, would be crushed to death on the spot. The fittest survive, the weakest go under. I don't make the rules, but there they are. If you play the game you must abide by them."

Once more he took up the pen. Despair held her nerveless for a moment. The clock had begun to strike! She dared not look round. Already she fancied she could hear stealthy footsteps.

She waved her hand frantically towards the unseen intruder. Then she wound her arms around her husband's neck and breathed for a moment more freely.

"Philip," she cried, "listen to me. I have been a good wife to you. I have begged for nothing as I am begging now. I may know nothing about business, but sometimes we women see the truth, even when it is hidden away in the darkest corner. I see the truth now, Philip," she continued, straining his face towards her. "I see it as though heaven itself were open. What are all these things worth – gold and jewels, the pride of great possessions, the power of wealth? Even if you stand to-day with your hands upon the levers that guide the world, death may come to-morrow; death may come at this moment to you, to me, to either of us. What about your rules then? What advantage has the strong man over the weak? Whose tale will reach God's ear the sooner – the cry of the beggared victim or the triumph of the conqueror? Philip, my husband, my love! You are so wonderful, so clever. I am very ignorant, but I have seen the truth. Tear up those papers, dear. For God's sake, tear them up! Let us have done for ever with this accursed money-making, with these bargains which leave behind the trail of misery and broken hearts. Give them to me, Philip. Only an hour ago you asked me what I would have for my Christmas present. I will have those papers. I will have you promise me that this man John Wilkinson shall come into your trust on fair terms, or that he shall be allowed to run his mills in his own way and for his own good."

Angus hesitated. For her it was a moment of agony. Already, in imagination, she could see close behind her the shining muzzle of that levelled revolver. He was signing his own death-warrant! If only she could make him understand!

The seconds ticked on. With a little shrug of the shoulders he handed over the papers.

"You are trying me pretty high, my dear Margaret," he said.

"You consent?" she cried. "You must consent!"

He smiled.

"You have always chosen your Christmas gift," he said. "We cannot break precedent."

The pieces of torn paper fluttered down on to the carpet. She fell on her knees with a little sob of relief. He stooped down and kissed her lips.

"I wonder if you have any idea," he said, "how much that little Christmas present of yours has cost me?"

She shook her head. Already her nervously strained ears had detected the closing of the window.

"There is another price," she murmured. "Thank God!"

FALSE GODS

T he two young men stood on the Embankment pavement. On their left the dark, turgid river, framed on the far side with a curving row of lamps; in the background a brilliant medley of sky signs; on their right, the two huge hotels, alight from basement to attic, pouring out warmth and brilliancy upon the chill November air. The younger and thinner of the two – also, by the way, the shabbier – pulled his companion by the arm.

"Richard," he exclaimed, "look! Our first walk in London is, after all, allegorical. We stand between the dark waters of despair and all the fire and splendour of life. We stand here with wet feet, cold, half starved, amongst the outcasts. Enough of it, Richard. There is no middle way. For me, at any rate, it shall be the pinnacles – or that!"

He pointed with a fierce downward gesture to the river. His companion – a youth of stouter build and more phlegmatic appearance – shook his head slowly.

"I am not sure that I agree with you, David," he said, slowly. "You want so much – you always have. I am ambitious, too, but I should be satisfied with something less than the topmost places, and nothing in the world would ever induce me to take my own life – nothing whatever!"

His companion laughed and dragged him along.

"Come," he said; "this is one of the backwaters of life. The whole place depresses me. Let us see what is on the other side of those palaces. Come quickly, Richard. You are always so slow."

They climbed the Savoy hill – tragical figures had they but known it – country lads called like moths to the candle by the far-off tumult of life. Three hundred miles north, the mother of David, wife of the Reverend David Barstow, Methodist and boot-maker, prayed by candle-light in her tiny bedroom for her truant son. And within a few hundred yards, Mr. Richard Skelmore, a grocer and coal-dealer, brooded in silence over his pipe, glancing sometimes into the fire, sometimes into the worn face of the woman who sat at the opposite corner of the hearth, pretending to darn his socks, weeping silently behind the shelter of her spectacles.

"Them boys'll come to no harm, mother," he said once. "They're young and strong. They can stand a lot of knocking about. Besides, from what one hears London's no such a bad place. There's money to be made there, and Richard's a shrewd lad. They'll come to no harm, mother."

His wife's reply was choked by a sob.

"Please God!" she murmured. "Please God!"...

Up the Savoy hill to the Strand, a few steps to the left, and they became entangled with the stream of carriages and motors turning slowly into the courtyard of the great hotel. Richard, diffident though stolid, would have hung back, but David laughed at his hesitation. Together they joined the supper-going throng. Speechless, they marvelled at the glossy silk hats, the white gloves, the strange uniformity of the men. But more wonderful still were the women – beautiful, fairy-like creatures, their lace skirts upraised as though to show their silk-clad ankles and satin slippers; women with golden hair and black, marvellously coiffured, flashing with ribbons or jewels, shaking perfume from their clothes which robbed the November night even of its dourness. Their voices, their laughter, their gestures were all strange. It was Venusberg to the peasant; the magic of it leaped through their veins. They pressed closer to the great glass front. They saw the splendour of the spreading vestibule, the blaze of lights, the banks of flowers, the women without their cloaks – bare-necked save for their jewels, the men in their immaculate dress-coats and white waist-coats, the servants with powdered hair and gorgeous livery. They even caught a whisper of the distant music – music which seemed to strike a keynote of this sudden glimpse of Paradise – thrilling, voluptuous, inspiring. David drew a long breath, a breath that came through his teeth like a sob.

"My father would call this Hell!" he whispered.

"Mine would never believe in such things," Richard muttered. "Man, it is wonderful."

Their presence became noticed, and a person in uniform – tall and splendid – swept them away. Loiterers were not allowed. Back into the Strand, into the streets, to the river – where they chose. David laughed harshly.

"Shall you ever forget that, Richard?" he asked.

"I shall never forget it!" Richard answered.

"They turn us away because we are poor!" David cried. "They are right! There is no place in this world for the poor! Some day we will come back, you and I, Richard! Some way or other we will forge the golden key!"

But Richard said nothing. His face was set and hard, and his eyes seemed to have grown closer together. But he, too, had sworn an oath!

Ten years of solid, strenuous labour, of dogged persistence, of mechanical industry which one by one overcame the barriers which guard promotion, slowly but surely Richard moved upwards. His clothes – characteristic clothes they were, too – marked his progress. He wore a silk hat now – a silk hat carefully chosen, bargained for, ironed every night himself by some secret process, glossier always than any other in the office, although none cost less. His trousers were freshly creased every morning in a home-made press. The age of his black coat – second-hand to start with – was incredible when one considered its smoothness and fit. His linen was a fraud, though its defects were hidden. His gloves – carried and never actually worn – seemed likely to remain new to all eternity. The great Mr. Driver, of Holmes and Driver, Holborn Viaduct, found nothing to complain of in the appearance of this young man whom he had just met by appointment in Spiers and Pond's bar at Cannon Street Station. He shook hands condescendingly. Richard had raised his hat.

"Until we have settled this little matter of business, Mr. Skelmore," the great merchant said, "it is just as well, perhaps, for your sake, that we are not seen too much together. My motor is outside, and, if convenient, I propose that we take our luncheon in the West-end."

"Just as you wish, Mr. Driver," Richard answered. "I am quite at your service."

So then, for the first time, Richard passed the threshold of the Milan Restaurant. A commonplace, insignificant young man, looking exactly what he was – a City clerk, a son of the people – took his place for the first time with those gayer and brighter children from the world he knew nothing of. He showed no signs of what he was feeling. His attitude of respectful attention to every word which fell from his companion's lips never wavered. And yet his heart was thumping against his ribs. It was premature – this. He had not meant to breathe this atmosphere as an outsider. He did his best to render himself unconscious of it – to forget the pleasant sense of warmth, the flutter of women's dresses, their soft laughter, the delicate cooking, the yellow wine. So far as he could, he steeled himself against his environment. Every day he lunched for sevenpence in a grimy hole underground, where the smells of countless dinners hung about the walls, where the few waiters were listless and dirty, where the appointments were coarse, the linen none too clean, and the gas burnt day and night. It was an interlude, this – no more. His day had not yet come.

"I see no reason, Mr. Skelmore," his host said, while they were waiting for a moment between courses, "why we should delay entering upon the subject which has brought us together. I understand that you are thinking of leaving the services of Messrs. Medbury, Smith, and Co.?"

"I am prepared to do so," Richard answered, cautiously, "if I can find a suitable position."

"And what," Mr. Driver asked, "should you consider a suitable position?"

Richard was silent for a moment.

"A suitable position," he said, slowly, "would be one where I should be paid, in actual salary or prospects, what I am worth."

Mr. Driver smiled. He had been told that this was a confident young man.

"Who is to decide," he asked, "that important question?"

"I shall be content to leave it to you, sir," Richard answered. "I will tell you only what I can do."

Mr. Driver nodded.

"That sounds reasonable," he said. "Please go on."

"Your turnover last year," Richard said, "was three hundred and forty-seven thousand pounds."

"How the deuce do you know that?" Mr. Driver exclaimed.

"Never mind," Richard answered. "The point is this. Next year I could raise your turnover to five hundred thousand pounds; the year after to seven hundred thousand pounds."

Mr. Driver raised his eyebrows.

"That's tall talking," he remarked.

"I speak within my figures," the young man said, calmly, producing a piece of paper from his pocket and laying it upon the table. "You will see transactions here, sir, to the value of two hundred thousand pounds. They have all been arranged by me. The blanks represent the source of supply and the customers' names. The day I joined your firm I could fill them in."

Mr. Driver glanced through the papers which his companion had gently pushed towards him. He checked off item after item, and his opinion of the young man with the wooden face and close-set eyes underwent a sudden change. It was genius. There was no other word for it.

"I might add, also," Richard said, "that the credit of your firm being better than the credit of Messrs. Medbury, Smith, and Co., I could doubtless obtain more liberal terms for you than those figures show. I refer more particularly to the export department, of which I have had sole control, and where cash payments are much appreciated."

"Supposing we come to terms and take over this business," Mr. Driver asked, after a short pause, "what would become of Medbury, Smith, and Co.?"

"Their business would be ruined," Richard answered, calmly. "They would be in the Gazette in two years' time."

Mr. Driver looked curiously across the table at his guest. He was a hard, unscrupulous man himself, but such callousness moved even him.

"I wonder you haven't approached them," he remarked. "They might give you a partnership."

"I should not accept it," Richard answered, deliberately. "They are on the downward grade. I prefer to associate with capital and enterprise. I want – to get on."

"I shouldn't wonder if you didn't," Mr. Driver remarked. "What salary are you getting now?"

"Four hundred a year," Richard answered.

"Married?"

"No."

"What do you want from us?" Mr. Driver continued.

"Five hundred a year, one per cent on the increase of your turnover, and a junior partnership in three years," Richard said, glibly.

"Prove your figures and it's a bargain," his companion declared.

Richard smiled for the first time.

"I am alone at the office after five this evening," he said. "You shall see the books. You can take any one of the items on that list and verify it."

They went out together half an hour later. A young man – pale, with dark eyes, clean-shaven, and with slightly worn features, rose suddenly from his chair and caught Richard by the arm.

"By Heaven, it's Richard!" he exclaimed.

"David!" the other exclaimed.

They shook hands. There was a moment's embarrassed silence. They had seen nothing of one another lately. Richard had been too engrossed for friendships.

"Curious that we should meet here, David," he remarked.

David laughed gaily, and pointed out of the window.

"That is where we stood," he remarked. "Have you been down below yet? Have you penetrated into the holy of holies?"

"Not yet," Richard answered.

"Nor I," David declared. "I'm afraid poetry will never take me there. You are doing all right?"

"Pretty well, thank you," Richard answered.

"We'll meet there some day yet," David declared, laughing. "Look me up when you've time. I change my abode pretty often, but I'm always to be heard of at the Wanderers' Club."

So they met and passed on, these two who had once been swayed by a common and passionate impulse. David was thoughtful for a moment. Then he turned to his companion – a middle-aged man, with classic features and flowing grey hair.

"Studley," he said, "that young man and I came from the same village in Westmorland. We literally ran away from home to make our fortunes. I remember the night after our arrival. We were walking along the Embankment – the river on one side, these palaces of light on the other. It was all fairyland to us. We were excited, emotional. We came over here, pressed our noses against the great windows, and watched the people going into the restaurant."

His companion laughed.

"I'd like to have seen you," he said.

"We were queer youngsters," David continued. "Remember that we came straight from a tiny village, that we had never even been in a town larger than Kendal, or seen a woman in evening dress. It was a sort of Arabian Nights to us – a Paradise, if you like. I remember even now how thrilled we were. I think we joined hands on our way homeward, and swore a common oath to attack the great citadel of Life from that moment. We went for our fortunes hammer and tongs, and I think that the height of our ambition at that time was to wear a swallow-tail coat, a white waistcoat, a white tie, and attend a lady with fair hair, a low-necked dress, black silk stockings, and high-heeled shoes down the corridor there and into the restaurant."

Studley laughed quietly.

"Your friend," he remarked, "seems to be still climbing. You, my dear David, might realize your ambition when you chose. If only you'll promise to write that story for me in the way I have pointed out, I'll advance you five hundred pounds on account."

David smiled. His eyes were suddenly fixed – reminiscent. He saw a country lane whose hedges were wreathed with honeysuckle and wild rose, a low privet hedge, more roses, pinks, and clematis, a cottage, and a girl. He smelt the new-mown hay. He heard the drowsy evening sounds. He heard the whisper of his own name as the girl came down the trim garden path. His lips parted – his smile became a laugh.

"Are you going to accept my offer?" Studley asked.

"Not I!" David answered. "I was just trying to think how Anna would look in a low-necked gown!"

There is a little space above the foyer at the Milan where the men-folk wait while their womenkind leave their theatre coats, smooth their hair, arrange their jewels, and bestow a final glance upon themselves in the long gilt mirrors before sallying forth to conquer. There David and Richard met once more, stared at one another doubtfully for a moment, and then exchanged embarrassed greetings. Richard had grown portly, his hair was a little grey, his cheeks were still pale, his eyes deeper set than ever. He was dressed in the very height of fashion – dressed, too, by a good tailor. His links and studs were all that they should be. His white waist coat was cut according to the fashion of the moment. His tie and collar were both correct. David, alas! fell very far short of such perfection. His dress-coat was a little shabby; his shirt had only one stud-hole and a distinct bulge; his tie, carefully arranged though it was, had evidently been through the cleaner's hands. His face, still thin, still a little worn, was brown with health; his mass of dark hair, sprinkled with grey, picturesque; his mouth and expression as delightful as ever.

"Queer thing that we should meet here, Richard!" he exclaimed, with a little laugh.

"It is certainly a coincidence," Richard declared.

David patted him on the back.

"I hear that you are a merchant prince," he said. "You look the part – you do, indeed, old man!"

Richard accepted the compliment unmoved.

"I have been fortunate," he admitted. "You remember we set our hands to the plough the same night."

"Remember! Of course I do," David answered, gaily. "Well, we've neither of us done so badly, eh? I'm a pauper still, but here and there a fool buys a copy of my poems, or an editor lets me spoil his pages. So I live! What can a man do more?"

Richard looked for a moment as though he scarcely understood.

"I am glad," he said, slowly, "that you are content."

David laughed.

"I am afraid my small measure of prosperity," he said, "would never satisfy you. Mine is a tiny income; but down in the country one doesn't need much. Studley is giving us some dinner here to-night – the editor I impose myself upon most frequently."

Richard – by the by, he was Sir Richard now – toyed with his gold chain for a moment.

"Your views on life," he said, with some show of curiosity, "have altered since we stood in the gutter and recorded our vow."

"Again and again," David laughed. "Thank God for it! What was a real picture to me that night has become allegorical. The gods have touched my eyes."

Sir Richard said nothing. He did not understand. But it was envy, no doubt, which made his less fortunate friend of former days change his point of view.

"You are married?" he asked.

"To the dearest little girl in the world," David declared. "You'll see her directly. By the by, I remember reading of your wedding. Half a column in the Morning Post, you lucky fellow!"

"I married the widow of my late partner," Sir Richard declared. "I am sorry that we are giving a dinner-party to-night, or I should have been glad for you to have joined us. We are entertaining the Lord Mayor unofficially – my wife's cousin. You will see our table as you go in – on the left, covered with pink roses."

"I'll look out for it," David declared, good-humouredly. "Ah, here's Anna!"

The women, curiously enough, came out together – as strange a contrast as any two figures in the ever-moving crowd. Lady Skelmore was short and stout. Her face, for all its coating of powder, was red; her hair, for all its blaze of diamonds, was stiff and ungainly; her gown of white satin was cut by a celebrated dressmaker, but her ladyship's instructions had been followed blindly and her figure was scarcely adapted to the Directoire style. Her neck blazed with jewels. She was very confident, very self-satisfied. And by her side came a tall girl, with large brown eyes and a sensitive, humorous mouth. She wore a simple black gown, which certainly was cut after the fashion of a few seasons ago. Her uncoiffured hair was arranged with the utmost simplicity. She wore no ornament nor any jewellery. Sir Richard did not flinch. The introductions followed and were duly acknowledged. Lady Skelmore, however, looked in something like amazement at this young woman whose acquaintance she had made. What was Richard about, she wondered! A girl here at the Milan in a home-made gown – such a cut – and not even a brooch! Lady Skelmore did not linger. She did not think it necessary to make any apology for her haste.

"My dear Richard!" she exclaimed, as they sailed through the foyer. "Whatever induced you to introduce me to such people?"

"I ran away to London as a boy with Barstow," he answered, apologetically. "I am afraid he has made rather a failure of things. But I came face to face with him there, and it was a little awkward."

His wife shrugged her profuse shoulders.

"One isn't likely to see them again," she murmured.

Anna was almost disturbed. The pleasure of her evening was threatened.

"David," she pleaded, "Is there anything wrong with me? Am I so very dowdy?"

David threw back his head and laughed – laughed like an angel.

"Here's old Studley!" he exclaimed. "Let's ask him!"

Southwards over the white roads, through the scented twilight, the great car with its two blazing eyes leaped and tore, always on fourth speed, always reckless alike of the police who challenged and the scattering crowds. On the front seat the chauffeur, leaning a little forward, and with face like a mask, sat alone. Inside was but one passenger – Sir Richard Skelmore, knight and member of Parliament. Richard was a little older now – a little shaken. The starch seemed to have gone from his frame, his cheeks were flabby, an unpleasant light was in his eyes. Sometimes he lifted the flap and looked behind. Sometimes he pored over the papers with which the little table in front of him was strewn. Sir Richard was ill at ease. He raised the india-rubber tube to his lips and spoke to the chauffeur.

"How far are we from Southampton, Murray?" he asked.

His tone was apologetic, for it was a question which he had asked often before. The man's answer, however, betrayed no sign of impatience.

"Thirty-seven miles, sir. Good road all the way."

Sir Richard laid down the speaking-tube and drew a little breath between his clenched teeth. After all, there might be a chance! Then there was a sharp corner, a grinding of brakes, a shout, a crash, chaos! The car had run into a half-a-dozen stray cows. Sir Richard crawled out. The chauffeur, covered with dust, limped his way to the engine.

"We're done, sir," he announced, half sobbing. "I did my best, but we had to take risks."

"Can't you tinker her up?" Sir Richard asked, hoarsely.

The man almost laughed.

"Not in a week, sir," he answered. "If it could be done, I should do it, you may be sure. A hundred pounds was a fortune to me. I did my best."

Sir Richard filled his hand with gold. Money was of little use to him now. Then he started down the lane. He had some vague idea of walking, he scarcely knew where. Perhaps he would come to a town where he could hire a car.

He walked swiftly, but he was unused to exercise. There were no lights in front – no sign even of a village. How far could he walk, he wondered. Already his feet were weary. Perhaps there would be an inn soon. Then he came to a sharp corner in the road, and immediately afterwards a small house lying a little way back – a long greystone building, almost covered with clematis and creeping shrubs. He paused in front of it for a minute and looked in. The air was almost faint with the perfume of roses. There were sweet peas and clematis, tall hollyhocks and fragrant borders of mignonette. Sir Richard hesitated for a moment. Then he lifted the latch and walked quietly up the path. There were no blinds. The curtains of the little drawing-room were undrawn. He could see a man lying in a basket chair. A lady at a piano was just finishing a song, the last word of which floated out to him as he walked softly up the grass border. She came toward the man, who rose from his chair holding out his hands. He passed his arm around her waist and suddenly pushed open the French windows.

"Come out and listen, Anna," he said. "Perhaps our nightingale is singing."

They came face to face with Richard, standing like a statue in the middle of their narrow path – Sir Richard, bare-headed (for he had lost his hat in the accident) and with the rising moonlight full in his face. The two men gazed at one another in amazement, and David removed his pipe from his teeth.

"By Jove, it's Richard!" he exclaimed. "Sir Richard, I beg your pardon," he continued, with a whimsical laugh. "Do you really mean that you have come to see us? You must have dropped out of a flying machine," he added, looking outside for some trace of a vehicle.

Sir Richard cleared his throat.

"I was motoring to Southampton," he said. "We had an accident a quarter of a mile back. I was walking to where I could find a vehicle to take me where I could hire another motor."

David laughed reassuringly.

"My dear fellow," he said, "you can't get any farther to-night. There's no town within miles of us, and no one round here has a motor-car. We can put you up, and glad to. Come along in and let me give you a drink to start with."

Sir Richard shook his head. The black fear was upon him. He showed it in his white face and twitching lips.

"I can't stop," he said. "I must get on board my yacht to-night. To-morrow will be too late."

"To-night!" David repeated, in amazement. "But, my dear fellow, be reasonable. It isn't possible. Make the best of things and have a shake-down with us."

"Do, please, stay, Sir Richard," the lady begged, and, even in his terrible plight, Sir Richard knew that the voice was sweet.

"We will do our best to make you comfortable. I will see about some dinner at once."

She turned toward the house. Sir Richard let her go.

"Is anything wrong, Richard?" David asked.

"Everything is wrong," the other answered. "Don't you read the papers?"

"Never, if I can help it," David declared.

"I am ruined, and worse than ruined!" Sir Richard said, unsteadily. "Worse than ruined! Do you hear that? Can you understand now why I must be on my yacht to-night? It is that or a convict prison!"

David dropped the pipe he was holding. All the natural gaiety seemed to have faded from his face.

"Richard," he said, gravely, "is it as bad as that, really?"

"It is that – no more nor less," Sir Richard declared. "Have you a telephone to your house?"

"There is no telephone within ten miles," David answered. "Perhaps you could rest quietly here, and they would not find you."

Sir Richard looked about him alike a hunted man. A cart drove by, and he drew back into the shadow. The two men were close up against the window of the little drawing-room. Suddenly he gripped David by the shoulder and pointed in.

"You are a weak creature, David," he muttered. "Don't you remember that night when you dragged me up from the Embankment? Don't you remember swearing that for you it should be the pinnacles or the river? Why, man," he continued, "your words ate into my brain. They rang in my ears year after year. They were the motto of my life. Didn't I set myself to conquer fate – to become one of those whom we saw? Thousands by thousands I built up my fortune. I cared not a whit for the stepping stones. I made myself into a machine for money-making. The rungs of the ladder for me were as though they had never existed. Every action of my life was shaped toward that one end. I reached the pinnacles, David. I have been there. And you – you whose words spurred me on – you have been content with the lesser things. Curse you, David! I wish that I had never seen your face, or heard you speak!"

He had turned toward the road, listening once more, but David rested his hand lightly upon his shoulder.

"Richard," he said, "I was a young fool in those days; but you, too, you were not over wise. You did not understand. When we looked in through the windows that night, what we saw – what we both saw – seemed to me to represent everything that was best in life. There was beauty and luxury, freedom from care, happiness. It was for that I strove, and, as the years go, the material goal changes, but the desire remains. I, Richard, I never sought anything less than the pinnacles, and I have found them – in there."

Sir Richard gazed, and his narrow eyes grew narrower. It was a long, low drawing-room, with a grand piano in one corner, water-colours hanging upon the white walls, bowls of flowers everywhere, red-shaded lamps, comfortable chairs. And coming toward them the beautiful woman, whose smile still brought the light into the younger man's eyes. Sir Richard turned away. He had no words. He walked a little into the shadow, and David did not follow him.

Then an unfamiliar sound broke the summer silence. A great car with flashing lights pulled up at the door. Two men sprang down. The voice of one of them rang out distinctly upon the silence.

"He must be here!" one said. "Watch the lane, Gregory."

Sir Richard held out his hand to his friend.

"Stay where you are," he said. "It shall not be here, I promise you that. It shall not be here!"

He moved farther back into the shadow – they heard him go crashing through the hedge. The two men stopped to listen. Then there was a sharp report, a groan, and silence! They all moved toward the spot. Anna came running out of the house.

"What is it, David?" she cried. "What has happened?"

He led her back.

"Nothing that you or I can help, dear," he said. "Nothing that concerns us."

"But Sir Richard? What has happened to him?" she asked, fearfully.

David shook his head.

"Dear," he answered, "he set up the false gods. Come into the house. There is nothing that we can do."

THE ILL-LAID ſCHEME OF MR. AMBROſE WEARE

Mr. Philip Letheringcourt, as he stepped out of his electric brougham and entered the premises of the London and Westminster Banking Company in Lombard Street, had certainly more the air of a man of fashion than of one interested in the everyday affairs of City life. He was immaculately dressed, handsome, debonair, from the tips of his patent boots to the bunch of violets which adorned his button-hole. He entered the bank with the air of one a little unaccustomed to his surroundings, and, approaching a vacant spot at the counter, drew a cheque from his waistcoat-pocket and carelessly filled it in for five hundred pounds.

"I'd like plenty of ten-pound notes, please," he said, holding it out to one of the clerks, "and one fifty."

The clerk accepted the cheque with a little bow, glanced at the amount, and then palpably hesitated.

"One moment, if you please, Mr. Letheringcourt," he said, turning away. "You want this in notes, I understand?"

Mr. Philip Letheringcourt raised his eyebrows.

"I certainly don't want gold, if that is what you mean," he replied.

The clerk hastened to a desk at the farther end of the bank and talked for a moment to a grey-headed man who sat there apparently entering up a ceaseless stream of amounts into a grand ledger. It was clear, even to Philip Letheringcourt – who felt only fairly interested – that the cheque which the clerk held in his hand was the subject of their conversation. The elder gentleman took up a telephone which stood by his side and spoke into it. When he replaced the receiver he nodded curtly to the clerk, who returned to his former place at the desk.

"One fifty, you said, and plenty of tens, I believe, Mr. Letheringcourt?" the latter remarked, beginning to count out the notes.

"That's right," Letheringcourt answered. "Why did you take the cheque up to the old gentleman? You didn't doubt my signature, I suppose?"

"Not in the least, sir," the man answered, civilly. "By the by, Mr. Jarndyse would like to speak to you, if you can spare half a moment."

"I haven't much time," Letheringcourt remarked, doubtfully. "If it's a matter of business, hadn't he better send for Weare? I don't interfere, you know, in the financial part of our affairs."

"I think Mr. Jarndyse would like to see you, sir," the clerk answered, "if you can spare half a minute. He is disengaged now, if you will come this way."

Letheringcourt stuffed the notes into his pocket and followed his guide into the private office of the bank manager. Mr. Jarndyse rose to his feet as they entered, and motioned the clerk to leave them.

"Some time since we met, Mr. Letheringcourt," the banker remarked, pleasantly. "You do not often favour us with a visit."

Letheringcourt smiled.

"Why should I?" he answered. "I leave everything connected with the financial conduct of our business to Weare. Your young man said that you would like to have a word with me."

"Just so, Mr. Letheringcourt," the bank manager said. "Sit down for a moment, will you?"

Letheringcourt sat down a little unwillingly.

"I'm afraid I can only spare you a moment," he said.

"I shall not detain you," the bank manager answered. "The fact of it is, Mr. Letheringcourt, I was looking into the figures connected with your firm this morning. You have, as doubtless you are aware, an authorized overdraft with us of twenty-five thousand pounds, against which we hold various securities. I find that you are overdrawn at the moment rather more than thirty thousand pounds, and that there is a draft of fifty-five thousand pounds to Cunliffe and Peabody due to-morrow."

Letheringcourt looked across at the manager in blank amazement.

"Really, Mr. Jarndyse," he said, "these are matters in which I never interfere at all. I presume that whatever obligations the firm has entered into will be duly met."

"I trust so, Mr. Letheringcourt," the bank manager answered. "At the same time I do not think that you should allow matters to be run quite so close. If you will pardon my saying so, I think that you ought to keep a stricter personal control over the financial side of your business."

Letheringcourt was a little taken aback.

"You don't mean to imply, Mr. Jarndyse," he said, "that Ambrose Weare is not so careful as he ought to be? He has been in our employ for over fifteen years, and for the last ten years, at least, he has absolutely controlled our finances."

"I wish to imply nothing," the bank manger answered; "but I do not think it is good financing to leave so large a sum as nearly sixty thousand pounds to be provided on the very day when the draft is due."

Letheringcourt took up his hat.

"I agree with you," he answered. "It doesn't sound exactly the thing. I'll speak to Weare about it. Very likely he has a number of bills of exchange which he did not wish to discount until the last moment. Bank rate's pretty stiff just now, isn't it?"

"There are, no doubt, explanations," the bank manager remarked. "At the same time, Mr. Letheringcourt, if you will pardon my saying so, I think that you will be well advised to take a little more personal interest in your business."

"Thanks!" Letheringcourt answered, a little curtly. "I'll remember what you say."

He was thoughtful during the drive home; he was thoughtful during the one rubber he had time for at the club; and he was even thoughtful over the tête-à-tête dinner alone with his wife, for which a series of mischances was responsible. Mrs. Letheringcourt, at the conclusion of the meal, rose to her feet with a little yawn and strolled to the mantle-piece.

"Philip," she remarked, lighting a cigarette, "a dinner à deux doesn't seem to amuse you."

He sat up with a little start; he had been gazing fixedly at the tablecloth, speechless, for the last five minutes.

"I am awfully sorry, Joan," he said. "I am afraid that you must have thought me a perfect bear."

"Your conversation certainly hasn't been brilliant," she remarked, quietly. "Please tell me what it is that you have been thinking about."

He shook his head.

"The affairs of Holt and Letheringcourt!" he answered.

She raised her eyebrows.

"Business?" she repeated. "Well, it isn't very often you allow that to trouble you."

"You are quite right," he admitted. "It is very seldom that I think about it at all. And yet this afternoon something happened – just a trifle – which gave me a most unpleasant quarter of an hour."

"Go on," she said. "Tell me about it."

They were sitting in one of the smaller rooms of their house in Berkeley Square, half study, half morning-room. It was an evening on which they had planned to dine out and to go to the theatre, but some friends had disappointed them, and at the last moment Letheringcourt himself had begged for a quiet evening. His wife, always good-natured, had acceded readily enough – it was not often that their social engagements permitted them to spend an evening together. A small dinner had been served to them in an impromptu fashion.

"Tell me, Philip," she said, "exactly what it is that is bothering you."

Letheringcourt threw away the cigar which had burned out between his fingers and lit a cigarette. In a few words he told his wife of his visit to the bank that afternoon. When he had finished she looked across at him with wide-open eyes.

"It certainly seems most odd!" she exclaimed. "What did you say to Mr. Jarndyse, Philip?"

"I told him, of course," Letheringcourt continued, "that for a great many years Ambrose Weare had had the sole control of the finances of my firm, that during all that time no complaint had been made, and that the business generally had been exceedingly prosperous. Yet I don't fancy that he was satisfied. I didn't like the way he twice advised me to take a more personal interest in my own affairs."

"Do you think that he mistrusts Ambrose Weare?" she asked.

"Such an idea is preposterous," Letheringcourt declared.

"You believe in him implicitly yourself, then?" she demanded.

"Implicitly!" Letheringcourt answered. "The man is as honest as the day. I am sure of it."

"I don't know much about business," his wife said, hesitatingly, "but to be thirty thousand pounds overdrawn at your bank and have nearly sixty thousand pounds to find the next day doesn't sound exactly comfortable to me."

"I agree with you," her husband answered. "I didn't like it at all."

"What have you done?" she asked.

"I rang Weare up from the club," Letheringcourt answered, "and asked him to come here to-night."

His wife nodded.

"He didn't make any difficulties, I suppose?" she asked. "He was willing enough to come?"

"Curiously enough, he wasn't," her husband replied. "He reminded me that never during the whole of our association had we transacted any business, or spoken of it, after office hours. He added that he personally, during all that time, had never set foot west of Temple Bar. He asked me to wait until the morning."

"You insisted upon his coming, I hope?" she exclaimed.

"I did," he answered. "He evidently did not like it, but he agreed to be here at half-past nine."

"What a curious sort of person he must be!" Mrs. Letheringcourt remarked. "Tell me, what is he like?"

Letheringcourt smiled faintly.

"He might have stepped out from some book of Dickens's or Anthony Trollope's," he answered. "Trim, grey-headed, old-fashioned, with formal manners; always dressed in black, never been known to be sixpence wrong in any account in his life. Everyone at the office swears by him."

"Ambrose Weare!" she remarked. "It's a singular name."

"He's a singular person," Letheringcourt answered. "I have never heard of his having a friend or a relative; no one even knows where he came from! By the by, there is someone in the hall now. He is coming up, I believe."

Joan Letheringcourt picked up her novel.

"I am going to my room for a little time," she said. "I shall be down again – perhaps before your man has gone. I am rather curious to see him."

She swept out of the room with a little farewell nod – graceful, good-natured, beautiful – a delightful wife and hostess. Outside, she passed with a pleasant smile a little man following a tall footman. The little old man started, but she had already gone by. The footman threw open the door.

"Mr. Ambrose Weare, sir, from the office," he announced.

Letheringcourt turned in his chair and welcomed his visitor.

"Come and sit down, Weare," he said. "Will you have a glass of port or some coffee? It is your first visit here and I shall expect you to take something."

The clerk bowed a little stiffly.

"Thank you, sir," he answered. "I am afraid that I must ask you to excuse me."

"As you will," Letheringcourt answered, carelessly. "Sit down there by the table, please. There are just one or two questions I wanted to ask you. I am sorry to have fetched you up after office hours, but the fact is that I have been a little uneasy."

The footman had left them; the two men were alone. Ambrose Weare was certainly a somewhat curious character. His face was white, and dry as parchment. His eyes were very bright, although he wore spectacles, and he had still an abundance of grey hair neatly parted in the middle. His clothes were old-fashioned, considering his position as head cashier of a well-known City firm. He wore a frock-coat, pepper-and-salt trousers, a black satin tie which resembled a stock, and a collar of ancient shape. He folded his gloves deliberately and placed them inside his silk hat. Then he turned towards his employer.

"I have come to answer any questions, sir," he said, "which you may care to ask."

"Oh, I am not going to put you through a catechism!" Letheringcourt declared. "You know much more about the conduct of the business than I do, of course. I will tell you exactly what it is that made me send for you. I happened to go into the bank this afternoon, and Jarndyse called me into his office. He pointed out that our account was thirty thousand pounds overdrawn, and that we had a draft due to-morrow for fifty-five thousand pounds. Of course, he didn't doubt but that it would be all right, for a moment, but he simply thought that it would be a great deal better not to run things so close. I must say that I agreed with him. It didn't seem to me to be exactly in accord with your methods, Weare, to leave so large a sum to be covered on the actual day."

Ambrose Weare inclined his head slowly. His fingers were interlocked. He was leaning a little across the table.

"There is not the slightest chance, sir," he said, "of its being covered!"

Letheringcourt looked at him for a moment as a man might look at a visitant from another world. It was impossible that Ambrose Weare should have said this. His hearing must have played him some strange trick.

"Do you mind repeating that, Weare?" he said.

"Certainly, sir," the clerk answered. "I regret to say that there is not the faintest chance of Messrs. Cunliffe and Peabody's draft for fifty-five thousand pounds being honoured to-morrow morning."

Letheringcourt sat like a man only half conscious of his surroundings.

"I don't understand," he said. "Do you mean to tell me that we are short of money, Weare? – that there is any real difficulty about meeting our engagements?"

"We are very short indeed, sir," the clerk answered. "We have been very short for a long time. The financing of your business has been an exceedingly difficult operation during the last few years. I must admit that the task has now grown beyond me."

Letheringcourt grasped the sides of his chair and looked around him wildly. For a moment he thought that he had fallen asleep and been visited by a nightmare. Everything else about him was as usual. There were all the evidences on every side of his luxurious home. And in the midst of it sat this strange, still figure – the Ambrose Weare whom he had known all these years, and yet – another man!

"If this is a joke," Letheringcourt exclaimed, hoarsely, "it's a – a bad one! Do you know what you're saying, Weare? You should know your place better —"

"I know it far too well," the man interrupted, "to joke upon such a subject. Your firm, sir – the firm of Holt, Letheringcourt, and Company – has been losing money for something like twelve years. Chiefly owning to my efforts, your credit has remained unimpaired. It is impossible, however, to preserve it any longer. To-morrow the crisis comes!"

"You must be mad!" Letheringcourt exclaimed, rising unsteadily to his feet. "Why, no one has ever breathed a word of this to me! You yourself have said nothing! Year by year you have brought me into my private office balance-sheets showing large profits. Last year you told me that we had made seventeen thousand pounds. I have been extravagant, but I have not spent money like this. What has become of it? Where is all this money? Our capital stood at one hundred and seventy thousand pounds seven years ago."

"It is all gone," Ambrose Weare said, calmly. "Perhaps it was never as much as that."

"But the balance-sheets!" Letheringcourt exclaimed – "the balance-sheets! You have brought them to me year by year. Not one has ever shown a loss."

"They were made out, alas," Ambrose Weare answered, "from the ledger of my imagination."

"In plain words, then," Letheringcourt cried, "we are ruined! – we have to fail! Is that what you mean?"

"Precisely!" Ambrose Weare declared. "I have not the figures with me, but I believe that we could not, at the moment, pay a fraction more than two shillings in the pound."

Letheringcourt swayed upon his feet. Then he leaned forward and struck the table before which the other man was sitting.

"Look here!" he said, fiercely, "if you are in earnest, answer me this. Why have you deceived me, year by year, with false balance-sheets? Why have you let me believe that the business was making large profits? Why have you even urged me to spend money – placed sums to my private account, time after time, which I scarcely needed? Tell me why you have done these things, Ambrose Weare?"

"It is a long story," the clerk answered, calmly.

Letheringcourt broke loose. Nothing but the sense of his own great strength and the other man's fail physique prevented his taking him by the throat and shaking the words from his lips.

"Long or short," he cried, "I must have it! Do you know what you have done? For the last ten years I have spent something like fifteen or sixteen thousand pounds a year, believing honestly that I was living within my income. I saved not a penny. Why should I? I knew nothing of the business myself. I have no idea how to do even a clerk's work. What am I to do? What am I to say to my wife?"

Ambrose Weare rose slowly to his feet. There was something almost spectral-like about his long, grey figure as he stood there, leaning slightly forward, his manner unruffled, his tone still calm and even.

"You have no wife!" he said.

Letheringcourt stared at him for a moment and then burst out laughing. After all, perhaps this was the explanation.

"You're mad!" he exclaimed – "mad or drunk, Weare! What is the matter with you, man? Has your mind given way?"

"I am sane enough," Ambrose Weare answered. "Better pray that you remain so. I repeat – you have no wife."

There was the sound of a trailing skirt. The door was softly opened. Joan Letheringcourt, humming a light tune, came in.

"Philip," she said, "have you nearly finished your talk? Shall I be in the way? I am tired of being alone."

"Yes, come in!" Letheringcourt answered. "Come here, Joan. Now tell me, Ambrose Weare," he added, pointing to his wife, who was crossing the room toward the two men, "who is that lady if she is not my wife?"

"She is mine!" Ambrose Weare answered, calmly.

Letheringcourt took him by the shoulders, lifted him up, and finding him as helpless as a baby flung him back into his chair. His wife ran forward with a little scream.

"Philip!" she cried. "Philip! What is the meaning of this? Who is this person? Why does he say these things?"

"God knows!" Letheringcourt answered. "For fifteen years he has called himself Ambrose Weare. If all that he has told me is true, I should say that he is the very Devil himself! Look at him, Joan. Have you seen him before?"

She bent forward, scanning his features eagerly. Ambrose Weare was pale and breathless, but he had strength enough left to rise to his feet. There was still no colour in his cheeks, no sign of emotion save the breath which came in little pants through his clenched teeth.

"Let her look!" he said. "Let her look! Perhaps she will understand."

There was an instant's breathless silence. Then her eyes seemed to be lit with a sudden, strange fear. She staggered back, holding her hands in front of her face as though to shut out some awful sight. She, too, was pale now. She, too, had the air of one who looks upon terrible things.

"No!" she cried. "No; it can't – it couldn't be!"

"Madam," Ambrose Weare said, "The impossible has happened. You have believed what you wished to believe – that the Nicholas Seton who died at St. Thomas's Hospital sixteen years ago was the man to whom you had been married. It was not so. I am Nicholas Seton, and, whatever you may call yourself, you are still my wife."

She shrank away to a corner of the sofa and sat there, sobbing quietly, pale, stricken, absolutely dazed. All the time she was muttering to herself. All the time she kept her back to the man who had told her this terrible thing.

Letheringcourt staggered toward the side-board and poured himself out some brandy. Then he came back and stood by the table, looking down upon the other man.

"Come," he said, "let us understand this matter. You are the Ambrose Weare who came to my firm as a cashier fifteen years ago whilst I was at college. My father trusted you implicitly; my uncle trusted you. When they were dead and I came into the business I found you all-powerful. There wasn't a clerk or a manager in the place who didn't speak of you with respect. I have believed in you – I have believed in the figures you have shown me; I have thought myself always a rich man. Now you sit there and tell me that your connection from the first with the firm has been one long tissue of lies and deceit. Why? What is the meaning of it all? Why has it pleased you to keep silent – to drive me on towards ruin?"

The man turned half round and pointed towards the woman who sat still upon the sofa. He pointed with long, trembling forefinger, but he said nothing.

"I have done you no harm," Letheringcourt cried.

"She was my wife," Ambrose Weare answered.

Letheringcourt was a strong man, and he kept sane.

"Even if this horrible thing were true," he said, "why should you seek to revenge yourself upon me? You deserted her. She had every reason to believe that you were dead. When I first knew her she told me of her former marriage. She honestly believed you dead."

"It is a lie!" Ambrose Weare said, slowly. "She saw luxury, and she stretched out her hand to grasp it. She took her risks. Things have gone her way for a good many years. I wrote to her. I told her that I would return when I had earned enough to keep her and the child in comfort. Her father hated me because I was poor. He allowed them enough to live on so long as I was out of the way."

"I had no letter," she sobbed. "If it came, my father destroyed it. He swore always that you had ruined my life – you knew that."

"So it is for these fancied wrongs that you have set yourself to ruin me!" Letheringcourt said, bitterly. "Well, there shall be a reckoning yet. If my money has gone as you say, where is it?"

"Safe," Ambrose Weare muttered, "in Paris, in Frankfort, in New York – a thousand or so here, a thousand or so there. For twelve years I have stripped the business. There is little enough now left for anyone except the bones. She left me once because I was poor," he cried, pointing to the woman who sat shivering upon the sofa. "To-day I am rich, if I choose, and you are a beggar!"

Letheringcourt laughed harshly. He touched the telephone which stood on the table by his side.

"Do you imagine," he said, "that I shall let you go scot-free? Do you imagine that I shall ever let you leave this room?"

"It makes no difference," the clerk answered. "I tell you to your face that I have robbed you, but I am the only one who knows. There are no books, no papers to prove it. On the contrary, there are bundles of accounts in the safe which I shall swear have been submitted to you year by year, and which show a steady loss. Those which it has been necessary to destroy I shall swear that you destroyed. You know you told me not long ago that I was the Napoleon of figures. It is true. I have used them like soldiers, and they have won my battle!"

Some new thing seemed to have come into Letheringcourt's face. Those of his friends who had known him for the last ten years might almost have failed to have recognised him now. At heart he was a man. He stood looking down at the thin, frail figure at the table with a curiosity almost impersonal.

"I wonder," he said, grimly, "that I can stand here and listen to you. I wonder I don't shake the life from your miserable bones. In all the world there cannot breathe a creature so despicable as you! You deserted your wife – you let her believe that you were dead," he added, pointing to the figure upon the sofa. "What kind of a creature can you be to bear an eternal grudge against me because I have tried to make her happy?"

"There was the child," Ambrose Weare said, and for the first time his thin, precise tone seemed to shake. "She deserted him."

The hands fell away from before her face. She looked across the room with blazing eyes.

"It is a lie!" she answered. "My husband has been as good a father to him as ever man could be. He is at Rugby now, captain of the school. Look!"

She sprang to her feet, and taking a photograph from the mantelpiece, she laid it on the table before him. Ambrose Weare staggered to his feet. He was like a man who has received a blow, but still withholds belief in the thing which he has heard.

"Look!" she cried again. "There is Nicholas! Don't you recognize him? Won't you believe now? He was going into the Army, and now, and now —" She sobbed.

Ambrose Weare took the photograph and turned his back upon them both. For a few moments there was nothing to be heard in the room but the ticking of the clock. Then there was another sound – the sound of a dry, hard sob. Ambrose Weare laid down the photograph and took up his carefully-brushed silk hat and gloves. There was no sign of emotion in his face. It seemed impossible that the sob could have come from him. He turned as though in farewell to Letheringcourt. His manner was once more the manner of the confidential clerk of fifteen years' service.

"There has been a mistake," he said. "You will be so kind, sir, as to overlook my rash statements. I have thought it better for the interests of the firm to invest large sums of money abroad. You will find the particulars here," he added, laying a roll of papers upon the table. "There are one hundred and forty thousand pounds invested in European banks, and nearly sixty thousand in New York. You can obtain credit to-morrow by cabling. You will excuse me, sir, if I hurry away? There is a little matter – a little matter left."

He was at the door before they could stop him. Husband and wife looked at one another in fear and wonder. The shadow of this terrible thing was still between them – the man who had left the room – Ambrose Weare, her husband!

"In God's name," she cried, "what can we do?"

From outside came the answer to her question. They heard the shot, the sound of a fall, the hurrying of servants. They did not need to be told! A white-faced footman threw open the door.

"The gentleman who has just left, sir!" he exclaimed, breathlessly.

"Well?" Letheringcourt asked.

"He has shot himself in the hall, sir," the man answered. "He is dead!"

THE THREE THIEVES

"That," Felix declared, pointing from the club window down into the square below, "is the one thing from which all the resources of our civilization seems powerless to save us. It is in that revolutions have been born."

His companions followed his gesture, and looked up at him as though for an explanation.

"We have school-boards," Felix continued, "charitable institutions, philanthropists without number in every great city. Theoretically there should be no such class as those who sit there. Yet there isn't a city that hasn't something of this sort to show."

The elder of his two companions, Mayne Richards, a lawyer, wealthy, and a professed cynic, smiled a little scornfully. "My dear Felix," he said, "no system of life can ever provide for people who declined to be provided for. The men who sit around down there are the men who will not help themselves. You will find them in every great city, and you will find exactly the same look in their faces. They are the men who will not be helped. They are the lazy good-for-nothings of life, the victims of drunkenness and the other vices of their order."

"You don't believe in such a thing as ill luck, then?" Felix asked quietly.

"Not to any extent," the other answered. "Nowadays, if a man comes to that, in ninety-nine cases out of a hundred it is his own fault. The very faces and attitudes of those people speak for themselves. They are a shiftless, impossible lot."

"I think Richards is right,' the third man remarked, taking a cigar from his mouth. "All this talk about the unemployed, and the hard life the laboring classes lead, is mostly electioneering trash. I bet you there isn't one of those fellows who couldn't get work if he wanted it."

"Put it this way," Richards said. "I should say there wasn't one of them who would do the work honestly if it was offered to him. There aren't many things which an employer demands of the British workman – reasonable honesty, reasonable sobriety, reasonable intelligence. I bet you'd find there isn't one of those fellows who spend their days lounging there who is to be trusted half a yard.

"I am willing to make a bet with you about that," Felix declared.

"Formulate it, then," Richards answered. "I'll back my opinion, with pleasure."

"Come down into the square with me," Felix said. "We will walk slowly round past the seats where the men are sitting. I will select three, and I will entrust them, each of them, with a different commission. Then I will make a bet with you that each one of those three will fulfill his errand honestly."

"They might deliver a letter," Richards said, "or anything of that sort, because there would be nothing to be gained by doing otherwise."

Felix laughed. "I mean a real test," he said. "The three men whom I select shall each have a sum of money to take to a certain place."

"Then I trust," Richards said, "that you will make the sum small, for you will certainly lose it as well as your bet."

"We shall see about that," Felix answered. "Remember, I choose the men and I choose the stakes. I will bet you fifty pounds that the three men whom I pick out will do their errands honestly."

"I will give you odds," Richards answered. "The bet as it stands isn't fair. I will bet you that two out of the three will not deliver the money with which you entrust them, and that you never hear of them again except by accident."

"Done!" Felix declared. "Get your hat, and we will go down into the square. Come, Andrewes," he added, turning to their companion, "you shall come, too, and be umpire."

The three men left the club, crossed the street, and entered the square together. It was by no means a cheerful-looking place. There were three or four flower-beds, empty now, for it was midwinter, and a deserted fountain-basin standing in the middle of the waste of asphalt. At regular intervals within the railing were iron seats, and upon these were dotted about here and there a miserable little company of human beings. At first glance they seemed all the same class – men upon whom misfortune had had a pernicious effect, men whose eyes were either fixed upon vacancy with dull, unseeing persistence, or who looked downward to the ground under their feet, most of them with their heads supported by their hands. They were of all ages, too, although the man who was a little past middle-age seemed to predominate. There was very little conversation among them, very little curiosity, very little interest in the passers-by or the traffic in the streets beyond.

Felix drew a little breath. "Poor chaps!" he said softly. "They look hungry, too, most of them. We must pretend to be talking as we walk round. I've picked out one already – and another. I shall take that boy for the third. Now I am going to ask them to come into the club while we explain what we want."

He went back and spoke to a strongly built, middle-aged man with hollow eyes and iron-grey beard.

"My man," he said, "do you want a job?"

"Yes!" was the prompt reply. "When?"

"At once," Felix answered. "Get up, please, and come with us. I want three altogether. I am going to speak to the other two."

He moved on a few seats, and spoke to a tall boy, thin and haggard of feature, miserably clothed, and with great holes in his shoes.

"Do you want a job?" he asked him.

"Yes!" was the quick, almost feverish, reply.

"Come with us, then," Felix said.

Then he stopped to speak to the third whom he had chosen – a tall, powerful-looking young man, apparently about twenty-five. He had a fair, smooth face, a little strained as though with hunger, a little reckless about the mouth and eyes, a little hard, too, about the jaw.

"Want a job?" Felix asked.

"Yes!" the man answered, almost fiercely.

"Come with us," Felix answered. "You see, there are two other of you. I want three altogether. Please follow us across to the club there."

Felix and his friends reentered the club, followed by the three men. They led the way into a small room on the ground floor. Felix placed three chairs in a row, and bade the men sit down. Then he rang the bell.

"Presently," he said to them, "I am going to give you something to eat. First of all, I am going to give you a cup of coffee. Then I will tell you what this job is."

"Is it something I can do?" the young man asked eagerly.

"And I?" the older one exclaimed.

"I will do it," the boy muttered, "whatever it is, if there's money to be earned!"

Felix smiled at them encouragingly. "It will be the easiest thing in the world," he said.

"We shall leave you for five minutes while you drink your coffee. I will tell the waiter to bring you some rolls with it. Afterward you shall have something more substantial."

They went out into the hall and entered the smoking-room. Richards was laughing softly.

"My dear Felix," he said, "you are the strangest mortal I ever met. There is no end to your experiments, but some day I think there will be an end to your optimism. However, why should I grumble?" he added, lighting a cigar. "I am going to make fifty pounds – fifty pounds, that is, I suppose, less the cost of the dinner, which I shall have to stand you."

"It's a foolish bet, Felix," the younger man declared. "There aren't many of those young fellows hanging about unless there is a reason for it."

"You don't believe that a man can have ill luck, then?" Felix asked.

"Not to that extent," Andrewes answered. "Odd bits of bad luck we all have now and then, but the man who's sober and honest, and who wants work, gets it. That's my experience, anyway."

Felix smiled. "My young friend," he said, "as you have been down from college only a year, and spend half of your time in town, I don't believe you know a thing about it. As for Richards, well, he has formed his opinions and I have formed mine. We shall see. I think we can go back to them now."

They were sitting just where they had been left. In front of each was an empty cup and an empty plate. Felix sat upon the edge of the table, a few feet away from them.

"Look here," he said. "I will tell you what I want you to do. I have three letters which I want delivered, one in London, one in Kettering, and one in Cambridge. These letters each contain a small sum of money, which I wish conveyed to the person to whom the letter is addressed. I shall give you your train-fare, and enough money for all your expenses. All that I ask is that at exactly this time, or as near it as possible, the day after to-morrow, you bring me back, from the people to whom the letters are addressed, a reply, and I shall then give you each a sovereign."

They were all clearly puzzled. The elderly man looked at him blankly.

"Perhaps I ought to explain," Felix continued, feeling for the first time a little diffidence, "that this offer of mine is the result of a bet. It doesn't make any difference to you, does it? All you have to do is to take the train to the place the letter is addressed to, and bring a reply back to me. It's easy work, and you will be well paid for it."

The elderly man and the boy rose to their feet eagerly.

"Are the letters ready?" the former asked.

"Will there be enough money for the night's lodging?" the boy demanded.

"Plenty," Felix answered. "While you sit there, I am going to write the letters."

The third man rose to his feet. There was something in his eyes which Felix did not altogether like. His lips were tightly drawn, and for the first time his unusual height seemed to become noticeable.

"So this is a bet, is it?" he asked, "a bet upon our honesty?"

Felix assented gravely. "One of my friends," he said, "has offered to wager me fifty pounds that I could not select three men from among you out there who would perform an errand like this honestly. I have accepted his bet. I have chosen you three, and I am quite sure that you will deliver your letters, bring me back the receipts, and earn the sovereigns which I promise you."

"And what about the fifty pounds that you win?" the man asked calmly.

"That is my business," Felix answered. "It is nothing to do with you. Will you take your letter?" he asked.

The man hesitated. "Yes, I'll take it," he answered shortly.

Felix went to the writing-table. He wrote three letters, and in each, without any concealment of the fact, he placed two five-pound notes. Then he sealed and addressed them, and took them back to the writing table.

"Now listen," he said. "if you cannot find the person to whom these letters are addressed, you can bring them back here. To-day is Monday. I shall expect you here on Wednesday afternoon between four and five o'clock. I am going to give you each a little more than you should need for your expenses. You can tell me what you have spent, and we can arrange for the balance.

He place a letter and two sovereigns in the hand of each one of them. The boy and the gray-haired man grasped theirs eagerly and went out with scarcely a word. The other one lingered.

"You don't ask for any promise from us?" he asked.

"No," Felix answered. "The promise goes without saying."

"Mind, I give none," the man said. "I do not promise to return. I do not promise I will not steal the notes which I saw you place in this letter."

"If you do so, it will be dishonest," Felix said. "I can only say that I hope you will do nothing of the sort."

The man wheeled about without a word and left the room. Richards, who was sitting in an easy chair, slapped his knee and burst out laughing.

"You silly ass, Felix!" he exclaimed. "Eighty-six pounds you have thrown away this afternoon. Eighty-six pound! Well, all I can hope is that you will learn a little wisdom from it."

At a quarter to four on Wednesday afternoon, Felix drove up in his motor-car and entered the club. "Anyone been asking for me?" he inquired of the doorkeeper.

"No one special, sir," the man answered. "Mr. Andrewes and Mr. Richards said that they were in the smoking-room when you came in."

Felix nodded, and joined his friends.

"I've ordered the dinner," Richards said. "I suppose we may as well have it tonight."

"Certainly," Felix answered; "only I am not at all prepared to say that I shall not be host. Wait a moment."

He sent a message down to the doorkeeper that anyone who asked for him should be admitted.

"In the meantime," Richards remarked, "we'll have a rubber of bridge."

At six o'clock Felix sent down another message, but the doorkeeper announced that no one had inquired after him. At seven o'clock he asked again, and met with the same reply. At eight o'clock they sat down to dinner. Richards raised his glass and proposed a toast.

"This is my wish for you," he said, "that to-night's lesson may teach you to keep your head from the clouds."

"And your feet upon the earth," Andrewes echoed.

Felix sighed. "I am disappointed," he admitted simply.

✳

"It's just about a year," Richards remarked, turning away from the club window, "since our friend Felix looked down into the square there and make the most ridiculous bet that was ever proposed."

"Three days before Christmas, wasn't it?" Andrewes remarked. "How the fellows did chaff him for weeks afterward!"

"He is an impossible person," Richards declared. "He needed just such a lesson as that. I only wish, for his own sake, that he'd learn a little common sense in the management of his business."

Andrewes nodded sympathetically. "Not doing over well, is he?"

Richards sighed, but made no answer. Almost at that moment Felix entered. Something of the old blitheness seemed to have gone from his manner. He looked much older, and there were lines in his face.

"Cut in for a rubber of bridge, old chap?" Andrewes asked.

"Oh, I don't know!" Felix answered. "Anything you like."

A servant from below came up with a letter upon a tray. Felix opened it listlessly enough, but as he read his face changed. He sat suddenly up in his chair. Something of the old enthusiasm lit up his features.

"Listen, Andrewes!" he exclaimed. "Listen, Richards! I want to read you this letter."

"It's from one of the three?" Richards exclaimed suddenly.

"It is," Felix admitted. "It's from the middle-aged man – the one with the iron-gray beard. His name is John Elwick. Listen to what he says:

33 High Street, Barnet.

Sir: I write you these few lines at last with much misgiving, and yet I cannot keep silence any longer.

You will doubtless remember who I am. A year ago you gave me a letter to deliver at an address in Kettering. I went there and found that there was no such place and no such person. I knew quite well what I ought to do – to go back to you and help you to win your bet. I didn't do it. I will tell you the truth. I was very angry. I had had a hard struggle, fighting against misfortune year after year. I have a wife, who has been my devoted companion, and who on the day I saw you was practically dying of starvation. I thought of her. I thought of my long fight against ill luck. And I thought of you, with your comfortable life and wealthy friends, to whom the sufferings of such as myself had become a jest. Never before had I done a dishonest act, but I did one then. I tore open your letter, and found, as I had expected, nothing but the two five-pound notes. I went for my wife, and I came to this place in search of work. I had had a small drapery business until I lost it through no fault of my own, and with your ten pounds I bought a share in a very small business in a side street here, from a man who was consumptive and could not work it himself.

Now I come to the strange part of this. Once when I was in a situation I saved sixty pounds. I bought a business with it, and I worked, I and my poor wife, till we were shadows, and it was all in vain. We lost our money, and I came to be what I was when you found me. Now, with this ten pounds which I stole from you, I made money from the first. Nothing could go wrong with me. I have moved three times during these twelve months, into larger premises. My wife is restored to health. I am sure now of a living for the rest of my days.

A week ago, for the first time, I told my wife the truth about that ten pounds – there was a distant relative from whom I had sworn that it had come. A few nights ago, as I say, I told her the truth. It is she who has made me do this. I send you back your ten pounds, with interest, and the address at which I live is at the head of this letter. If you think it worth while, you can send me to prison. You know my story, and from what I remember of you, you did not look like a man who would be too severe upon his fellow creatures. Let me off, sir, and send me a line to set our minds at ease. If it is any pleasure for you to know it, that ten pounds has been the making of me, and saved my wife's life.

I am, sir,
Your obedient servant,
John Elwick.

"What do you think of that?" Felix exclaimed breathlessly.

Richards laughed. "Well," he said, "I should call it a lucky theft."

"I don't care what you call it," Felix declared, rising and making his way to the writing-table. "I'm thankful now that I made the bet, and I'm thankful that I lost it. I shall write and tell the poor fellow so tonight."

"What about the other two?" Andrewes asked.

"A young man is in the hall, wishing to see you, sir," the servant who had brought up the letter announced.

Felix went down-stairs. From the first, he had a presentiment as to whom it would be. A tall, ungainly figure was waiting in the hall. Felix threw open the door of the strangers' room and bade him enter. Then he pulled up the blind and shook his head slowly.

"Well," he said, "what have you come to say?"

"I've come to see," the boy said sullenly, hanging his head, "whether you can't do something for me."

Felix shook his head slowly. He was an optimist, he had been an enthusiast all his days, but there are things which no man can mistake. The boy who stood before him bore, in his face and attitude and manner, every sign of evil. His hair was close cropped; his speech was sullen, almost defiant; his eyes were shifty; his clothes were ragged and untidy.

"Why should I do anything for you?" Felix asked.

"Because it was you that made me a thief," the boy answered. "I wasn't much of a chap, but I'd never stolen before until you played that silly trick on us. I dunno what the other two did. I know I just took out those two five-pound notes, and went for having a bit of fun. I'd starved long enough. When it had gone I stole more. I've been in prison twice. Give us something, guvnor, to help me along."

"Until you can find an opportunity to steal again?" Felix asked quietly.

"I'll make a fresh start," the young fellow whined.

Felix rang the bell. There were limits even to his optimism. "You can go," he said. "I have nothing for you."

✳

Felix knew that he was ruined. He sat in his office, and looked at the figures which a sympathetic but plain-spoken accountant had just laid before him.

"I am very sorry, Mr. Felix," the later said. "There is nothing for it but to call a meeting of your creditors at once. I should advise your doing so without any delay. Times have been bad, and there has been no one in your business who seems to have got a proper grip of things. You have given away a great deal more than you could afford, if you will allow me to say so – not only of your money, but of your time and thoughts. The result, I am afraid, has been disastrous."

"If you will come back in an hour, Mr. Malcolm," Felix said, "I will tell you exactly what I propose to do."

Mr. Malcolm took up his hat and went out. As he left the office, a tall man pushed his way in, followed by a protesting clerk.

"I cannot see anyone to-night," Felix said, rising to his feet.

"You will see me," the newcomer answered. "I shall not keep you long."

Felix was suddenly silent. It was the third man. He signed to the clerk to close the door and leave them.

"Well?" he said.

The newcomer took a seat. "You remember me?" he said. "My name is John Watts."

"I remember you," Felix answered. "Have you brought me back my ten pounds?"

"It would serve you right," John Watts said slowly, "if you never saw that ten pounds again. I am not sure that it would not serve you right if I took you by the shoulders and shook you. Do you know that you made a thief of me?"

"I deny it," Felix answered. "I put you to a test, and you failed."

"It was an unfair test," John Watts said. "Never mind, I made a deliberate choice. The fates have been against me all my life, although I had played the game straight. I thought I'd try my luck a little differently. I have done fairly well," he continued, "and so have you."

"So have I?" Felix repeated.

"Yes," John Watts answered. "I was an honest thief – I will say that for myself. You and I went into business together over in Mexico. You'll know all about it later. We've done well."

"Oh! Have we?" Felix answered.

"I put your ten pounds together with my muscle and experience," John Watts said, "but where the luck came from God only knows, for I've had the wickedest luck of any man that ever breathed – I should say that we had."

"You are not talking nonsense by any chance, are you?" Felix asked.

"You may call it nonsense if you like," John Watts said, "but the fact remains that you and I are the owners of the Infanta Silver Mine, and if you like to take three hundred thousand pounds for your shares, you can have it to-morrow. I'm not selling mine."

"You're mad!" Felix faltered.

"I'm not nearly so mad as I was at you once," John Watts said, "but I think we'd better shake hands and forget it. My lawyer's down at the hotel. You'd better put on your hat and come along with me. He'll show you just how things are. But first of all, let me ask you this. What became of the other two?"

Felix told him. John Watts nodded thoughtfully.

"Well, after all," he said, "two of us were honest thieves. I'm not sure that you didn't win your bet."

Felix arose with sparkling eyes. "We'll call in at the club and find Richards," he declared. "Come on."

THE TURNING WHEEL

"I say, aren't we going on to Bushey at all?"

The boy stirred his head, lazy, yet impatient.

"Why should we?" he asked. "We won't find a better place than this."

The girl was apparently disappointed.

"A young lady in our room was there last week and said that the chestnuts were glorious," she announced.

"Think of the crowds!" he murmured, half-closing his eyes. "We have it almost to ourselves here."

The girl looked around with an air of mild discontent. Her back was against the trunk of an ancient oak. Her companion was stretched upon the ground by her side with his head in her lap. Their clothes, bicycles, and the fact that they had so disposed themselves within a few yards of one of the roads leading through Richmond Park sufficiently proclaimed their status. They were the toilers whom the June sunshine had drawn out from the hidden places of the great city.

"I have never known it so quiet here on a fine Sunday," the girl remarked.

"So much the better," the youth muttered. "Heavens! Don't we see enough of our fellow-creatures and hear their voice often enough six days in the week? It's a treat to hear something else – the wind in the leaves and the grasses, and the singing of the birds."

The subject was manifestly one which, if argued, might lead to misunderstandings. The girl stifled a yawn and changed her position a little, as though cramped. The boy, flat on his back, his hands pressed deep down in the cool grass, looked upward through the green leaves to the sky, dotted all over with little fleecy specks of white clouds.

"Can't you feel the quiet of it?" he asked. "No hum of machinery, no foreman rushing about the place to know when that work will be finished. I wonder —"

He stopped short. The frown upon his forehead deepened. He changed his position so that he could see into the pale, anaemic face of the girl with whom he sat.

"I wonder what we do it for?" he remarked, curiously.

"Do what?" she asked.

"Make bond-slaves of ourselves," he answered. "Ten hours a day for me, and nearly as much for you, and I don't suppose that my engineer's shop is a much livelier place than your dressmaker's room. One day's peace, of a sort, and six days with both feet upon the mill. What do we do it for, Agnes?"

"To live," she answered, with a hard little laugh. "Do you suppose I'd stand a single hour of the life if I hadn't got to?"

The boy was answered, but unsatisfied. He looked away from his companion, but the frown remained deep-graven upon his face.

"To live!" he repeated. "I'm not so sure. It seems to me that we do it so that other people may live. It isn't for ourselves we work – it's for the others."

"I work for fourteen shillings a week," the girl said, bluntly.

The boy shook his head.

"You don't," he declared. "You work so that the woman who employs you, and who calls herself a modiste, and has a flat in town and a little cottage up the river, can get all there is to be got out of life. You are one of the parts of the machine, and so am I. I think that we are foolish."

"What would you do?" the girl asked, curiously.

"I don't know," he answered. "I haven't thought about it."

"I shouldn't bother," the girl said.

"Perhaps you are satisfied with your life," he went on, pulling out a handful of grass and throwing it from him. "I'm not. Three times last week I thought of things which improved the working of the room. I reckoned it out on the back of an old envelope. Someone must have made pounds and pounds by my idea. I altered one of our filing machines on Monday, and it's done its work a lot better since. What do I get for it?"

"Twenty-eight shillings a week," the girl answered. "You see, we are labourers. I suppose you are one of them who call themselves Socialist?"

"I don't think I am," the boy answered. "I never talked with one, that I know of, in my life. And as for books, I never look inside them. But there's something wrong. If only one had time I would try and think out what it is."

"Better rest," the girl said, curtly. "You look as though you need it."

"And what about yourself?" he answered. "I haven't seen you with a speck of colour in your cheeks since the first time we met up on the hill there."

"What chance should I have to get colour in my cheeks, I wonder?" she asked. "Anyhow, it doesn't matter; I'm strong enough."

He turned his head and looked at her with new-born criticism in his eyes. Her cheeks were pallid, her eyes lustreless. Even her hair was dull and without life. Her mouth, well shaped once, had taken to itself a discontented turn. Her features, though good enough, were expressionless. Yet she was not without a certain natural prettiness, barely surviving the environment of her life. She bridled a little under his scrutiny and threw some grass into his face.

"Well, Mr. Impertinent," she said, "what do you think of me?"

He sighed.

"You are well enough, Agnes," he said, "but you've got the brand upon you. So have I. So has every man in my workshop. So has every girl, I expect, in your room. I don't understand it."

"Let's go down and get some tea," the girl suggested, yawning. "It won't do you no good to lie there puzzling your head about things that don't amount to anything. My, that's a fine motor-car."

The boy turned his head. The car had come to a standstill in the road, a few yards away. The man and the girl who were its sole occupants had turned to look at the view. In front, the chauffeur and footman, immaculate both in spotless livery, looked stolidly into space.

"In many respects," the man in the car was saying, "London is wonderfully fortunate. Our parks are magnificent. Fancy these thousands of acres free for all Londoners to come and sit about and enjoy themselves!"

His companion inclined her head faintly towards the boy and girl beneath the tree.

"Like that," she remarked, smiling. "Yes, I suppose they find pleasure in it."

The man at her side followed her gesture. It seemed as though the eyes of the four met at the same moment.

"Quite an idyll," he remarked, good-humouredly. "These people must do their love-making somewhere, I suppose."

"Why not?" the girl answered, nonchalantly. "How tired they look, though!"

She withdrew her eyes, into which, perhaps, for a moment, had passed some faint glint of pity. The man touched a button and the car glided on. The boy raised his head from the girl's lap and followed it with his eyes. His gaze was no ordinary one. It seemed as though within these last few minutes he had seen farther into life, as though the passing of these two, denizens of an unknown world, had kindled in him a new seriousness.

"I don't understand it," he muttered.

"Then you're a fool," the girl declared, hardly. "It's simple enough. They're rich and we're poor. They ride in motor-cars and we on hired bicycles. The girl wears silks and laces, and I have to be thankful for cheap linen. The man smokes cigars, and you can just run to a packet of Woodbines. It's easy enough to understand. They're rich and we're poor."

The boy seemed as though he scarcely heard her.

"I wonder!" he said to himself.

"Are you going to stand tea or aren't you?" the girl asked, a little wearily. "I'm almost famished, and the places'll be full unless we hurry."

He rose to his feet – five feet ten of long, lanky humanity, dressed in a ready-made blue serge suit, a clean collar, and a black tie, good-looking enough in his way, but with his shoulders already bowed beneath the burden – the burden of the toiler. Even as he held his companion's bicycle for her to mount, his eyes watched the cloud of dust left by the motor-car.

A year later he stood, perfectly at his ease, in the prisoners' dock, waiting for the sentence which was obviously deserved and would certainly be forthcoming. Throughout the brief proceeding he had listened to the evidence against him with the intelligent interest of someone quite removed from personal association with the case. The speech for his defence he had ignored. His attitude, in fact, for a first offender, had been so puzzling that the magistrate was prompted to ask whether he had anything to say on his own behalf. He shook his head.

"The gentleman who was kind enough to defend me," he remarked, "said a great deal more for me than I should have ventured to say for myself. It is quite true that I took the money – a hundred and seventy pounds, I think it was. I hoped to have got away with it, but the luck was against me."

"You realized," the magistrate asked, "that you were committing a dishonest action?"

"Not in the least," was the prompt reply. "The money to which I endeavoured to help myself was a very small portion of a great fortune which had been amassed by my employers by means of my brains and the brains of others like me. I have no personal grudge against the gentlemen who are prosecuting me, but morally I consider them at least as guilty as myself. They are not productive members of society in any sense of the word. They have left us, I and my fellow-labourers, to do the work, and they have spent the results in luxuries whilst we have been starved for necessities. I myself, in one room of that man's factory" – pointing to the somewhat pompous figure of the prosecutor – "have inaugurated changes and improvements which must have saved him in a single year ten times the sum I am accused of stealing. For this my wages were advanced two shillings a week. I am not saying," he continued, "that I could have got more elsewhere. None of my ideas were worth anything without the capital to buy the machinery and the established business in which to make use of it. But the fact remains that mine were the brains and his the opportunity. I was the worker and he the parasite. It didn't seem to me to be a fair bargain, and I saw no way of getting it set right, so I helped myself. I am willing to serve any sentence you may give me, but if you, sir, and the society proclaim me dishonest, I venture, with the utmost heartiness, to disagree with you."

The magistrate stared at him. There was a little ripple of interest though the court. A moment or two later the sentence was pronounced: "Six months' imprisonment in the second division!"

The youth, as he was being led from the dock, met the eyes of his employer fixed a little curiously upon him. It was thus almost that they had exchanged glances in Richmond Park twelve months before. There was nothing threatening about the appearance of this younger man, who followed the policeman obediently from the dock, yet his late employer went back to his works with an uneasy feeling that a new force was abroad in the world – something which he did not understand. He thought of it at dinner that night, and his daughter feared that things had gone ill in the City, and felt a moment's alarm lest anything might happen to prevent the purchase of a new steam yacht in which they had planned a cruise.

"Nothing wrong in the City, I hope?" she asked, after the servants had left.

Her father shook his head.

"Nothing at all," he answered. "Rather a curious thing happened today, though. Do you remember driving through the Richmond Park a year ago? We stopped to look at the view, and a boy and a girl who were lying on the grass under one of the trees stared at us curiously. I told you at the time the boy's face seemed familiar to me. I discovered afterwards that he was one of my employees."

"I remember perfectly," the girl answered, with interest. "I told you that I liked his face."

"To-day I had to prosecute him," her father continued. "He robbed us of a hundred and seventy pounds, and very nearly got away."

She raised her eyebrows.

"I am sorry," she remarked, quietly. "He didn't look like a thief."

"Nor did he look like one in the dock," her father answered. "Nor did he talk like one. He even tried to justify himself. It's this infernal Socialism that's doing all the mischief with the half-educated working classes. Young men like this take it up and imbibe the most absurd ideas."

"Did he have to go to prison?" the girl asked, anxiously.

Her father nodded.

"Yes," he declared. "I couldn't have got him off if I would. He's gone to prison for six months."

Being naturally of a law-abiding temperament, and conducting himself, therefore, in prison with rare discretion, John Selwyn was a free man again in five months and eight days. Twenty-four hours after that period, however, he stood once more in the dock upon another and very different charge. This time he was certainly paler, and he was dressed in borrowed clothes, but his manner had lost nothing of its earnest composure.

"The most determined case, sir, I ever did see," a policeman explained. "Got on the steamboat pier and threw himself off in the deepest part of the river."

The magistrate nodded.

"I read the particulars," he said. "I understand that he even struggled with the lighterman who saved his life."

"Naturally," the young man in the dock interrupted. "I did not throw myself into the river with the object of being picked out again."

The magistrate looked at him earnestly.

"Do you consider," he asked, "that you have a right to dispose of your own life in this fashion."

"Why not?" the young man answered. "It appears to me that for any-one in my position it is the most sensible and reasonable thing to do. I lived like a slave for a great many years. I made an attempt to better myself, and it failed. Now that I have been in prison my chances of getting on in the world are certainly less than they were. I really do not feel under the slightest compulsion to continue an unequal struggle."

"There is a place for every man in the world," the magistrate said, "if only he has the courage and wit enough to find it."

"You are doubtless right, sir," the prisoner answered, politely. "I would suggest, in that case, that a few signposts would be an advantage. I have never considered myself lacking in intelligence, but, so far as I am concerned, I have failed to find that place."

"You became a thief," the magistrate reminded him.

"That is a point," the prisoner answered, "upon which I regret to say that we disagree. But, in any case, I was driven to it. The day before I took that money, if it interests you to know this, I went to a physician. He explained to me that ten hours' work a day in an unwholesome atmosphere, without proper food or under sanitary conditions of life, was rapidly undermining my constitution. Another year of it and I should have been a dead man. I felt that it was time for me to make a change."

"If I discharge you," the magistrate asked, "will you promise not to repeat the attempt?"

The young man hesitated.

"Really," he said, "I have no wish to become a burden to the State, and I do not exactly see —"

The magistrate stopped him.

"There has come into my hands," he said, gravely, "a sum of twenty pounds. That sum is yours if you will promise to leave the country at once and not to repeat the offence with which you are at present charged."

"My I inquire the price of a third-class ticket to New York, and the sum of money I should be required to have to be allowed to land?" the prisoner asked.

"The police-court missionary," the magistrate answered, "will take you from here to an emigrant office, when you can learn all particulars."

"In that case," the young man declared, "I am willing to give my promise."

Eight years later Sir Henry Rathbone and his daughter stood talking together in the reception-room of one of London's principal restaurants. The eight years had dealt kindly enough with the girl, who had become a beautiful woman. The man had not improved. His face bore the marks of a life of pleasure. Here and there were lines which seemed to indicate anxiety. Just at present he had very little the look of a prosperous man.

"You can have the car for Ranelagh, of course, Violet," he said, "but I am quite sure that I shall not be able to go. My luncheon appointment here is a very important one."

She shrugged her shoulders.

"I wonder you men don't do all your business in the City," she remarked.

Her father laughed hardly.

"My dear girl," he said, "It is only with the utmost difficulty that I have managed to get this fellow Selwyn to meet me at all. He declined to come to the works, and it is only to oblige Haregood, his solicitor, that he agreed to lunch here to-day."

"I really cannot understand," she remarked, watching the people as they came in, "why a little machinery should be so important to you."

Her father frowned irritably – his temper had not improved during the last few years.

"You don't understand anything about it, you see, Violet," he declared. "This man has invented some machines by which he can make my screws at about half the price it costs me to turn them out. Unless he'll lease me some machines, or sell me some, or amalgamate, Messrs. Rathbone and Co. may as well close their doors."

"What does it matter?" the girl answered, carelessly. "You have plenty of money."

Her father seemed to grow pale underneath his flushed cheeks.

"Plenty of money," he agreed, "but every penny in the business. Here they come."

"And here," the girl remarked, "is Lady Angerton. Good-bye for the present, then."

She went forward to meet her hostess at the same time that her father shook hands with his two guests. Selwyn had changed beyond recognition, yet as they took their places at the table Sir Henry was conscious of a vague sense of familiarity.

"Where did you learn the practical part of our industry, may I ask, Mr. Selwyn?" he inquired, as soon as it was possible to turn the conversation toward business.

"In your workshops, Sir Henry," the young man answered. "I was there eight years ago. By the by, perhaps I ought to remind you before I accept your invitation that I have been in prison. I stole a hundred and seventy pounds of yours once, you know. You got the money back again, but some people have prejudices about that sort of thing."

Sir Henry shook in his chair.

"Of course," he muttered, "I remember. I remember you now."

There was an awkward pause.

"I ought to have explained before," the young man murmured, with a quiet smile.

"Not at all – not at all," his host declared, hastily. "These things are best forgotten. This is a business meeting, Mr. Selwyn. I want to talk to you about those machines of yours."

"I shall be glad," the young man said, "to hear what you have to say."

They talked throughout luncheon, and in the smoking-room afterwards, and Mr. John Selwyn only resisted with difficulty an attempt on the part of his host to take him round to his club. He declined politely but firmly to pledge himself to anything. His idea in coming to England, he admitted, was to set down the machines to manufacture screws for himself. Sir Henry felt the perspiration break out on his forehead at the mere idea.

"Between ourselves," he said, "we need not mince words. You know, and I know, that if you do so, and if you refuse to sell or lease your machines, my firm will have to close their doors."

"Precisely," Mr. Selwyn admitted. "The fact had occurred to me."

"You mean to make us do it, by God!" Sir Henry exclaimed, suddenly.

"If you want the truth," the young man answered, "I do."

Sir Henry went away from the interview disturbed and uneasy. Nevertheless, negotiations were not wholly broken off. There were times when Selwyn seemed on the point of accepting some of the offers which the solicitors of Messrs. Rathbone and Co., Limited, were continually making him. Sir Henry himself spared no effort to win the good-will of his former employé. He invited him to his house – an invitation which, curiously enough, John Selwyn accepted. On one of these occasions he met Violet, and their mutual interest was so obvious a thing that she was feverishly incited by her father to take a hand in the game. Mr. Selwyn listened to all that she had to say, and was very polite. He even accepted further invitations, and more than once he was seen about with Violet Rathbone.

They sat together one Sunday morning in the Park. Her father, at the first opportunity, had made some excuse to hurry off and leave them alone. They talked the usual banalities, watched the people, and made remarks about them. Finally, Violet rose a little suddenly.

"Come and sit further back, Mr. Selwyn," she said. "I want to talk to you."

He obeyed at once. No one could have judged from his face what effect her words had upon him. They found two seats a little apart from the others. She looked for a moment at the lace of her parasol and then into his expressionless eyes.

"Mr. Selwyn," she said, "I am beginning to find the present position embarrassing. You know very well why my father leaves me alone with you, why he is always asking you to the house. I do not see why we should play at misunderstanding one another. My father tells me that it rests with you whether or not he is to lose the whole of his fortune and to watch the ruin of his business."

The young man nodded his head thoughtfully.

"Your father is quite right, Miss Rathbone," he said. "It rests entirely with me."

"There are ways," she continued, "of avoiding this, are there not? Compromises, I mean, which could be made? You would lose very little, for instance, if you leased your machines to my father or went into partnership with Rathbone and Co., Limited?"

"So far as the financial side of the matter is concerned," the young man admitted, blandly, "it would be a very reasonable and satisfactory settlement."

"It does not appeal to you, though?" she continued.

"It does not," he admitted.

She raised her eyebrows. They were coming to it at last, then!

"From your manner," she said, "one would imagine that you had some grievance against my father."

"I have," he admitted. "Not a personal one altogether, and yet, perhaps, it is a personal one. I have been in prison, you know, Miss Rathbone, for stealing from your father."

She laid her hand upon his arm.

"You must not talk about it, please," she said. "We have forgotten all that."

She did not move her fingers for a moment. She was twenty-six years old, very beautiful, but as yet heart-whole. She was beginning to feel that there was something remarkably attractive about this young man, if only he would be reasonable.

"I wonder if you remember," he said, "somewhere about nine years ago, driving through Richmond Park and stopping on the hill?"

"I remember perfectly," she agreed. "You sat on the grass with your head in a young woman's lap. I considered it at the time most shocking behaviour."

"It was the way of the world in which I moved," he answered, "the way of the world in which Fate and your father kept me. It is not that I have a personal animus against Sir Henry. He was my employer in those days, and he only did what others did and are doing; but, none the less, the wealth which he is so anxious that I should preserve for him has been built up on the bodies and the souls of hundreds such as I. Labour to him was labour, a weapon towards his end – some dead, inanimate thing, to be used as cheaply as possible and as effectively as could be. I had my brains picked week by week for your father's benefit. Those days are hard to forget, Miss Rathbone."

"I am not a political economist," the girl said, "but you must surely understand that it was not my father who fixed the conditions. What he did, he did because others were doing it. It is not possible, Mr. Selwyn, that you bear him a real and personal grudge for those days?"

The young man looked out across the Park, but he said nothing.

"It is an opportunity which makes the employer," the girl went on. "You yourself speak of starting great works. Will your men be better treated than my father treated you?"

"I intend to make some efforts, Miss Rathbone, in that direction," he remarked.

She looked down at her little patent shoe and beat the ground impatiently for a moment or two.

"You are so enigmatic," she protested, softly. "Can't we understand one another, Mr. Selwyn? Please speak out and tell me what is in your mind."

He looked at her thoughtfully. She represented the last word in wealth and elegance and education. Her delightful carriage was the outcome of her healthy, untrammeled life. No trouble had ever dimmed her beautiful eyes or carved a single line upon her still girlish face.

"Miss Rathbone," he said, "you and your father are both anxious to know my plans. It is better, perhaps, that I should tell you them. I will not admit that I have any personal feelings against your father. On the other hand, I hate, with a hatred which has been absolutely the mainspring of these recent years of my life, the means by which he made his wealth, the means by which he holds it. You have been very kind to me. Perhaps I have not deserved it. You beg for peace and I tell you that it must be war. I am here for that purpose and no other. Already the plans are out for my new factories. In two years' time – before, if your father is wise – he will close his doors. I shall find employment for his workpeople, and I promise you that I shall find it on very different conditions to any that Messrs. Rathbone, Limited, ever offered."

She looked at him, suddenly pale to the lips.

"Is this final?" she whispered.

"It is final," he answered.

They were very nearly alone, and she leaned so closely towards him that her soft breath fell upon his cheek.

"You are very hard, Mr. Selwyn. Could nothing – could nobody move you?"

She was offering herself to him – he knew that quite well.

"Nobody," he answered. "Not even the woman whom, in a few weeks' time, I hope to make my wife."

For a moment she neither moved nor spoke. Then she drew away and rose to her feet with a little shiver. Amongst the crowd at the corner came her father. She hurried toward him.

"Please leave me," she begged her companion. "I am going home. I have taken too much of your time already. Forgive me."

Late on the following afternoon John Selwyn set out to pay a call which he had already delayed for several weeks. He found his way to a certain address in Hanover Street, mounted to the first floor, and knocked at the door. A young woman dressed in black, with pins and needles stuck all over the front of her dress, threw it open. She stared at the visitor in surprise.

"The shop's downstairs," she remarked, "There's no one allowed up here. Madame is very strict about it."

John Selwyn's eyes travelled down the room. There were at least twenty girls sitting there at work – twenty girls with pale cheeks, and only one small window open. His conscience smote him because of those three weeks' delay.

"I am sorry," he said. "I came to make inquiries about a Miss Agnes Carton."

"Agnes Carton!" the young woman exclaimed. "Why, she left nearly four years ago. You'll find her at No. 55, Grosvenor Street."

John Selwyn raised his hat and departed.

"I ought to have come before," he said to himself, repentantly. "Perhaps it is too late."

He walked quickly to No. 55, Grosvenor Street. The appearance of the place was a distinct relief to him. It was a neat little milliner's shop, clean and smart. He opened the door and found himself in a cool, handsomely-furnished apartment, which to his inexperience seemed almost like the drawing-room of a private house. A young lady came hurrying forward.

"I am in search of Miss Agnes Carton," he announced. "I was told that she was to be heard of here."

The girl was puzzled for a moment, then she smiled.

"Why, you mean madame!" she exclaimed.

"Madame?" he repeated.

"Certainly," the girl answered. "That was her name before she was married. Here she is. It is a gentleman, madame, who asks for you."

A tall young lady, very elegant, very stylishly dressed, and apparently very prosperous, came towards him with an inquiring smile. John Selwyn recognized her with a little gasp.

"My dear Agnes!" he exclaimed.

"Why, it's – it's John Selwyn!" she declared.

The assistant slipped discreetly away. They shook hands a little perfunctorily.

"I have come to ask you to marry me," he announced.

She laughed heartily.

"Well, if it isn't just like you!" she answered. "You haven't changed a bit."

"I mean it," he assured her.

"But you're three years too late," she laughed. "The idea of going away like you did and never writing me a single line, and then walking in one morning and expecting me to marry you off-hand!"

"I had no time for letters," he said. "I have been working hard."

"From your appearance, I should say that you've been making money," she declared.

"More than I shall ever be able to spend," he assured her. "If only you'd waited."

She laughed again.

"Don't be foolish," she said. "I want you to meet my husband. He's such a dear. We should never have been able to marry, though, but for —"

A sudden change came into her face.

"Why, of course," she continued, "you were there. Let me tell you of my adventure. About a year after you left for America I was called down into the showroom one day and found a young lady there, looking at evening gowns. I was very tired – we had been up late the night before – and she was very impatient and hard to please. Well, I got trying on things for half an hour or so, and at last I fainted. I couldn't help it, but madame was very angry."

"And the girl?" he asked.

"Madame sent me away the next day, and I saw her in the street on my way home. She stopped her carriage and came up to me. I told her that I had lost my situation, and she was so angry that she went straight back to madame and told her that she would never set foot in her shop again. Afterwards she sent me to Hastings for two months, and when I was quite strong again she lent me the money to start in business here. I am proud to say that in less than eighteen months I was able to pay her back every penny."

"But what about this husband?" he asked.

"You remember my telling you about Mr. Mallison," she said. "He used to travel in silks, and I saw him now and then at madame's. He called here when I started and was very attentive. In a business like this, you know, one needs a man."

John Selwyn laughed. He was astonished to find how relieved he was.

"That's all very well," he said, "but I consider you've treated me shamefully."

"You shall tell my husband so," she declared. "He'll be here in a few minutes."

"We'll all go out to lunch," he suggested.

"And in the meantime," madame said, "let me tell you something strange. Do you know who the young lady was?"

"How should I?" he asked.

"Do you remember sitting in Richmond Park one Sunday afternoon when two people went by in a motor-car – a man and a girl? We all stared at one another rather strangely, and you told me afterwards that the man was your employer."

John Selwyn stood perfectly still.

"I remember," he said. "Go on."

"That was the girl – Miss Rathbone – who has done all this for me," madame declared, with tears in her eyes.

John Selwyn sat down in one of the padded chairs.

"Upon my word," he said, slowly, "in those days I used to admit that I couldn't understand life. I don't understand it now."

Late that afternoon he called at Berkeley Square. Miss Rathbone was at home, the butler thought, after a moment's hesitation, but she had gone to her room with a headache, and was refusing to see callers. Selwyn persisted, and twenty minutes later she came to him in the darkened drawing-room. He was standing when she entered, and she did not ask him to take a seat.

"I did not expect to see you here again, Mr. Selwyn," she said. "Under the circumstances, I think perhaps you might have stayed away."

"I could not," he answered, simply.

She gave a little start.

"Perhaps it was my father whom you wished to see?" she murmured.

"No," he answered, "it was you."

She came a few steps farther into the room. He saw then that she was paler than he had ever seen her. It was the beginning of trouble, this – the beginning of the blow which he had dealt.

"I do not know," she said, "what you can have to say to me."

"You look tired!" he exclaimed, abruptly. "Won't you sit down?"

She hesitated and then obeyed him, sinking on to a couch with a little gesture of weariness.

"Miss Rathbone," he said, "I have come to thank you for your kindness to the woman whom I was expecting to marry."

She looked at him for a moment without comprehension.

"I mean the young lady," he reminded her, "whom you set up in business in Grosvenor Street, whom you saw with me nine years ago in Richmond Park."

She suddenly understood.

"It was she, then, whom you spoke of in the Park yesterday?"

"Of course," he answered. "I was going to marry her. It was only right. She and I were sufferers together. We belonged to the same world. My prosperity was to have been her prosperity. You know," he continued, with a sudden smile, "even amongst the lower orders you can't sit in Richmond Park with your head on a girl's lap for nothing."

"You were going to marry her, but you didn't care," she said, in a broken voice.

"I certainly did not care," he admitted. "I did not know," he continued, coming close to her, "that I cared for anybody. I did not believe that there was any room in my life for that sort of thing. I rather fancy that I have been mistaken."

"It's horribly like the end of a story," she murmured, loosening her arms for a moment from around his neck.

"Not the end, sweetheart," he answered; "the beginning."

THE SOVEREIGN
IN THE GUTTER

It was over at last, the five days' cause célèbre, the five days' long-drawn-out agony. To the man who sat alone upon the hard bench fixed close to the whitewashed wall of the little cell the whole thing seemed, now that it was over, very much like a dream. He was plunged once more into solitude. The distant sounds came to his ears in a sort of muffled chaos. The crowded court with its insufferable atmosphere; the white, parchment-like face of the judge; the bewigged barristers with their strange callousness, their slight jests, their artificial earnestness; the sea of closely-packed faces extending even to the door; the faces of friends, acquaintances, enemies – all seemed, now that the curtain had fallen, as though they were but images of what might have been, as though they had never had – never could have had – any real existence. And then the story – the hateful, impossible story – twisted and turned against him at every point, the lies of another man put into his mouth, the evil deeds of his partner heaped upon his shoulders. His first sense of fierce martyrdom had burned away into ashes through the furnace of those long days of torture and suffering. The result had come at last scarcely even as a blow. The horror of it had been discounted a hundred times over, discounted by all those curious, inimical faces, the scathing words of the prosecuting barrister – a member of his club, once a guest at his house – discounted even by the cold, carefully-balanced words of the judge himself, so studiously impartial, so weightily censorious. It seemed to him that nothing remained – no pain, no loneliness, no humiliation. His senses were steeped in a sort of torpor. He was barely conscious of the opening of his door, of the entrance of the visitor, fresh from the court, who was sitting now by his side in grave silence.

"I am very sorry, indeed, Mr. Harewood," the lawyer was saying, "that the case went so badly. Personally, I am quite convinced that a serious injustice has been done. If Carelton had only been alive, he would have been able to clear you in many ways. Without his evidence the Court, of course, have assumed that you shared equally with him in his speculations and rash schemes."

The convicted man made no reply. He appeared indeed almost to have lost the power of speech. The solicitor, who was really exceedingly sorry for his client, and honestly believed him guilty of little more than the folly of a pleasure-loving man of the world who has left his affairs to an unscrupulous partner, tried to impart a consoling note to his next speech.

"The sentence," he declared, "was far too severe. I have heard it universally condemned. I can assure you that we do not intend to let the matter remain here. There will be a petition to the Home Secretary, and I believe I may say that it will be signed by the principal counsel for the prosecution. In the meantime, if you have any messages, you will be allowed to see your wife for a few minutes. And as to letters —"

There was a considerable space of wooden bench between the two men, and Harewood's fist suddenly smote it a terrible blow.

"Enough!" he said. "The thing is finished – my life is finished! I have no wife – no children! I wish to see no one. I will see no one."

"Mr. Harewood!" the lawyer protested.

A sudden fire flashed in the eyes of the convicted man.

"Silence!" he ordered. "You did your best. I am grateful. For the rest, I repeat that what has happened takes me out of this world as surely as death itself. You can tell my people that from me. They had better make their minds up to it, for it is inevitable. My wife is a widow and my children fatherless. I suppose there is a little money left somewhere. They must shift for themselves, as well as they can. But as for visits or letters, no! Not the thinnest thread shall bind me to the past when once I enter the convict prison. Understand that finally."

"In a few months' time —," the lawyer began, soothingly.

"In a few months' time," Harewood repeated, "things will be with me exactly as they are now. I have been hardly judged, perhaps, yet according to my strict deserts. Mine was the sin of omission. I left Carelton to play ducks and drakes with our clients' money while I enjoyed life in my own way. I trusted Carelton and I had no right to trust him, or any man, with other people's money. It was more than foolish – it was wicked. I admit the justice of my sentence. I am prepared to pay."

"With regards to Mrs. Harewood —," the lawyer recommenced.

"So far as I am concerned," the convicted man interrupted, "there is no such person. Let her understand that, and let my children understand it. God himself could not blot out these last five days, or the memory of them. They have come and gone like an avalanche, and they have swept me from the face of the earth. You understand?" he wound up, rising to his feet at the sound of a key in the door. "Letters I shall not open. Visitors I will not receive. I shall enter the convict prison without a name, and if ever I leave it I shall leave it without a name."

"You will leave it a good deal before fifteen years," the lawyer declared.

"As to that I am indifferent," Harewood answered. "Indifferent, that is to say," he added, slowly, "save for one thing."

"Your children?" the lawyer murmured.

"No," Harewood answered, with a note of repressed passion in his tone; "the children of Stephen Carelton!"

The sovereign lay on the edge of the kerbstone, half hidden by a little sprinkling of dust. Carelton's companion pointed it out to him.

"Your sovereign, Stephen," he remarked. "Lucky fellow, as usual! A few more rolls and it would have gone down the drain."

Carleton stood on the middle of the pavement looking at the spot where the glittering edge of the coin was clearly visible. He made no motion to pick it up. His friend looked at him in surprise.

"I know you're a veritable Croesus, Stephen," he remarked, "making money hand over fist, and all the rest of it, but I presume you don't intend to leave that sovereign for the sweepers?"

The young man drew a cigarette-case from his pocket and, selecting one, tapped it against the side and calmly lit it.

"For the sweepers, my dear Cyril," he answered, "I think not. To tell you the truth, I believe that Providence has some other destination in view for that luckless coin. That is the fourth time within the last five minutes that I have dropped it."

His companion adopted a practical attitude.

"Why don't you keep your gold in your waistcoat pocket?" he suggested.

"You are missing the whole point of my statement," Carelton declared. "I am convinced that it was not carelessness alone which caused the coin to drop from my fingers twice in the taxi-cab and twice when I sought for that loose silver to pay the man. Depend upon it, Cyril, Fate has its own use for that sovereign. I am clearly dispossessed."

His friend looked at him doubtfully. Carelton was a man of whims; but surely this was absurd!

"You can't mean," he said, "that you are going to leave it there?"

"Precisely what I do mean, my dear fellow," Carelton answered. "Come into the club and stand in the bay window. We shall be able to see the person whom Fortune has taken under her wing."

"There is not the slightest doubt about it," his friend remarked, decisively, "that you are more or less a fool, Stephen."

"I hope so," Carelton declared, fervently. "This world was not made for wise men. The workhouses and prisons are full of them. Come inside, Cyril, there's a good fellow. I am really interested to see into whose hands my sovereign is fated to pass."

The two men stood in the bay window of the club and watched. Stephen Carelton was tall and dark, with pale face, humorous mouth, and keen, grey eyes deep-set under his level eyebrows. He was still a young man, but ten years of exceptionally hard work, successful though it had been, had left its traces upon his features. Cyril Hanneford, his companion, was a man of slighter physique, more carefully dressed, a person of less marked characteristics, a loiterer amongst the byways of life, in the broad thoroughfares of which Carelton had already found for himself a place. As regards this particular incident, however, the two seemed to have changed identities. Carelton, the practical man of affairs, had yielded to the idlest of superstitions. Hanneford, the person to whom such things might well have seemed likely to appeal, was adopting the pose and tone of a cynic.

"A sovereign," he remarked, looking out upon the pavement, "is relatively a small sum. Yet, after all, my dear Stephen, there are possibilities about it. It is the price of a bottle of wine, a basket of violets for your good-looking typist, a stall at the Opera, a tip to a maître d'hôtel. You might, even," he added, "entertain me modestly to luncheon upon that sum. And behold! there it lies," he wound up, pointing out of the window, "chucked away as a thing of no worth, left there to gratify the vaguest of superstitions. Upon my word, I've a good mind to go out and fetch it myself."

"Don't talk rot, Cyril," Carelton declared, good-humouredly. "Stay here with me instead and watch for the lucky person. See, there is someone coming now."

A boy went by with a parcel under his arm, whistling loudly, with his eyes fixed upon the windows of the great club. He did not even look upon the pavement. Then there came a couple of men, arm in arm, talking intently as though engrossed upon some matter of business. They, too, passed on without a downward glance. A woman leading a dog by a string followed, but she only looked at the ground to admire her well-shod feet. A beggar-woman came slowly along, and Carelton found it hard work to prevent his friend from rushing out.

"If someone's going to pick it up," he protested, "why not that poor woman? It looks as though it might do her a bit of good."

Carelton held his arm.

"If it is meant for her, she will see it," he declared.

"You are not such a superstitious ass," Hanneford demanded, "as to believe —"

"I believe nothing," Carelton assured him. "Only I intend that Chance, which four times brought that particular coin from my pocket, shall choose the person into whose hands it shall pass."

"To judge by his walk, then, here he comes," Hanneford declared. "He's got his eyes glued on the pavement all right. Two to one he'll see it! No, he's going by! By Jove, he's stopped! He's got it, Stephen! Did you see him pick it up? You can say good-bye to your sovereign now, old man. He doesn't look the sort of chap to part easily."

Carelton was watching eagerly the face of the man who, after a covert glance around, was preparing to quit the scene. He was certainly not a person of prepossessing appearance; but, on the other hand, his clothes and general air seemed to indicate the fact of his belonging to that class to whom a sovereign is a distinct consideration. He was of powerful build, thin but sinewy, with hard, weather-stained face and undistinguished slouch. He wore a ready-made suit of clothes, and he carried no gloves or stick. Yet there was something about him a little different from the ordinary wayfarer, something which excited the curiosity of both men as they watched him hurry off.

"The sort of man, that, who would take a great deal of placing," Carelton remarked, thoughtfully. "He was no ordinary waster, I'm sure."

"It's good-bye to your sovereign, at any rate," Hanneford laughed. "Hadn't you better order those whiskies and sodas?"

The man with a sovereign gripped in his hand passed down the street and disappeared. There was a curious lack of vitality about him and the way he moved. His walk was a tired plod – a physical action which seemed purely mechanical. If he brushed the sleeve of a passer-by, he started, as though alarmed, and shrank away. Notwithstanding his somewhat forbidding appearance, he had an air which was almost timid. An acute physiognomist might easily have placed him. His were the mannerisms and deportment of a man finding himself once more amongst his fellows after a long period of solitude.

He reached the Strand and pursued his way steadily along as far as Chancery Lane. Here he turned into a little square and came to a sudden standstill before a venerable pile of offices. Then, for the first time since he had stopped to pick up that sovereign, the light swept across his face. Exactly opposite to him was a large brass plate, on which was engraved the name of Mr. Stephen Carelton, Junior, with a list of legal distinctions in smaller type. The place had an undoubtedly thriving appearance. Through the wire blinds of the offices he could see rows of clerks. There were visitors coming and going all the time – barristers' clerks with silk hats and small black bags, and others more obviously clients. The man stood there for several minutes, motionless. His lips were slightly parted, his face had gradually become hard and cruel. He spoke to himself for the first time.

"Mr. Stephen Carelton, Junior!" he muttered; "the boy who was at Oxford. It is well that one of them is alive."

He hesitated for a moment as though about to enter the offices. Then he looked at the sovereign in his hand and changed his mind. Slowly he turned round to face another shock before he had taken half-a-dozen steps. A carriage was drawn up close to the kerb in Chancery Lane. A woman with uplifted skirts was in the act of descending from it. She was tall, graceful, and young; fashionably dressed, with pleasant smile and clear brown eyes, which rested for a moment upon the man who was staring at her. She was suddenly perplexed. A frown wrinkled her forehead. She even stood still in the middle of the pavement. The man shuffled on and her eyes followed him. Then she went on her way slowly. She entered the offices of Mr. Stephen Carelton, Junior, with a puzzled frown lingering upon her face.

Harewood strode on towards the Strand, with the fires of hate suddenly loosed within him – the yearning of a moment changed already to that passionate desire to kill which for many years had been all that had remained to him of sensation. He came to a standstill in front of a small shop in the Strand, where various secondhand articles were for sale. He looked in at the window, and after a casual glance entered the shop.

"How much for the small revolver?" he asked.

The shopman took it from the window and examined it.

"Fifteen and sixpence," he answered, laying it upon the counter. "Nice little weapon, too – good as new."

Harewood took it up and examined it.

"What about cartridges?" he asked.

"You'll have to buy those at a gunsmith's," the man told him; "but there are three or four here somewhere which came with it. You can have them, if you like."

He rummaged about for several minutes and produced them at last from a large box filled with oddments.

"They've been lying here for some time," he remarked, "but I expect you'll find them all right."

Harewood inserted them into the chambers of the revolver, thrust it into his pocket, and placed the sovereign upon the table. The shopman handed him four and sixpence.

"I wouldn't carry it like that if I were you," he advised. "A loaded revolver's not too safe a thing to have loose in the pocket."

Harewood nodded, but left the place without making any answer. In the street he was conscious of a sudden giddiness. He stopped short for a moment, and remembered that as yet he had tasted no food that day. His hand was shaking like a drunken man's. Reluctantly he crossed the road and entered a small eating-house. It was a waste of time this, but it was necessary. When he emerged, half an hour later, he walked with a new decision and with more rapid footsteps. In a few moments he had found his way once more to the little square off Chancery Lane, and, presenting himself at the offices of Mr. Stephen Carelton, Junior, made his inquiry at the clerk's desk.

"Mr. Stephen Carelton has just come in from lunch, sir," the boy told him. "Have you an appointment?"

"Yes," Harewood answered.

The youth took up a book and glanced down it searchingly.

"We can't seem to have any record of an appointment with anyone of your name," he remarked. "When was it made?"

"A long time ago," Harewood answered, grimly; "perhaps before you were in a position to record it. Tell Mr. Carelton that Mr. Harewood wishes to see him at once."

The name, audible this time to the other clerks, elicited a slight stir of interest, but it did not occur to anyone to connect the speaker with the quondam head of the firm. After a brief delay Harewood was shown upstairs. Trembling a little at the knees, he passed along the familiar way. Soon he was ushered into the private office which had once been his. Stephen Carelton looked up and greeted him with a brief nod.

"You wished to see me I understand?" he said. "I am Mr. Stephen Carelton. I didn't quite catch your name."

The boy had disappeared and closed the door behind him. Harewood calmly seated himself in the empty chair opposite to the young lawyer.

"My name is Harewood," he announced.

They looked at one another across the table. Stephen Carelton's expression was at first one of puzzled doubt. Suddenly a light seemed to break in upon him.

"My God!" he exclaimed. "You are Julian Harewood?"

"Julian Harewood – yes!"

The younger man held out his hand.

"You have taken us completely by surprise, sir," he said. "Allow me to say, however, that I am very glad to see you. We had no idea that – that you would be here so soon. Your behaviour as to letters has been a little extraordinary, you know."

Harewood looked at the outstretched hand as though at some poisonous thing. Carelton slowly withdrew it.

"You're not going to bear malice against me, I hope, Mr. Harewood?" he said, frankly. "I know that my father used you ill, but it was before my time. I know, too —"

"Be quiet!" Harewood ordered.

He drew the revolver from his pocket and fingered it almost affectionately.

"I was released from prison early this morning," he said, slowly. "I had only one desire when I came out; I have had only one desire all the time I have been a prisoner, and that was that I might kill you, or anyone else who bore your name, before night."

"What have I done to injure you, Mr. Harewood?" the young man asked, calmly.

"You are your father's son," Harewood answered. "Look at me. I am the broken-down wreck of a man, the shell of a man in whom the heart and the soul are dead. I am what your father made me. Fortunately for him, he is dead. Unfortunately for you, you are alive. Stephen Carelton's son, indeed! I, too, had children. What has become of them God only knows! A wife – she is dead, I hope. Say your prayers quickly, young man. A word will have to do. A few hours ago I was terrified lest I should lack the strength of this thing. I feared that I might have to kill you with my hands. Chance sent me the money to buy this," he added, patting the revolver; "a blessed chance. My curses on you, Stephen Carelton!"

He raised the revolver and, pointing it deliberately at the other's head, pulled the trigger. There was an empty click. He tried once more. Again the fall of the hammer upon some unresponsive substance. Carelton, who had been paralyzed by the unexpectedness of the attack, sprang up and gripped his assailant's wrists so that the revolver fell on to the office table.

"Harewood!" he exclaimed. "My God, are you mad?"

Harewood answered nothing. He seemed suddenly turned into stone. The failure of his weapon was a thing uncontemplated – an unimaginable catastrophe. He suffered himself to be pushed back into his chair. Carelton looked at him wonderingly.

"I know you now!" he exclaimed. "You are the man who picked up my sovereign in Pall Mall! Is that what you bought with it?" he asked, pointing to the revolver.

"Yes!" Harewood answered mechanically, "that and a meal. I wish I had never seen the sovereign. I should have killed you then, sure enough."

The young man felt his forehead. He was scarcely surprised to discover that it was wet.

"Mr. Harewood," he said, "if you had killed me you would have killed your son-in-law. I was married to Louise two years ago. I know that my father treated you badly, but I have done all that I can to make up for it. And so far as regards the business, why, I have been more successful than I deserved even. There's money for you and a new life, and there isn't one of your people, or even your old friends, who won't be glad to see you. There isn't a soul who hasn't come to the conclusion that your sentence was ridiculously severe, and for the last twelve months there has been quite a series of agitations for your release. It's your own fault that we haven't been able to let you know. We've tried every means in vain. One moment."

He walked to the door of an inner room and called to somebody. Harewood pressed the barrel of the revolver against his own temple.

"One of them must be good," he muttered.

He pulled the trigger – again the empty click.

"One more – the last one!" he whispered to himself, and stiffened his finger.

Suddenly the weapon was wrenched from his hand. He turned swiftly round. The girl whom he had seen stepping from the carriage was there on her knees by his side; her arms were around his neck; marvellous, incredible words were pouring from her lips; her cheek, even her lips themselves were pressed to his. He rocked in his chair. There was a lump in his throat, burning fire behind his eyes. The years were falling away with the hot tears – nothing could stop them now. It was a nightmare which had passed...

Carelton walked to the window which overlooked the square, with the revolver in his hand. He pulled the trigger idly. It went off at once with a loud report. He stood gazing at it in amazement – it was the fourth cartridge which had been good! Through the little cloud of smoke he seemed to see the sovereign lying in the gutter below.

MR. HARDROW'S SECRETARY

The man looked up from his writing-table impatiently. Once more the door had opened and closed. He forgot even to be polite.

"What the dickens do you want?" he asked.

"I am your new secretary, Mr. Hardrow," the girl announced.

He laid down his pen and looked at her. She was very neatly though shabbily dressed, and very pretty.

"My new what?" he replied.

"Secretary," she answered, calmly.

"There's some mistake," he protested. "I haven't got a secretary; don't want one. I'm not looking for one."

"Pardon me, you do want one," she objected, firmly. "I arrived here an hour ago on quite different business, and found you were keeping no end of people waiting while you answered a few rubbishy letters yourself. Of course you want a secretary. A man who has just come back to England with a great fortune, and is getting invitations every minute, and visits from politicians, and all that sort of thing, must want a secretary. The only trouble seems to be that you did not know it. Shall I fetch my typewriter?"

He looked at her steadfastly for several moments. Notwithstanding the trim sobriety of her toilet, she was a most attractive-looking young person. She met his gaze quite fearlessly, and seemed to be absolutely unconscious that there was anything at all unusual about her attitude.

"What salary do you require?" he asked.

She considered the subject briefly.

"I get twenty-eight shillings a week at present," she said, "as I am a very rapid typist. You would doubtless be able to give more than that, but I am not sure how much. Suppose you give me thirty shillings a week for a month, and at the end of that time, if you keep me on, I expect I shall be worth a great deal more to you."

He nodded.

"I should think it very probable," he agreed, pushing a pile of letters away from him with an obvious air of relief. "By the by, what is your name?"

She hesitated for a moment, and there was something a little unconvincing about her statement.

"Miss Robinson," she said.

"Very well, then, Miss Robinson," he continued, "you may as well get your typewriter, and I will leave these letters until you return. The people who are waiting outside had better be shown in – one at a time, of course. Will you leave word as you go out?"

"Certainly," she answered. "I shall be back in less than an hour. By the by," she added, with a slight rush of colour to her cheeks, "would you mind advancing me two shillings?"

"Two shillings!" he gasped. "Why, with pleasure! What for?"

"To pay my cab," she told him, composedly. "It's Friday morning, you know, and I have spent my last week's salary. Thank you. I shall come back as quickly as I can."

She went out, and Hardrow looked after her with amazement.

"If she had asked for two pounds," he said to himself, "I should be pretty sure that she never meant turning up again. But two shillings! She is the most extraordinary young person —"

In rather less than an hour Hardrow returned to his rooms after a temporary absence to find his new secretary already installed, carefully wiping the keys of her instrument. She had taken off her hat, and looked very neat and workmanlike.

"Halloa! So you've come back?" he remarked, a little tritely.

"Naturally," she answered. "If you are ready to give me down those letters, I shall be glad to have something to do. You can give them down in shorthand, if you like, but I am afraid I am not very quick."

He frowned. A confession of incompetency from her seemed somehow out of place.

"A secretary should be quick at everything," he grumbled.

"Very likely I shall be able to take them down as fast as you are able to dictate them," she declared, with composure. "At any rate, we shall be through them in half the time you have been taking. Some of those, I should think," she added, glancing at the pile in his hand, "you can tell me what to say and leave the wording to me."

He nodded.

"There are at least forty letters amongst this pile," he said, "asking for donations to some institution or another. You had better go through those and mark them according to your idea of their deserts. Begging letters you can destroy at once."

"There is one here," she remarked, "from a man who says that he used to know you before you went abroad."

He glanced it through.

"Can't remember him," he declared. "Tear it up."

"He seems in a very bad way," she said, doubtfully.

"Send him ten pounds, then!" Hardrow exclaimed, with a note of impatience in his voice. "By the by, there is an envelope there with the Stoke Pagnall post-mark."

She knew very well where it was, and she slipped it underneath the rest.

"I'll let you know when I come across it," she promised.

"Don't forget," he said. "It's a begging letter, I suppose," he went on, carelessly, "but it comes from the place where I used to live before I went abroad. It's astonishing how people remember you when you've done well in the world, especially those who've made a mess of things themselves."

She bent a little lower over the machine. There was a dull streak of colour in her cheeks of which, however, he remained unconscious. If he had only known it, he had effectually destroyed all chances of ever seeing the contents of the letter in question.

"The invitations?" he said, dubiously. "Well, I scarcely know what to do about them. They're a hideous nuisance."

"I will get a plain calendar," she suggested, "and write them all in on the proper dates. Then you can just put your pencil through those you wish to refuse and a tick against those I am to accept."

"Good idea," he answered. "Excellent! I am going out now. I shall be back at four o'clock. You had better ring the bell and order lunch up here when you want some."

"Before you go," she said, looking fixedly at the sheet of paper which she had thrust into her machine, "I think that I ought to tell you something."

He stopped short in his journey toward the door.

"Well, what is it?" he asked.

She went on without looking at him.

"I told you that I had been getting twenty-eight shillings a week. It wasn't exactly true. It was what I wanted; but I have never had a permanent situation."

"I don't see that that matters," he answered. "You're engaged to me, anyhow, for a month at thirty shillings a week."

"And then as regards references?" she continued.

"Oh, don't bother me about trifles," he answered, turning abruptly away. "I'll take you on spec."

Miss Robinson went home that night with a smile playing around her lips and an entire absence of that strained look about the eyes with which she had commenced the day. She rode on top of a bus to Camberwell, and afterwards walked briskly for a quarter of an hour. She soon arrived at a tiny cottage at the end of a row – little creations of brick and mortar, all brand-new, which seemed as though they had come out of a German toy-box, and the road to which was as yet barely made. The front door, which she could easily reach from the street, opened into a sitting room, where she was welcomed with a shriek of delight by a very much smaller edition of herself.

"Mary, is it all right?" the child exclaimed. "Did you find him, and is he nice? Do tell me! And I'm so hungry!"

Miss Robinson smiled, and the sigh of relief which followed came from the bottom of her heart.

"It's absolutely all right, dear," she answered, kissing the child.

"Tell me what he was like, and everything about him!" the latter exclaimed. "Did he recognize you? What did he say? And when shall I see him? Is he coming here?"

Miss Robinson looked for a moment grave.

"Nora, dear," she said, "to tell you the honest truth, he hasn't any idea who I am. He didn't recognize me and he hadn't even opened my letter. When I found myself in the room and saw that he didn't know who I was, I simply couldn't tell him. I engaged myself to him as his secretary instead."

The child clapped her hands.

"How clever!" she exclaimed. "Did he mind?"

Miss Robinson laughed outright. It could not have been for vanity, because there was no one there to see, but her laugh certainly made her appear an extraordinarily attractive young woman.

"I rather took him by storm, I'm afraid," she confessed, throwing off her hat, "but I can see that I am going to be exceedingly useful to him. He was trying to deal with his correspondence himself, without a typist or anything. I was only just in time. It absolutely must have occurred either to him or to someone else, before the day was over, that he needed a secretary."

"But what fun his not recognizing you, Mary!" the child exclaimed. "And all the time you know who he was and all about him."

Miss Robinson turned away and hid her head in a cupboard. The humour of this non-recognition seemed scarcely to appeal to her; in fact, her lip had quivered for a moment.

"Now, I'm just going to make one cup of tea," she said, "and then I'll go out and get something to eat."

"But have you any money, Mary?" the child asked.

Miss Robinson looked searchingly around the sitting-room. Her eyes rested upon a little water-colour – their last – and she sighed.

"We soon shall have," she declared, cheerfully. "To-morrow I am going to ask him to pay me a week's money in advance. I've had to borrow two shillings already to get my machine taken up on a barrow. I told him a cab, because it sounded better."

The child looked perplexed.

"But why don't you tell him, Mary, who you are and all about us? I believe he'd give you a great deal more money. You always said that he was such a nice boy."

Miss Robinson let her hand rest for a moment on her sister's head.

"Dear," she said, "you are wonderfully wise for your years, but there are some things which you cannot understand, and this is one of them. Unless Mr. Hardrow finds out for himself, I would rather not tell him."

The child sighed and remained puzzled. She was only nine years old, but life had already shown her something of its complex side. The change from a comfortable country house, with large gardens and plenty of young friends, to a cottage on the outskirts of London at two shillings a week, with no servant, a few scraps of furniture, sometimes barely enough to eat, sometimes a grim suspicion that Mary had less even than she, was a change such as could scarcely fail to leave its mark. Somehow or other she had looked forward to Hardrow's return as likely to alter all this. He was to have been the fairy prince who provided all manner of desirable things. On the whole, she was a little disappointed with her sister's visit.

"Well," she said, wistfully, "I hope he finds out."

Miss Robinson laughed.

"If he doesn't," she declared bravely, "we are going to have quite a good time now. Thirty shillings a week! One can do a great deal with thirty shillings a week. You must go to school – even if it is only a very tiny school – in the mornings. And perhaps, later on, we may be able to take a cottage out in the country."

"Supposing," the child asked, shrewdly, "Mr. Hardrow goes back to Africa and doesn't want you any more?"

Miss Robinson was a little disturbed at the thought, but she only laughed.

"He'll want me, right enough," she declared. "I'm going to make myself so useful that he won't be able to do without me."

In a sense, her words undoubtedly came true. Hardrow scarcely realized even himself how much easier the days went because of her rigorous supervision of his affairs. He was always seeking her advice, too, and continually adopting it. One day he leaned back from a mass of correspondence with a perplexed frown upon his forehead.

"Stop that for a moment, Miss Robinson," he said. "I want to ask you something."

She ceased her work and turned around on her stool.

"You know that I have been refusing all invitations of a certain sort," he began. "I find that I shall have to change my front. It is necessary for me to go into society more or less. Some of my schemes – one in particular – must be pushed by people who have influence there."

She nodded and touched the keys of her instrument carelessly.

"There is not much difficulty about that," she remarked.

"Perhaps not," he admitted; "but I have got out of the way of it. I've lived in the open air too long, in wooden shanties or in a tent, fed out of tin things, cooked for myself, and played the boor generally. I want civilizing. How should you start about it?"

She looked at him critically.

"I should take off that ugly beard of yours," she declared.

He stroked it for a moment, and looked at himself in the glass.

"I suppose you're right," he admitted. "Anyhow, there's no need to keep the thing over here. Telephone down for the barber, please. Anything else?"

"You don't dress very well," she told him.

"Hang it all!" he objected. "I went to the best tailor in London."

She nodded.

"Yes, and I can see you there," she said, with a faint smile at the corner of her lips. "You probably marched into the place, caught hold of half-a-dozen bales of cloth, told them to make you a suit of each, and came out again in about three minutes."

"Just what I did," he agreed. "What do you suggest?"

"Let the tailor choose for you, if he's a good one," she answered, "and ask him about the ties and shirts to go with the clothes he sends you."

"You're a jewel," he declared; "I'll do it. And you'd better accept those last five or six invitations I gave you."

Thenceforth Miss Robinson saw a deal less of her employer. Vastly improved in his bearing, he became quite a popular figure at a great many social gatherings. The appearance, toward the end of a rather dull London season, of a good-looking bachelor, who was reputed to be a millionaire, and who had acquired his wealth in an exceedingly romantic fashion, was almost a godsend. Invitations came faster and faster, so that even Hardrow, whose energy was boundless and whose zest for this new amusement extraordinary, found it impossible to keep pace with them. Nevertheless, he managed fairly well, and kept in touch, too, with his affairs in the City. One day he suddenly realized how invaluable Miss Robinson was to him. He turned abruptly in the act of leaving the room.

"Miss Robinson," he said, "I don't know what I should do without you."

"I don't know what you would," she agreed.

"Our month has been up for some time," he continued. "Please double your salary."

"I am very much obliged," she answered, with beating heart. "Do you mean really double it?"

"Certainly," he declared. "You're very cheap at that."

He stood looking down at her. It seemed to him that he had forgotten for weeks how pretty she was. Her slim figure, too, looked at its best in the absolutely plain, tight-fitting black dress that she wore at her work. Her hand was resting upon the table. He took it up and held it in his. She snatched it away.

"Mr. Hardrow!" she exclaimed, breathlessly.

He laughed, and looked at her for a moment as though half deriding her agitation. Just then there was a knock at the door. He turned away. In a few minutes he left the room with his visitor, and when he reappeared the incident seemed to have escaped his memory.

Hardrow was by no means a bad fellow, but he was more or less what is usually described as being a man of the world. If Miss Robinson had been a trifle less good-looking, or the fascination of her quiet, demure speech a little less apparent, he would probably, in a few weeks more, have forgotten that she was a woman at all, and looked upon her as a very excellent part of his well-ordered life, whose use to him was purely a mechanical one. Unfortunately, she forgot one morning the strict control which she usually kept over her features, and laughed at some remark of his in perfectly dazzling fashion. Perhaps he considered the few words which she flung out, the quick upward glance which came naturally enough at that moment, as an invitation. At any rate, he stooped and kissed her. For a moment she seemed almost passive. Then she rose slowly to her feet.

"Mr. Hardrow —" she began, with trembling voice.

He took her face between his hands and kissed her again.

"Don't be a goose!" he exclaimed, and went out.

When he came back she was gone. Not only had she departed, but she had taken her typewriter with her. Upon his desk was a neat little statement of her account and a little pile of money, from which he noticed that, although it was Friday morning, she had omitted to draw any salary for the week. For several minutes he stood and swore profusely. He remembered with dismay that he did not know her address. His servant, whom he summoned at once, was equally ignorant of it. He dashed off two advertisements to the evening papers, commanding – begging for her return. He even sought out for himself the hall-porter of the residential hotel in which his quarters were situated, and endeavoured to discover whether in her comings and goings she had ever left any trace of her abode. But the suburb in which Miss Robinson lived was a very long way from Mayfair, and she certainly had no money now to spend in evening papers. The days passed by and he heard nothing. He advertised for a temporary secretary and selected a young man, who robbed him; replaced him with another, who was honest but stupid; and finally, leaving him behind to mismanage his affairs, went off to Scotland in disgust.

And in the meantime things went very ill indeed for Miss Robinson. Naturally of a sanguine disposition, and over-anxious to provide once more the necessary comforts for the child whom she loved so dearly, she found that she had saved very little. Early the next morning she recommenced the search for work in which she had been engaged when she read of the return of Mr. Hardrow to his native land and paid him that eventful visit. Alas! the search was no more successful than it had been before. Never, it seemed, were there so many typists wanting situations; never so few people who wanted typing done. The child Nora, too, was fretful and pale. The summer had been a long one and hotter than usual. In a week's time Miss Robinson had made up her mind to ask her employer for a fortnight's holiday, and to have taken the child into the country. All that, of course, was out of the question now. There was no holiday because there was no work to take a holiday from. And no work came. September passed away, and the tiny house was barer than ever. Nora was becoming alarmingly thin and often peevish. She was never tired of asking what had become of Mr. Hardrow, why Mary had left, why she did not go back and ask him to help her find another place.

At last the time came when the rent was not forthcoming. With a little sob Miss Robinson put her pride in her pocket and walked to Mayfair. Mr. Hardrow was still away, she was told, travelling on the Continent. His secretary was upstairs in his rooms, and she could go up if she chose. She presented herself at the familiar door and, knocking timidly, turned the handle. She was a very different-looking person to the trim young woman who had taken Mr. Hardrow by storm a few months ago. Her clothes were worse than shabby now. She was much paler, her cheeks were hollow, and her eyes had lost all their brightness. The immaculate young man who occupied her former position scrutinized her closely though his eyeglass, and formed by no means a favourable opinion of her or of her errand.

"Mr. Hardrow is away," he announced, in reply to her inquiry. "It is quite impossible to say when he will be back in London."

"Will you give me his address, please?" Miss Robinson asked.

The young man dropped his eyeglass and stroked his chin.

"Impossible!" he declared. "Mr. Hardrow is away for a holiday. He gets too much – er – correspondence and that sort of thing when he is in England."

"Will you send on a note to him?" she persisted.

The young man was bored, and showed it.

"Mr. Hardrow does not wish letters forwarded," he said. "Do you mind closing the door as you go out?"

As Miss Robinson stepped out of the lift and passed from the hotel a new fear came to her. The streets and buildings seemed, somehow, strange. There was a pain in her head. Her knees shook so that people stared at her, and for a moment she had even to clutch at a lamp-post. She told herself that this was madness. If she were to give in now, what would happen? Then she remembered that she had had very little food that day, and less still the day before. She entered a shop, and, though her heart ached to part with it, she laid down sixpence and ordered some milk and a bun. Afterwards she walked back to Camberwell – a long walk and not a very cheerful one. Nora met her with red eyes. The man had called again for the rent and had been very rude. The child was trembling and obviously terrified.

"Mary, dear," she cried, "we must get some money! We must! Is there no one we can write to?"

"We've tried everyone," Mary reminded her, sinking into a chair. "I don't know, just for the moment, what there is that we can do."

"I know that I am very hungry!" the child exclaimed, bursting into tears.

It was the last blow. The room went suddenly round, and the rumbling in her ears became like thunder. Mary was unconscious for nearly an hour. When she recovered, the child was still by her side, almost in an agony of terror.

"Oh, Mary, Mary!" she cried. "What are we to do? You're going to be ill, I'm sure! I'm so frightened!"

"I'm going to be nothing of the sort," Miss Robinson declared. "I was just a little tired. You'll find threepence in my pocket. Do stop that milkman and buy threepennyworth of milk for your supper. Afterwards, we'll go to bed."

The child sighed.

"I should like something to eat," she murmured. "I'm so tired of milk, and so hungry."

They went to bed, and Nora, at any rate, slept. Mary lay awake most of the night, with hot eyes and a pain at her heart.

She got up in the morning, trembling a little and terrified. Before midday they were in the streets and the key turned against them. Their few remaining scraps of furniture would never pay the rent that was owing. The typewriter had long ago gone. Mary made a supreme effort.

"This must be the worst that can happen to us, dear," she said to Nora. "We'll go somewhere and sit down, and I'm sure we shall be able to think of something."

The child was half terrified, half starved. They walked wearily from the first – footsore and tired to death before they arrived at their destination. Somehow or other, they reached the Embankment and sank down upon one of the seats, and a few minutes later, though he was supposed to be on the Continent, Hardrow came along taking his first lesson at driving his new motor-car. By chance she turned and saw him, and, staggering to her feet, came out into the road, waving her hand. He barely escaped running over her, and the chauffeur shouted angrily. Just at that moment, however, Hardrow recognized her and sprang from the car.

"Miss Robinson!" he exclaimed, and suddenly took it all in. "Good heavens!"

She had meant to greet him with, at any rate, some attempt at dignity, to explain that a series of misfortunes of a temporary character had placed her in a very uncomfortable position – any rubbish so that she might have looked him in the face and held her own in words at least. But it was all of no use and all quite unnecessary. The faces of the two girls told their own story with pitiless truth. In a minute or two she found herself in the back of the car, with Nora by her side holding her fingers tightly. Hardrow relinquished his place at the wheel and ordered the chauffeur to drive to some restaurant.

THE REɅTLEɅɅ TRAVELLER

From Paris to Boulogne the man had seemed inspired with a perfect demon of restlessness. He had secured a comfortable corner seat facing the engine, for he had reached the Gare du Nord at least an hour before the train was due to leave, but instead of occupying it he seemed to spend most of his time wandering aimlessly up and down the corridor – a gaunt, disquieting figure. Fever had set its brand upon his features; something more than fever seemed occasionally to flash from his unnaturally brilliant eyes. A couple of women, travelling alone, shivered as he passed.

"I shouldn't like to be alone in the carriage with that man," one of them remarked.

"He looks ill," the other murmured, sympathetically. "I should think he was an Army officer who has had a touch of sunstroke."

He was almost the first to leave the train and make his way along the gangway on to the steamer, hurrying as though there were not a second to be lost. During the short voyage across the Channel he walked with nervous, ceaseless footsteps backwards and forwards upon the upper deck. The cool night wind seemed to bring him no relief. If indeed he had been abroad for many years, as seemed possible from his luggage, the familiar sights which he was now reaching appeared to afford him but little pleasure. The level line of lights along the Folkestone esplanade moved him to no emotion save a renewed impatience. Arrived in the harbour he was once more almost the first to cross the gangway, almost the first to take his place in the train. There he sat in a corner seat, his arms folded, staring grimly out of the window, till a man who had passed along the platform twice and looked at him curiously on each occasion entered the carriage and touched him on the shoulder.

"Why, Bulwer, old man!" the new-comer exclaimed. "Glad to see you home again. I saw in the *Gazette* that you were on your way. How goes it?"

Major John Bulwer, for that was indeed the name of the uneasy man, looked into the questioner's face for a moment without recognition. Then he slowly extended a hand.

"It's Murray, isn't it, of the Carbineers?" he said. "How are you?"

"Jolly fit, thanks," the other answered. "I'll travel up with you, if you don't mind. You look as though you wanted a holiday, by Jove!" he added, as he settled himself down.

"I have had a touch of sunstroke," Bulwer admitted, slowly; "rather a bad touch, in its way. My head has been a little queer ever since."

He closed his eyes presently and showed no further disposition to talk. His companion made a few spasmodic efforts at conversation, but met with no encouragement. At Charing Cross they stood together for a moment upon the platform.

"Come round to the club and have one drink," Murray suggested, "before you go to your rooms. I suppose you've nothing here for the Customs?"

Bulwer shook his head.

"My heavy baggage I left on the boat," he said. "Yes, I'll come for a few minutes."

They drove off together. Bulwer drank a couple of whiskies and sodas in the smoking-room of the club whilst he was gloomily receiving the salutations and welcome of some of his old friends. Now that he had actually arrived at his destination, some part of the nervous impatience of the last few hours seemed to have disappeared. His manner, however, was still sufficiently curious to attract remark. Men whispered to one another as they strolled away to join some other group.

"I tell you what: he wants looking after, that fellow," one remarked. "He's got a touch of India. By the by, Carstairs — "

His companion – a tall, fair man – shrugged his shoulders.

"I think I can guess what was in your mind," he said. "You are quite right. Bulwer was engaged to Helen Tremlett. I am not sure whether he knows."

"I'd leave him alone for a bit, anyway, if I were you," his friend remarked.

"Nonsense," Carstairs answered. "I must go and speak to him."

He crossed the room and held out his hand to Bulwer, who took it after just a second's hesitation.

"Welcome back, Bulwer!" he said.

"Thank you," the other man answered.

At close quarters the change in Bulwer, to one who had known him well, was almost tragic. Carstairs' voice, despite himself, took a sympathetic note.

"I am afraid you are not very fit, are you?" he remarked.

"I am all right," Bulwer answered. "A little tired, perhaps – nothing more."

They were standing together in the farther corner of the smoking-room – Carstairs, Bulwer, and Murray, and one or two others. Carstairs drew a cigarette-case from his pocket. It was attached to a chain with several other trifles. Among them was a curiously-shaped Yale key, washed in gold.

"Have a cigarette?" he asked Bulwer.

Bulwer made no answer – his eyes were fixed upon the key. The other men looked at one another gravely. Bulwer had seemed queer from the moment of his appearance in the club, but there was something in his face now which spoke of tragedy. They all knew that trouble was ahead, close at hand. Yet the calmness of Bulwer's voice, when he spoke, surprised them.

"Where did you get that key?" he asked.

Carstairs looked at his questioner at first with blank surprise. Then he understood, and cursed himself for a fool; it was not a thing to have shown Bulwer, this.

"The key is mine," he answered, coldly.

"You are a liar," Bulwer told him.

There was a moment's ugly silence; then Murray passed his arm through Bulwer's.

"Look here," he said, "we can't have a row here. You are a bit excited, old man, and not quite up to the mark. Come along with me and I'll see you to your rooms. You can talk to Carstairs in the morning, if you want to."

Bulwer seemed suddenly calmer.

"I do not wish to make a row here, but I have this much to say, and to say now, to Captain Carstairs," he declared, lowering his voice so that no one outside the little group should hear. "He has stated that that key is his, and I repeat that he lies."

Carstairs shrugged his shoulders.

"It would be absurd of me to take offence, Bulwer," he said, calmly, "because you do not know what you are talking about. You have been away from England for some years, and there have been changes. This is the key to a flat which belongs to me, and which I shall use when and as often as I choose. If you will accept a word of advice from me, Bulwer – and I give it to you earnestly and in all friendship – I would beg you to go to your rooms at once and read your letters."

Bulwer preserved his almost unnatural calm.

"I thank you for your advice," he said. "Let me, in return, give you one word of warning. If you make use of that key to-night, or any other night whilst I am in London, it will cost you your life. That is all."

Then those few who were friends of both began to understand things. They remembered that Bulwer, when he had left England, had made over the lease of his flat to Helen Tremlett and her brother. Murray even remembered the day when Bulwer had left the key of his flat at a jeweller's to have it washed in gold before he handed it over to its new tenant. An uncomfortable silence followed. Carstairs' lips were sealed by a promise; the others knew that it was not for them to speak. Then Bulwer went quietly away.

It was a few minutes past midnight when the silence of the darkened and deserted little sitting-room of flat No. 10 of Ellesden Mansions, Mayfair, was suddenly broken by the tinkle of the telephone. The woman who had been asleep in the next room awoke suddenly, sat up in bed, and listened. It was her telephone, without a doubt. She slipped on a dressing-gown and, opening the door which communicated between the two rooms, groped her way to the instrument without waiting to turn on the electric lights. She took the receiver and placed it to her ear.

"Well? Well? Who is it?" she asked, a little impatiently. "Oh, it's you, Maggie, is it?" she went on, in an altered tone. "Why, how are you, dear, and whatever do you want at this time of night?... What do you say?... What?... John Bulwer home?... Yes, I knew he was coming, but I didn't think he was due yet – not till next week... Why, Maggie, I don't understand why you should ask me a question like that over the telephone at this hour of the night!... Well, yes, if you insist upon knowing, there was something between us when he went out to India, but it's all over now, of course... I am sure I don't know whether he guesses or not. I should think he ought to have done from the tone of my last few letters. Anyhow, he will find a letter from me at his rooms when he gets there. Tell me why... What did you say?... Oh, wait a moment please."

The woman stood away from the telephone, her hand pressed to her heart. Her face went whiter than ever. It had come so suddenly – this message through the night. Once again she gripped the receiver in her hand.

"Tell me about it, Maggie. You say that he saw Captain Carstairs at the club. Did they quarrel?... What's that, dear? I can't hear. I think I am nervous. Please speak distinctly.... There was something about a key, you said.... What an idiot Ronald was to let him see it! He used to live here, you know. He would recognize it, of course.... Do you mean that he is mad?... Oh, I am sorry! I knew he'd have a sunstroke; I didn't think it was so bad as that.... Oh, I am not afraid of his coming here! He wouldn't think of that, I am sure. My letter was quite clear. And it hasn't been altogether my fault, either. Some of the things he wrote me a month or so ago were simply abominable.... No, I think it's sweet of you, dear, and your husband to think of warning me. You are the only people who know the truth about Captain Carstairs and myself.... Nervous? Not I!... Good night, Maggie! Good night, dear!... Yes; I'll ring you up in the morning.... Good-bye!"

The woman put the receiver down. Notwithstanding her assurance that she was not nervous, she found herself trembling all over. Slowly she made her way to the other end of the room and turned on the electric switch. Then for a moment she stood as though turned to stone, petrified with the horror of what she saw. Within a few feet of her, sitting in a high-backed chair facing the door, his arms folded, his traveling clothes unchanged, with a small revolver upon his knees, sat the man whom three years ago she had been engaged to marry.

"John!" she cried at last. "John! Why, how did you get here? Who let you in?"

"I did not need to be let in," he answered, slowly. "I have the second key. I have kept it as a memento."

"B—but what do you want?" she exclaimed.

He did not reply, although he was looking steadfastly at her. Then she, too, saw that thing in his eyes which had made other people afraid.

"You mustn't stay here," she faltered. "You frighten me."

She crept away toward the telephone. Then he spoke.

"Leave that thing alone," he said. "You can go back into your room, if you like."

"But what are you doing here?" she asked, still white to the lips. "What are you waiting for?"

"To shoot Carstairs," he answered, "if he comes in through that door."

She threw up her arms; the place was going round with her.

"John, are you mad?" she cried.

"I am not sure," he answered. "Perhaps I am. That doesn't matter, does it?"

"Have you been to your rooms?" she asked.

"No," he replied. "I reached Charing Cross at ten forty-five. I called at the club and came straight on here."

She was at heart a brave woman, and the situation began to get clearer to her. She struggled to speak calmly, yet all the time every nerve in her body was strained to an effort of listening.

"John," she said, "did you hear what I was saying on the telephone?"

"Some of it," he answered.

"Madge Murray rang me up. Her husband was at the club. She was telling me about it. You saw—Captain Carstairs."

"Yes."

"Did you quarrel with him?"

"I saw something which belonged to me upon his watch-chain, and I asked him what he was doing with my property," Bulwer replied, grimly. "Come here and kiss me, Helen."

She shrank away.

"I can't, John. That's all over."

The man's lips parted, but there was no smile upon his face.

"I have lost my beauty, haven't I?" he muttered. "You haven't, Helen. You're just the same."

Once more she began to tremble.

"John," she said, "I am sorry. I wish you'd been to your rooms before you went to the club. You would have understood then; you would have found a letter from me."

"A letter," he repeated, "from you! Was it to break off our engagement, Helen?"

She came over again to his side.

"Yes, John," she said. "I am sorry, but it had to be. Your letters lately have been so strange and queer, and I am afraid that I have changed myself. It was a foolish engagement. Don't be too hard upon me, John. Don't think me too fickle. I told you at the time I wasn't sure that I cared, I wasn't sure that I could wait. Soon after you left I met someone else, and then I knew that I hadn't really cared for anyone before in all my life."

"Carstairs is the man, of course?" he asked, hoarsely.

"Yes," she admitted.

"Carstairs!" he muttered. "I whipped him at school. I wish I'd killed him then."

She laid her hand gently upon his shoulder.

"John," she pleaded, "please don't talk like that. Why do you sit there and look so terrible with that – that thing upon your knees? You are not really thinking of shooting anyone, are you? Let me take it away."

His fingers gripped it – a passing sound on the stairs had attracted his attention. He pushed her on one side. The footsteps died away, but she found herself trembling. She came a little nearer still. The fear for her own safety was passing away; the courage of a woman, strong to defend the thing she loves, was stealing into her blood.

"John," she said, softly, "Ronald Carstairs is the man I am really fond of – the man I love better than anything else on earth. There is a story to be told about this. You don't understand."

"I understand this, at any rate," he muttered. "I have challenged him to use that key to-night. If he does, I shall shoot him."

"John, you mustn't talk like this," she pleaded. "Ronald Carstairs is my husband – he is everything in the world to me."

The man heard her with unmoved face.

"If he is your husband," he said, "he's stolen what belongs to me, and you are a false woman. I have been thinking about this all the way, all the time. I have made up my mind. That is why I am here – I am going to shoot him."

She was suddenly rigid, her finger held out, her whole attitude one of concentrated listening. They both heard the tinkle of the hansom bell stopping below, the slamming of the apron, a man's cheery "Good night" to the driver. Bulwer's eyes gleamed, his right hand gripped the revolver, his left hand kept away the woman who tried to fling herself upon him.

"John," she cried, "you won't think of this! Why, it would be murder. Let him come in and help me tell you all about it. It wasn't his fault. He didn't even know that I had been engaged to you until the last few days. John, I love him so much. Put that thing away, for Heaven's sake!"

She ran half-way to the door, screaming, but the man only laughed.

"The more you do that, the quicker he'll come," he muttered.

They heard his step now outside. One last inspiration came to her aid. She sprang across the room and turned out the electric lights. Once more the room was in darkness; then the door was opened.

"Ronald, John Bulwer is here – just opposite. Throw you cigarette down quick. Go away and leave us, please. He swears he is going to shoot you. He won't hurt me; I'm not afraid. Please go."

The little red spot of light went down at her first words. The shot rang out, and there was the crash of a fallen picture. Carstairs, unhurt, stole slowly on tiptoe across the room. They heard Bulwer rise and grope his way toward the wall.

"Turn on the lights," he shouted, "and let me see you. Where are you, Ronald Carstairs? Stand up, like a man!"

Then once more there was a crash of breaking glass. The woman, failing to unfasten the window at her first effort, had thrown a great vase through it and was blowing a whistle furiously. There were two more shots and the sound of a man's groans. An eternity of silence followed; the woman was groping her way about, moaning with fear. Then suddenly the room was once more flooded with light. It was Carstairs who stood with his finger upon the switch and a small revolver gripped in his right hand. Bulwer was lying upon the floor, his limbs twitching convulsively, his revolver smoking by his side. The girl looked from one to the other wildly.

"Ronald," she cried, "you are safe – you are really safe?"

Carstairs was pale as death; it was he now who was afraid.

"I am safe enough," he answered, "but I've shot the fellow. I never thought that he was in earnest at the club. I thought he was mad. I wish to Heaven I hadn't brought this cursed thing!"

He threw it down with a gesture of disgust. They could hear footsteps now upon the stairs. She stooped down and hid the revolver behind the curtains.

"Helen!" he cried.

She held out both her hands; her lips framed an injunction to silence. The door was opened. A policeman, followed by an inspector, entered. Behind was a cab-driver and several other street loiterers. The policeman turned the key in the door, shutting them all out.

"What's wrong here?" the inspector asked, quickly. "What's happened to that man?"

Bulwer raised himself a little and looked at them.

"I am shot," he muttered. "I am dying."

The policeman hurried to his side, the inspector took out his note-book from his pocket.

"Will you ring up for a doctor, madam, if you have a telephone?" he asked. "No one must leave the room."

They looked suspiciously at Carstairs. Bulwer, gasping a little for breath, seemed suddenly changed. His eyes once more were human, his expression ghastly but natural. He was like a man from whose blood a fever has passed.

"I am sorry," he faltered. "Mrs. Carstairs!"

She flung down the receiver of the telephone and hurried to his side.

"I am sorry," he repeated. "I meant to shoot myself to-day. The doctor of the regiment – he knew. They will all tell you – I had only a month or so – to live. I thought I'd get back home and stick it out – if I could. But it was too much for me to land here and know I had to die – so soon. But I didn't mean to do it here. I am sorry to give everyone – so much trouble."

Her arm was around his head, her hand was smoothing his. The inspector bent down.

"Are we to understand that you shot yourself, sir?" he asked.

"What else?" Bulwer murmured. "Of course – I shot myself."

He fell back. They brought brandy and forced it between his lips. The doctor arrived within a few minutes, but it was too late. The inspector, as he bade them a respectful "Good night," was inclined to be sympathetic.

"It's just as well, madam," he remarked, "if you'll allow me to say so, that the poor fellow lived long enough to tell the truth. This sort of thing always leaves an awkward feeling behind unless it is cleared up properly at the time."

Then they were left alone in the little room. They heard the heavy tramp of footsteps descending the stairs, the tramp of the men who carried the ambulance with its terrible burden. They heard the footsteps grow fainter and fainter. The man's restless journey was over.

ONE LUCKLE*ſſ* HOUR

He stood upon the edge of the lawn at Ascot, looking towards the band, apparently listening to the music, in reality seeing nothing, hearing nothing, realizing only the slow torture of a live and sickly fear. To the casual observer the Honourable Ralph Fausitt looked all that a fashionable young man of good breeding, education, and parentage should look. His clothes were selected with unerring taste, and he wore them with that air of distinction which was presumably an inheritance from a long line of aristocratic forbears, coupled with a devotion to athletics which until lately had been paramount in his life. He was sufficiently well-off; he had already received at least half-a-dozen invitations to luncheon; he had never in his life made a bet which he could not afford to lose; the paddock was full of his friends, and the prettiest girl there, to whom – at any rate, up to a month ago – he had been devoted, was even at that moment sitting anxiously in her box awaiting a visit from him. Yet all these things counted for nothing, and less than nothing. In his eyes was the nameless terror of a man who has never felt a twinge of cowardice, who feels fear now for the first time. The flower-decked lawn was a barren waste. Life had become, during the last twenty-four hours, an ugly phantasm, a scarlet terror. Before his eyes seemed to float the memory of a tiny room, a luxurious, over-furnished, bijou chamber in a toy palace, and there upon the soft green carpet, with a broken ornament by his side, always the central figure, a dead man, the body of a man lying there white and still, a man killed by his hand. Already outside the gates newspaper boys were probably calling out the news: "Horrible murder in the flat of a celebrated actress!" He fancied that even where he stood he could hear their voices, the raucous relish of their cry. He was a murderer! It was for him that Scotland Yard in a few hours would be sending out far and wide their greyhounds of the chase, against him the whole wonderful machinery of their elaborate system would be set at work. How could he hope to escape? What chance was there for one so ignorant, so young in crime? Already he was giving himself away every minute. The most harmless of policemen sent a shiver of fear through him. What chance was there when the hunt should begin in earnest? None – absolutely none!

A hand fell upon his shoulder. The voice was the voice of a friend, yet he started as though he had been shot.

"Why, Ralph, old chap, you look as though you'd been backing the wrong 'uns, and no mistake," the new-comer remarked, carelessly. "What's up with you? Why haven't you been up to luncheon?"

Fausitt turned slowly round. He was still shaking, and his friend's casual interest was quickly changed into something like amazement.

"Why, what in thunder's the matter with you, man?" he exclaimed, dropping his voice a little. "You look as though you were seeing ghosts."

"I've a headache," Fausitt stammered; "the sun, I suppose – and you startled me."

His friend – Captain Guy Darnell, of the Argylls – whistled softly under his breath. He was a young man of resource, and he came to a rapid decision.

"What you want is a drink," he declared, "and I should say that you wanted it quick. Come along."

Fausitt suffered himself to be led away. Yes, he needed a drink – anything to drown the torture of those grisly memories!

"Netta's been asking for you," Darnell remarked, as they strolled along the gravel path. "She said that you promised to take her into the paddock."

Fausitt almost groaned. He could see Netta sitting in a corner of the box, waiting, a trifle wistful, too proud to complain, but still feeling his neglect. Dear little Netta! He began to wonder drearily if there had ever been a moment in his life when he had not been in love with her. If only he could wipe out his last month of small follies – above all, these last few hours of supreme, consummate idiocy! He had held everything in his hands; he had thrown life itself away to gratify a moment's impulse.

"I am going up presently," he muttered, feverishly. "I hadn't forgotten. There was a man I wanted to speak to."

Darnell said no more for the moment, although his eyebrows rose a little curiously when he saw Fausitt dispose of his tumbler of brandy and soda-water at a single gulp. They made their way outside again. Darnell passed his arm through his friend's.

"Look here, old chap," he said, "I am going to talk like an ass. Just listen to me, though, there's a good fellow."

Fausitt nodded indifferently. They had just passed a policeman, and he was shivering all over.

"It's about Netta," her brother continued, pausing to light a cigarette. "Now, we've always been pals, of course, Ralph," he continued, taking his companion's arm again, "and I've always been jolly glad to have you round so much, and so thick with Netta. She's a nice little thing – although she's my sister – and I've something to say about her. Don't think I'm a prig, old chap, but here goes. You'll have to chuck going about with a so much advertised young lady as Mlle. Lafère if you're going to keep on making the running with Netta."

Fausitt nodded in a spiritless fashion.

"Is that all, Guy?" he asked.

"Not quite," Darnell replied. "You know, Ralph, I'm not setting up for being a saint, or anything of that sort, but dash it all, I think that class of people need keeping in their places. I was jolly glad to find you alone just now, and if you think of coming up to see Netta, as I hope you do, why, then, just give Mlle. Nina the go-by to-day."

"What the mischief do you mean?" Fausitt exclaimed.

"Sorry I didn't make myself clear, old fellow," Darnell answered. "I'll have another shot at it. If you're going to be seen about this place with Mlle. Nina Lafère, I'd rather you didn't come up to see Netta – that's all."

Fausitt laughed. It wasn't at all a pleasant-sounding laugh; there was nothing which even suggested mirth about it.

"You needn't have bothered about that, Guy," he replied; "Mlle. Nina won't be here to-day."

Darnell shrugged his shoulders.

"Well, I'm glad to find that you didn't bring her, old chap," he answered; "but as for her not being here – well, I've just passed her in the paddock, not ten minutes ago."

Fausitt was almost past any further display of emotion. Nevertheless, he sat down abruptly upon an empty seat. His cheeks were livid, his eyes were hot and burning. Mlle. Nina here! The thing was terrible.

"You don't mean it, Guy?" he muttered. "You don't mean to tell me that she is here?"

"She's here, right enough," Darnell assured him. "She favoured me with a most gracious bow. I ran into Somerville and her talking together just outside the subway."

There was a short silence. Darnell was watching his friend more curiously than ever. By degrees he had come to understand that this was no ordinary fit of nerves, no ordinary indisposition with which Fausitt was afflicted. The music rose and fell, the breeze rustled pleasantly in the trees, there was a murmur of cheerful voices, and much laughter around them. But tragedy sat by his side upon that seat, and Darnell recognized it. He, too, had grown a little paler. The June sunshine had lost its warmth for both of them.

"What's wrong, Ralph, old man?" he demanded, laying his hand upon the other's shoulder. "There's no one within hearing, and you can trust me – you know that. Out with it."

"I must tell someone," Fausitt answered, thickly, "or go mad. Here goes."

He took off his immaculate silk hat. His forehead was wet with perspiration, yet as he sat there he shivered – shivered though the blazing sun fell upon his uncovered head. When he began to speak the words seemed to tumble from his mouth.

"I have killed a man, Guy – shot him through the heart – last night! He is dead; I murdered him!"

Darnell drew a little away. Incredulity and horror struggled together in his face.

"You are not serious, Ralph?" he gasped.

"Shot him through the heart," Fausitt repeated with dull reiteration. "I saw him fall, saw the blood come through his coat. Guy, don't ever kill a man if you can help it – it's ghastly!"

They stared at one another, speechless for countless seconds, Darnell almost as livid now as his friend. At first he refused to credit his senses; then he saw the horror alive in the other's face, distorting, paralyzing, and he believed.

"Where was it?" he faltered.

"In Mlle. Lafère's rooms," Ralph answered.

"Does anyone know?"

"She does. I suppose others do by now," Fausitt muttered. "She let me out after it was over."

"And the – the man?" Darnell asked.

"I left him lying upon the floor."

"Was there a quarrel?"

Fausitt nodded.

"You know, I've been rather a fool about Mille. Nina," he said, slowly. "I didn't care a jot about her, but she was amusing to take round, and the fellows all envied me, and that sort of thing. There's something else I'd like to tell you, Guy, while we are about it, and it seemed to make her more attractive in a way. She was straight – upon my word she was."

"Go on," Darnell insisted. "If you say so, that's good enough for me. Tell me how it happened."

"Last night I fetched her from the theatre," Fausitt continued, "and we had supper together. Afterwards I took her home. In her rooms there was a man waiting – a Portuguese. Directly we entered the row began. You know, I can't understand their beastly language, but I could guess that he was jealous, and that it was about me. He went on talking till I didn't know where I was. At last he snapped his fingers in my face. She tried to get between us, and he pushed her away. Then I lost my temper and punched his head. He was coming for me like a madman – a great bull of a fellow, over six feet high, and as strong as a giant. You know I am only just about again after influenza. Nina knew it too, and she pushed a little revolver into my hand and screamed at the man like a Paris gutter-child. He struck her across the cheek brutally. He was going to do it again – then I fired."

"You hit him?" Darnell whispered, hoarsely.

"Just over the heart," Fausitt groaned. "He simply collapsed upon the floor. I saw – the blood. Nina pushed me out of the room. She locked the door and sent me off."

"You think there is no chance? You are sure that he is dead?" Darnell asked.

Fausitt shook his head with a gesture of despair.

"I shot at him deliberately," he answered. "I was only a few feet away."

A race was just over, and the people were beginning to stream back again down the walks and on to the lawn. The band were remounting to their places. Darnell rose unwillingly to his feet.

"Ralph, old chap," he declared, "I must go and look the people up for a few minutes. I'll come back afterwards and sit with you, unless you'd rather be alone."

"It's very good of you, Guy," Fausitt replied, drearily. "I think, if you don't mind – I won't if you'd rather not – I'd like to come and say good-bye to Netta."

Darnell hesitated, but only for a moment.

"Come along in a few minutes," he said. "I had better get there first and just prepare them for your looking a bit queer."

He patted his friend affectionately on the shoulder and strode off, swinging his field-glasses in his hand, trying to realize this thing, and failing utterly. Fausitt remained upon the seat, starting with glazed eyes at the apparition which confronted him. Darnell had spoken the truth, then. Not a dozen yards away Mlle. Nina herself was sitting at a small table, talking to a man whom he himself had introduced to her not many evenings ago. She was a little paler than usual, perhaps, but otherwise there was nothing remarkable about her appearance. More than once he heard her laugh – the sound maddened him. There was a hollow ring about her mirth, perhaps, but to him it seemed ghastly. He rose to his feet and made his way unsteadily toward the table. Nina looked at him strangely. Her black eyes seemed larger than ever, her cheeks more pallid. She showed no signs of surprise. Probably, he reflected, someone had told her that he was there. The man by her side greeted him casually. Some foolish questions and answers passed between them. Then mademoiselle's escort, who was a man of the world, rose to his feet and bowed.

"Mademoiselle will excuse me," he said, smiling. "We shall meet again, I trust."

He passed away, leaving them alone. Fausitt took his place almost mechanically. Mlle. Nina leaned towards him.

"Why is it that you look at me like that?" she murmured.

"What are you doing here?" he demanded. "How could you come?"

"Or you, then?" she replied. "What about you? It is the same thing, is it not?"

"Does anyone know yet?" he faltered.

She shrugged her shoulders, opened her lips, and closed them again. She seemed to be in two minds as to how to answer his question.

"No," she said at last; "as yet I do not believe that anyone knows."

Her face had lost a little of its brilliant hardness; she was looking at him now more kindly; her eyes were soft, as though the tears were not far away.

"My God!" he muttered, half to himself. "What made me do it? What made you give me that accursed thing, Nina? You could have called for help – anything sooner than that!"

She was looking down toward the point of her parasol.

"Monsieur Ralph," she begged, "please to go now. There is someone here with whom I wish to speak. In ten minutes you will return. You promise? It will perhaps be for the last time."

"For the last time!" Fausitt muttered, as he plunged into the crowd.

He had meant to go at once to the Darnells' box, yet whenever he turned that way his courage failed him. To see Netta for the last time, to say good-bye to her before all these people – the agony of it was inconceivable. Perhaps after the races were over he might meet them coming out, might draw her aside for a single moment in the crush. Anything was better than a formal entry into the box, Lady Darnell's polite inquiries as to his headache, Guy's forced cheerfulness, Netta's serious, remonstrating eyes. She might even be piqued by his neglect, refuse to speak to him. He might have to come away without even a touch of her fingers. For the last time he turned away from the staircase. He would not go up; he came to that decision finally.

For something more than the ten minutes he wandered aimlessly about. Then he remembered his promise to Mlle. Nina, and he turned back toward where he had left her. The lawn was crowded now with people sitting out taking wine and fruit under the trees, and he had forgotten exactly at which table she was. He came upon it quite suddenly. It was, indeed, the sound of her voice which first attracted him. He stood quite still; his feet were rooted to the ground. He was absolutely unable to move another step. Then up went the earth and round the faces of the people, the tents, the pavilion, the whole panorama. Conversation, music, laughter, everything was merged into one dull humming, beating against his ears. For a moment the world was black. And then – he was sitting down at the table. They were both there – mademoiselle and the man, mademoiselle and the man whom he had killed! Mademoiselle was holding a glass of wine to his lips.

"Drink, Monsieur Ralph," she whispered. "Oh, I am sorry!"

He drank – afterwards he knew that it was champagne. Then he set the glass down, but he could not move his eyes from the man's face opposite. There were no such things as ghosts, he told himself. This was the man himself. His pallid skin, his sleepy eyes, his fiercely upturned moustache and unnaturally white teeth; it was the man himself, no other. Mlle. Nina's fingers were gripping his. A few people were looking at them curiously. Could they, too, see the man? he wondered. Was he really a substantial person, a human being, alive like the others?

"Monsieur Ralph," Mlle. Nina continued in his ear, "it is my husband, this. He would speak to you now himself, but you do not understand. Last night we quarrelled together, it is true. He was jealous, and of you. It was absurd. He said cruel things, and I was angry, but there was no wish in my heart to kill. When I pushed the little revolver into your hand I never imagined but that you must recognize it. It is the one I use every night – always – at the music-hall, in my sketch. You remember now? Ah, I can see that you remember! The burglar comes from under the couch, and I shoot. The cartridges are full of that red fluid; there is no bullet. They are made for me, these cartridges, in Paris. It was one of these which you used. I put it into your hand that you might frighten Miguel, my husband. We love one another, indeed, very dearly, but if I am alone for one week – oh, he is so jealous!"

She rested her hand upon her husband's. In broken French, and with many expressive gestures, he was doing his best to corroborate her words. Fausitt felt his breath come quickly. Again there was a little uncertainty about the faces, the hurrying waiters, the moving branches of the trees. The man spoke rapidly to mademoiselle in their own language, and she poured out more wine and passed it along the table.

"Please drink this, Monsieur Ralph, and do not be angry with either of us," she begged. "It was cruel of my husband; but he was so jealous, and I promised that I would not tell all at once, because he hoped that you would be frightened, as he was. But it was cruel. Now you understand – it must be that you understand. You have not hurt anyone. My husband, he will shake hands with you for we are all three to be the good friends, is it not so?"

Then Fausitt began to grasp the truth. All of a sudden he realized one of the great dramatic emotions. He came back from the shadows into the full warmth and vigour of splendid life. Again the blood was warm in his veins, the joy of existence a fire in his heart. With every second his understanding of this thing became more intense. He was free; he had killed no one! Mlle. Nina and her husband were two very delightful acquaintances who were passing with smiles and bows from his life – and Netta was waiting for him. He held out his glass, which Nina's husband, with a polite little gesture, filled. They all three drank together.

"Monsieur et madame," Fausitt exclaimed, "I congratulate you upon your reconciliation! I drink to your very good health."

"And Monsieur Ralph forgives?" Mlle. Nina murmured. "It was all so foolish, so cruel."

Fausitt drained his glass and held out his hands.

"I'd forgive anybody anything," he declared.

He was never quite sure of the way he went across the lawn, amongst the chairs, past the band, across the gravel path, and up the wooden staircase. People stared after him and made remarks – he had probably won a great bet; he had heard some wonderful news. There was something, at any rate, quite extraordinary about the joyful haste with which this well-dressed young man pushed his way along, regardless alike of manners and safety. He threw open the door of the box. Opposite was Guy Darnell, pale and worried. Netta's blue eyes, as she half rose from her place, were full of plaintive sympathy. Lady Darnell welcomed him a little coldly, a fact of which he was entirely unconscious.

"I have just been telling them all," Darnell explained, laboriously, "about your head, and that you are obliged to get back home. It seems to me as though you might possibly have another touch of the 'flu' coming."

Fausitt laughed, and his friend stared at him as though he had taken leave of his senses.

"My headache's gone!" he exclaimed. "I never felt better in my life. I have come to make my most humble apologies and to beg Miss Netta, if it isn't too late, to take just one turn in the paddock with me."

She arose at once with alacrity.

"I am not sure that you deserve it," she answered, smiling. "I had nearly given you up. Guy's account was so pathetic, though, that we none of us had anything but sympathy left. According to him you were almost prostrate."

"Worst of your brother, he does exaggerate so," Fausitt remarked, lightly.

Guy, who was feeling a little dazed, followed them out on to the corridor. Fausitt leaned back toward him.

"I was fooled," he whispered. "I shot the fellow with mademoiselle's stage revolver – you know, the beastly thing she uses at the Palace. I have just had a drink with the man and wished Mlle. Nina farewell."

"By Jove, that's splendid!" Darnell exclaimed. "Congratulations, old fellow!"

Fausitt grasped his friend's hand.

"Keep them till I come back, old chap," he replied.

"What were you saying to Guy?" Netta asked him, as they descended the steps.

"He was congratulating me upon something," Fausitt answered, leaning a little towards her. "I told him to wait – until we got back."

She looked up at him and then suddenly away.

"Bother the horses!" he whispered. "Let's go and sit under the trees and listen to the music."

Darnell watched them cross the lawn. Then he whistled softly to himself for several moments, drew a long breath of relief, and, turning back into the box, rang the bell.

"I am sending for some champagne," he explained. "We shall need it when they come back."

QUITS

They were both presumably seeking shelter, only whereas the girl achieved it in a scientific and exceedingly feminine fashion, the man stood half exposed to the driving rain, and with the drops from a chink in the awning falling fast down his neck. There came a time – she was proverbially a soft-hearted little woman – when she could stand it no longer.

"Monsieur will be wet through!" she exclaimed, timidly. "There is plenty of room. Here where I am standing it is quite dry."

He moved his position slightly with some muttered words of thanks, half careless, half sulky. Then he chanced to catch a glimpse of her face by the light of the glittering gas-jet, and he was at once ashamed of his surliness. He raised his hat and did his best to seem grateful.

"Very kind of you to notice," he said. "I will come and stand by you, if I may."

By his side she appeared smaller than ever. He was not only tall, but broad in proportion; good-looking enough in a negative, boyish sort of fashion, though just now the scowl upon his face would have disfigured the countenance of an Adonis. She was quite small, quietly but somewhat shabbily dressed, her cheeks white with the pallid complexion of an unhealthy life, large, soft brown eyes, and a tremulous mouth. The man, as was common with him – his best quality, perhaps – forgot himself.

"You seem tired," he remarked.

"Not more than usual," she replied. "I think I am hungry. I was on my way to dinner when the rain came on."

She looked anxiously outside. The young man seemed struck with a sudden idea.

"Do you know," he said, "I believe that's what's the matter with me. Let's go and dine somewhere together."

"Thank you," she answered; "I could not do that."

"Why not?" he urged. "I have just one five-pound note left in the world, and I am longing to spend it. Come with me and we'll get the best dinner Luigi can give us."

She frowned at him a little disapprovingly.

"If you were thinking of spending five pounds upon a dinner," she declared, "I consider that you are very reckless. I should not think," she added, severely, "of going anywhere with anybody who had such ideas."

He looked her over curiously.

"Come, then," he said, "you were going somewhere to dine. Why mayn't I go with you?"

She laughed softly.

"You wouldn't care to," she answered.

"Try me," he begged. "If I am really to take care of my five-pound note, I must go somewhere cheap."

"I generally go to Pierelli's, in Oxford Street," she told him. "One pays eighteen-pence, and there is a glass of wine included."

He hailed a passing taxicab, which drew up before them. Even then she hesitated for a moment.

"I pay for my own dinner," she insisted.

"Just as you like," he answered, laughing at her.

In the restaurant, which was hot and crowded, they were lucky enough to find a retired corner, which a noisy little company of diners were just evacuating. There was no ordering to be done. They just sat still and waited for what was brought to them.

"Macaroni!" he exclaimed. "How good it is, too! I certainly was hungry. Listen, little mortal!"

"I am listening," she assured him.

"I am going to introduce myself," he said. "My name is Clifford Ford. I am twenty-five years old, and I have been a failure at everything I have tried. To tell you the truth, I have been waiting for the last three years for an uncle to die and leave me fifty thousand pounds. He died last month and left me – a hundred pounds."

"And what have you done with the hundred pounds?" his very practical companion demanded.

He leaned back in his seat and roared with laughter. "I have spent it," he declared at last, "all except the five-pound note I told you about. I haven't even been able to pay my bills."

She looked at him for a moment with a little less favour.

"My name," she said, "is Gertrud Huber. I come from Switzerland, as I dare say you could tell from my accent. I am a typist at the Milan Hotel. I earn only thirty-two shillings a week, but I live with a very pleasant family at Denmark Hill, and I take care never to owe anything. I do not think it is right to owe money one cannot pay."

"I don't suppose it is," he admitted, suddenly sobered. "It depends upon one's bringing up, though, doesn't it?"

"Perhaps so," she assented. "My father and my mother were very strict when we were children. I think that it is best so."

The head waiter, in passing, stopped to pay his respects to her. Clifford Ford took the opportunity to watch her for a moment unnoticed. She was very neat, but she wore no ornaments. Her pallor was unnatural. It spoke of bad ventilation, lack of fresh air and exercise. It was a pity. She would have been so pretty.

"You dine here every night, I suppose?" he asked, when the man had passed on.

"Nearly every night," she answered.

"And alone?"

She flushed – most becomingly, but she was not pleased.

"I do not think that you should ask me that," she replied.

He apologized humbly. She inclined her head.

"It was foolish of me, perhaps, to mind," she said, slowly. "If it interests you really to know, I have had three invitations to dinner this evening."

"And you did not accept one of them?" he remarked, curiously. "You chose to dine here alone? Why?"

"I will tell you, if you like," she answered, simply. "The invitations came from my clients – the men for whom I do typing in the hotel. I should never dream of accepting favours from any one of them. I have nothing to give in return. I do not care to be under an obligation. I came here with you – but I pay for myself. It is different. You looked lonely and I was lonely. And I thought – I thought," she added, hesitatingly, "that you looked unhappy. I thought, perhaps, that you had lost your situation, or were in trouble of some sort. I do not think that I quite understood."

"Dear Miss Huber," he said, earnestly, "you understood better than you imagined. If I am not quite the sort of person you believed me, it is my misfortune. I was at least lonely enough, and if it had not been for you I should certainly have done very stupid things with myself and my five-pound note."

She frowned at the laughter in his eyes, and regarded his broad shoulders and sun-burnt cheeks a little disparagingly.

"Why do you talk so foolishly?" she exclaimed. "You ought to find some work to do."

"Can't get anything," he answered, promptly.

"You were well educated, I suppose?" she asked.

He nodded.

"Public school and Oxford – only, you see, I was in the eleven and played cricket all the time."

"That was very idle of you," she said, severely.

Clifford Ford, to whom this was a new point of view, looked at her doubtfully.

"I suppose it was idle," he admitted. "No one seemed to think so there, though."

"What are you going to do with yourself, then?" she asked.

He shrugged his shoulders.

"I have a good many friends and some relations down in the country who are decently well off," he remarked, vaguely. "I suppose I shall have to look some of them up. Perhaps between them they'll be able to find me a job of some sort."

She frowned at him severely.

"You mean that you will have to go to your relations," she said, "and ask favours, or borrow money from them?"

"Can you suggest any alternative?" he asked, feeling suddenly small.

"Certainly," she replied, with a swift look at his shoulders. "I should work."

He was half amused, half bitter. To be lectured by a little Swiss typist in a cheap eating-house was distinctly a new experience for him. Yet there was something in her words which stung.

"Come," he said, "tell me what you think would be a suitable post for me?"

"You are young and strong," she replied. "There are many places you could take."

"You mean work with my hands?"

She seemed surprised.

"Why not – if you are not clever enough for the other things?"

"Oh, I say!" he exclaimed, flushing up to his temples.

"Is it not what you call false shame," she asked, "to mind what manner of work you do, so long as it is honest and you are paid for it?"

"I suppose it is," he admitted.

"For myself," she continued, "I learned shorthand and typing. That is what I do now. It is not much that I earn, but every week I send five shillings to my mother, who is not well off, and I save something too."

He looked at her and felt his sense of manhood weaken. She was such a small being, her dress, her gloves, her hat, all so very cheap, so very tidy. Even the little white bow at her throat, spotlessly clean, was worn and shrunken. Her boots were thick and ready-made. And withal there was the too great delicacy of her complexion, the hollow cheeks, the tired eyes, the many evidences of an ill-nurtured body. Yet life, and the desire of life, flowed in her veins as in the veins of those others – the whole army of gaily-dressed young women who went blindly through life with their hands open to receive what it might bring; who had their young men, their clothes and cheap jewellery, their theatres, and all the pleasures they could gather in. He suddenly felt very humble.

"You are right," he said. "I have been looking at this matter from a wrong point of view. I would break stones to-morrow if someone would offer me a job."

She smiled at him approvingly. It was astonishing how pretty she was.

"Do you really mean that?" she asked.

"I do," he replied.

"You would not mind carrying things about – trunks and luggage?" she persisted. "You look so beautifully strong."

"I shouldn't care a bit," he declared.

"Very well, then," she went on; "I am quite friendly with Mr. Dennis, the head porter at the hotel where I am engage, and I will speak to him about you to-morrow morning. I know that he is two men short. He may engage you at once."

Clifford Ford laughed till the tears were in his eyes. Then he saw the perplexed frown gathering upon her forehead, and he stopped abruptly.

"The Milan Hotel," he explained; "that's where my cousin, to whom my uncle left the money instead of me, has taken a suite. Shall I have to wear a uniform, little woman?"

"After you have been there a month, if you suit them, you will have to," she told him. "It is a very nice uniform, and I wish you would not laugh so much. You will get a pound a week and your meals, to start with, and there are the tips."

"The tips," he repeated, wiping the tears from his eyes. "I hope the other tenants are more generous than Ralph, or I am afraid they won't amount to much."

She opened her purse and counted out one and ninepence, which she placed upon the table.

"Please pay the bill," she directed. "Wait one moment, though."

She took it from his fingers, and in fluent French pointed out a mistake of a penny to an apologetic waiter. She watched her companion produce his share of the amount, and frowned severely at the size of the tip which he gave.

"It was too much," she objected, as they passed out into the street. "You should have given him sixpence – no more."

"I am sorry," he answered. "I'm afraid I am a bit careless in those things."

"It is wicked not to think of money," she told him; "wicked to spend or give away more than you can afford. It means that later on in life someone has to help you. Whilst one is young, one should save."

"Don't you ever spend anything on yourself?" he asked.

"Of course I do," she replied. "I bought a pair of gloves last week and a new umbrella. It seemed terribly extravagant," she sighed, "but I had to have an umbrella. Mine was all holes. Would you like to walk home with me, Mr. Ford? You see, it is quite fine now."

Clifford Ford did like. In fact, he felt that at that moment there was nothing else he wanted so much to do. They were creatures of very different worlds, and yet he thoroughly enjoyed that walk and their conversation. She described, with many little bursts of enthusiasm, her home, the village under the mountains, their simple customs, the intimate social and family life of the people, their many innocent gaieties, of which she spoke wistfully, with kindling eyes. Her father was dead, and her mother was hard put to it to bring up a second family. Gertrud had been her only child until she had married again – now it was she who helped in the struggle. Seven children to feed and educate! The little figure who walked by his side was eloquent about their needs and tastes. It was for their sake that she toiled in this ugly London – ill-fed, ill-clothed, and without the simplest of pleasures. And she told it all unconsciously. When they parted before a dreary house in an ugly back street, Clifford Ford shook hands with her, and his bared head meant something more than ordinary courtesy. He felt as he had never done before to any human being toward this strange little mortal, whose cheeks were a trifle flushed now with the walk, and whose eyes were bright with interest.

"To-morrow, then, at twelve o'clock," she told him. "If you can get a character of any sort you had better bring it."

"I will do the best I can," he answered, clasping her fingers; "and I sha'n't forget."

He watched her pass into that gloomy abode, whose rest seemed to be the only thing she had to hope for in life, and walked slowly back. For the first time for years he found himself thinking seriously. He had looked for a minute or two into another person's life!

Clifford Ford had been porter at the Milan Hotel for more than three weeks before he saw his cousin. Then they met face to face in a narrow corridor, and Clifford dropped a heavy trunk within a few inches of his cousin's toes. Mr. Ralph Ford was nervous. He first jumped and then swore heartily.

"You clumsy idiot!" he exclaimed. "What the mischief are you doing?"

"Jolly heavy trunk, this," Clifford answered, wiping his forehead. "You might give me a hand."

Ralph gazed at his cousin in blank amazement. Then he began to laugh contemptuously.

"Clifford!" he cried. "Well, I'm dashed!"

He passed on without further speech, but still laughing, into his apartments. A young man – dressed in the height of fashion, with sleepy, dissipated eyes – was lolling upon a sofa, awaiting him.

"Halloa, Ralph! What's the joke?" he asked.

Ralph grinned again.

"One you'll appreciate, Sidney," he answered. "Whom do you think I just passed outside, carrying a heavy trunk? Seems he's engaged as a porter here."

"No idea."

"My cousin Clifford!"

Ralph began to laugh again, but suddenly stopped. There was no answering gleam of amusement in his companion's face. On the contrary, Mr. Sidney Lenton had the appearance of a young man altogether thunderstruck.

"What the dickens is the matter with you, Sid?" his friend demanded.

The young solicitor was ill at ease.

"You mean that Clifford's here working as a porter?" he asked.

Ralph assented.

"Got up in the uniform, too. Why, what are you looking like a scared rabbit about it for? Funniest thing I ever knew!"

"Give me a drink, Ralph," his friend said, shortly.

Ralph produced a bottle of brandy, some soda-water, and two glasses from a cupboard. All the time he watched his visitor curiously.

"Well?" he inquired, as the latter set his tumbler down empty.

Sidney Lenton lit a cigarette and leaned toward his friend. "Look here, Ralph," he declared, "we're pals, and it goes without saying that I'm more interested in your affairs than any ordinary client's. I am going to do something which is beastly unprofessional. If the governor knew it, or ever found it out, he'd kick me out of the office."

"Anything about Clifford?" Ralph asked, uneasily.

His friend nodded.

"It's that codicil," he said. "It was to be opened in two months, you know."

Ralph was suddenly serious.

"Go on," he muttered.

"I know what's in it," Lenton continued. "Only the governor and I know, and you can guess what would happen to me if it ever got about that I'd given it away. It provides — Listen, Ralph! It provides that if at anytime before it is opened Clifford has held any post of any sort whatever for one month, and been paid a salary, that he is to share equally with you."

"It can't be true!" Ralph faltered.

"There is no doubt about it," his friend insisted, impatiently. "Tell me, how long has Clifford been here?"

"I have no idea," Ralph replied. "Can't be long, anyhow, or I should have seen him."

"We must get him the sack – or, rather, you must," Sidney Lenton declared. "You're a resident here; it ought to be quite easy. Complain about him all the time – anything will do. Bring all the girls he used to know here to see him. Get Lily and that lot to come and laugh at him. Get him to realize what a fool he's making of himself... Who the mischief is this?"

Ralph turned quickly round. With her note-book in hand, Gertrud was standing just inside the door.

"I beg your pardon, Mr. Ford," she said. "I knocked twice, and I thought that I heard you say, 'Come in.'"

"That's all right," Ralph answered her. "Please sit down for a moment. I shall be disengaged directly."

He thrust his arm through his friend's and led him out into the passage. "Come back to luncheon, Sid," he said. "We'll think out some scheme."

"Who's the girl?" the young solicitor asked, suspiciously.

"Oh, she's all right," Ralph declared. "She types my letters for me. Good-looking little thing, too, in her way. I ordered her up for eleven o'clock. Even if she heard anything, she wouldn't understand. So long!"

Ralph re-entered his sitting-room. Gertrud was still standing up. He wheeled an easy-chair toward her.

"Now, then, Miss Gertrud," he began, with a smile which he did his best to make ingratiating, "come and make yourself comfortable while I think out my letter."

She sat down, choosing, however, an ordinary chair.

"I am quite ready, Mr. Ford," she replied, quietly.

The young man frowned; her manner was certainly not encouraging.

"Wonder why you're always so unkind to me, Miss Gertrud?" he remarked, throwing himself on to the sofa and lighting a cigarette.

She looked at him with faintly uplifted eyebrows.

"I don't understand," she replied. "I am here to take down your letters and then to type them. I am always anxious to do my duty properly. Please begin. I have another appointment presently."

"Can't collect my ideas all at once," he declared. "Look at me, please, Miss Gertrud. Why, what have you been doing to yourself? You look quite smart."

She looked at him steadily without any change of countenance, and then glanced away out of the window. Ralph laughed softly. He was of the order of young men who do not recognize snubs.

"Don't be unkind, please, Miss Gertrud," he begged, rising to his feet. "Tell me, when are you coming out to dinner with me?"

"Never," she answered, firmly. "You know that quite well. If you have no letters to give me, I will go."

"But I have some letters," he assured her. "Wait for a moment, please. I want to ask Dennis a few questions."

He went to the telephone in the next room, and returned almost at once.

"I am ready now," he announced. "Please take this down: 'To Sidney Lenton, Esquire, 17, Jermyn Street. Dear Sidney, — I have made all inquiries. C. has been here a month next Saturday. I feel sure we'll be able to get rid of him, though. I have been making complaints already. Come up to lunch. I am asking Flo and some of the girls, and giving them the tip what to do. So long!'"

"Any copy?" she inquired, calmly.

He shook his head.

"Bring it back yourself as soon as you've done it," he directed.

In ten minutes she was back again. Ralph looked through the letter and signed it.

"I said 'no copy,'" he remarked. "This sheet feels quite damp."

"I quite forgot, sir," she answered. "I will destroy the copy."

He laid his hand upon her shoulder.

"Very careless of you, Gertrud," he declared. "You'll have to pay a fine."

She moved contemptuously toward the door. He followed her.

"If you touch me, Mr. Ford," she exclaimed, "I shall cry out!"

Ralph laughed unpleasantly.

"I wouldn't," he said.

He caught her by the wrist and held her. She called loudly for help, and before he could raise her head the door was opened. A moment later Ralph was lying in the carpet, and a porter in the hotel uniform standing over him.

"Your old tricks, eh, Ralph?" Clifford exclaimed, contemptuously. "What an unpleasant brute you are!"

He turned away and joined Gertrud, who was waiting for him in the passage. She clutched at his arm.

"Mr. Clifford," she begged, "promise me something."

He nodded. "All right. What is it?"

"Don't leave here – don't let them send you away, whatever happens – not this week, at any rate. Promise."

"I haven't the slightest idea of going," he assured her.

She was trembling still. He took her hand in his and found it for a moment passive. Then she drew it away.

"Please don't," she whispered. "I feel just a little foolish."

She ran away down the corridor and he knew that there were tears in her eyes, tears which she hated to show. He looked back and shook his fist in the direction of Ralph's room.

At three o'clock that afternoon he met her in the front hall. He was carrying an immense portmanteau, which he at once swung to the ground.

"Miss Gertrud," he said, "I was hoping to see you. You've got to let me off that promise."

She looked at him steadfastly. His cheeks were flushed and his eyes unnaturally bright.

"That brute of a cousin of mine," he explained, "is taking the meanest sort of revenge. He's been asking all the people I used to know here to lunch, and pointing me out."

"Do you mind that?" she asked, coldly.

"Of course I mind it," he answered, impatiently. "I don't think I am a snob, but it isn't exactly pleasant to have a lot of people one used to know, the girls one used to take out to lunch oneself, come and stare at me in this beastly uniform, and have that cad of a Ralph handing me a shilling for taking a note. You'll have to let me off that promise, Miss Gertrud."

"I should not worry about friends who thought the less of you for working in an honest situation," she declared.

"Little girl," he insisted, "you don't understand. I know they're not worth taking notice of. They're the sort who like you when you're up, and haven't a word for you when you're down; but it hurts all the same. And to-night," he continued, "that sweet cousin of mine has asked some people to dinner – a young lady especially whom I used to fancy that I cared for. I'll look for work, honestly – anything I can get; but you'll have to let me off that promise, please."

She shook her head firmly.

"I shall not do that."

He frowned.

"But, Miss Gertrud," he protested, "you don't want to be unreasonable, do you? My uncle's solicitor, or, rather, his son, was here a few minutes ago. He said that it was a great shock to his father to hear what I was doing, and he offered to lend me fifty or a hundred pounds for immediate use, and to find me a place in an estate agent's office, if I cared to stay in England. I don't think I shall accept anything, but it's decent of them to offer it, all the same. And, Miss Gertrud," he went on, "the long and short of it is, I want to clear out quick, before the dinner to-night. Coming, sir. Coming at once."

Clifford hurried off and helped load a bus, with zest. He accepted a half-crown tip from an elderly American lady with complete sang-froid, and stood on the pavement to watch the vehicle out of sight, with a quite professional interested in the piled-up trunks. When he turned back he found Gertrud still in the hall, pretending to study a time-table. She called him to her.

"Mr. Ford," she said, "I have always been told that the promise of an English gentleman is a very sacred thing. Is that not so?"

"Certainly," he answered; "but —"

"Please let that be enough," she interrupted. "I claim the fulfillment of your promise. You must remain here until Saturday."

She left him standing there, swearing softly to himself. Sidney Lenton came up and touched him on the shoulder. Ralph was by his side.

"Do your duties here include a flirtation with the typist?" Lenton inquired, smiling.

"Miss Huber is an old friend of mine," Clifford answered.

Lenton nodded.

"What time are you off?" he asked.

"Not at all to-day," Clifford replied. "I have made up my mind to stay till Saturday."

Ralph came forward, frowning.

"What, you mean that you will let Mrs. Lethbridge and Alice, and all of them, see you in that infernal livery!" he exclaimed, angrily.

Clifford did not even flush.

"I shall keep out of the way if I can," he said. "If not, they can please themselves whether they speak to me or not."

Ralph was very pale. He drew out his pocket-book. Lenton pushed him on one side.

"Look here, Clifford," he said; "can't you see that it's deuced unpleasant for Ralph to have you here? Now, it can't make any real difference to you. Go and have a few days' holiday. I'll slip you a fifty-pound note into your waistcoat-pocket."

Clifford shook his head.

"I am very sorry," he replied. "I tell you frankly I'd like to go, but I've given my word of honour to stay until Saturday, and I can't break it."

The two young men exchanged glances. Suddenly Ralph understood.

"To Miss Huber!" he exclaimed.

Clifford turned away.

"It doesn't matter. I have given my word. I shall stop."

Lenton did not at once understand. Ralph took his arm.

"We are done," he muttered. "She typed that letter to you."

Ralph Ford was a young man of mean disposition, and he went straight to the manager's office.

"Mr. Krudlong," he said, "I have a complaint to make."

The manger was very sorry to hear it, and waited, gravely attentive.

"This morning," Ralph continued, "I engaged a young lady typist from your office – Miss Gertrud Huber. She took down an important letter for me, and has since divulged its contents to a person in this hotel."

"This is a very serious charge, Mr. Ford," the manager answered, ringing the bell.

"The young lady will not be able to deny it," Ralph replied.

In a moment or two she appeared. Her lips trembled when she saw who it was, and, if possible, she was paler than ever. This was the one thing which she feared in life – dismissal.

"Miss Huber," the manger said, "this gentleman believes that you have divulged the contents of a letter, which he dictated to you, to a person in this hotel."

"That is not true," Gertrud answered.

"Put it another way," Ralph broke in, unpleasantly. "She has given advice to a person, founded upon her knowledge of that letter, in a way very prejudicial to my interests."

"Is that a fact?" the manager asked. "Please be careful, Miss Huber. We have been so satisfied with your services."

"It is true," she admitted, "that I did advise someone because of what I had seen in that letter, but —"

The manager interrupted. He was holding the door open.

"You need not continue, Miss Huber."

"It was an injustice," she exclaimed. "A conspiracy."

The manager shook his head.

"Even if that were so," he said, "there is no excuse. A week's salary shall be sent to your address, Miss Huber. Kindly leave within ten minutes."

She walked out of the office with her head in the air and a little flush in her cheeks. She pinned on her hat and drew the cheap veil down over her eyes with trembling fingers. It was not until she was out in the Strand and on the way to her lodgings that the tears came.

Ralph Ford's first attempt at making himself disagreeable was a success; his second a failure. The manager absolutely declined his request to send Clifford away. The head porter spoke well of him; there was no authentic complaint which could be made. Ralph played his last card in despair. He made a personal appeal to the manager.

"The fact of it is, Mr. Krudlong," he explained, "he's a distant connection of mine, and we can't both remain here. There you have it straight. Which is it to be?"

"As a matter of principle, Mr. Ford," the manager answered, gravely, "I cannot send away a servant who is doing his duty, even to oblige a client."

"You prefer to lose me, then?" Ralph declared, furiously.

The manager bowed.

"We shall hear of your departure with much regret, Mr. Ford," he said. "You will excuse me now."

Ralph's dinner guests fell in with his wishes more readily. They certainly made themselves as disagreeable as a little company of ill-bred people could do. Only one – an American chorus-girl whom Clifford knew slightly – listened to his cousin's story and took her own course. She went up to where Clifford was standing by the lift and held out her hand.

"Mr. Ford," she exclaimed, "I want to tell you that I am very glad to see you!"

Clifford had stood everything else, but this almost upset him. As soon as she was gone, however, he knew that her words had done him good. For the rest of the evening he thought of nothing but his work. There was only one really sore feeling in his heart. For the first time he was angry with Gertrud for holding him to his promise. He did not even, after he had changed his clothes, wait for her in the Strand as he usually did when he was not on night duty.

Three weeks later Clifford Ford, who had resumed his accustomed appearance, drove up in a taxi to the Milan Hotel, and, to the head porter's great embarrassment, insisted upon shaking him by the hand.

"Seen anything of my amiable cousin lately?" he asked.

"Not lately, sir," Dennis replied. "Mr. Ford left here very soon after you."

Clifford laughed.

"The poor beggar's fifty thousand pounds worse off than he expected," he remarked. "Is Miss Gertrud about anywhere, do you know?"

Dennis looked a little surprised.

"Miss Gertrud Huber, sir? Why, she left on the Thursday before you left on Saturday."

"Left?" Clifford exclaimed, thunderstruck.

Dennis leaned toward him confidentially.

"I understand, sir, that there was some complains made by Mr. Ford," the man told him. "She was accused of divulging the contents of a letter Mr. Ford had written to his solicitor."

The place swam round for a moment with Clifford. Then his heart began to ache. If only he had understood!

"The hound!" he muttered. "Get me a taxicab at once, please, Dennis – a good one."

He drove down to Denmark Hill and found out her rooms. The lady of the family with whom Gertrud had boarded was there, but Gertrud herself was gone.

"This very day, monsieur," the woman announced – "this very day she left me. It is most unfortunate."

"Left you!" Clifford repeated. "But where has she gone? Where can I find her?"

"For the last three weeks," madame declared, "she has tried for a situation every day, in vain. It was the fault of the hotel, who refused her a character. Behaviour the most extraordinary! Never, monsieur," the woman continued, energetically, "had I a young lady in this house so regular, so careful, so thoroughly respectable. Yet from that hotel they sent her away without a character. It was infamous!"

"But I must find her," Clifford persisted. "It was my fault that she was turned away."

Madame was much interested.

"Only last night," she continued, "Miss Gertrud decided to give it up and return home. Indeed, it was the best thing, for the poor girl was half starved, and she would accept nothing from anyone without payment. Only the day before she was sent away she received a letter from her mother with some bad news, and she sent all her savings to Switzerland. To-day she had even to sell some of her clothes to buy her ticket. She has gone by the two-twenty."

"Does she owe anything?" Clifford asked, with his hands in his pockets.

"Not one penny, sir," the woman replies, vigorously. "There never was such a young lady for refusing to get into debt. She was one in a thousand was Mlle. Gertrud."

Clifford reached Charing Cross at a quarter-past two, and hurried on to the platform. He found her wedged in a third-class carriage, looking very white and miserable, with a German commercial traveller on one side, a waiter on the other, and four other people of various nationalities in the compartment. She gave a little cry as she saw him and half jumped up, eagerly. The guard blew the whistle.

"Good-bye!" she faltered. "Oh, Mr. Clifford, you are just in time to say good-bye!"

"Good-bye be hanged!" he answered, lifting her bodily out of the carriage.

The guard called out angrily.

"The young lady is not going on," Clifford remarked.

She was quite speechless. The train was now moving out of the station. She looked after it with a helpless air.

"My luggage!" she cried. "And my bag is in the carriage."

"Let it go," he laughed. "We'll buy your trousseau this afternoon, after we are married."

The colour streamed again into her cheeks.

"Mr. Clifford!" she exclaimed.

He nodded.

"I've got the license in my pocket," he declared. "Now kiss me and say you are glad."

She had never looked more charming, though her eyes were misty and her cheeks hollower than ever. He had kissed her for the first time in his life, boldly, here upon the platform! She had to keep on telling herself that it was not a dream.

"You can't mean it," she faltered.

He almost carried her out to a taxicab.

"We'll be married in half an hour," he said, "buy clothes till five, come to the hotel here, dine quietly, do a theatre, and start for Switzerland to see your people to-morrow. How does that sound?"

The taxi was moving now. It was real! She crept into his arms. Such happiness for her was incomprehensible, a thing undreamed of, a thing to be read about and wondered about, but to happen – never!

"I am quite poor," she whispered. "I ought not to marry you."

He laughed.

"I owe you fifty thousand pounds," he declared. "We'll divide it and call it quits."

THE DE/ERTER

I.

Peter Mayes made his way homeward from the office in a depressed frame of mind. He was a small man, with slight, sandy whiskers, and hair brushed back over his ears in two little tufts. He had weak eyes, a mouth excellent in shape but a trifle too humorous for his position, and a general appearance wholesomely and completely insignificant. He sat on the extreme edge of his seat in a non-smoking compartment of the Golder's Green Tube, and as his arms were full of parcels and the evening paper was tucked away in his pocket he busied himself trying to imagine what sort of homes the remainder of the passengers were returning to. The season of the year failed altogether to enliven his spirits. He found a great bunch of holly which a woman was carrying on his left a disagreeable and painful nuisance, and the air of slightly bibulous hilarity which seemed common amongst his fellow-passengers was scarcely likely to prove attractive to a man who had tasted nothing stronger than ginger-ale for six years.

Arrived at his destination, he walked for some distance along a broad street lined with very new houses and equally new shops. Most of the shops were still to let, and nearly all of them had notices displayed in the windows overhead, announcing almost hysterically that flats, apartments, or offices were to be procured there. At the end of the shops was a building estate in the course of development. Peter Mayes, with a little sigh, took the first turning to the left and came presently to a long row of model dwelling-houses. He opened the gate of No. 7, which, so far as outward appearance went, might just as well have been No. 17 or No. 70, let himself in with a latchkey, and went softly into the sitting-room on the left-hand side of the passage.

Now, it was part of the arrangement of these model dwelling-houses that the sitting-room and the dining-room should be connected – that is to say, that they should be separated only with curtains of such design as the householder might chance to fancy. Peter Mayes was accordingly made aware, from the moment of his entrance, that in the farther room were gathered not only all the members of his family, but a visitor. Some indication of Peter Mayes's position in the household might be gathered from the fact that, having softly deposited his parcels, instead of boldly entering the inner room he set himself down to watch and listen.

Evidently this was no ordinary visitor. Mrs. Peter Mayes, large, expansive, with flushed face and raiment a trifle disarranged, possibly from the pursuit of some household avocation, sat – from reasons of safety as well as comfort – in the largest chair the room afforded. Standing by her side was Belinda – Miss Belinda Mayes, that is to say – eldest daughter of the household. She was nineteen years old, and her dress, arrangement of the hair, and deportment were exactly what Golder's Green might have been expected to have borrowed from Piccadilly. There was a younger daughter, Amy, negligible, because she was a youthful replica of Belinda. There was also a young man, from sixteen to seventeen years old, budding clerk in a City warehouse, who distinctly took after his mother. He had a coarse, thick-looking face, he was untidily but flashily dressed, and he was puffing a cigarette furiously. The little gentleman seated at the table was so obviously a lawyer that he might have had it written all over him. It was also immediately apparent to Peter Mayes that the occasion was a great one.

"I do not think," the lawyer said, "that there are any further details I can give you at present. Your sister, madam," he went on, addressing Mrs. Mayes, "wished specially that you should be acquainted immediately after her decease with the fact that she had left her entire property to you to pass on to your children. The funeral, as I said before, will take place on Thursday. If I can be of any service – you will forgive my mentioning it, but an advance of money on account of mourning expenses is sometimes acceptable – you can command me."

Mrs. Mayes was sitting with her mouth very wide open and a very high colour. Her expansive bosom showed signs of emotion.

"Well, to think of this!" she exclaimed, not for the first time. "And poor Jane would never promise anything. To think she should have left the whole of it to us!"

"How much is it?" the boy asked.

"The amount of my deceased client's property is somewhat vaguely stated," the lawyer replied; "nor am I exactly aware in what manner it is invested. I have reason to believe, however, that it is between twenty-five and thirty-five thousand pounds."

Mrs. Mayes was stupefied. The younger girl began to dance. Her sister Belinda, whose own eyes were sparkling, restrained her.

"It's a tidy sum," young Mr. Mayes vouchsafed, his own voice none too steady.

"Whatever shall we do with it?" Mrs. Mayes gasped, looking helplessly around her.

"Do with it, mother!" Belinda cried, almost reproachfully. "Do with it, indeed! What a thing to say, when you consider what a pinched, semi-genteel sort of life we've had to live. Why, we can take Laburnum Lodge, the house with the gates to it and the drive. We can move in there at once, and all those people who go to the tennis club will be sure to call on us. Just think of the new clothes!"

"Hooray! Perhaps I'll go to boarding-school instead of that horrid shop!" Amy exclaimed.

Her sister frowned.

"There no necessity to mention the shop," she said, sharply. "That's the worst of you, Amy."

"I shall chuck old Bunderby the moment after the holidays," Mr. Mayes, junior, declared, with enthusiasm. "Just stroll into the office, you know, and say, 'Sorry, I'm taking a few months' holiday. Probably run over to Paris or somewhere, eh?' Jove, won't the other fellows be surprised! I shall just look about me for a bit. Sha'n't be driven into anything. Phew! Sounds like a fairy tale."

Mrs. Mayes patted her daughter on the arm.

"What about Mr. Hargreaves now, Belinda?" she whispered, archly.

Belinda blushed.

"I hope he will get to hear of it soon," she replied.

"We shall all," Mrs. Mayes declared, "be able to live in an altogether different fashion. I shall keep two servants and we shall dine late. I think, too, that it would be a very fitting compliment to my departed sister if we took her name along with the fortune. Mayes – plain Mrs. Mayes – never did appeal to me much. What do you say, girls, to Mrs. Horrington-Mayes?"

Mr. Mayes, junior, whistled. Belinda nodded her head approvingly.

"The only trouble that I can see in front of us," Mrs. Mayes continued, leaning forward and taking the lawyer into her confidence, "is Mr. Mayes."

She sighed. Belinda nodded. Mr. Mayes, junior, looked blank.

"You know what your father is, my dears," Mrs. Mayes went on. "You know how he will insist on sitting without a coat when he wants to. It's the only thing I've ever had trouble with him about. He's easy enough in most ways," she continued, nodding her head toward her visitor, who was showing signs of uneasiness; "but as regards his dress and little habits, I've had trouble with him ever since we were married, and there's no denying it. It took me two years to get him off his pipe, and another two to stop his beer and whisky. When it comes to getting him to drink claret and leave off his carpet slippers, and wear even a black coat for dinner – well, I can see there's going to be trouble for us. He'll be a stumbling-block, children. Mark my words, he'll be a stumbling-block."

"He must be spoken to," Belinda declared, sharply. "It's bad enough as it is to see the shabby way he goes about and the people he talks to."

"Does us no good, anyway," Mr. Mayes, junior, grumbled. "He went out fishing only three Sundays ago with old man Seddon, the fishmonger. I was up at the Dewhirsts' in the afternoon and they told me. They'd seen them start off together."

Mrs. Mayes nodded sympathetically.

"We must all be firm," she declared, her face and manner alike becoming portentous.

"Firm," Belinda echoed, looking for a moment rather like her mother.

Mr. Peter Mayes picked up his parcels, tiptoed his way out of the room into the street, and walked briskly back in the direction from which he had come.

II.

The actions of Mr. Peter Mayes on leaving his model abode were, in the first instance, somewhat peculiar. The brown-paper parcel from under his arm, consisting of two pounds of bacon – it was already making its presence felt by means of a greasy stain – he surreptitiously dropped down an area. Another package which had considerably impaired the set of his coat, from the space it occupied in his pocket, and which, from its odour, appeared to be a portion of some highly-seasoned cheese, he gaily threw over the palings amongst the rubbish and building materials collecting around a proposed dwelling-house. Similarly he dealt with a half-pound of tea which he had to bring from a certain shop in the City because it carried with it a coupon, three mutton-chops which were intended for the evening meal of the family, and a few slices of cold ham which he had purchased on his own, having had some experience of the appetites of his family with reference to mutton-chops. Having disposed of the last of these packages with great adroitness in an empty basket outside a greengrocer's shop, he stretched himself for a moment as though glad to be rid of his burden, and calmly crossing the street, entered, for the first time in four years, the doors of a public-house.

He ordered a tankard of bitter and a mild cigar. The appearance of Mr. Peter Mayes as he sipped his beer and lit that cigar would certainly have disgusted the little company who were even at that moment engaged in framing rules to be submitted to him presently for the purpose of aiding him in the acquisition of a more genteel deportment. He had picked up a newspaper and was leaning back upon the cushioned seat. The cigar had reached a somewhat rakish angle at the corner of his mouth, his feet were supported upon an empty stool. He read his paper, smoked his cigar, and drank his beer with an air of great relish. He even contemplated renewing the dissipation, but on second thoughts changed his mind. He left the place, purchased a stick for ninepence at the shop next door, and walking jauntily to the Tube Station shook the dust of Golder's Green off his feet for ever. Only, instead of returning on his daily track to the City, he changed and went out to Piccadilly. Here he emerged into the crowded streets, found a hairdressing saloon, where he had his hair cut and a shave, washed his hands, bought a new collar and a lavender tie, which he arranged with great care, and had a complete brush. Still in high good spirits, he made his way to a small restaurant, where he dined, having two mutton-chops all to himself, and a pint of beer. Afterwards he lit a cigar, and pushed his way good-humouredly amongst the throng waiting outside the doors of a music-hall. He managed, with considerable ingenuity, to get almost into the front row of the cheaper seats, and made himself so agreeable to several of his neighbours that drinks were freely exchanged during the evening. At twelve o'clock he presented himself at the door of a small commercial hotel and, regretting the loss of his luggage, paid for a room, where he turned in and slept like a top till morning.

The next day was Christmas Eve. He awoke a little after his usual time with a curious sense of lightness which he had not felt since he was a boy. Quickly realizing the position, he stayed in bed an hour longer than his usual time for the sheer pleasure of being able to do so, ordered a cup of tea in his room because he had never been allowed such a thing since he had been married, and, descending just when he chose, ate a hearty breakfast of bacon and eggs. A visit to a neighbouring tobacconist's provided him with a half-a-dozen cigars, yellow in colour and dotted with faint spots, which, however, he secured, with a paper case, for the moderate sum of one and fourpence. He then set out for the offices of the nearest steamship company and booked a steerage berth to New York on a steamer sailing in three days' time. His next proceeding was one upon which he only entered with considerable deliberation. The issue was between his claims and the claims of his family. He decided in his own favour.

"They have got," he reasoned to himself, "between twenty-five and thirty-five thousand pounds, and a lawyer who is willing to advance them what they like. I have got forty. Maria's welcome to her little lot. I think I have a right to mine."

So he formed one of a string withdrawing deposits at a well-known savings bank, and came out with forty pounds in his pocket. With the money safely concealed about his person, he hesitated for a moment as to how to spend Christmas Day. The vastness of his fortune decided him against remaining in so dangerous a spot as the Metropolis. He strolled about, looking in the shops and enjoying himself thoroughly, until one o'clock, when he dined, again with great heartiness. Afterwards he took the three o'clock train down to a village in Oxfordshire of which he had never heard before, and found a small country inn, where they received him with much surprise but open arms. Here, before the shops closed, he bought himself a few very humble necessities and a brown bag. He ate a hearty tea and supper combined, and walked about the small town with great interest during the evening, finally dropping in and spending a pleasant hour in the bar-parlour, where he was looked upon with some respect as a commercial gentleman without family ties, uncertain how to spend the festive season.

On the next day he tramped fifteen miles, leaving the road when he could, and climbing every hill he saw. He lingered about in the country till it was almost dusk, breathing the air as though it were one of the rarest of luxuries, watching the colouring of the woods as though indeed it meant something to him, strolling many times backwards and forwards through a thick plantation of firs on top of a hill, wondering at the silence, delighting in the leaf-framed peeps of the country he could see now and then through low-hanging branches. At night he dined alone but plentifully. For a few minutes before he accepted his host's invitation to join the little party in the private room he sat and looked into the fire.

He looked back through the years; he saw himself a young man, born of working folk, not more than ordinarily ambitious, not more than ordinarily intelligent, yet starting out in life blithely and with every desire to do well for himself and for others. His heart quickened a little as he thought of Maria and their wedding-day, the coming of Belinda, their first Christmas together; but the throb of sentiment soon passed. He saw the slow strangulation of all his hopes. From the first he had been dominated by the coarser, stronger nature of his wife. Perhaps, he thought with a sigh, she had not known what she was doing, but she had certainly driven him along the narrowest of narrow roads with a grip of iron. If he would have wandered ever so little, if he would have tried to gather in even the most human of pleasures into his life, her voice was in his ears, her grip upon his shoulders; the thing which he coveted was spoilt already by her shrill tongue, her torrent of remonstrance. The natural niceness of the man had saved him from the ways of dissipation, and left him nothing but silent endurance. As he sat there he wondered, not at his flight, but at the years of misery which he had suffered. In a way they were dear to him – his ungainly son, his hard-voiced, narrow-minded wife, who had never thought it worth while to keep alight a single flicker of sentiment between them; his daughter, with her prim ways and false ambitions; Amy, growing up in the same path – all with a certain measure of contempt for the shabby little man who was the slave of every one of them, whose use it was to bring the money and the parcels on Saturday night, and to bear the rough edge of their mother's tongue. It was over! He had almost given up hope, but the way of escape had been shown to him in that great moment of inspiration.

He rose, and with the smile upon his face of one who has thrown away the old burdens and commenced a new life he made his way into the land-lord's sitting-room, where he was welcomed with much cordiality.

"To absent friends!" someone proposed towards the end of the evening, and Peter Mayes lifted his tumbler high.

"To absent friends!" he murmured.

He wished them well, he wished them the detached house, the membership of the lawn-tennis club. He wished Belinda the young man whom she secretly coveted, he wished for Amy her boarding-school, and for his son that he might play the young man of fashion in the local bars and even in the West-end, after the manner dear to his heart. Let them have their hearts' desire, let him have his! A year or so of freedom before the turning of the wheel!

III.

Peter Mayes went out to America, steerage, where he suffered many discomforts which he thoroughly enjoyed. He was popular amongst his fellow-passengers and made many friends. He discovered that he could still sing a song, and some humorous recitations which had been forbidden in No. 7 of the model dwellings on account of their possible vulgarity came back into his memory and were much appreciated. He landed in New York not a bit abashed by the size of the place, and carrying his bag in his hand walked about the city for two days, perfectly happy. He lived soberly, but well. His appetite for mutton-chops seemed unappeasable. He always ordered two and always left the tails, thinking with a little gleam in his eyes of the time when they had constituted the major portion of his diet.

At the end of the third day he decided that it was time to work. He had been employed all his life in a land-agent's office, and he knew that he was a good man. He walked into an office in Broadway and offered his services. They laughed at him at first, but he managed to impress them.

"I've got enough to live on for a fortnight," he said. "Let me come here for nothing for a few days. You watch me. If I'm worth anything, give me a job. If I'm not, you can soon tell me so, and I'll try and find someone who knows a good thing when they see it."

He got his chance, and at the end of the first day he had secured a post. The methods of the firm rather staggered him at first, but he did his work thoroughly and well. At the end of the week he ventured to advise. At the end of a month his advice was often sought. Peter Mayes was a man in whom shrewdness, when he chose to make use of it, was a natural gift. In his London office the principals were pompous and unapproachable people, who played golf every other day and held no converse with their employés. Peter Mayes, therefore, had been repressed. Here, however, he found things very different. Everyone in the office seemed to talk together on a basis of equality. Very soon his position in the firm was unassailable. They were making money fast.

The whole of this period of his life was a joy to him. He first rented an attic, terrified at the prices asked for apartments, but very soon discovered the principle of the American boarding-house. He was fortunate in stumbling across a fairly good one, and before he had been established there a week he was very nearly the most popular inmate. He had had quite enough of the repressed life, and his sociability made him popular from the first. He sat at the largest table because there were more people there to talk to. He addressed everyone, and there was something about his manner, without being familiar, so friendly, so unsuspicious of any possibility that his acquaintance was not desired, that in turn everyone spoke to him. He made friends right and left. Some of them provided him with free entertainment at the theatres, some of them were useful to him in his business, some of them would have lent him money if he had wanted it, some of them did succeed in borrowing such small sums as he could afford. And all the time he prospered. His salary was doubled before he had been with his firm a month. It was quadrupled at the end of the year, and he began to have a nice little sum laid by. He grew somewhat stouter, he was chaffed into shaving off his side-whiskers, and an American barber treated his hair in a new and becoming fashion. He bought the sort of clothes he liked and he looked well in them. He was always agreeable and pleasant to ladies, but it was obvious that he preferred men's society. He was never drunk, he never even had too much to drink, yet he never seemed to refuse a sociable invitation. He smoked a good deal, but it seemed to agree with him. It was very seldom that anyone saw him without a smile on his face.

At the end of two years he was made a junior partner. Within a fortnight he had suggested a speculation into which the firm entered, and which realized within a week a profit larger than any they had made for many years. His partner stood him a dinner at Delmonico's and introduced him to his wife and daughters.

"Say, you ought to marry, old chap," his partner declared more than once. "You're spoilt as a bachelor, and I tell you our American women are all right."

Peter Mayes laughed and turned the conversation. Once a week he got the Morning Post from a newsvender in Fifth Avenue and read carefully through the Fashionable Intelligence. Never was there any mention of the doings of Mrs. Horrington-Mayes. Each time when he folded it up he was just a little disappointed. He would have liked to have heard that they were doing well and fulfilling their ambitions. Sometimes he would have liked to have known whether they believed him dead, whether they ever thought of him. More than once he half made up his mind to write. In the end, however, he never did. After all, he had always been a stranger to his wife and family. They hadn't understood him, and he had understood them so well as to perceive the futility of attempting to improve their relations. Besides, there had always been the guiding hand of Mrs. Peter Mayes upon his shoulder. There was no escaping from that. In his earlier days in America he had more than once awakened as though from a nightmare and sat up in his bed, vaguely terrified. In his dream he had heard the commanding voice of the lady who had ruled his life!

The years slipped easily away. Peter Mayes was a rich man. He was also almost a good-looking one. His partner died suddenly, and a few months afterwards his partner's widow invited him to lunch. The lady in question was an American woman of business.

"You see, Mr. Mayes, it's this way," she said, after she had fed him exceedingly well. "You and I are, as it were, equal partners in the business, and it's too good for me to give up. I need money for myself and the girls. We've always been used to having it, and we've got to have it. Now, I don't want to come down to the office every day, but I want to stay a partner in this business. Is there anything that occurs to you."

The first thing that occurred to Peter Mayes was to go, which he did, with perfect courtesy but much dispatch. In a week he had sold his share of the business, and found himself worth one hundred and sixty thousand dollars. He did then what most successful American business men do immediately they retired. He booked a passage – saloon this time – and came over to England.

On the whole, it was a thrilling trip. They made much of him in the smoking-room and even in the saloon, for his manners were delightful, his humour inexhaustible, his name as a successful man of business well known to some of them. As usual, he made friends and received half-a-dozen invitations, most of which, however, contrary to his custom, he evaded. He stayed at a very fine hotel on the Embankment, and walked about the City and the West-end on the night of his arrival with the keenest interest and pleasure.

Early on the next morning he took a ticket and went down to Golder's Green by the Tube.

The place was changed indeed. The shops had lost their newness, others had sprung up, the streets now were crowded, and a general air of prosperity abounded. Peter Mayes walked along, swinging his cane, smoking a cigar, looking at his well-dressed irreproachable figure now and then in the plate-glass windows, and laughing softly at the thoughts of that moment when, depositing his parcels right and left in obscure hiding-places, he had fled from the tyrannies of the domestic hearth.

He walked first to Laburnum Lodge, which was still standing and much improved in appearance. There was a gardener in the drive whom he addressed by name, knowing him well. The gardener was surprised, but he certainly did not recognize Mr. Peter Mayes.

"Can you tell me who lives here, Jackson?" he asked.

"Parties of the name of Hammerton," the man replied, pausing from his task. "Six children there are, and I wish they'd keep off the flower-beds."

"Hammerton," Peter Mayes repeated, as though surprised. "I had a sort of an idea that a Mrs. Horrington-Mayes lived here."

Jackson shook his head.

"There ain't no person of that name round here," he decided. "There's a Mrs. Mayes, a poor sort of widow-woman as lives in Crescent Row – pretty bad way she's in, too, I understand."

"In Crescent Row!" Peter Mayes gasped. "Why that's where she used to live seven years ago."

"Been living there ever since," the man replied, curiously.

"But I thought she'd been left a fortune!" Peter Mayes exclaimed.

"It worn't much of a one, I don't think," the man remarked. "I never heered the rights of it; but I think it was a lot of money in some shares that burst. Anyway, she's still there, and the daughters. And the son too, for that matter. And they owe me two-and-ninepence which I can't get, and I did hear as 'ow there was an execution going in directly after Christmas, if not before."

Peter Mayes turned away and walked a little unsteadily toward Crescent Row. This was a view of things which had never presented itself to him. A sudden sense of guilt was in his heart. He saw himself under different colours. He was a deserter! Perhaps — He drew a quick breath and walked more rapidly.

When he came to No. 7 of the model dwelling-houses he found the door ajar, and he walked softly in. He entered the sitting-room. Again he heard voices in the farther apartment. It reminded him very much of a day seven years ago, only there was a difference. There wasn't a picture and not much furniture left in the room, and the voices – they were all very changed. He looked past the faded curtain. Surely that was not Maria! She was thinner, her hair was grey, there was a queer look of suffering about her mouth. And Belinda – Belinda to his mind was better-looking than ever, but she wore no fringe and she was pale; and she, too, had that look about the mouth. Maria was working a sewing-machine, and Belinda was bending over some work. Amy was sitting huddled up before the fire, so that he could not see her face, but it was obvious that she was crying.

"I wonder how much Jim will get for it?" Mrs. Mayes remarked, in a tired voice.

"Not more than five shillings, I shouldn't think," Belinda answered. "A lot of good, isn't it, when we owe three pounds for rent, and it's Christmas Day to-morrow and not a thing in the house!"

"We shall have to do the best we can," Mrs. Mayes said, and her voice no longer had a strident note in it. It was almost soft, almost the voice of a girl. "Jim may get work directly after Christmas."

The girl who had been crying looked around; her mother had leaned over and patted her on the shoulder.

"I can't help it mother," she said. "It's seven years ago to-day since that beastly lawyer came here and told us about Aunt Jane's property. Aunt Jane's property, indeed."

"We had two thousand pounds," he mother reminded her, bending over her work.

"And what good was that," the girl exclaimed, "when we expected a fortune? Why, it was all spent before we knew where we were!"

Mrs. Mayes sighed.

"I am afraid we were all a little extravagant," she admitted, "and Jim's trip to Paris cost a good deal of money."

"I only wish father would come back," Amy declared, looking into the fire. "We always had plenty to eat, anyhow, then, and you and Belinda were different."

"I'm here," Peter Mayes announced, stepping into the room.

Mrs. Mayes laid down her spectacles and looked at him. Then her fingers began to twitch, she caught at the tablecloth with one hand and held the back of her chair with the other. Belinda frankly opened her mouth as well as he eyes. Amy began to scream.

"It is father!" she cried. "I know him, although he's shaved off his whiskers."

She was the first to come to his arms. No one else seemed able to speak at all. Peter Mayes came forward and laid his hand upon his wife's shoulder.

"I'm knocked all of a heap," he said, quietly. "Seven years ago to-day I was in that room and heard the lawyer tell you about your sister Jane's fortune. I heard all the things you were going to do with me and yourselves, and I – well, I funked it," he declared, with his irresistible little laugh. "I went out to America thinking all the time that you were living in the lap of luxury and didn't want me."

"We only got – two thousand pounds," Mrs. Mayes faltered. "Peter, is that really you – you – my husband?"

"It's the American accent and the clothes, I suppose," he remarked. "You'll recognize me presently."

"I should have known you anywhere," Belinda insisted; "but you have improved, you know."

"Great country, America," Peter Mayes declared, cheerfully. "I am sorry about these seven years, but you can have Laburnum Lodge now and call yourselves Horrington-Mayes, and if your young man hasn't gone you can have him too, Belinda. I am afraid Amy's a bit too old for boarding-school, but perhaps she'd like to go abroad for a year. I've made plenty of money."

Mrs. Mayes began to sob. Then there was a heavy footstep and Jim came in.

"Three-and-sixpence was all I could get," he called out, bitterly, before he entered the room. "Never mind," he added, "we'll do the best we can with it. It's better than nothing."

His father smote him on the back.

"It's sound philosophy, Jim," he declared. "You can stand me a drink with that three-and-sixpence when we get up West. Now then, all of you put your things on. I'm staying at the Milan, and I think we'll move in there for a day or two. As for shopping, we shall just have time to see to it, if you look alive."

He was overwhelmed. Only Mrs. Mayes sat still. She was sobbing quietly.

"I drove you away from me once," she said. "I've thought of it often since. I don't know that I wonder at it."

He kissed her again, and patted her on the shoulder consolingly.

"Been the making of all of us," he declared. "You've had the worst of it, I'm afraid, these seven years; but perhaps I had a bit of the worst of it the seven years before. My own fault, and let's call it quits. Hurry up."

They walked down Crescent Row, feeling somehow as though their feet fell upon the air. One or two of the neighbors looked out of the window and wondered.

"Had another fortune left her, perhaps," No. 5 suggested, ironically.

"Her scamp of a husband come back, perhaps," No. 4 echoed.

Mr. Peter Mayes, who was always sharp of hearing, turned quickly round and waved his hat.

"Right first time!" he declared.

THE OUTCAST

The girl was, as usual, the centre of a little group of admirers gathered together in front of the hotel. The man, as usual, was alone. He was standing with his hands behind him, leaning against the trunk of a fir tree, looking down upon the vineyard-covered plain which stretched to the Mediterranean. The girl was watching him. He had been for several moments the topic of their conversation.

"You all seem trying to put me off," she remarked, "but you are really not succeeding a bit. If I were a man, I think I should be a gambler myself. And as for the rest, how can the poor fellow be sociable if none of you speak to him?"

"He divides his time," one of them said, "between the smoke-room and the hills. When he goes into the smoke-room, he plays bridge diabolically well for the highest stakes he can get. When he goes to the hills, he walks out of the hotel with his head in the air, and doesn't even say good morning to anyone. What can you do with a man like that?"

"I don't know," Pamela replied, rising to her feet. "I'll tell you presently."

She walked across to him and stood by his side.

"It is a beautiful view, isn't it?" she remarked, following the direction of his gaze.

"Mademoiselle —"

He recognized her nationality and corrected his speech. It was the American girl, this, with whom he had travelled in the motor-omnibus from the station a few days ago. She was no longer wearing her trim blue-serge travelling costume. She was even more attractive in golf clothes and without a hat. She had exactly the coloured hair and eyes he most admired, a fact which he had realized vaguely during those few moments they had spent together, and since done his best to forget. He was a little taken aback by her unexpected presence.

"It is, indeed," he assented.

"I do not seem to have found an opportunity to thank you for your kindness at the station the other day," she said. "I got my trunk all right during the morning. It was very good of you."

"I am delighted to have been of any service," he declared. "It was a very slight matter."

"Not so slight to me, I can assure you," she replied, laughing. "Six evening frocks to a travelling young woman are of some consequence. If it hadn't been for you, I should have had to dine that first night in a shirt waist.

"Instead of which," he remarked, "you wore some marvellous arrangement of white muslin with blue underneath, which made you look like —"

"Like what?"

He shrugged his shoulders and turned a little away.

"I am glad to have been of any service to you," he repeated, relapsing into his former moodiness.

Miss Pamela Wilcox almost gasped. The man was positively indicating that he had had enough of their conversation! Her first impulse was to leave him at once. Then she remembered that there were others who were watching her enterprise, and she swallowed her resentment.

"I should like to know what I looked like, please?" she asked, meekly.

"Too charming for the peace of mind of a susceptible person like myself," he answered, with faint irony.

"So you are susceptible, are you?" she remarked. "Is that the reason you avoid everyone in the hotel?"

"Your sex has always been fatal to my peace of mind," he assured her, solemnly; "hence my seclusion."

"A matter of cowardice?"

"Of infinite discretion," he retorted.

Her eyes followed the flight of a bird for a moment across the plain.

"Will you dance with me this evening?" she asked.

He turned deliberately and looked at her. She smiled into his face with unflinching good-humour. The abrupt negative seemed to crumble away from his lips.

"I have been here for a fortnight," he said, "and I have not been near the ballroom."

"Quite time you became more sociable," she declared. "We'll have the first two."

"How do you know I can dance?" he asked.

"I don't, but I'll risk it," she replied.

"Or that I am a respectable person for you to dance with?"

"I'll risk that too," she decided, laughing. "Mind you don't go sneaking off to that wretched cardroom. I shall be waiting for you in the lounge."

"But, Miss Wilcox —"

She only turned and waved her hand. Already she was on her way to rejoin her friends. Calveley slowly resumed his former position. His expression, in fact, was if possible, even more morose and discontented. He would have strenuously denied that the few words which he had exchanged with one of his fellow-creatures had altered in the slightest his outlook upon life. Yet it was certain that there was something more attractive about the prospect at which he was gazing. Some miraculous weaver of colours seemed to have been there during the last few moments, working with strange flashes of colour, little touches of light and shade. The dull earth of the ploughed vineyards gleamed with a rich and comely brown. Delicate patches of green seemed to have sprung up from invisible places. The plain white farmhouse set in the valley was, after all, no such ugly place – its red roof and bright green shutters had their own peculiar picturesqueness. The distant hills were grey no longer. A faint mauve halo rose like mist from their summit. The Mediterranean was gleaming like molten silver. Down in the garden hollows a bird was singing. Calveley felt the change, and for a moment he revelled in it. His pulses were warm with life. The girl's voice seemed to live in the air around him, a music to which his heart kept tune. He had always been a dreamer, and he told himself that this was not the effect of her personality; it was simply that she stood for things which seemed for a time to have slipped past him. He revelled in those few moments of her imagined presence. He saw her as clearly as though she were actually by his side. Fair brown hair and plenty of it, complexion a little freckled, mouth very sweet, but not too small. She was scarcely more than average height, slim, and yet by no means thin. Her voice was delightful; there was the slightest possible suspicion of a transatlantic accent, just enough to redeem it from monotony, and there was a thrill in it, some nameless quality, which had already set it far apart from any other sound in the world.

Calveley came suddenly to his senses and laughed at himself shortly. He looked out upon his folly and he was amazed. These were the sentimental vapourings of a boy!...

She was surrounded by her friends in the lounge after dinner, but she left them directly Calveley approached. He told himself that he was over his folly now, but he wished that she had not worn white, that her eyes had not met his so kindly. He addressed her with much formality.

"May I speak to you for a moment, Miss Wilcox?" he asked.

"Why, certainly," she replied, drawing a little apart with him. "Shall we sit down? The music has not begun yet."

"I am sorry to say I cannot dance with you," he said.

She looked at him for a moment without any attempt at speech. Then she looked down at the tips of her shoes.

"That seems a pity," she remarked. "I have been rather looking forward to it."

"I am sorry," he muttered.

She said no more, but she made no attempt to get up and go away. He saw something in her face which suddenly upset all his resolutions. He had meant to be purposely and finally brutal. Instead, he threw all his resolutions to the wind.

"Miss Wilcox," he said, "you know everyone in the hotel. Haven't people told you anything about me?"

"I really forget," she replied, calmly. "Gossip never interested me."

"But gossip is sometimes true," he reminded her.

She nodded.

"Very likely. Now you mention it, I believe that I have heard a few things about you. You can tell me if they are true, if you like."

"I will," he promised.

"They say that you are quite nice-looking – I suppose we must start with that."

His eyes flashed, and she hurried on.

"That you are exceedingly morose, that your only form of recreation consists of long and solitary walks, that you are very rude to anyone who tries to be agreeable to you, and that you spend most of your time in the smoking-room, playing cards for high stakes with some very horrid men."

"Anything else?"

"Opinions, on the whole, are a little divided about you," she went on. "Your name is familiar to no one. Your appearance is – shall I say somewhat distinguished? – for a nobody. And you play cards and billiards remarkably well. Consequently —"

"Now we are coming to it," he murmured.

"Consequently," she continued, smoothly, "there are people who whisper the mysterious word 'Adventurer'! I have been solemnly warned against you by a dozen kind friends."

"Your friends are right," he said, hardly. "'Adventurer' is a fairly accurate and somewhat kindly description of me."

She smiled at him sweetly.

"I knew you were going to turn out interesting," she declared.

He set his teeth.

"Miss Wilcox," he said, leaning towards her, "I am here under a false name. I left Monte Carlo because of a gambling scandal — I was asked to leave. I am not a proper person for you to associate with."

She sat up in her chair.

"The music!" she exclaimed. "I believe it is 'The Chocolate Soldier' waltz."

Her eyes flashed into his; her body was swaying a little.

"Don't you understand?" he asked, harshly. "I am here under a false name – a confessed gambler, suspected of cheating. If people knew —"

"I was right," she interrupted suddenly. "It is 'The Chocolate Soldier.' Come."

She leaned towards him as she rose. Calveley laughed at Fate then, as she slipped into his arms.

There followed days which the gossips of the hotel, and perhaps a few others, considered a scandal. Pamela and her new friend were inseparable. She made a few efforts to draw him into the little circle of her immediate friends, but, though his manners were always perfect, he met their advances with so much restraint, and was so obviously uncomfortable, that she finally desisted. They took long walks together and played golf. His first appearance on the golf links with borrowed clubs was the occasion of a little episode which, if possible, increased the gossip. He had been persuaded to play in a mixed foursome, with Pamela for his partner, and on the tee, which was somewhat crowded, the question of handicaps came up.

"I am afraid," he admitted, apologetically, "that my handicap will sound ridiculous nowadays. I haven't played for a long time, but I used to owe four."

"Plus four!" his opponents gasped. "Horrors!"

"It was when I used to play golf regularly," he explained. "I played for the 'Varsity and stuck to it for a bit. I don't think that you need worry. I shall probably be quite useless now."

One of Pamela's disappointed admirers spoke up from amongst the little crowd.

"I don't remember anyone of your name playing for the 'Varsity in recent years," he remarked.

Calveley ignored him. It was his turn to drive, and he gave his caddie brief instructions as to the building of his tee. The young man was persistent.

"Did you play for Cambridge or Oxford?" he asked, pointedly.

Calveley hesitated. Then he remembered that his own careless statement had provoked the question.

"I played for Oxford," he said, and mentioned the year.

"There was no one of your name in the team," the young man declared, bluntly.

"I not only played for Oxford, but I captained the team," he said, quietly.

"Then you did so under another name," the young man asserted.

"Is that your business or mine?" Calveley asked, quietly.

There was a tense silence. The young man shrugged his shoulders and turned away. Calveley smote his ball far down the course, provoking a little cry of delight from his partner. His opponent followed suit according to his capacity, and they all strolled off together.

"You are really a delightful person to play golf with," Pamela declared, cheerfully. "Remember, please, that you are not to think of anything but the game until we have finished. We have to give them half a stroke, and I want to win."

"We'll win," Calveley asserted, grimly; "but I must have my walk this afternoon."

"It shall be your reward," Pamela promised.

They won five up and four. In the afternoon Calveley had his walk. They started out to climb the pine-wooded hill at the back of the hotel. Near the summit they paused. For some time they had not spoken. It was a silence which became more and more emotional.

"Sit down," he begged.

She obeyed him. The air was fragrant with the perfume of the pine trees, the land below sleepy and beautiful after the heat of the day.

"Do you know that you have been very kind to me these last few days, Miss Pamela?" he asked, abruptly.

"Yes, I know it," she admitted.

"Why?" he demanded.

"Because I like you," she replied.

He leaned towards her. He had the appearance of a man placing himself under restraint.

"You have been very good," he said. "You see what I am – nearly forty years old, a tired, worthless person, with no aim in life, no purpose save to drift on ignobly down the stream. I had forgotten all the beautiful things; I did not even think that I had any emotions left. Then you came."

She half looked up and then away.

"Do you mind, I wonder, if I talk to you like this?" he went on, gravely. "It is hard for me to keep silence altogether. I think that you came when my very soul was poisoned with bitterness and loathing of the whole world. I hated even my life; and there were moments —"

Her fingers held his. He smiled.

"They will never come again," he promised. "Dear, it is more wonderful to make a weary man feel than anything else in life. I caught a glimpse of you that first day; I watched you with your friends; I didn't understand why the sight of you seemed to fill me with vague regrets. I found myself thinking of you. Do you know what it means to a morbid man when he finds his thoughts engrossed by someone else besides himself?"

She raised her eyes and looked at him steadfastly. There was a new softness in her face, something wonderful.

"I think that you are far too morbid," she declared. "You speak and think only of the present and the past. There is the future."

"That is what I dare not think of," he answered, softly. "A man who has misused his past as I have done has no right to count upon the future."

"You are foolish," she whispered.

"Heaven knows, I soon shall be if I stay here much longer!" he replied, a little wildly. "Pamela, can't you see – don't you understand – that my heart is full of things I must not dream of saying to you? Come!"

She held her place obstinately.

"What sort of things?" she whispered.

He flung himself away from her, but returned almost at once.

"Little lady," he pleaded, "don't spoil my wonderful dream. You have made a little corner of fairyland in my heart, a little treasure-chamber into which I can creep sometimes when the black days come. Don't force me to destroy it."

"But what about me?" she whispered, with a tremble in her voice.

"God forgive me!" he answered, and took her in his arms.

Through an unreal world they walked down the winding path to the hotel. Theirs was the golden silence, the one tense period when the finger of the gods is laid upon the wheel of time. But the awakening had come. A huge touring motor-car was discharging its load in front of the hotel – a funny little man with a huge fur coat, a loud voice, and many diamonds, a wife and children to match; an unpleasant crowd to look upon, but notable patrons of the hotel. Calveley half paused as he saw the man, then he walked firmly on with Pamela by his side.

"The Goldbergs," she whispered. "Horrid people. They come every year and pay a fabulous price for their rooms. Whatever is the matter with the little man?"

Mr. Goldberg was suddenly excited. He caught hold of the hotel proprietor's shoulder and pointed to Calveley.

"Is that person staying in the hotel?" he demanded.

His raucous voice was audible to everyone around. Calveley came to a standstill before him. The contrast between the two men as they faced one another was absurd.

"If you are alluding to me, sir," he said, "I certainly am staying here. Have you any objections?"

Mr. Goldberg turned to the porters.

"Stop unloading my trunks," he ordered. "Huber," he went on, excitedly, "either that person leaves the hotel or I do not enter it. Which is it to be? Now, then!"

The proprietor turned a bewildered face towards his angry patron.

"I do not understand, sir!" he protested. "What is the objection to Mr. Calveley, sir?"

The new-comer turned back towards Calveley with an ugly sneer upon his face.

"So it's Calveley here, is it?" he demanded. "It was the Honourable Ronald Calveley Trent at Monte Carlo. The fellow is a sharper and adventurer," he continued, raising his voice so that those who were standing around could hear. "With two others of his own kidney he robbed me of four thousand pounds last month at baccarat."

The listeners all drew a little nearer. There was a breathless silence. Only Pamela laughed aloud, quite naturally, but a little scornfully.

"Robbed you, indeed!" she exclaimed. "No one is likely to believe that, Mr. Goldberg."

"It's the solemn truth," Goldberg declared, "and, what's more, he can't deny it."

There was one awful moment of silence, during which Pamela's heart stood still. Then Calveley replied, and though he did not raise his voice in the slightest, every word he said was distinctly audible to all of them.

"I do deny it absolutely and completely," he asserted. "I regret having to admit that I was in company with men who have been pronounced card-sharpers, but I was ignorant of the fact, and directly I knew it I returned the whole of my winnings to the directors of the club where the affair took place."

"Rubbish!" Mr. Goldberg cried, excitedly. "It was seven hundred pounds out of four thousand. You were one of the gang, Calveley, or whatever you call yourself; and if you're the sort of person they admit here – well, I don't set foot in the hotel, that's all. It's in your hands, Mr. Huber, entirely in your hands."

The hotel proprietor shrugged his shoulders. He gesticulated with the palms of his hands, turning as though in appeal for their sympathies to the little crowd of bystanders. How was it possible for him to arrive at any decision save one? Mr. Calveley occupied a single room, for which he paid a moderate price. He had no friends in the hotel, nor any following. Mr. Goldberg, on the other hand, occupied, with his wife and family and servants, the greater part of one floor, for which accommodations he paid a sum befitting his means. The rooms had been kept waiting for him, there was no one else likely to engage them. Mr. Huber turned regretfully towards Calveley. There could be little doubt as to what his decision would have been if he had ever been called upon to make it. At that moment, however, Fate intervened. Almost unnoticed during the progress of the little scene, another large touring-car had drawn up behind Mr. Goldberg. Its solitary occupant – a tall, dark man, good-looking, and obviously English, came strolling up towards the group. He looked around him for a moment with a slightly bewildered expression. Then he came up and laid his hand familiarly upon Calveley's shoulder.

"Halloa, Ronny!" he exclaimed. "What's going on here? Who's the funny little man who can't keep still?"

Calveley started. He looked at the new-comer in amazement.

"Morchester!" he exclaimed. "Dicky! Why, what on earth are you doing here?"

"First of all, tell me what's the trouble," the new-comer insisted. "It may be my fancy, but you seem to be mixed up in it somehow."

"This is the person who lost his money that night at baccarat," he explained. "He has just arrived here and recognized me. Now he refuses to stay unless I am turned out, that's all."

Calveley's new friend whistled softly. Mr. Goldberg elbowed his way to their side.

"I don't know who you may be, sir," he declared, loudly, "and I don't much care; but my charge against that young man is that he was one of a gang of sharpers who robbed me of four thousand pounds at baccarat last month."

The new-comer nodded.

"So you're Mr. Goldberg, are you?" he said. "Well, sir, I am very pleased to be able to tell you that, under the presidency of the Grand Duke and one of the Governors, a small committee to whom my cousin here appealed has pronounced him innocent of any complicity in the matter. His membership of the club and his entrance to the Rooms have been restored, and I have an autograph letter in my pocket here from his Serene Highness congratulating him on the result."

Mr. Goldberg stared at the speaker, open-mouthed. He made one more attempt at bluster.

"That's all very well," he declared. "But I don't know who you are from Adam."

"I don't suppose you do," the new-comer remarked, dryly. "There are several people in the hotel, however, who do, including, I think, Mr. Huber."

"Certainly, your Grace," the latter replied, with a low bow. "The Duke of Morchester," he added, in an awed whisper, to Mr. Goldberg.

Mr. Goldberg was plainly nonplussed. The characteristic of his race, however, saved him from wholly abandoning his position.

"But what about my money?" he cried – "my four thousand pounds?"

The Duke looked at him for a moment through his eyeglass, as one might look at some interesting specimen of the insect world.

"Confound you and your money, sir!" he said, turning on his heel. "Come on, Ronny, and show me where we can get a drink," he added, passing his arm through his cousin's. "It's a dusty ride from Monte Carlo."

"You're sure it's all right?" Calveley gasped.

"Right as rain," Morchester declared. "Who's the pretty, fair-haired girl slipping away there? She was standing by your side when the row was on."

"The dearest little woman in the world!" Calveley exclaimed, fervently.

"Glad you've found her at last," his cousin remarked, dryly. "It was about time."

Pamela the next morning was elusive. It was not until within a few minutes of the time fixed for his departure that Calveley found her. She was sitting on the trunk of a fallen pine tree near one of the paths at the back of the hotel. Something about her discomposure at the sight of him seemed to suggest that she was hiding. Calveley looked at her reproachfully.

"Since ten o'clock," he declared, seating himself by her side, "I have been looking for you."

"That's too bad," she replied, with a touch of her old lightness, "especially as I must go directly. My aunt is waiting for me to take her for a walk."

"Then your aunt must wait," he said, firmly. "I am going away in a few minutes with Morchester. There is something I want to say to you first – something I must say."

"Going away!" she repeated, a little blankly.

"My cousin wants me to stay with him for a few days at Monte Carlo," he explained. "I think perhaps it would be best for me to do so. Please don't look so nervous," he went on, a shade of bitterness creeping into his tone. "I only want to tell you that I haven't misunderstood anything. I am not quite such an idiot as that."

She looked at him wonderingly, and almost immediately dropped her eyes.

"I have come," he continued, "to thank you from the very bottom of my heart for your kindness to a poor outcast. I am glad that Morchester turned up, and that you know that I am not entirely a wrong 'un. But I am bad enough, Heaven knows!"

"Are you?" she murmured.

He looked at her with a curious wistfulness.

"I don't think," he went on, "that I have ever regretted it quite so much as I do now. You see, I have lived in the darkness so long that it never seemed possible to me that my day too might come; that you, Pamela dear, were anywhere alive in the world to touch the clouds with your fairy fingers and let the sunlight through. If I had known —"

"If you had known?" she whispered.

"I should have lived a different life," he declared, with quiet passion. "I should not be sitting here by your side, a tired, pleasure-sated man of forty, with no profession nor any useful place in the world, with simply a taste for athletics and a weakness for gambling. To my dying day there is nothing else in life I shall regret like this."

"Is this what you wanted to tell me?" she asked.

"This, and to thank you," he replied. "Those are poor words, aren't they? They mean a good deal to me, though. And I want you above all to know," he went on, earnestly, "that I haven't really misunderstood, and that it was your dear, kind little heart which made you come and talk to me because you saw I was miserable. You needn't have hidden away from me this morning. I understood."

"Did you?" she murmured.

His fingers closed upon hers.

"So much so," he continued, "that I nearly went away without seeing you at all, only I thought that you might like to know this. I have finished with my present life. Morchester and I talked it out last night. It's late to make a start, but he's going to get me a job out in Africa somewhere. That's one reason why we're hurrying off. There's a man at Mentone who's in the Government, and Dicky hopes to have it all fixed up by the end of this week. And it's all you," he added, with a curious little break in his voice.

She leaned towards him, so close that her breath fell upon his cheek, her lips almost touched his.

"After all, you are a very stupid person," she declared. "I should like to come to Africa, too."

THE PERFIDY OF
HENRY MIDGLEY

Mr. Henry Midgley glanced a little apprehensively over the top of the letter which he was reading toward his wife. Mrs. Midgley, however, was busy boiling eggs. She went on talking with her eyes rigidly fixed upon the minute-glass and a spoon clutched determinedly in her hand.

"If it's a matter of a hundred pounds or so," she declared, "why, what I should say is, take no notice of it at all. Put it into the Post Office Savings Bank, and let it be for a rainy day. If it's more – well, there's heaps of ways of having a good time, and the sooner we know about it the better. You'd better trot along and see those people, Henry, in your dinner-hour."

Mr. Midgley was slight and sandy, with a fair moustache and a mass of obstreperous hair. At present the repose of his features was somewhat marred by an expression of nervous anxiety. He looked first at the letter which he was holding and then at his wife. More than once he seemed on the point of saying something, but at the last moment changed his mind. He was evidently in a state of indecision. Mrs. Midgley, however, had just then only two objects in life – to see that those eggs were perfectly boiled and to start her husband off by the eight-forty train to the City with a satisfied inner man and a well-brushed exterior.

"Suppose it was more, now," Mr. Midgley began at last. "Just for the sake of argument, say it was enough to launch out a bit, eh – for me to join the golf club and for you to go up town for a matinée now and then. How does that strike you, Rose? What do you want to do about it, eh?"

Mrs. Midgley, with a sigh of relief, pounced upon the two eggs and set them up in their cups. She placed both before her husband and glanced at the clock. Then she poured out the tea.

"First of all," she declared, "I should buy the Fernery."

Mr. Midgley's face fell. It was clear that the acquisition of the Fernery, which was an ugly red-brick structure with a stucco front at the corner of the street, did not appeal to him at all. He thought of the broken-down arbor in a corner of the untidy garden, the decapitated statue, and the stone bay-window, with a little shiver.

"Buy the Fernery!" he repeated, a little despondent. "It isn't a pretty house, Rose."

"It has an appearance," Mrs. Midgley declared. "Besides, it's to be bought cheap."

"You wouldn't care about leaving this neighborhood, then?" Mr. Midgley ventured.

"Certainly not," his wife replied. "I like it, and because one gets on a bit in the world, I see no reason for shaking off one's old friends and trying to buy new ones. Besides, an earthquake wouldn't move mother; and, so long as she's here, I hope I know my duty too well to think of moving. Keep one eye on the clock, Henry."

Mr. Midgley, who had often wished that an earthquake or some less violent eruption of Nature would remove his mother-in-law from the next house but one in the row, scratched his chin thoughtfully.

"Very well, then," he said. "We'll take it that you'd like to buy the Fernery to start with. What else?"

"I should insist upon it," she declared firmly, "that you never left home in the morning with a nasty pipe in your mouth. I like to see a gentleman smoking a cigar."

Mr. Midgley, who loved his briar and hated all manner of cigars, groaned under his breath.

"Go on," he begged. "Go on, Rose."

Mrs. Midgley continued promptly.

"I should take two front sittings in St. Paul's Church," she announced; "and, as you probably wouldn't have to work so hard in the week, there would be no excuse for your not occupying them with me twice a day on Sundays."

Mr. Midgley wiped his forehead. His tone seemed to become fainter.

"Go on," he murmured. "Please go on, Rose."

Mrs. Midgley began to warm to the subject. She was a pretty little woman, but she had an exceedingly determined mouth.

"I should have a parlor-maid with strings to her cap, and late dinners," she declared. "Also I should be 'at home' one afternoon a week and give tea with two sorts of cake. You would have to come home early from the office and hand things round."

"It might be inconvenient," Mr. Midgley protested, weakly.

"You would have to make it convenient," his wife insisted. "No good starting on that piece of toast, Henry. You have to leave in three minutes, and I must brush you first."

Mr. Midgley gulped down his tea hurriedly.

"While we are on this subject," he remarked, in a tone which had sunk almost to a whisper, "is there anything else you'd be particular about?"

"A good many more," Mrs. Midgley replied. "But I can't think of them all on the spur of the moment. Besides, I never did hold with this fancying business. There's just a little matter, however, I should make a point of. With good claret like they have at the grocers' at the corner of the street at a shilling and three-ha'pence a bottle I'd take care that there wasn't a drop of beer in the house. I can't bear the sight or smell of the stuff – reminds me always of public-houses and the weakness of poor pa who's gone."

Mr. Midgley waited for his opportunity, thrust the letter which he had been reading in his pocket, and buttoned up his coat. This had been the last straw. He was a temperate man, but he liked his glass of beer and he loathed claret.

"Well, well," he said, as he stood up in the passage and submitted himself to vigorous flagellations with the clothes-brush, "it's a pity things ain't likely to turn out our way. A hundred pounds, with ten of it for a mourning-ring, is about my guess."

"And a very nice sum, too, let me tell you, Mr. Midgley," his wife declared, standing back for a moment and surveying her handiwork. "Not a penny of it do we spend, mind. Gracious goodness, give me your hat. You don't mean to tell me that you were going out like that? Why, there's a perfect rim of dust round it. Where you get it all from I can't imagine. There, now, put it on straight. Never mind lighting your pipe; you've only four and a half minutes for the train. Bring home the bacon and the tea for mother, and be sure that you go to the lawyers in the dinner-hour, and don't say a word about any legacy at the office. If they think you've come into money they may keep back your next rise. Hurry off, stupid – no time for nonsense."

Mr. Midgley started for the City without his pipe or a farewell kiss from his wife. That is to say, he started as though he were going to the City, but as soon as he turned the corner of the street he apparently changed his mind. From that moment his subsequent proceedings became more or less mysterious. He first of all entered a tobacconist's shop, where he purchased an expensive pipe and two ounces of tobacco. On emerging once more into the street, he lingered upon the pavement for a moment, glancing up and down with a casual expression which was distinctly overdone. Satisfied at last that there was no one in sight whom he knew, he summoned a four-wheeled cab from the other side of the road, and threw himself into a corner of the vehicle with a lordly air.

"Station, sir?" the man inquired.

"Drive me to the golf club," Mr. Midgley directed.

The man, who knew him by sight, stared.

"To the golf club," Mr. Midgley repeated sharply. "I'm not going to the City this morning."

Arrived at his destination, Mr. Midgley sought out the professional.

"I am going to join the golf club here," he announced. "I have a spare morning and should like a lesson."

The professional, who found the week-day mornings dull, accepted the suggestion with enthusiasm.

"Have you any clubs, sir?" he asked.

"Not at present," Mr. Midgley admitted.

"I waited to buy them from you. Make me up a bagful. The best, mind. I like the look of the shiny ones there. See that I have plenty of them."

"How many balls, sir?"

"I shall want a great many balls," Mr. Midgley replied, firmly. "Several boxes full, at least. Where can we go for our lesson?"

For more than two hours, with his well-brushed silk hat reposing on the turf a few feet away, Mr. Midgley suffered the alternate joys and pangs of the novice. At the end of that time, streaming with perspiration and stiff in every joint, he settled his account with the professional, fee'd him handsomely, and retired to the club-house. Regardless of the fact that his membership was as yet incomplete, he ordered and consumed with much enjoyment a large-size bottle of the beverage against which his wife had just issued her dictum. Afterwards he telephoned for a cab, stretched himself out upon the cushions with a pipe in his mouth, caught the eleven-thirty-eight train to town, and strolled into the office, where he was due at five minutes past nine, at precisely a quarter past twelve.

The manner of his entrance upon the scene of his neglected labours was by no means apologetic. It was, in fact, almost jaunty. The newly-purchased pipe was still in his mouth, his shoes were caked with mud, his collar was broken down with the warmth of the exercise, and his ready-made tie was on its way to the back of his ear. From the office-boy to the head clerk they all stared at him speechless. The principal of the firm, who happened to be passing through the office, surveyed him with strong disapproval.

"Is this your first appearance this morning, may I ask?" he inquired.

Mr. Midgley nodded amiably, and glanced at the clock.

"I am a bit late, aren't I?" he remarked, in a friendly fashion.

"Have you any excuse to offer?" his employer demanded.

Mr. Midgley shook his head.

"Can't think of one," he admitted. "The fact is, it was such a fine morning that I stopped to have a golf lesson."

Mr. Welby, the head of the firm, was a fat man, with red cheeks and beady eyes. Somehow the fact of these physical deficiencies had never seemed more apparent than at the present moment. The longer he gazed at his clerk the fatter and redder he seemed to become. He was positively bristling with rage.

"Are you drunk, Mr. Midgley?" he demanded. "How dare you come to business over three hours late and talk about golf lessons? Have you taken leave of your senses, may I ask, sir?"

"The fact is," Mr. Midgley explained, genially, "I've only come to get my office coat. I've decided to leave. It's a rotten sort of shop, this, anyway. Hours too long and screw too short. I'm fed up with it. Hand over my coat, there's a good fellow, Matthew."

Mr. Welby was threatened with apoplexy. Mr. Midgley listened to his flow of language with an interest which speedily merged into something like admiration. He backed slowly out and stood with the open door in his hand for the last few seconds.

"Steady, sir, steady!" he interposed at last. "Don't overdo it, Mr. Welby, sir. It's as good as anything I ever listened to of its sort, but go steady, sir, or you'll do yourself an injury. Is that all?"

Mr. Midgley dodged a letter-book and thrust his head through the door again a moment later.

"About that trifle of salary you were speaking of depriving me of, sir," he said; "put it in your own pocket and stand yourself a drink from me. I'm feeling a bit independent this morning about the ha'pence. I dare say it's the spring coming on. Ta-ta, Welby! So long, you fellows!"

Hot, but triumphant, Mr. Midgley stepped into the street with his office coat on his arm. Every now and then, as he made his leisurely progress toward a restaurant which up till today had been only a name to him, he stopped to chuckle. Then a sudden thought send a cold shiver through him. He snatched out the letter from his pocket and hurried to the address of the lawyers from whom it had come. His reception there should have itself been sufficient reassurance. He put it into plain words, however.

"There's no possibility of any mistake about this letter of yours?" he demanded.

The lawyer shook his head.

"None whatever."

"It is an absolute fact, then," Mr. Midgley persisted, "that I, Henry Midgley, of St. Clement Villas, Golder's Green, am entitled by the will of the late Charles Midgley, of Huddersfield, to the sum of thirty-five thousand pounds?"

"Quite correct," the lawyer agreed. "If you are still feeling any doubt about it we shall be able to advance you any reasonable sum that you may require. Your banking account will be in order for you tomorrow."

Mr. Midgley accepted fifty pounds and went on his way to the restaurant for which he had been bound when assailed by that sudden wave of doubt. Undeterred by its splendors, he ordered a hearty lunch, his enjoyment of which was greatly enhanced by the near presence of his late employer, whose stony stare he met with a genial nod and an upraised glass. Mr. Welby changed his seat, breathing heavily.

"Surly old gentleman," Mr. Midgley declared, pleasantly, to the head waiter, with whom he was talking. "I sha'n't ask him to play me a game of billiards afterwards."

In due course he finished his lunch, paid his bill, and went out. He drank coffee at a Mecca close at hand, played dominoes, and afterwards billiards, with a lordly disregard of time. He caught the proper train home, however, and sat down to his evening meal at the appointed hour.

"Fifty pounds, I guess, and half of it to go for a mourning-ring," Mrs. Midgley declared, as she bustled in with the sardines and cold mutton. "I hate those mourning-rings anyway."

"Wrong," Mr. Midgley declared, cheerfully. "It's a hundred."

Mrs. Midgley looked intently into the teapot. Her husband looked at her and sighed. In her way she was distinctly pretty, but her devotion to her household duties was almost an obsession. Mr. Midgley sometimes wished she would remember that he too was one of them. It was a regrettable fact that she devoted much more pains toward keeping his house spotless and himself well-clothed and fed than to anything else in life.

"One hundred pounds is a real nest-egg," she declared, swaying the teapot to and fro. "You'll remember what I decided, Henry. It's to be the Post Office Savings Bank, mind."

Midgley sighed and told a falsehood. He was beginning to find this sort of thing quite easy.

"It's there already, my dear," he murmured.

Henceforth, Mr. Midgley embarked upon a course of deceit, in the meshes of which he became more completely involved day by day. He left home always at the usual time, but never, alas, for the City. The mornings he spent at the golf club, to the great enrichment of the fortunate professional there, who was speedily coming to regard this eccentric visitor as his chief source of income. In a suit of clothes sent by stealth from the establishment of a sporting tailor directly to the golf club, Mr. Midgley, who changed there every morning, pursued his new avocation with relentless and amazing industry. At midday he traveled first-class to London and lunched at a popular restaurant, generally standing treat to one of his late fellow-clerks or acquaintances. Every evening he returned by his usual train to his usual meal. And every evening he felt the same twinges of conscience as he entered his neat little home and received the methodical and conscientious caress of his managing little wife. He dared not bring her presents for fear of being rebuked for extravagance, and their visits to the theatre were laid down by law as enterprises to be taken three times in the year only. With a sort of morbid desire for relief at any price, he led her on to talk of the Fernery, the greenhouse she would have built from the drawing-room, her scheme of linoleum for the hall. He probed her base worship of a mirror-tainted suite of plush-covered furniture in a neighboring emporium. He encouraged her to dilate upon gentility with special reference to silk hats in the day-time, visits from the vicar's wife, regular attendance at church, and the supreme advantages of red wine over malt liquors. After such times he felt stronger.

Nevertheless, Nemesis was inevitable, and Nemesis came. Mrs. Midgley's cousin, who was on the stage – quite respectably – and engaged to a clerk in a wholesale drapery firm, made a special visit to Golder's Green, and brought with her the full account of Mr. Midgley's misdeeds, so far as regards the City part of them, at any rate. It being the morning sacred to the offices of the local charwoman, the two ladies proceeded out into the country to indulge in their confidential talk. And their way lay across the golf-links.

"Fore!" cried Mr. Midgley, who, with only two strokes a hole, was one up on the professional and wanted to approach the green.

The two ladies never moved. Miss Ellen Darcy – which was the stage name of the cousin – was gripping Mrs. Midgley by the arm.

"What he's doing, my dear, is plain enough," she exclaimed, with vigour. "He never banked that hundred pounds, not he! He's having the time of his life, that's what he's having! Half-crown tips to porters and warehousemen; free lunches and wine to all his friends; and travelling first-class, if you please, just as bold as anything! Why, it makes one's blood boil! And you mean to tell me, my dear, that he hasn't given you so much as a pair of gloves?"

"Fore!" cried Mr. Midgley, who was getting impatient.

"He's been home to supper at the usual time every evening," Mrs. Midgley declared, with a little catch in her voice. "Not once has he even missed the train."

"There's plenty of mischief to be got into in the afternoons, my dear," Miss Darcy reminded her cousin. "Besides, he wants to keep it all dark until the money's gone, so that he can have his fling properly. What on earth does that funny little man want?"

Mr. Midgely, who stood now upon the edge of the green, was brandishing his putter and shaking with virtuous indignation.

"Get out of the way, there!" he cried. "Can't you see you're stopping my ball? How dare – Rose!"

Mr. Midgley, notwithstanding the disguise of his tweed knickerbockers suit, was discovered. He broke off in the middle of his sentence; but, unfortunately for the dignity of his appearance, he forgot to close his mouth. His wife, who, save once or twice on Bank Holidays, had never seen him except in a black coat and silk hat, looked him up and down in an amazement which was at first pitiful. Then she took one step toward him.

"Mind my ball!" he cried, weakly.

Mrs. Midgley, who, for reasons of economy, wore thick boots, kicked his ball, and kicked it more fairly in the middle than her disconsolate husband often hit it with his drive. She gathered up her skirts and turned her back upon him.

"You and your ball!" she cried, furiously. "You and your ball, indeed!"

The two ladies, with their heads in the air, walked off together. Mr. Midgley, who was something of a philosopher, discussed the fate of the hole with the professional, yielded it to him with a sigh, and finished his round. Afterwards he went manfully to St. Clement Villas, and found the house locked up.

"Gone away with all her luggage," the next-door neighbor declared, with gusto. "Such a to-do as never was, sending for cabs and that, and a man to help with the boxes. Went off with a young lady, too, who might be all she should be, but didn't look it. Such goings on! Come and sit down a bit, Mr. Midgley, and have a chat."

Mr. Midgley went instead to the station, and saw the back of the train. He then solaced himself with half a pint of beer and filed his pipe while he waited for the next.

"I'll have to take on the Fernery and the red wine," he admitted to himself, cheerlessly.

"Never mind. It's been all right this last month, and it's the little woman's turn, anyway."

Mrs. Midgley was a young woman of resources and determination, and, having made up her mind to disappear, she did so most completely and effectually. Mr. Midgley visited one after another of her relations without the slightest result, except the provocation of a stream of curious questions. Last of all, he tackled Miss Darcy.

"Now, it's no use your telling me you don't know where Rose is, because you do," he declared, having finally cornered her.

"Of course I know," she admitted; "but wild horses will never drag her address from me, you deceitful, faithless spendthrift. Why, to look at you makes me boil. You and your smart clothes, indeed! Have you paid for them yet?"

Mr. Midgley took no offence. He was far too much in earnest.

"I've paid for them all right, and I'll pay for a diamond ring for you if you'll tell me where to find Rose," he declared.

Miss Darcy laughed scornfully.

"Diamond ring, indeed!" she exclaimed. "Haven't you come to the end of that hundred pounds yet?"

"It was more than a hundred pounds," Mr. Midgely said, firmly. "It was a great deal more."

"The greater pig you, then," Miss Darcy declared. "Although, mind you, I don't believe a word of it. Now be off with you. If you follow me about I'll speak to the police straight away."

"But I want my wife," Mr. Midgely protested.

"Find her, then," Miss Darcy retorted. "You don't deserve a wife. Makes a respectable girl feel like a Suffragette to think of such as you!"

Mr. Midgely did his best. He bought the Fernery, installed his mother-in-law there in splendour which seemed to her positively regal, ordered in two dozen of claret, and began to smoke cigars. Then he took a suite of rooms in Duke Street, replenished his wardrobe, and plunged into life. Being handicapped, however, by a weak stomach, an indifferent digestion, and an unquenchable fidelity to his wife, he found the process alike painful and unsatisfying. At the end of a month he was sick of it. He sought out Miss Darcy again, but this time he was wise. He took the ring with him. Miss Darcy was swept off her feet.

"Well, I never did!" she gasped, turning it over in her hand. "So you're really rich, are you, Mr. Midgely?"

"I've got thirty-five thousand pounds," Mr. Midgley declared, sadly; "and it's no use to me without my wife."

Miss Darcy relented.

"Well, I will say you are one to persevere," she admitted; "I've got Rose a shop at the Hilarity with me. She's in the third row of the chorus. Her stage name is Miss Morris."

Mr. Midgley, with evidence before him of the power of diamonds, paid another visit to the jewelers. Long before the curtain went up that evening he was in his place in the stalls, fidgeting restlessly about. When the first act did begin he was almost demented because Rose was certainly not there. With the second scene, however, he felt a wave of relief. A mist was before his eyes. His heart pounded against his ribs. Rose was sitting upon an upturned milking-tub, wearing the abbreviated costume of a shepherdess in some presumably tropical country. He almost blushed when he realized what she must have been through before she had consented to don that costume. On the whole, he was bound to admit it was becoming.

He never took his eyes off her until the curtain went down. Then he made his way boldly back and handed the little note which he had prepared to the box-keeper, together with a liberal offering.

Miss Morris was requested to take supper with an unknown admirer.

When the answer came back in the affirmative he boiled with rage. The box-keeper stared at him as he strode out. He could not even console himself with the hope that she might have recognized his handwriting, for he had carefully printed his few words of invitation. It was disgraceful of her! Supper with an unknown admirer, indeed!

It was a wet night, and long before the last act was over Mr. Midgley was making a nuisance of himself, crushed up against the stage-door with an umbrella in his hand and a taxicab waiting. He received at least half-a-dozen snubs from young ladies who were perfect strangers to him, reverses which he bore with the utmost equanimity as soon as he discovered his mistake. When at last Rose came out, she was so heavily veiled that if she had not been wearing the jacket in which she had gone away he might almost have failed to recognize her.

"Miss Morris?" he said, timidly, holding the umbrella over her with one hand and raising his hat with the other.

She looked at him in the face, and he quailed.

"Are you my unknown admirer?" she asked.

"I am," he admitted, humbly.

"If you'd been another day without letting me know about it," she declared, "I'd never have spoken to you again. This your taxi?"

"Yes, dear."

She gave him her hand, and let him squeeze it as he handed her in.

"Savoy!" he called out, boldly, and immediately pulled both windows up.

"Do wait until I loosen my veil!" she begged.

THE END

A COLLECTOR'S BIBLIOGRAPHY OF OPPENHEIM BOOKS

C ompiling a complete bibliography of the works of E. Phillips Oppenheim is a thorny task. To begin with, the sheer number of Oppenheim titles is daunting. In addition, many Oppenheim books were published under different titles in the United States and the United Kingdom. Pirated titles – seven are listed in this bibliography – add further confusion. And then there is the strange problem of phantom titles – titles that were never published but which appear in various catalogs and lists of "Other Works by E. Phillips Oppenheim" printed inside a few of his books. A final difficulty stems from the fact that Oppenheim's career spanned so many years – from the appearance of *Expiation* in 1887 until the posthumous publication of *The Oppenheim Secret Service Omnibus Number One* in 1946. During that period, cataloging standards changed, making certain information available in some years, but not in others.

I believe this bibliography is unique among all that have been published thus far in that it is not primarily a compilation of data collected from catalogs and indexes – a standard method of creating bibliographies. Because there are errors and omissions in even the best catalogs and indexes, a bibliography based primarily on these sources must repeat those errors. In contrast, the foundation of this bibliography is data gleaned from my 400+ volume collection of Oppenheims as well as the 100+ volume collection of Oppenheims at the Firestone Library of Princeton University. Every piece of information gathered from those Oppenheim volumes has been compared with information contained in six important catalogs: *The English Catalogue* (EC), *The American Catalog* (AC), the *Cumulative Book Index* (CBI), the *National Union Catalog, Pre-1956 Imprints* (NUC), the *British Museum General Catalogue of Printed Books* (BM), and the Online Computer Library Center's WorldCat (OCLC). The EC, AC and CBI are compiled from information provided to the catalog editors by publishers regarding books they have published. The massive 754-volume NUC is a compilation of the entire card catalog of the Library of Congress along with catalogs of a number of other American libraries. The British Museum is the UK equivalent of the Library of Congress, and thus the BM is similar to the NUC. The OCLC is a union cata-

log of more than 52 million items at more than 9,000 libraries world-
wide. It is the 21st century digital online version of the NUC.

In cases of a conflict between the catalogs and the first editions, this
bibliography follows the first editions, recording any differences in the
footnotes. For example, *The American Catalog* lists a November 1909 Little Brown publication date of *Jeanne of the Marshes,* while the first edition
bears the date October 1909; this bibliography uses the October 1909
date.

Ellen Wellman and Wray D. Brown (WB) provided important information in their article "Collecting E. Phillips Oppenheim" which
appeared in the Summer 1983 issue of *The Private Library.* In compiling
this bibliography, I have also consulted the useful list published in Les-
ley Henderson's *Twentieth Century Crime and Mystery Writers* (CMW).

I use the abbreviation LB to refer to the list of titles published in the
back pages of the Little Brown edition of *The Man Who Changed His Plea.*
The LB list indicates the year of the first publication of a work in book
form.

Novels and Story Collections

Expiation: a Novel of England and our Canadian Dominion. London, J. & R.
Maxwell, 1887.

A Monk of Cruta. London, Ward Lock, Dec. 1894; New York, Neely, 1894;
as *The Tragedy of Andrea,* New York, J. S. Ogilvie, Sept. 1906.[1]

The Peer and the Woman. London, Ward Lock, May 1895; New York, J. A.
Taylor, 1892.[2]

A Daughter of the Marionis. London, Ward and Downey, Sept. 1895;
Boston, Little Brown, Sept. 1910; as *To Win the Love He Sought,* New
York, D. W. Newton, 1910.[3]

A Modern Prometheus. London, Unwin, Feb. 1896; New York, Neely,
1897.[4]

The World's Great Snare. London, Ward and Downey, 1896; Philadelphia,
Lippincott, 1896.[5]

The Mystery of Mr. Bernard Brown. London, Bentley, March 1896; Boston,
Little Brown, Sept. 1910; as *The New Tenant,* New York, D. W. Newton,
1910;[3] as *His Father's Crime,* New York, Street and Smith, April 1929.[6]

The Wooing of Fortune. London, Ward and Downey, July 1896.[7]

False Evidence. London, Ward Lock, Dec. 1896; New York, Ward Lock,
1897.

The Postmaster of Market Deighton. London, George Routledge, Sept. 1897.

The Amazing Judgment. London, Downey, Nov. 1897.[8]

A Daughter of Astrea. Bristol, Arrowsmith, Feb. 1898; New York, D. W. Newton, 1910(?).[9]

As a Man Lives. London, Ward Lock, May 1898; Boston, Little Brown, Dec. 1908; as *The Yellow House*, New York, C. H. Doscher, Dec. 1908.[3]

Mysterious Mr. Sabin. London, Ward Lock, Oct. 1898; Boston, Little Brown, Feb. 1905.

Mr. Marx's Secret. London, Simpkin Marshall, April 1899; Boston, Little Brown, Jan. 1916.[10]

The Man and His Kingdom. London, Ward Lock, April 1899; Philadelphia, Lippincott, 1900.[11]

A Millionaire of Yesterday. London, Ward Lock, July 1900; Philadelphia, Lippincott, July 1900.[12]

The Survivor. London, Ward Lock, Feb. 1901; New York, Brentano's, Dec. 1901.

A Master of Men. London, Methuen, Sept. 1901; as *Enoch Strone*, New York, Dillingham, March 1902.

The Great Awakening. London, Ward Lock, June 1902; as *A Sleeping Memory*, New York, Dillingham, Oct. 1902.[13]

The Traitors. London, Ward Lock, Oct. 1902; New York, Dodd Mead, March 1903.

A Prince of Sinners. London, Ward Lock, March 1903; Boston, Little Brown, May 1903.[14]

The Yellow Crayon. New York, Dodd Mead, Sept. 1903; London, Ward Lock, Oct. 1903.

Anna the Adventuress. London, Ward Lock, March 1904; Boston, Little Brown, May 1904.

The Betrayal. New York, Dodd Mead, Oct. 1904; London, Ward Lock, Aug. 1907.[15]

The Master Mummer. London, Ward Lock, April 1905; Boston, Little Brown, May 1905.

A Maker of History. London, Ward Lock, Oct. 1905; Boston, Little Brown, Jan. 1906.

Mr. Wingrave, Millionaire. London, Ward Lock, March 1906; as *The Male-factor*, Boston, Little Brown, Jan. 1907.

A Lost Leader. London, Ward Lock, Sept. 1906; Boston, Little Brown, Aug. 1907.

The Secret. London, Ward Lock, March 1907; as *The Great Secret*, Boston, Little Brown, Jan. 1908.[16]

The Conspirators. London, Ward Lock Sept. 1907; as *The Avenger,* Boston, Little Brown, May 1908.

The Missioner. London, Ward Lock, April 1908; Boston, Little Brown, Jan. 1909.

The Governors. London, Ward Lock, Sept. 1908; Boston, Little Brown, June 1909.

The Ghosts of Society. (Anthony Partridge) London, Hodder and Stoughton, Sept. 1908; as *The Distributors*, New York, McClure, Nov. 1908.

The Long Arm of Mannister.[†] Boston, Little Brown, Oct. 1908; as *The Long Arm*, London, Ward Lock, Jan. 1909.

Jeanne of the Marshes. London, Ward Lock, May 1909; Boston, Little Brown, Oct. 1909.[17]

The Kingdom of Earth. (Anthony Partridge) Boston, Little Brown, May 1909; London, Mills and Boon, Aug. 1909; as *The Black Watcher*, as E. Phillips Oppenheim, London, Hodder and Stoughton, Sept. 1912.

Passers-By. (Anthony Partridge) Boston, Little Brown, Jan. 1910; London, Ward Lock, Feb. 1911; as E. Phillips Oppenheim, London, Lloyd's, March 1918.

The Illustrious Prince. London, Hodder and Stoughton, April 1910; Boston, Little Brown, May 1910.

The Missing Delora. London, Methuen, Sept. 1910; as *The Lost Ambassador, or, the Search for the Missing Delora*, Boston, Little Brown, Sept. 1910.[18]

Berenice. London, Ward Lock, 1910; Boston, Little Brown, Jan. 1911.[19]

The Golden Web (Anthony Partridge) Boston, Little Brown, Jan. 1911; as E. Phillips Oppenheim, London, Lloyd's, Nov. 1918; as *The Plunderers*, as E. Phillips Oppenheim, London, Hodder and Stoughton, March 1912.

The Falling Star. London, Hodder and Stoughton, Feb. 1911; as *The Moving Finger,* Boston, Little Brown, May 1911.

Havoc. Boston, Little Brown, Oct. 1911; London, Hodder and Stoughton, Jan. 1912.

The Double Four.[†] London, Cassell, 1911; combined with *Peter Ruff* and published in US as *Peter Ruff and the Double Four*, Boston, Little Brown, Jan. 1912.[20]

For the Queen.[†] London, Ward Lock, Feb. 1912; Boston, Little Brown, June 1913.

Peter Ruff.[†] London, Hodder and Stoughton, April 1912; as *The Adventures of Peter Ruff,* London, Hodder and Stoughton, Aug. 1916; combined with *The Double Four* and published in US as *Peter Ruff and the Double Four,* Boston, Little Brown, Jan. 1912.

Those Other Days.[†] London, Ward Lock, July 1912; Boston, Little Brown, June 1913.

The Court of St. Simon. (Anthony Partridge) Boston, Little Brown, Aug. 1912; as *Seeing Life,* as E. Phillips Oppenheim, London, Lloyds, 1919.[21]

The Lighted Way. Boston, Little Brown, May 1912; London, Hodder and Stoughton, Sept. 1912.

The Tempting of Tavernake. Boston, Little Brown, Oct. 1912; as *The Temptation of Tavernake,* London, Hodder and Stoughton, April 1913.

The Mischief-Maker. Boston, Little Brown, March 1913; London, Hodder and Stoughton, Aug. 1913.

Mr. Laxworthy's Adventures.[†] London, Cassell, May 1913.

The Double Life of Mr. Alfred Burton. Boston, Little Brown, Aug. 1913; London, Methuen, Sept. 1914.[22]

A People's Man. Boston, Little Brown, Jan. 1914; London, Methuen, Jan. 1915.

The Way of These Women. London, Methuen, Feb. 1914; Boston, Little Brown, Sept. 1915.

The Amazing Partnership.[†] London, Cassell, Feb. 1914.[23]

The Vanished Messenger. Boston, Little Brown, Aug. 1914; London, Methuen, Feb. 1916.

Mr. Grex of Monte Carlo. Boston, Little Brown, Jan. 1915; London, Methuen, Sept. 1915.

The Double Traitor. Boston, Little Brown, May 1915; London, Hodder and Stoughton, March 1918.

The Game of Liberty.[†] London, Cassell, June 1915; as *The Amiable Charlatan*, Boston, Little Brown, April 1916.

The Black Box. New York, Grosset and Dunlap, 1915; London, Hodder and Stoughton, Feb. 1917.

Mysteries of the Riviera.[†] London, Cassell, June 1916.

The Kingdom of the Blind. Boston, Little Brown, Oct. 1916; London, Hodder and Stoughton, July 1917.

The Hillman. Boston, Little Brown, Jan. 1917; London, Methuen, Feb. 1917.

The Cinema Murder. Boston, Little Brown, June 1917; as *The Other Romilly*, London, Hodder and Stoughton, July 1918.

The Pawns Count. Boston, Little Brown, March 1918; London, Hodder and Stoughton, Nov. 1918.

The Zeppelin's Passenger. Boston, Little Brown, Sept. 1918; as *Mr. Lessingham Goes Home*, London, Hodder and Stoughton, April 1919.

The Wicked Marquis. London, Hodder and Stoughton, July 1919; Boston, Little Brown, 1919.[24]

The Box with Broken Seals, Boston, Little Brown, Oct. 1919; as *The Strange Case of Mr. Jocelyn Thew*, London, Hodder and Stoughton, Jan. 1920.[25]

The Curious Quest. Boston, Little Brown, 1919; as *The Amazing Quest of Mr. Ernest Bliss*, London, Hodder and Stoughton, Jan. 1924.[26]

The Great Impersonation. Boston, Little Brown, Jan. 1920; London, Hodder and Stoughton, Oct. 1920.

Aaron Rodd, Diviner.[†] London, Hodder and Stoughton, May 1920.[27]

Ambrose Lavendale, Diplomat.[†] London, Hodder and Stoughton, May 1920.

The Honourable Algernon Knox, Detective.[†] London, Hodder and Stoughton, May 1920.

The Devil's Paw. Boston, Little Brown, Sept. 1920; London, Hodder and Stoughton, May 1921.

Jacob's Ladder. Boston, Little Brown, Feb. 1921; London, Hodder and Stoughton, Aug. 1921.

The Profiteers. Boston, Little Brown, June 1921; London, Hodder and Stoughton, Jan. 1922.

Nobody's Man. Boston, Little Brown, Nov. 1921; London, Hodder and Stoughton, Nov. 1922.

The Great Prince Shan. Boston, Little Brown, March 1922; London, Hodder and Stoughton, Aug. 1922.

The Evil Shepherd. Boston, Little Brown, Sept. 1922; London, Hodder and Stoughton, March 1923.

The Seven Conundrums.† Boston, Little Brown, Feb. 1923; London, Hodder and Stoughton, Feb. 1924.

The Mystery Road. Boston, Little Brown, May 1923; London, Hodder and Stoughton, Feb. 1924.

The Inevitable Millionaires. London, Hodder and Stoughton, Oct. 1923; Boston, Little Brown, Jan. 1925.

Michael's Evil Deeds.† Boston, Little Brown, Nov. 1923; London, Hodder and Stoughton, April 1924.

The Wrath to Come. Boston, Little Brown, April 1924; London, Hodder and Stoughton, April 1925.

The Passionate Quest. London, Hodder and Stoughton, July 1924; Boston, Little Brown, Oct. 1924.

The Terrible Hobby of Sir Joseph Londe, Bart.† London, Hodder and Stoughton, Oct. 1924; Boston, Little Brown, Jan. 1927.

Stolen Idols. London, Hodder and Stoughton, July 1925; Boston, Little Brown, May 1925.

The Adventures of Mr. Joseph P. Cray.† London, Hodder and Stoughton, Aug. 1925; Boston, Little Brown, 1927.

Gabriel Samara. London, Hodder and Stoughton, Oct. 1925; as *Gabriel Samara, Peacemaker, Boston*, Little Brown, Oct. 1925.

The Golden Beast. Boston, Little Brown, Feb. 1926; London, Hodder and Stoughton, May 1926.

The Little Gentleman from Okehampstead.† London, Hodder and Stoughton, Feb. 1926.

Prodigals of Monte Carlo. Boston, Little Brown, June 1926; London, Hodder and Stoughton, Aug. 1926.

Harvey Garrard's Crime. Boston, Little Brown, Oct. 1926; London, Hodder and Stoughton, Feb. 1927.

Madame.[†] London, Hodder and Stoughton, Jan. 1927; as *Madame and Her Twelve Virgins*, Boston, Little Brown, Jan. 1927.

The Channay Syndicate.[†] London, Hodder and Stoughton, Jan. 1927; Boston, Little Brown, Jan. 1927.

Mr. Billingham, the Marquis and Madelon.[†] London, Hodder and Stoughton, March 1927; Boston, Little Brown, May 1929.

Nicholas Goade, Detective.[†] London, Hodder and Stoughton, April 1927; Boston, Little Brown, Nov. 1929.

The Interloper. Boston, Little Brown, April 1927; as *The Ex-Duke*, London, Hodder and Stoughton, Aug. 1927.[28]

Miss Brown of X.Y.O. Boston, Little Brown, Aug. 1927; London, Hodder and Stoughton, Oct. 1927.

The Light Beyond. London, Hodder and Stoughton, Jan. 1928; Boston, Little Brown, Jan. 1928.

The Exploits of Pudgy Pete & Co.[†] London, Hodder and Stoughton, March 1928.

The Fortunate Wayfarer. Boston, Little Brown, May 1928; London, Hodder and Stoughton, Sept. 1928.

Chronicles of Melhampton.[†] London, Hodder and Stoughton, July 1928.

Matorni's Vineyard. Boston, Little Brown, Oct. 1928; London, Hodder and Stoughton, Feb. 1929.

The Treasure House of Martin Hews. Boston, Little Brown, Jan. 1929; London, Hodder and Stoughton, June 1929.

Jennerton & Co.[†] London, Hodder and Stoughton, Jan. 1929.

The Human Chase.[†] London, Hodder and Stoughton, April 1929.

The Glenlitten Murder. Boston, Little Brown, Aug. 1929; London, Hodder and Stoughton, Oct. 1929.

What Happened to Forester.[†] London, Hodder and Stoughton, Dec. 1929; Boston, Little Brown, May 1930.

Blackman's Wood. Story included with Agatha Christie's "The Under Dog" in *Two Thrillers*, London, Readers Library, 1929.

The Million Pound Deposit. Boston, Little Brown, Jan. 1930; London, Hodder and Stoughton, March 1930.

Slane's Long Shots.[†] London, Hodder and Stoughton, July 1930; Boston, Little Brown, Nov. 1930.

The Lion and the Lamb. London, Hodder and Stoughton, Aug. 1930; Boston, Little Brown, Aug. 1930.

Up the Ladder of Gold. London, Hodder and Stoughton, Jan. 1931; Boston, Little Brown, Jan. 1931.

Inspector Dickins Retires.[†] London, Hodder and Stoughton, Feb. 1931; as *Gangsters' Glory*, Boston, Little Brown, Nov. 1931.

Simple Peter Cradd. London, Hodder and Stoughton, July 1931; Boston, Little Brown, July 1931.

Sinners Beware.[†] London, Hodder and Stoughton, Oct. 1931; Boston, Little Brown, April 1932.

Moran Chambers Smiled. London, Hodder and Stoughton, Jan. 1932; as *The Man from Sing Sing,* Boston, Little Brown, Jan. 1932.

The Ostrekoff Jewels. London, Hodder and Stoughton, Aug. 1932; Boston, Little Brown, Oct. 1932.

Crooks in the Sunshine.[†] London, Hodder and Stoughton, Sept. 1932; Boston, Little Brown, 1933.

Murder at Monte Carlo. Boston, Little Brown, Jan. 1933; London, Hodder and Stoughton, June 1933.

Jeremiah and the Princess. London, Hodder and Stoughton, Jan. 1933; Boston, Little Brown, July 1933.

The Ex-Detective[†] London, Hodder and Stoughton, Sept. 1933; Boston, Little Brown, Nov. 1933.

The Gallows of Chance. London, Hodder and Stoughton, Jan. 1934; Boston, Little Brown, Jan. 1934.

The Man Without Nerves. Little Brown, May 1934; as *The Bank Manager,* London, Hodder and Stoughton, June 1934.

The Strange Borders of Palace Crescent. Boston, Little Brown, Sept. 1934; London, Hodder and Stoughton, Jan. 1935.

The Spy Paramount. Boston, Little Brown, Jan. 1935; London, Hodder and Stoughton, July 1935.[29]

General Besserley's Puzzle Box.[†] London, Hodder and Stoughton, May 1935; Boston, Little Brown, May 1935.

The Battle of Basinghall Street. Boston, Little Brown, Sept. 1935; London, Hodder and Stoughton, Nov. 1935.

Advice, Limited.[†] London, Hodder and Stoughton, Sept. 1935; Boston, Little Brown, May 1936.[30]

Floating Peril. Boston, Little Brown, Jan. 1936; as *The Bird of Paradise*, London, Hodder and Stoughton, March 1936.

Ask Miss Mott.[†] London, Hodder and Stoughton, May 1936; Boston, Little Brown, May 1937.

The Magnificent Hoax. Boston, Little Brown, July 1936; as *Judy of Bunter's Buildings*, London, Hodder and Stoughton, Sept. 1936.

The Dumb Gods Speak. Boston, Little Brown, Jan. 1937; London, Hodder and Stoughton, Feb. 1937.

Envoy Extraordinary. London, Hodder and Stoughton, July 1937; Boston, Little Brown, July 1937.

Curious Happenings to the Rooke Legatees.[†] London, Hodder and Stoughton, Oct. 1937; Boston, Little Brown, March 1938.

The Mayor on Horseback. Boston, Little Brown, Nov. 1937.

The Colossus of Arcadia. London, Hodder and Stoughton, Jan. 1938; Boston, Little Brown, June 1938.

A Pulpit in the Grill Room.[†] London, Hodder and Stoughton, June 1938; Boston, Little Brown, March 1939.

The Spymaster. Boston, Little Brown, Nov. 1938; London, Hodder and Stoughton, Jan. 1939.

And Still I Cheat the Gallows.[†] London, Hodder and Stoughton, Nov. 1938.[31]

Sir Adam Disappeared. Boston, Little Brown, May 1939; London, Hodder and Stoughton, Sept. 1939.

General Besserley's Second Puzzle Box.[†] London, Hodder and Stoughton, July 1939; Boston, Little Brown, Feb. 1940.

Exit a Dictator. Boston, Little Brown, Aug. 1939; London, Hodder and Stoughton, Nov. 1939.

The Strangers' Gate. Boston, Little Brown, Nov. 1939; London, Hodder and Stoughton, Feb. 1940.

The Milan Grill Room: Further Adventures of Louis, the Manager, and Major Lyson, the Raconteur.† London, Hodder and Stoughton, Jan. 1940; Boston, Little Brown, 1941.

The Grassleyes Mystery. London, Hodder and Stoughton, July 1940; Boston, Little Brown, July 1940.

Last Train Out. Boston, Little Brown, Nov. 1940; London, Hodder Stoughton, Feb. 1941.

The Shy Plutocrat. Boston, Little Brown, July 1941; London, Hodder and Stoughton, Nov. 1941.

The Man Who Changed His Plea. London, Hodder and Stoughton, March 1942; Boston, Little Brown, April 1942.

Mr. Mirakel. London, Hodder and Stoughton, June 1943; Boston, Little Brown, Oct. 1943.

Burglars Must Dine. London, Todd Publishing Co., 1943.[32]

The Great Bear. London, Todd Publishing Co., 1943.[33]

The Man Who Thought He Was a Pauper. London, Todd Publishing Co., 1943.[34]

The Hour of Reckoning and The Mayor of Ballydaghan. London, Todd Publishing Co. 1944.[35]

Plays[36]

The Money-Spider. (produced 1908).

The King's Cup. [co-written with H. Dennis Bradley] London and New York, Samuel French, 1913. (produced 1909).

The Gilded Key. (produced 1910).

The Eclipse. [co-written with Fred Thompson] (produced at Garrick Theatre, London, 1919).

Omnibus Volumes

The Oppenheim Omnibus: Forty-One Stories by E. P. O. London, Hodder and Stoughton, March 1931.

The Oppenheim Omnibus: Clowns and Criminals. Boston, Little Brown, April 1931. Contains: *Michael's Evil Deeds; Peter Ruff and the Double Four; Recalled by the Double Four;* and *Jennerton & Co.*[37]

Shudders and Thrills: The Second Oppenheim Omnibus. Boston, Little Brown, July 1932. Contains: *The Evil Shepherd; Ghosts of Society; The Amazing Partnership; The Channay Syndicate;* and *The Human Chase*.

The Secret Service Omnibus: Five Full Length Novels of International Intrigue. London, Hodder and Stoughton, Sept. 1932. Contains: *Miss Brown of X.Y.O.; The Wrath to Come; Matorni's Vineyard; The Great Impersonation;* and *Gabriel Samara*.

Spies and Intrigues: The Oppenheim Secret Service Omnibus. Boston, Little Brown, Oct. 1936. Contains: *The Wrath to Come; The Great Impersonation; Gabriel Samara, Peacemaker;* and *Mr. Billingham, the Marquis and Madelon.*[38]

The Oppenheim Secret Service Omnibus Number One. Boston, Little Brown, May 1946. Contains: *Mysterious Mr. Sabin; A Maker of History;* and *The Illustrious Prince*.

Autobiographical

My Books and Myself. Boston, Little Brown, 1922.[39]

The Quest for Winter Sunshine. [travel] London, Methuen, Nov. 1926; Boston, Little Brown, Jan. 1927.[40]

E. Phillips Oppenheim: The Prince of Story Tellers Tells His Own Story. Boston, Little Brown, 1927.[41]

The Pool of Memory. London, Hodder and Stoughton, Nov. 1941; Boston, Little Brown, Feb. 1942.[42]

Collections

Many Mysteries. Selected by E. Phillips Oppenheim. London, Rich & Cowan, May 1933.

Phantom Titles[43]

A Woman's Blindness
The Lesser Sin
The Vindicator

† Short story collection

[1] First UK edition of *A Monk of Cruta was* a *Beeton's Christmas Annual*. Many catalogs indicated that *The Tragedy of Andrea* as an alternate title of *A Monk of Cruta*. LB, however, lists it as an entirely separate book. I have not seen a copy of *The Tragedy of Andrea* so I cannot confirm either claim.

[2] Taylor edition a paperback and is No. 4 of the Mayflower Library series. It bears a 1892 copyright date but no publication date given. LB indicates that first publication of *The Peer and the Woman* is 1895.

[3] *The Yellow House, The New Tenant*, and *To Win the Love He Sought* are three pirate titles first published by C. H. Doscher & Co. AC lists Dec. 5, 1908 Doscher publication of *The Yellow House*. Doscher editions of *The New Tenant* and *To Win the Love He Sought* do not appear in AC or CBI, however Donald W. Newton editions of *The New Tenant* and *To Win the Love He Sought* list a 1910 Doscher copyright date. The Newton editions also do not appear in AC or CBI. Subsequently, P. F. Collier & Sons, New York, published a three-volume set containing: vol. 1) *The Yellow House* and abridged version of *Master of Men*; vol. 2) *The New Tenant* and abridged version of *A Daughter of Astrea*; and vol. 3) *To Win the Love He Lost* and abridged version of *The Great Awakening*. CBI lists a Feb. 1915 publication for the three-volume set. This set has gone through at least three separate editions.

[4] Neely edition not listed in AC; Neely edition has 1897 copyright date, but no publication information.

[5] AC lists Lippincott edition; EC does not list 1896 Ward and Downey edition, it appears, however, in Yale University Library catalog. LB lists 1900 as the date of publication.

[6] Title does not appear in NUC, but is listed as to be published March 1929 by Street & Smith, in *The Great Awakening*, (No. 110 The Adventure Library), Street & Smith Corp., New York.

[7] WB notes: "In 1896 the first rare title was presumably published, since it is listed in the English Catalogue of Books for 1890-1897 as *Wooing of Fortune*, 8vo, 304 pp. 8s., Ward and Downey. Some of the *aficionados* do not think that it was ever published but probably rewritten and published under another title. Mr. Nicholas Davies, the English publisher, recently deceased, was the foremost Oppenheim collector and had never heard of a copy."

[8] According to WB, "the King or Queen of hard-to-find Oppenheims is *Amazing Judgment* (Downey & Co., 1897). There is a copy in the British Museum and a copy appears for sale about every ten years."

[9] AC does not list 1910 Newton edition; it does appear in NUC.

[10] CMW lists 1899 Street and Smith edition, but there is no such listing in AC, OCLC or NUC. CBI lists US first as 1916 Little Brown.

[11] Little Brown edition lists first as March 1906.

[12] CMW lists 1899 publication date for Lippincott edition; AC lists 1900 Lippincott publication date with 1899 copyright date.

[13] Dillingham edition lists Oct. 1902 publication date, while AC lists Nov. 1902.

[14] Little Brown edition lists May 1903 publication date, while AC lists June 1903.

[15] First EC listing is Ward Lock, August 1907; BM lists Ward Lock, 1904, likely a reference to copyright date rather than publication date. AC lists Dodd, October 1, 1904.

[16] LB lists 1908 date of first publication of *The Secret*. AC, however, indicates first publication was by Ward Lock in March 1907.

[17] Little Brown edition lists Oct. 1909 publication date, while AC lists Nov. 1909.

[18] Little Brown edition lists Sept. 1910 publication date, while AC lists Oct. 1910.

[19] CMW lists 1907 Little Brown edition. Little Brown first edition is Jan. 1911, copyright date is 1907. First listing in EC is Sept. 1911 for a cheap edition, however the Ward Lock first edition bears the date 1910, with no month indicated. Additionally, LB lists first as 1907.

[20] CMW lists 1911 Cassell edition. Earliest EC listing is July 1913 for a popular edition, however there are multiple OCLC listings for a 1911 Cassell edition.

[21] *Seeing Life* listed in BM, but not in EC or NUC.

[22] LB lists first as 1913.

[23] Cassell edition bears Feb. 1914 publication date, while EC lists March 1914.

[24] Little Brown edition does not list month of publication.

[25] EC lists publication date for *The Strange Case of Jocelyn Thew* as January 1920 while the book's title page carries a 1919 date.

[26] OCLC has multiple listings of *The Amazing Quest of Mr. Ernest Bliss* with a 1922 publication date. CMW also lists this date. EC, however, first lists this title with the date Jan. 1924. The Little Brown edition does not list month of publication.

[27] CMW lists a 1927 Little Brown edition of *Aaron Rodd, Diviner*, but OCLC and NUC do not list an Little Brown edition.

[28] CMW mistakenly lists the Little Brown publication date as 1926. The copyright date of this work is, however, 1926.

[29] LB lists 1934 publication date, however, the Little Brown first edition of *The Spy Paramount* bears a January 1935 publication date.

[30] LB lists 1936 publication date; EC indicates Hodder and Stoughton edition was published September 1935.

[31] LB lists 1939 publication date; EC lists Feb. 1939 publication date; Hodder and Stoughton first edition, however, bears a Nov. 1938 date.

[32] BM claims that this title is 16-page pulp edition of a story from *Ask Miss Mott*. There is, however, no story named "Burglars Must Dine" in *Ask Miss Mott*. Reprinted in 1945 by Vallancey Press of London. Listed in BM.

[33] Title is 16-page pulp edition of a story from *Jennerton & Co*. Reprinted in 1945 by Vallancey Press of London. Listed in BM.

[34] Title is 16-page pulp edition of a story from *General Besserley's Puzzle Box*. Listed in BM.

[35] Title is a 16-page pulp edition of two stories from *A Pulpit in the Grill Room*. Listed in BM.

[36] Oppenheim's plays are not listed in AC, EC, NUC, BM or OCLC. I have a copy of *The King's Cup*, but have never seen scripts of the other plays.

[37] The 20 stories listed in this omnibus as the contents *Peter Ruff and the Double-Four* and *Recalled by the Double-Four* are, in fact, equivalent to 21 stories contained in the Little Brown edition of *Peter Ruff and the Double-Four*. The Little Brown volume is divided into Book One, containing 10 stories, and Book Two, containing 11 stories. There has never been a book published with the title *Recalled by the Double-Four*. In the *Omnibus* edition, the first two stories of the Little Brown edi-

tion's Book Two are combined to form a single story, thus accounting for the reduction of 21 stories to 20.

[38] EC lists Oct. 1932 publication date; Hodder and Stoughton first edition carries Sept. 1932 publication date.

[39] Pamphlet reprint of an article from *The New York Times Book Review*.

[40] LB lists 1927 publication date; EC lists Nov. 1926 publication of Methuen edition.

[41] This is a 13-page pamphlet.

[42] EC lists publication date for the Hodder and Stoughton edition as Dec. 1941 while the book itself carries Nov. 1941 publication date.

[43] There are a number of titles that appear on various lists that have not been located by even the most advanced Oppenheim collectors. It seems that publishers announced the titles before the books were actually published and subsequently published the books under a different title. WB writes: "*A Woman's Blindness* is in a panel listing in *Mr. Marx's Secret* (*Sheffield Weekly Telegraph*, 1899) though no one has found a copy of it. So, too, *The Lesser Sin* is included in a list of Oppenheims in *The Honourable Algernon Knox, Detective* (Hodder & Stoughton, 1920). If *Lesser Sin* was published, where is it now? The Library of Congress had a card for *The Vindicator* but removed it after it was unable to find the book. We think that it was a reprint of *The Avenger* (Little, Brown & Co., 1908)."

Acknowledgements

E. Phillips Oppenheim: The Prince of
Story Tellers Tells His Own Story.
Boston:
Little Brown, 1927.

The Ambassador's Dilemma
Windsor Magazine, v. 12,
pp. 452-458.
(1900)

Mr. Ashley's Failure
Windsor Magazine, v. 14,
pp. 350-356.
(1901)

The Man Who Saved the
President's Life
Windsor Magazine, v. 17,
pp. 715-722.
(1903)

The Man Whom Nobody Liked
Windsor Magazine, v. 19, pp. 25-30.
(1903)

The Great Fortuna Mine
Harmsworthy London Magazine, v. 10,
pp. 554-564.
(1903)

John Garland the Deliverer
Strand Magazine, v. 36, pp. 185-192.
(August 1908)

The Money-Spider
Strand Magazine, v. 36, pp. 483-490.
(November 1908)

False Gods
Strand Magazine, v. 37, pp. 277-285
(March 1909)

The Ill-Laid Scheme of
Mr. Ambrose Weare
Strand Magazine, v. 37, pp. 380-387.
(April 1909)

The Three Thieves
Cosmopolitan, v. pp. 497-502.
(April 1909)

The Turning Wheel
Strand Magazine, v. 38, pp. 356-365.
(September 1909)

The Sovereign in the Gutter
Strand Magazine, v. 38, pp. 610-616.
(November 1909)

Mr. Hardrows Secretary
Strand Magazine, v. 38, pp. 741-747.
(December 1909)

The Restless Traveller
Strand Magazine, v. 39, pp. 643-649.
(June 1910)

One Luckless Hour
Strand Magazine, v. 40, pp. 275-281
(September 1910)

Quits
Strand Magazine, v. 40, pp. 579-588.
(November 1910)

The Deserter
Strand Magazine, v. 40, pp. 729-737.
(December 1910)

The Outcast
Strand Magazine, v. 41, pp. 711-718
(June 1911)

The Perfidy of Henry Midgley
Strand Magazine, v. 42, pp. 83-89.
(July 1911)

The Best in Mystery & Noir Fiction Past & Present

1-933586-26-5 **Benjamin Appel** Sweet Money Girl / Life and Death of a Tough Guy $21.95
1-933586-03-6 **Malcolm Braly** Shake Him Till He Rattles / It's Cold Out There $19.95
1-933586-10-9 **Gil Brewer** Wild to Possess / A Taste for Sin $19.95
1-933586-20-6 **Gil Brewer** A Devil for O'Shaugnessy / The Three-Way Split $14.95
1-933586-24-9 **W. R. Burnett** It's Always Four O'Clock / Iron Man $19.95
1-933586-31-1 **Catherine Butzen** Thief of Midnight $15.95
1-933586-38-9 **James Hadley Chase** Come Easy--Go Easy / In a Vain Shadow $19.95
0-9667848-0-4 **Storm Constantine** Oracle Lips (limited hb) $45.00
1-933586-30-3 **Jada M. Davis** One for Hell $19.95
1-933586-43-5 **Bruce Elliot** One is a Lonely Number /
                    Elliott Chaze Black Wings Has My Angel $19.95
1-933586-34-6 **Don Elliott** Gang Girl / Sex Bum $19.95
1-933586-12-5 **A. S. Fleischman** Look Behind You Lady / The Venetian Blonde $19.95
1-933568-28-1 **A. S. Fleischman** Danger in Paradise / Malay Woman $19.95
1-933586-35-4 **Orrie Hitt** The Cheaters / Dial "M" for Man $19.95
0-9667848-7-1 **Elisabeth Sanxay Holding** Lady Killer / Miasma $19.95
0-9667848-9-8 **Elisabeth Sanxay Holding** The Death Wish / Net of Cobwebs $19.95
0-9749438-5-1 **Elisabeth Sanxay Holding** Strange Crime in Bermuda / Too Many Bottles $19.95
1-933586-16-8 **Elisabeth Sanxay Holding** The Old Battle Ax / Dark Power $19.95
1-933586-17-6 **Russell James** Underground / Collected Stories $14.95
0-9749438-8-6 **Day Keene** Framed in Guilt / My Flesh is Sweet $19.95
1-933586-33-8 **Day Keene** Dead Dolls Don't Talk / Hunt the Killer / Too Hot to Hold $23.95
1-933586-21-4 **Mercedes Lambert** Dogtown / Soultown $14.95
1-933586-14-1 **Dan Marlowe/Fletcher Flora/Charles Runyon** Trio of Gold Medals $15.95
1-933586-07-9 **Ed by McCarthy & Gorman** Invasion of the Body Snatchers: A Tribute $19.95
1-933586-09-5 **Margaret Millar** An Air That Kills / Do Evil in Return $19.95
1-933586-23-0 **Wade Miller** The Killer / Devil on Two Sticks $17.95
1-933586-27-3 **E. Phillips Oppenheim** The Amazing Judgment / Mr. Laxworthy's Adventures $19.95
0-9749438-3-5 **Vin Packer** Something in the Shadows / Intimate Victims $19.95
1-933586-05-2 **Vin Packer** Whisper His Sin / The Evil Friendship $19.95
1-933586-18-4 **Richard Powell** A Shot in the Dark / Shell Game $14.95
1-933586-19-2 **Bill Pronzini** Snowbound / Games $14.95
0-9667848-8-x **Peter Rabe** The Box / Journey Into Terror $21.95
0-9749438-4-3 **Peter Rabe** Murder Me for Nickels / Benny Muscles In $19.95
1-933586-00-1 **Peter Rabe** Blood on the Desert / A House in Naples $21.95
1-933586-11-7 **Peter Rabe** My Lovely Executioner / Agreement to Kill $19.95
1-933586-22-2 **Peter Rabe** Anatomy of a Killer / A Shroud for Jesso $14.95
1-933586-32-x **Peter Rabe** The Silent Wall / The Return of Marvin Palaver $19.95
0-9749438-2-7 **Douglas Sanderson** Pure Sweet Hell / Catch a Fallen Starlet $19.95
1-933586-06-0 **Douglas Sanderson** The Deadly Dames / A Dum-Dum for the President $19.95
1-933586-29-X **Charlie Stella** Johnny Porno $15.95
1-933586-39-7 **Charlie Stella** Rough Riders $15.95
1-933586-08-7 **Harry Whittington** A Night for Screaming / Any Woman He Wanted $19.95
1-933586-25-7 **Harry Whittington** To Find Cora / Like Mink Like Murder / Body and Passion $23.95
1-933586-36-2 **Harry Whittington** Rapture Alley / Winter Girl / Strictly for the Boys $23.95

STARK HOUSE PRESS
www.StarkHousePress.com